# HAMMER OF THOR

## BY

## S. EVAN TOWNSEND

**World Castle Publishing**
http://www.worldcastlepublishing.com

**World Castle Publishing**
Pensacola, Florida

Copyright © S. Evan Townsend 2011
ISBN: 9781937593872
Library of Congress Catalogue Number 2011937307

First Edition World Castle Publishing September 1, 2011
http://www.worldcastlepublishing.com

Cover: Karen Fuller
Editor: Maxine Bringenberg

# DEDICATION

Dedicated to OAS: My so-smart-it's-scary children.

# BOOK ONE
# ARROWHEAD
# 1932

# CHAPTER ONE

I stood erect despite my fatigue, sweat forming a puddle in the small of my back, running down into my eyes, beading on my arms. I was breathing hard, sucking in the cool air, and grinning from ear to ear.

Newmark was looking at me intently. We were standing near the summit of Mount Sutro in San Francisco.

"In which guild did you apprentice?" Newmark asked casually. He seemed hardly winded.

"Minne-apolis," I replied, my rapid breathing turning it into two words.

"They trained you well, Student," he said, smiling. "And you say we have you to thank for killing Weiss?"

I nodded. "Yes, you do. He angered the leader of my guild by trying to prove adepts were as fraudulent as he. So I was ordered to kill him, and I did."

"He angered all the guilds," Newmark stated. "How did you do it?"

"A simple rune," I stated. My breathing was becoming more regular. "He didn't even bother to hide his real name. He got sicker and sicker until he collapsed on stage in Detroit and died Halloween night." I chuckled; I'd been in the audience and seen it.

"Yes," Newmark said. "I remember reading about it in the papers. You must have been young then."

It had been six years ago. "Twenty-five," I bragged. "Just four years after my first trials."

"That's very impressive," Newmark commented.

"Thank you, Teacher." I was still smiling; I enjoyed telling others about killing that fraud, Weiss.

The older adept walked to me and smiled. "Joining my guild will not cause problems with your old guild?"

"No, Teacher, I had permission to leave the guild."

"And why the West Coast Guild?"

"It doesn't snow here, Teacher," I said with a laugh. I was frankly sick of snow, having grown up on America's northern plains.

Newmark laughed. "It doesn't snow here, but it's not like southern California either. Wait until you see our chilly summers, when the fog rolls in during the afternoon."

I smiled at that. It was hard to believe on this beautiful spring day.

7

"Let's go," Newmark said. He started walking down the hill to where the auto that had brought us was waiting. I had started to follow when he suddenly turned.

I still had my hand on my arrowhead talisman as his finger came up. The lightning bolt hit me, but my protection spell was up in time and the blast only physically knocked me back a bit.

Newmark smiled again. "Very good. Welcome to the West Coast Guild."

"Thank you, Teacher." I allowed myself to relax. He'd just welcomed me to the guild; he wouldn't attack me again.

Trials to join guilds were not on a pass-or-fail basis; they were pass-or-die. Newmark, the head of the guild I wished to join, had spent the last hour trying to kill me. I was sure he could have if he really desired. But he only wished to test me to determine whether I was powerful enough to join his guild—I apparently had just proven myself so—and hadn't used all of his power.

The hike down the mountain was leisurely. I got the feeling he was also tired, but trying to hide it. I couldn't help but laugh. I knew I could do it: I'd worn him out.

There was a gravel road which led from the city and sitting where we'd left them were a warrior who was leaning against the long green auto smoking a cigarette, and a driver who was sitting behind the wheel looking bored. The warrior opened the back door for Newmark—I had to open my own door to enter—and then got in the front. The auto's roof only covered the back seats, which were as plush as the most comfortable parlor furniture I'd ever seen. There was a windshield between the front and back seats. The front seats were in the open, and I wondered what the driver did when it rained. The driver started the machine and piloted it down the road.

"Where are you staying?" Newmark asked over the wind noise.

I told him the name of the cheap hotel I'd found near the Union Pacific station. Transcontinental sleeping berths weren't cheap, and I'd yet to find a place where rich men congregated to supplement my funds.

Newmark shook his head and reached through the open window to smack the right arm of the warrior. "Samuel, give me some money."

The warrior handed back a roll of bills. Newmark handed me the roll. "Find someplace nice."

I looked at the roll of bills and then back at him. Was this another test? I handed the roll back to him. "No, thank you, Teacher," I said.

Newmark smiled as he pocketed the money. "You were trained well. You know what guilds are for."

"Mutual protection," I stated. "Killing a member of a guild will cause that guild to avenge his death."

"That is correct, Student," Newmark replied.

Guilds are also for companionship, I didn't add. But guilds weren't mutual aid societies. An adept who asked for help was showing his weakness. Even accepting help was giving other adepts a signal that you were less than able to protect yourself. And while guilds protected you from members of rival guilds, they did nothing to protect you from the member of your guild who would like your talisman or your position in the guild. The leader of a guild was always the strongest and most powerful member.

When we entered San Francisco proper, the streets became paved, some with cobblestones. I saw a line of shabbily dressed men stretched along the sidewalks of one block. I immediately recognized it as the line for a soup kitchen—they were in every American city, including Minneapolis. Even adepts couldn't help but know about the Depression that had gripped the country. Luckily, we were exempt from such lesser matters.

A man was trying to sell pencils on a street corner for a nickel. Our eyes met for a moment and I had to look away. The despair and pain I saw in his face was almost unbearable. I thought about Newmark's money and the cash I would soon be accumulating and was glad I was an adept.

When the auto stopped in front of the Huntington Apartments on Nob Hill, Newmark got out and I followed. The warrior also exited the vehicle and hovered nearby. As I stood waiting on the sidewalk, the driver drove the auto away, and I assumed he was going to go park it somewhere.

"Come see me tomorrow about noon," Newmark told me. "You'll also meet other members of the guild then."

"Yes, Teacher."

He entered the lobby of the apartment building. It was later converted to a hotel but it remained the guild headquarters, with our guild renting the thirteenth floor.

I wandered around the town looking for men of means. With the Depression there weren't many, but I was able to lighten the wallets of some imprudent gentlemen.

When I hailed a taxi and told the driver to take me to a nice hotel, he dropped me at the Drake-Wiltshire, not too far away on Stockton Street. It was nicer than any place I'd ever stayed in my life—certainly like nothing in Grand Forks.

In North Dakota, one only heard rumors of adepts, although there were occasional stories in the newspapers about their exploits in big cities. The stories were almost universally reproving and my parents usually added their own opinions. But I didn't care. I wanted to be an adept and knew I had the talent, ambition, and brains to be one. I also knew I didn't want to stay in Grand Forks a moment longer than necessary.

Once, on a school field trip to a museum, there were Indian artifacts displayed under glass. One artifact, an arrowhead with markings scratched into it, seemed to me to be emanating power. I asked my friend, standing close by, if he noticed anything, and he just laughed at me.

Everyone knew adepts used "talismans" to increase their power. I was sure that the arrowhead was a talisman, probably for an Indian medicine man. So, at age 17, I broke into the museum, stole the arrowhead, and with my other scant belongings and all the money I could rustle up in a carpetbag, I took a train to Minneapolis in search of a guild. The train was full of men going to Chicago to Navy boot camp because of the war in Europe. I felt young and out-of-place even though I was just a year younger than most of them. They were excited to go stop the Huns, and I was glad that I was embarking on a path that would, if successful, preclude my fighting for my country in the war to end all wars, or any other wars that might come along. Even though I did feel some pangs of guilt, I forgot them quickly.

I'd never been to a city like Minneapolis before. It was a wonder; the streets were paved, there were electric lights everywhere, even in the buildings, and street cars and automobiles moved along like magic. I'd never even seen an automobile before.

I had no idea how to find a guild, but I needn't have worried as they found me, apparently feeling the arrowhead's power. After a five-year apprenticeship, I passed my trials to join soon after my twenty-first birthday.

I spent almost ten years with that guild, but after the summer of '29 and the winter of '30 I decided it was time to leave. It had been over 100 degrees in June, July, and August, and 104 in September. Then five months later it was below zero; February and March were absolutely, miserably cold. After giving it careful thought I concluded that I wanted to move to a milder climate, so I asked the head of my guild for permission to attempt to join the West Coast Guild. She was unhappy to see me go, but wished me luck. I got on the next train for San Francisco.

There was not much to do in the hotel other than read or listen to the radio, and I quickly became bored. I felt like celebrating (and wanted to wash the face of the man selling pencils from my consciousness). I'd need to find a speakeasy and maybe a pretty girl to seduce, or to use a persuasion spell on, for a proper celebration. The doorman or bell captain could probably help me find a hooch joint, preferably a classy one.

My plans were pleasantly changed. As I walked through the lobby of the Drake-Wiltshire, I saw her. First I glimpsed her from behind and I admired her slender form in her stylish dress. I could see her dark, dark hair that came to the nape of her neck, and her shapely ankles. Then she turned and I practically gasped out loud. She was Oriental, and one of the most beautiful women I'd ever seen in my life. She was so lovely it almost hurt to look at her. She was dressed in a two-tone western-style dress, slim down to her silk-covered calves. She wore high-heeled shoes and a small hat on her black hair, hair that was so black it seemed to have blue highlights. And, I could feel it; she was an adept.

Our eyes locked and I found I couldn't look away. She didn't avert her eyes, either, and we continued to stare at one another. I slowly approached her.

"Greetings," I said in the ancient language, afraid she might not speak English.

At that she looked down. "Greetings, Teacher," she replied in the same language.

I was surprised at that; I'd rarely been called teacher, and then only by the most junior adepts. "What name do you use?" I asked her. All adepts use pseudonyms, for if someone knows your name they have power over you.

"Pak Meyoung," she said, still not meeting my gaze.

I changed languages. "Do you speak English, Pak?"

"*Ahnioh*," she whispered.

Although it was difficult to hear her voice, what I heard made me blink in surprise; I could not understand what she'd said. Reaching for my talisman, I wrapped my fingers around it and worked up a translation spell. I wanted to talk to her, desperately.

I didn't know what it was. I had met attractive women before, but I felt drawn to her immediately, and it seemed she felt the same. Boldly I reached out, cupped her chin and lifted her face. She smiled shyly and tried to look away, but I didn't allow it. "I'm Joe Kader," I whispered to her, hoping the translation spell was working properly.

"Hello, Joe," she whispered back.

I chuckled. "Hello, Pak."

She shook her head. "Pak is my family name. We say family names first."

I wasn't sure what she meant. "Well, I'll call you..." I had to think for a moment, "Peg. Are you Nisei?"

For a moment I saw anger or hurt in her face, but she covered it quickly. "No. I'm from Chosun."

"Chosun?" I asked, not ever having heard of it.

She shook her head. "Americans call it Korea."

"Wherever that is," I laughed, thinking maybe it was part of Japan or China. "Are you staying here at the hotel?"

"Yes."

"May I buy you dinner, Peg?"

She hesitated. I could tell she was in turmoil about it. But finally she shook her head.

"No, thank you," she said.

I looked at her. I should have accepted her answer, but with the way I felt about her and the way I thought she felt about me, I couldn't. "Why?"

She didn't answer but stepped away. Then she turned. "I'm sorry, I cannot."

\*\*\*

By using a persuasion spell on the desk clerk, I learned she was staying at the hotel and in what room. I also learned she was alone; however, she'd come to the hotel with an Oriental man who had paid for her room for four months in advance and then left. One of those months was gone. He had also paid for the room of a man, also Oriental. The man was easy to find. The evening after I met Peg, there was a pounding on my room door. I used a far seeing spell to see that it was a tall, angry-looking Oriental man. I made sure my hand was around my talisman when I opened the door.

Without preamble he stated in English, "You stay away from Chosun woman."

He wasn't an adept unless he was masking, so I just said, "Why?"

"She not your business. She not free."

I blinked at that, wondering what he meant.

"What are you going to do about it?" I asked.

He reached inside his western business suit and pulled out a revolver. "I can make you not want to see her," he said. The man must have wanted to sound menacing, but with his accent and Pidgin English, he sounded almost silly.

Up to this point, the man's face had shown only anger. However, when I pointed and he felt what I had done to him, his face became twisted with fear.

"Leave her alone," I told him, "or I'll finish the job." I released him.

He looked at me. "You have trouble when he gets here."

"He, who?" I asked.

"You see," he spat and walked away.

Well, I decided, if this man was representative of my competition, I had little to worry about.

The next day I waited in the lobby until I saw her again. I approached her carefully, but was surprised and happy to find that her attitude was different and she was not as shy as before.

"Did you scare off Ito?" she asked in the ancient tongue.

"If that was his name, yes."

She smiled, which made her face all the more beautiful. "Thank you. I hate that man."

"Why didn't you do anything about him, then?" I asked. She was an adept.

She simply did not answer.

"Would you like to go for a walk, Peg?" I asked her.

She thought for a moment, then almost giggled, covering her mouth shyly. "That would be nice, Mr. Kader."

\*\*\*

Peg's body was next to mine, nude, in the bed. We were awake, resting and relaxing. The three months since I'd come to San Francisco had been the most amazing of my life. I had passed the trials to enter one of the most powerful guilds in the country and I knew I was in love with Peg. The language barrier was slowly being eroded; she was learning some English and we used translation spells and the ancient language to back us up.

She and I had spent almost every moment together, except when I went to see Newmark or to have other contact with members of my guild. It wasn't that I was ashamed of her—rather the opposite. But she was not a member of the guild (and wouldn't tell me what guild she belonged to, if any) and would not be welcome.

We had explored the city together and it was a wonderful time. I did see some people stare—both Caucasians and Orientals—as her hand would rest in the crook of my arm.

There were also some strange incidents. We ran into some Nisei on the street and she acted scared; I didn't understand what an adept would have to fear from any lesser, even Japanese. I took her to a speakeasy one night, thinking she'd enjoy the music and I could teach her to dance. Minneapolis was close enough to Chicago that it had a thriving hooch trade and I often visited speakeasies there, sampling the bathtub gin or smuggled-in Canadian booze in high-class joints. I wanted to share that with Peg. However, the guard at the door took one look at her and said, "No niggers, chinks, or Irish." It probably took a week for the spell I put on him to wear off, keeping him mute the entire time. We didn't patronize the dive, as I wasn't going to give the bastards my money. But we brushed these incidents off as easily as we ignored the stares and whispers. I only saw her as a beautiful woman with black hair, lovely dark eyes, and skin that contrasted nicely with my northern plains pallor.

I did, occasionally, see Ito lurking in the shadows, looking angry and frustrated. When I tried to ask Peg about it, she would refuse to speak of it.

She told me that, before my arrival, she'd been imprisoned in the Drake-Wiltshire by Ito. I still could not understand why she'd allowed a lesser to control her. He must have had some power over her before I had chased him off.

There was something about her, a sadness or a hurt, that I could sense but could not bring her to share. I didn't like the feeling; I just wished I could break down her reserve. It was as if, despite our physical and emotional closeness, she still held me at arm's length.

"Sweet one," I said.

"Yes, *yuhbo*?" She had taken to calling me that, explaining it meant "dear" in her language.

"I want to tell you something but, I'm afraid."

She turned in my arms to look at me, her face inches from mine, her breath warm on my nose, the length of her body against mine. "Why are you afraid?"

"I'm afraid if I tell you it will scare you off." And I was.

Her dark eyes studied my face. "Why would it scare me off for you to tell me something?"

I had no answer to that. "It just might."

She looked deep into my eyes then. "I want to tell you something but I am afraid."

"Afraid of what, dear?"

"Afraid that you will think me foolish."

I smiled. "How could I?" I was sure we were both talking of the same thing. "If I promise not to think you foolish, do you promise not to be scared away?"

She nodded, a serious look on her face.

I took a deep breath. "Peg, I love you."

She smiled and lowered her eyes. "And I love you, Joe."

I laughed. "See, that was not so hard."

"No, *yuhbo*, it was not," she agreed.

I pulled her closer. But I still felt the presence of something: the secret she could not share.

***

A few days later, I returned to our hotel from the Huntington and when I entered our room—she'd moved in with me weeks ago—she was gone. I tried to feel for her: nothing. I physically searched the room, then the hotel. Both she and Ito were gone. The desk clerk informed me that Ito had vacated his room and the two of them—Ito and Peg—had left with an Oriental man.

I searched the city, starting with the hotels, assuming that a beautiful Oriental woman should be easy to find. But despite truth and persuasion spells, I found no trace of her. I even tried the small Japanese community in the city, but I got nothing there but hostility, and no one knew anything about any Peg or Pak. Those were the only names I knew for her.

About a week after she had disappeared I returned to the Drake-Wiltshire late in the afternoon, exhausted. I lay on the bed, my mind unable to find rest, but my body needing it. There was a gentle knock on the hotel room door, and I bounded off the bed, crossed over to the door in two leaps, and pulled it open saying, "Peg?"

A young, Oriental man stood outside my door. He looked at me and said softly, "My name is Takada. What I do now endangers my life and my guild's honor." He was an adept, I could feel it.

As I looked at him, wondering what he had meant, he handed me a folded piece of paper.

I pulled it open, still standing in the doorway. It was a handwritten note, and I had to use a translation spell to read the strange writing. "I am sorry, I must go now. Don't try to follow me. I will love you forever and never forget you." She had signed it in symbols I didn't bother to translate but assumed were her Korean pseudonym. It didn't matter; I reached out and grabbed the man's shoulders.

"Where is she?" I demanded, nearly shouting.

He didn't resist, even though he could have, being an adept.

"Her ship leaves from Pier 22 at the Embarcadero; the *Reinan Maru*."

"When?" I grunted, my hands gripping his shoulders.

"Soon; you must hurry."

As the realization that I might lose her hit me, I blinked. Then I pushed him back and started running down the hall for the elevator. A thought occurred to me and I turned back to face him. "Why are you telling me this?"

He looked at me for a long moment before answering. "I have my reasons. You can find me on the west end, in the Japanese area." The way he said it, it was plain that he didn't expect to see me again.

I turned and ran to the elevator and pressed the call button. When it didn't come soon enough, I raced down the stairs, across the lobby, and out to the street. The doorman waved down a taxi and I jumped in.

"The Embarcadero," I ordered, "Pier 22."

"You got it," the driver replied around a half-smoked cigar in his mouth.

"And fast," I added, hitting him with a persuasion spell.

As the taxi left the curb, I looked down and realized that I still had Peg's note clutched in my hand. I carefully folded it and put it in my shirt pocket.

The taxi stopped at Pier 22, between a warehouse and a big black steamship. From the pier the ship looked like a massive steel wall many stories tall. From my taxi window I saw Peg standing near the bottom of the gangplank about to board the ship. At the top of the gangplank was a dark hole in the black metal of the side of the ship. It seemed as if that hole led to another world and if I allowed her to enter it, she'd be gone forever. I bounced out of the car and called her name. "Peg!" I had not meant to play this scene out here on the docks of the Embarcadero in front of lessers but I didn't seem to have a choice.

She turned and looked at me, tears in her eyes. "*Yuhbo!*" she cried out.

Standing beside her were Ito and another Oriental man whom I could sense was a powerful adept. But I had been an adept for ten years and had passed the trials for two guilds. I wasn't a pushover, and I kept moving toward the ship.

Upon seeing me, Ito spoke excitedly to the adept, who nodded his understanding and then spoke back to Ito. He nodded, bowed, and rushed up the gangplank and entered the ship.

"Who the hell are you?" I demanded of the adept, forgetting he might not speak English.

"I call myself Nakamura," he said calmly. "My guild is the *Omi Uji*." His English was nearly perfect and unaccented.

I'd never heard of it and didn't really care. How was I to know at the time that they were the most powerful guild—the only guild in fact—in Japan?

"What are you doing with Peg?" I asked.

"Her name," he said, "is Miko. And she is mine."

Adept names are rather fluid, and at the time I didn't understand that he called her by a Japanese name, or the significance of that.

"What do you mean, 'mine'? Is she your wife?"

"No, she's just mine."

"You can't take her," I wailed. "We love each other."

15

Nakamura laughed. "Your 'love' means nothing. She is mine; she is my property."

"She is an adept, as free as you are," I tried.

He laughed again. "You do not understand our ways, Westerner. She is mine!" I was really getting tired of hearing him say that. He turned and spoke to her in what I assumed was Japanese. I didn't understand it but I got the gist: We're leaving.

"Stop!" I commanded, pointing at him. "I won't let you take her."

He turned quickly. I dodged left as his airbolt whizzed by my right ear. I heard it hit something solid, probably the wall of the warehouse behind me, which sent lessers gasping and screaming. Battles between adepts in public were rare, but they did happen, and most lessers knew the best thing to do was to get as far away as possible.

As I recovered, standing up straight, Ito stepped out of the ship and pointed at me. Two Oriental men emerged from the dark opening and rushed down the gangplank. They were dressed in dark, robe-like costumes. Each carried above his head a slim curved sword—I would later learn they were called "*katana*." They rushed at me, screaming ferociously.

I shot an airbolt at one and knocked him down. The other, screaming, slashed at my head with his sword, and I heard the blade hum by my ear as I ducked. My hand grasped my arrowhead talisman and I pointed at him. Since he was a lesser, I could affect him directly. He stopped moving, his sword stationary in its arc as he was bringing it up again for another swing. I kept the holding spell on him and turned my attention to Nakamura's second warrior—I assumed that was who these armed men were—who had jumped to his feet again almost effortlessly and came at me, the point of his sword level and aimed for my gut. I jumped out of the way and tried to reach out to touch him, but he ducked my grasp, probably knowing what I could do if I laid a finger on his skin.

While some of my attention was focused on holding the first warrior, the second turned, sword held out in front of him, and attacked again, probably trying to keep me from using a spell on him. It worked. He slashed at me and the blade cut through the bicep of my left arm. I howled in pain as blood cascaded from the gash.

He turned so rapidly that I wondered if he was an adept, using some meta to move inhumanly fast. He slashed again, so quickly that the sword was nothing but a blur that I managed to avoid before the blade removed my head. I ignored the steel's whistle as it cut through the air, and reached for him. He brought the sword around and practically severed my right arm, blood splashing from the wound, but I got my hand around his neck, and he dropped to the wooden dock, dead, his red-stained sword clattering to the planks next to him. I did the same for the first, motionless warrior, not having the time or inclination to show mercy.

While I was busy with his warriors, Nakamura had pulled Peg up the gangplank and was about to enter the black hole at the top with her. I healed myself enough to stop the bleeding, which left me tired and in no shape to face him. But I had to try.

I pointed, and fire arced from my finger toward Nakamura. He put a hand up and the flames stopped a few feet from him. My next shot was more powerful, but he walked towards me, undeterred, back down the gangplank. Then, with his black eyes beaming hatred toward me, he pushed the flames back at me. When they hit I screamed as my head was engulfed in pain. I dropped to the ground, scrambling through the agony to find a spell to stop the fire.

Suddenly, the flames died and I looked up to see Peg using a spell to douse them. Nakamura looked at her angrily and pointed at her; she became motionless. While he was distracted, I shot lightning at him. It smacked into the side of his ribcage, knocking him back. He hit the railing on the gangplank, flipped over it, and fell to the dock. The impact must have knocked the wind out of him, as he didn't immediately rise. I shot fire at him again, this time hitting him full-on. He yelled in pain and surprise and rolled off the dock into the greasy water between the ship and the quay.

I rushed up the gangplank to Peg and took her forearm in my hand. "Come on!" I said, tugging.

She looked at me and didn't move—couldn't move. I didn't understand; as an adept, she should have been immune to spells that directly affected her.

Unless Nakamura knew her real name.

As the spell on her dissipated, I could see the torment in her eyes. Fear kept her planted where she was as effectively as had the spell.

Nakamura flew out of the water and landed, wet but alive, on the dock. I'd never seen an adept fly without a carpet or broom or some type of device before. Nakamura screamed angrily and pointed both hands at me. The airbolt knocked me backwards across the gangplank's rail, and I flew through the air until I smashed into the dock. I must have lost consciousness for a moment because the next thing I knew, Nakamura was standing over me, his foot pressing down on my chest. He was pulling my talisman from my hand.

"Shall I kill you now, *gaijin*?" he asked, holding the arrowhead.

I shook my head. I knew he could kill me without much effort, and I could do little to stop him.

"The woman is mine," he growled. "Understand?"

No! I screamed inside my head. But I knew to say that would be to die. "Yes," I whispered.

"I am taking her back to Japan," he stated. "If you try to follow, if I ever see you again, I will kill both of you."

I nodded, defeated.

He looked at my talisman. "Interesting. I assume this is an Indian artifact. I'm keeping this as payment for my warriors."

I had no way to stop him.

He pocketed the talisman, lifted his foot from me and walked to Peg, who had come back down to the bottom of the gangplank. He said something to her in Japanese, took her arm, and pulled her back up the gangplank. She glanced back at me, giving me one last look at her beautiful eyes before she passed out of sight into the stygian interior of the black ship.

I stood slowly, carefully. No bones seemed to be broken, but I hurt all over. Lessers were staring at me but I continued to ignore them. I ran as best I could to the bottom of the gangplank, debating momentarily whether to follow them into the ship. But I knew Nakamura could, and would, kill me if I tried. Instead I called out: "Peg! I love you! I'll find you. I promise!"

There was no response, not even from Nakamura.

I turned and hobbled away. My taxi had left so I simply walked, fully aware of all the eyes that were fixed upon me. I felt the need to lash out at something. I shot a weak fireball into a warehouse. It hit a stack of crates and lit them on fire. It was about all I could do without a talisman, but it was effective. The lessers turned and started minding their own business.

# CHAPTER TWO

Without a talisman I couldn't do a healing spell, and my body ached all over from being slammed on the dock. My right arm where the sword had cut it was healed enough that I could use it, but it still hurt, and the left side of my scalp was throbbing painfully. Some feeling of dread warned me not to touch it. I made my way to the street somehow, since my world had become a haze of physical and emotional agony. I waved down a taxi and got in, grateful to sit down. My thoughts were fighting through the pain; I'd get a talisman, sneak on that ship, and get Peg off before it sailed. I just didn't know where I'd get a talisman, yet.

The taxi driver looked at me. "You okay, bud?"

I realized my clothes were singed and bloodstained. "Yeah, I'm fine," I said softly. "Get me to the Drake-Wiltshire on Stockton." Needed to change clothes before—before whatever I was going to do to get a talisman. Go beg Newmark for one? Find a weak adept and take his?

"You ain't fine, buddy," the driver protested. "I think I need to take you to a hospital."

I wondered if I looked worse than I felt. That hardly seemed possible.

"The Drake-Wiltshire," I mumbled, suddenly feeling light-headed.

The driver turned his rearview mirror so I could see myself. "Take a look, bud."

I did. The hair was gone on the left side of my head. Instead there was a bright red skin that was starting to blister. When I saw this, the pain increased exponentially and the world went gray, then black.

\*\*\*

Pain woke me up.

The room was painted white and I was in a white iron bed. My left arm was strapped down and a needle was inserted near the elbow. A tube ran from it to an upside-down glass bottle hanging from a metal rack beside the bed. The rack was painted white. The side of my head felt as if someone had spread a layer of hurt over it, like frosting on a cake. I touched it without thinking and felt cloth. My head had been bandaged. But just that slight amount of pressure increased the pain to nearly unbearable levels. I involuntarily sucked in a sharp breath.

An old man in the bed next to me said, "Good morning."

I looked at him. It had been afternoon when I had gone to the Embarcadero. There was an eight-pane window near my bed. I could see that it was daytime, but since I had no idea what direction the window faced, that gave me no clue to the time.

"The nurse will want to know that you're awake," the man said.

He had no outward signs of trauma, so I didn't know why he in a hospital bed. I just stared at him, my brain not quite seeming to work right. He seemed to have yellow ears and the whites of his eyes were almost saffron-colored.

"Pull that string," he said, pointing at something on my bed. His fingernails were also tinged with yellow.

I looked—it hurt like hell to move—and there was a string connected to a chain like that on a pull cord for a light. It was resting on my pillow next to my head.

"Go ahead," he said, trying to sound encouraging. "Pull it."

I fumbled for it with my hand, found it, and tugged. I felt as if I had no energy, so I kept tugging, not knowing if it had done any good. I kept clumsily pulling it until a nurse walked in.

"Keep pulling that cord and I'll wrap it around your neck," she said, striding in like a white-mantled centurion. "Oh, you're conscious," she said, looking at me. "Good. The doctor will want to talk to you." She turned around and left, her white shoes squeaking on the tile floor.

"She's a mean one, that one," the old man said. "But the night nurse is pretty."

I lay back on the pillow and breathed deeply. I reached for my talisman that should be in my trouser or vest pocket, but of course I was wearing a hospital gown. And then I remembered; I had no talisman.

I hoped the doctor would do something for the pain. It hadn't hurt like this before I passed out in that taxi.

A man walked in wearing a white smock and a reflector strapped to his head. This must be the doctor, I thought. He was short and overweight with thinning black hair. It hung like black strings that contrasted with his pale skull. The nurse followed the doctor and stood at the foot of the bed as if trying to keep me from escaping.

"Now," he said, looking at me. "You're conscious. Are you in pain?" He had a German accent, making me wonder how long he'd been in America.

"Yes," I replied to his question.

"Do you have a name?"

"Joe," I said. "Joe Kader." It hurt to talk; the skin on my face moving caused the burned skin on my skull to move painfully. I also felt tired and weak, and my mouth was dry, as were my eyes.

"Well, Mr. Kader," the doctor continued, "you were burned very badly. I would be interested to know how this happened. You were brought in by taxi, did you know?"

20

"Yes," I said.

"You are lucky to be alive," he stated. "We treated your burned head with the most modern methods, treating the wound with tannic acid, silver nitrate, and a sterile dressing. We're giving you saline to replace lost liquids. The biggest fear now is infection, *Staphylococcus* and such."

I looked at the man in the other bed.

"Don't worry about that," the doctor said, whispering, "cirrhosis of the liver. When he starts vomiting, we'll move him."

That didn't sound encouraging, but I didn't say anything, so he continued. "Let me take a look at this." He swung the reflector over his eye and leaned over me to examine my head. "Nurse, the light," he ordered and the nurse left her post at the foot of the bed and moved a lamp on a table near my head to shine the light on him. He spent some time looking at my head, leaving me to look at his chin. I was grateful he didn't touch it. I heard him sniffing. "No smell of infectious decay," he said, apparently talking to himself. "That is good; the silver nitrate must be working."

He sat back and looked at me. "We'll have to change this dressing. I'm afraid you'll find that unpleasant."

I worried about that; if merely touching the dressing was intolerably painful, I couldn't imagine what pulling the bandage off would feel like.

He took my hand and squeezed the base of my fingernail between his thumb and index finger for a few moments, then released it and studied the result. "Good," he said. "You're only slightly dehydrated and no sign of shock." He stood up and swung the reflector up again. "I am afraid you'll be scarred for life. Nothing we can do about that. Such a shame; such a young man, too. Are you married?"

"No."

"Such a shame." He looked at me with a look of pity I did not enjoy. "Is there anyone we can contact for you? Family or friends?"

I didn't want Newmark to see me in this condition so I just shook my head.

"You said you are in pain?" the doctor asked.

"Yes," I whispered.

"I'll have the nurse bring in a morphine injection. We might as well change that dressing as soon as it takes effect. That will help a little."

I don't know whether the morphine helped. I remember screaming uncontrollably as they removed the old dressing. And they did this daily, although the pain slowly decreased to being merely unbearable.

\*\*\*

About the third day I was in the hospital, a man wearing a suit came in to ask if I could pay for my treatment. What money they'd found on me had quickly been consumed. When I told him I couldn't pay, he informed me that, in that situation, I was a "charity case" with my medical expenses paid by a combination of city monies and various philanthropic groups. That was part of the reason, despite the fear of infection; I had to share a room with a dying alcoholic. A policeman came in another day and asked how I had been burned. I told him I didn't remember. He looked as if he didn't believe me, so I used a persuasion spell, albeit a very weak one, and he left satisfied. He probably wondered later why he'd believed me.

And because I was a charity case, I was apparently obligated to listen to a man from a church talking to me about my sinful ways. I tried to spend the time sleeping.

After three weeks of excruciating pain during dressing changes lessened slightly by morphine and what little meta I could muster in my weakened state, horrifying morphine dreams, and people asking me stupid questions, my roommate looked at me and said, "Is that stench coming from you?"

I didn't know; I didn't smell anything.

Later that day the doctor sniffed my head and smiled. "Good news," he said, a little too happily, "we don't need to change your dressings anymore. I'll bet you're glad to hear that."

I looked at him as he showed me a forced smile, then patted me on the shoulder and walked away. He stopped to talk to the battle-ax day nurse. Their voices were low, so I used a spell to increase my hearing.

"Just as I feared: infection," he was saying. "We can try to treat it with more silver nitrate, but I'm afraid it won't do much good."

The nurse nodded gravely. "We'll keep him as comfortable as possible."

"If the infection spreads too much, start a morphine drip," the doctor ordered.

"Yes, doctor."

"Poor bastard," he said and walked out of the room.

I knew then that they expected me to die. My burn was infected and there was nothing they could do. And without a talisman, there was nothing I could do.

I refused my next morphine injection.

I had to fight to stay awake, and the pain helped. I watched the sky darken through the room's window and listened to the lush's snoring. Somewhere I heard a clock chime. When it chimed twelve times, I removed the needle from my arm and sat up in the bed. I felt lightheaded but was determined to get out of there. There was a closet I'd never seen opened. I stumbled to it and jerked the door open. My blood-stained clothes were inside. It probably took me half an hour to dress, with numerous rest periods. I wondered how I was going to walk out of there. I looked out the window and, this close to it, could tell I was on the second floor. I debated jumping out the window as the fastest escape, but decided that was foolish.

Then I remembered something. I reached into my shirt pocket. Peg's note was in there, folded neatly by someone other than me. But I could feel her presence in the note. It wasn't a talisman—it could become one in time—but it did have power. Not enough to heal, but enough for some strength.

I walked out of the room. The night nurse, a voluptuous strawberry blonde with a constellation of freckles across her nose, looked at me aghast.

"Mr. Kader," she called out, "what are you doing out of your bed?"

I pointed at her. "I've been released."

"You've been released," she repeated.

"Call me a taxi," I ordered.

She picked up the phone and called a taxi company.

"Escort me outside," I said.

She came to me and took my arm. "It's good to see you going home," she said. "We were worried about you."

"Thank you," I replied.

Having her with me, I was not challenged. I had to reinforce the persuasion spell continuously, something I wouldn't have had to do if I'd had a talisman, but we made it to the main entrance without incident. We stepped outside into a foggy, damp night.

"You can go," I told her. "Thank you."

She smiled and walked back into the building. I collapsed on a bench, weakened by the spells and my condition.

I hoped the spell on her would hold until the taxi got there.

It must have, as she hadn't come to get me by the time the yellow and black auto stopped.

"You call for a taxi?"

I got in. "The Huntington Apartments on California," I said. "You know where that is?"

"Top of Nob Hill?" the driver asked.

"Yes." I leaned back in the seat.

"You okay, buddy? You don't look too good."

"I'm fine; get me to the Huntington, now!" I added a persuasion spell to get him to move.

"Yes, sir!" he said.

The bouncing of the car caused pain to run across my scalp with every bump. I probably would have slept, otherwise.

At the Huntington, the elevator operator didn't recognize me and didn't want to let me on the thirteenth floor until I gave him the pass phrase. I was greeted by a warrior I didn't know.

"Where's Newmark?" I asked.

"Sleeping," the warrior said gruffly. "Who are you?"

"Kader," I said, leaning against the wall of the corridor.

He looked at me with big eyes. "We thought you were dead."

"I almost am," I groaned. "I need Newmark."

There was a flurry of movement that I was barely aware of. I remembered sitting in a chair with Newmark looking me over.

"We thought you were dead," he said harshly. "Who did this to you, someone from another guild?"

I nodded.

Newmark's attitude changed to one that was almost fatherly. "Those bastards. Looks as if you got here just in time, son." He turned to the warriors. "Help him."

Of course, I thought, this is the job of the guild, to help a member when attacked. Mutual protection.

He searched my clothes, finding only Peg's note. He glanced at it and set it aside. "No talisman. That explains why he hasn't healed himself," he said to the warrior looking over his shoulder. "Watch him," he said and walked away. The warrior looked at me, and twisted his face in a manner that I could only understand as meaning he didn't like what he saw.

Newmark returned and picked up my hand. He placed an object in it.

It was a talisman. I felt the power. I smiled. "Thank you," I said. I healed my head until I passed out. I woke up lying on a bed that was apparently in one of the bedrooms of Newmark's apartments. Peg's note was on a table by the bed, along with the talisman. I folded her note carefully and placed it in my pocket. Then I picked up the talisman and healed my head some more. I tested it by pulling off the dressing, which was about the size of a sheet of typewriter paper folded in half. It was smaller than I had thought given the pain that it had caused me. And it smelled bad. I dropped it on the floor, and healed my head completely. I'd have to wait for the hair to grow back, though. I healed my arm that the Japanese warrior had cut and then took another nap.

***

Newmark was sitting in a leather chair and smiled when I came into the room. The shades were up and it was a lovely day outside. From there I could see the Golden Gate: the narrow entrance to San Francisco Bay. There'd been talk of putting a bridge over it, but many thought that would prove impossible with the currents and the winds. I figured it would be tried; lessers trust their iron and steel wonders so much. There was even talk of a bridge to Oakland which, considering the distance, seemed even less likely.

"Joe," Newmark called out upon seeing me. "You're looking almost healed."

"Thank you, Teacher," I said, sitting on a couch across from him.

"Although," he added with a chuckle, "you might want to even out your haircut."

I ran my hand through my hair. One side needed cutting, and the other was stubble like a three-day beard. "Yes, I'll do that," I said.

He looked at me as if trying to see through me. "Now, tell me, what happened. I must confess I read the note, apparently from the—" he paused as if trying to think of the correct words "—Jap lady you've been seen with around town."

"Korean," I corrected.

He waved his hand dismissively. "They're all slopes to me."

I kept my anger in check. My Peg was not a slope like other Orientals and I didn't want him calling her one. But there wasn't any point in confronting him.

"Tell me what happened," he ordered.

I nodded, and began the story with my meeting Peg in my hotel lobby. When I explained about Ito, he looked at me.

"This didn't strike you as strange?" he demanded.

"The whole situation was so… exotic, I didn't know what was normal."

"I wish you had come to me, Student. I could have saved you some pain." He said it as a statement of fact, with no feeling.

I continued with the story, up until the confrontation on the Embarcadero.

"What did you say he called himself?" Newmark demanded, sitting forward in his chair.

"Nakamura," I said.

"Of the *Omi Uji*?"

"Yes, Teacher."

Newmark just looked at me, anger obviously seething behind the mask of his face. Then he turned to his warrior. "Call the leadership, Fitzgerald, Swartz, and Gordon if you can find him."

"Yes, sir," the warrior said and hurried to a phone.

"What is it, Teacher?" I asked.

He glared at me. "The *Omi Uji* is one of the most powerful guilds on the planet. They united all the Japanese guilds about four hundred years ago. Nakamura has extended their power to Korea and now he's working on Manchuria. If he thinks our guild had anything to do with this unprovoked attack on their leader…"

"Unprovoked?" I cried. "He was—" I stopped; I wasn't sure what he was doing.

"He was stealing your girlfriend," Newmark said in a tone that reduced the whole situation to a foolish schoolboy crush. "But your 'girlfriend,'" he said the word sarcastically, "is his consort. We knew she was here. An upstart rival in his guild was trying to assassinate him, so he had sent her to America to keep her safe. If I'd known that was the woman you were seeing…" he let his voice trail off.

"But she doesn't love him," I whispered.

Newmark almost spat. "Love is irrelevant. Their ways are different from ours."

"I'm sorry, Teacher," I said softly.

"Don't call me that," he said.

I looked at him. "What?"

"I am not your Teacher. You are banished from the guild. If you return, I'll kill you."

I looked at him, hoping he wasn't serious.

"And," he added, "I'll take my talisman back." He held out his hand. "I'm sorry I helped you heal. Take that as the last aid this guild will ever bestow on you." His voice was so calm it was more frightening than if he had been screaming.

I could have fought him for the talisman. But he would have won and I would have died. I was sure the talisman he'd given me was no match in power for his. Also, I was still weak from my ordeal. He'd probably make quick work of me.

I reached in my pocket and handed over the carved piece of ivory.

"Get out of here," Newmark said dismissively.

I stood and walked out.

***

I had no money, so I had to use a persuasion spell on a cabby to get him to take me where I wanted. At the Drake-Wiltshire I learned they had sold my things to cover my unpaid bill. I learned there that I'd been missing for almost a month.

As I left the lobby, I bumped into an older, well-to-do-looking gentleman. I apologized and moved on, leaving him with a little spell to help him forget my face and lopsided haircut. He must have been very well off; there was over a hundred dollars in his wallet.

I found a barber, a haberdasher, then a café. Money was easier than constant persuasion spells, especially without a talisman.

I could only think of one place to turn, although I had no reason to think he'd help me. Takada had said I could find him in the Japanese section of town on the west side. Since I had no idea where, I stood quietly in the street and tried to sense the presence of an adept. After wandering a bit, I finally found a storefront. I walked inside, noting that it sold herbal medicines and mysterious Oriental trinkets I couldn't identify. Takada was standing behind the counter and looking at me.

"You look well," he said without a hint of sarcasm. "Come in the back." He lifted a hinged section of counter and I walked through the opening. He set it down and then called out in Japanese. I didn't get a translation spell going in time, but an old Japanese woman emerged from the back. She wasn't an adept. They spoke a few words and Takada led me through the door the woman had used.

The back of the store was lined with wooden shelves and pigeonholes full of more small bottles of herbs and the same kind of devices as the front. Takada led me to some stairs that went up to an apartment. At the top of the stairs he took off his shoes and placed them next to a line of other shoes. I followed him and he looked at me with an expression of exasperation. I wondered for a moment what I'd done wrong, until I saw his gaze move to my feet

I took off my shoes and placed them next to his. I wondered what the hell the point was.

He pointed me to a chair. "Forgive my poor hospitality; I have little to offer you. Perhaps some tea?"

"Nothing, thank you," I said.

"I will be back with some tea," he said as if he hadn't heard me, and went to a doorway, slid back the curtain covering it to show it was the kitchen, and went in.

I sat in the wooden chair and looked around the apartment. It was decorated with Oriental paintings, some lacquer pieces, but mostly old and worn-out furniture that looked as if it had been bought second-hand. I wondered why his guild didn't have the wealth my guild—my former guild—had.

He returned in a few minutes. "The water is heating."

"Really, I don't need anything," I tried.

"It's no bother." He sat in another chair that was covered in threadbare upholstery.

I looked at him, wondering what I should say. He saved me by speaking first.

"I am surprised to see you alive."

"Why is that?"

"Sending you to that ship, I thought it would be a situation where you could not win."

"Why?"

"Nakamura is very powerful."

I nodded in agreement. "He took my talisman and almost killed me. I've been in a hospital most of the time since then, unable to heal myself."

Takada was quiet, seeming to look at the wall over my head. I wondered what he was doing. "He might have deduced how you found him," he finally said.

"I don't know," I replied, shrugging my shoulders.

"That could be unfortunate."

"Why did you give me that note and tell me where to find him? You said it risked your life and your guild's honor, if I remember right."

Takada looked at me, a blaze in his black eyes. "You remember correctly. Nakamura seeks power for himself. He has crushed the Chosun and Manchukuo guilds. Now he wishes to control the Oriental guilds in America, including mine. I had small hope you may have been successful and killed him—or at least diverted his attention to your guild. I decided it was worth the risk. And telling you that, you may have been less likely to tell him who gave you the information."

I was angry for a moment, thinking he'd set me up to do his guild's dirty work. But actually, I was grateful for the chance to fight for Peg.

I spoke slowly, carefully, "I have lost my talisman and been exiled from my guild."

"If I had not given you that note, and told you where to find her, this would not have happened?"

I nodded.

Again he was quiet, not looking at me, but at the wall behind me, it seemed.

"Don't get me wrong," I said, feeling the need to fill the silence. "I'm glad I know what happened to her."

He looked at me. "Do you wish to find her?"

I nodded. "Yes, very much."

"Nakamura was going to Japan; that is all I know. He may also travel from there to Chosun—Westerners call it Korea—or Manchukuo."

"Manchukuo?" That was the second time he'd mentioned that place.

"Manchuria, I believe is the more common name," he explained.

That didn't help; I hadn't heard of it, either. I decided to change the subject.

"I need a talisman," I stated as a matter of fact. It would be suicidal to face Nakamura without a talisman. Hell, it probably was with one.

"One moment, please," he stood and went to the kitchen.

I sat back in the chair and waited; apparently I was getting tea whether I wanted it or not. I decided it would be rude to refuse.

He returned in a few minutes carrying a tray with a simple blue teapot with a bamboo handle and two matching porcelain cups. They were shallow and without handles, and covered in intricate designs, inside and out. He set the tray on a small, low chest and began pouring the tea. He held out a cup for me with both his hands. I reached out with my left hand to take it.

He looked at me angrily. "If you are going to Japan, you should learn some manners."

I looked at him, wondering what I had done wrong.

"Take it with both hands and a bow," he stated crisply, as if controlling his rage.

I reached out with both hands and took the cup, and tried a bow, bending at the waist.

"You'll need practice," he said, letting me have the cup.

He watched me as I held the teacup, looking at the liquid which was, to my surprise, green.

"You must taste it," he said.

I took a sip. It was bitter and yet sweet, not at all like what I was used to calling "tea."

He was looking at me expectantly.

28

"Thank you?" I said.

"Bah!" he spat. "I will have to teach you manners."

He walked away angrily and pulled an iron box from a shelf. He carried it over and set it down next to the tea tray. I saw that the lid was intricately designed with squares at multiple angles so each caught the light a little differently.

Takada pulled off the lid and reached inside. He held out an object with both hands. "You'll need this," he said.

I decided I should humor him since I needed his help. I remembered to reach for it with both hands and attempted to bow. Touching it I knew exactly what it was: a talisman.

"Are you going to kill Nakamura?" he asked me as I pulled the object to me.

"I'm going to get Peg back," I said.

He looked at me questioningly. "'Pag'?"

"Peg," I repeated. "It was what I called her. She said her name was Pak. I didn't think that was a proper name for a beautiful girl."

"Such arrogance," he whispered.

I looked at him, wondering what he meant.

He looked at me as if debating something, then spoke. "She used the name Pak Meyoung. 'Pak' is the family name she chose to use. Like 'Kader' for you. Orientals say family names first. She must have truly cared for you to allow you to call her 'Peg.' Meyoung is the given name she used. What you would call a 'first name.'"

"Meyoung?" I asked, letting the strange sound roll around my mouth.

"Yes. 'Me' means 'beautiful' and 'young' is her generational name and means 'forever.'"

"Beautiful forever," I whispered. It fit her—fit her better than "Peg." I felt like an idiot. "Nakamura called her 'Miko,'" I said.

Takada nodded. "The 'mi' also means 'beautiful' and is the same *Kanji*."

I shook my head. "I don't understand. What's a *Kanji*?"

He let out a sigh of exasperation and stood and walked to a desk. He came back with a blank piece of paper, an ink bottle, and a small paintbrush like one would use to paint a picture. He dipped the brush in the bottle and in fluid, practiced motions drew:

"That is 'mi,'" he explained. "It is a Chinese character—or in Japanese, *Kanji*—and it means the same thing in Chinese, Korean, or Japanese: beautiful.

There are slight variations on pronunciation: 'me' in Korean, 'mi' or 'bi' in Japanese depending on what other *Kanji* it's paired with, and 'mei' in Chinese.

"I see," I said, not really understanding.

Takada looked frustrated. "Yes, I'm sure you do. Also, there are differences between *Kanji*, Chinese characters, and Korean *Hanja*. But there are enough similarities that if you know one system, you can work with the others."

I looked at him. "Why do you know so much about Korean and Chinese?"

"There are Chinese, Japanese, and Koreans living in San Francisco, some of them adepts. I find it useful to know as much as I can about other cultures and languages, including yours."

We were both quiet, me looking at the picture, trying to figure out how one was supposed to get "beautiful" out of that.

I pulled out Peg's-Meyoung's note and pointed to the symbols at the bottom. "What are those?"

"*Hangul*, the Korean phonetic alphabet. It says 'Pak Meyoung.'"

I looked at the three marks, mystified as to how one could get her name out of them.

Finally Takada spoke. "You still plan to pursue Meyoung?"

"Yes," I said firmly.

"Then you'll have to kill Nakamura," Takada explained.

"I realize that."

While we were talking, I let the power of the talisman flow into my nerves. It was almost as powerful as my arrowhead. I looked at it. It was a brass button with an eagle perched on an anchor design. There was a red stain on it that I knew immediately was blood. I'd have to be careful not to allow the blood to be removed as then it would lose some, if not all, of its power.

"One of Admiral Perry's sailors gave up that button," Takada said with a smile.

"Thank you," I said, again trying to bow.

"Better," Takada said, smiling.

"One thing," I said, "it seemed Nakamura could control Peg—Meyoung, as if he knew her name, her real name."

Takada looked at me seriously. "I don't know how that could be," he said slowly. "She wouldn't have given him her name willingly."

"I know, but I could swear he was controlling her."

"Perhaps emotionally, but not with his powers," Takada said.

"Perhaps," I said, but I didn't believe it. I'd seen him control her as if she were a mere lesser on that gangplank.

There was a long silence. Then I asked, "And you want nothing in return?" This was unprecedented, one guild member helping another, even though I had no guild.

"Kill Nakamura," Takada said. "And if you succeed, my guild's talisman returned."

I nodded. I noticed that he didn't sound very optimistic about getting his talisman back.

\*\*\*

Money was not a large problem. I had learned the parts of town where men could be counted upon to have fat wallets. Takada tried to train me on manners, and to humor him I learned some; never again did I fail to remove my shoes or receive a gift with both hands. But, when he started talking about why the Japanese acted the way they did, I didn't really listen. I didn't see the use of knowing any more about Oriental culture than needed to keep Takada happy. I was going to go to Japan, kill Nakamura, and come back home where people didn't bow or take off their shoes when entering an apartment. Their barbarian culture did not interest me in the least.

It was nearly two months after I'd last seen Peg, or Meyoung as I had started calling her in my thoughts, when Takada and I were on the Embarcadero not far from where Nakamura had almost killed me. I was going to board a tramp steamer for Tokyo because Takada said he'd heard rumors Nakamura was there with his consort.

"Good luck," he said with a bow.

I returned it clumsily, thinking what the whites around us would think of seeing me bow to a Jap. "Goodbye," I said.

"Farewell." He looked as if he never expected to see me again.

# CHAPTER THREE

It was early morning when I arrived in Fusan, as the Japanese called it, on a freighter from Matsue, Japan. After six months in Nippon, I hadn't found Nakamura or Meyoung. I had met the occasional member of the *Omi Uji* or their warriors, who wanted to kill me. One warrior told me, before I killed him, that Nakamura might be in Korea or Manchuria. Japan had invaded Manchuria the year before on some pretext. It was a huge international incident, apparently.

I could feel my button talisman grow stronger as I used it to defeat Japanese adepts and warriors. Many of the warriors were actual samurai—like those I had defeated on the Embarcadero—remnants of Japan's past, finding purpose hiring out their services to adepts. I was sure I still wasn't strong enough to take on Nakamura, but I hoped I could find Meyoung—I was still getting used to calling her that—and steal her away from him without a direct confrontation.

Japan was an interesting society. It seemed a medieval feudal society had had modernity grafted onto it. The Emperor was the unquestioned absolute ruler, although the military seemed to be running things. But Tokyo was as modern as San Francisco, at least in terms of technology, with phones, electricity, streetcars, and the occasional automobile. Most of the women and some of the men wore robe-like clothes called kimonos, but most men wore Western-style suits or uniforms. As one got further from Tokyo, the level of technology decreased and people tended to dress more traditionally. But this wasn't surprising. Even in the U.S., Grand Forks was still on gaslights when Minneapolis had electricity.

Chosun, or Korea as most Westerners called it, had been a Japanese colony for more than twenty years. The ship I arrived on carried military equipment. As I disembarked, I noticed bags of rice stacked on the pier, apparently to be loaded onto the ship to be taken back to Japan.

Fusan was not, I discovered as I walked from the port area, as modern as even Matsue. One of the first things to hit me was the smell. The entire city had the unpleasant odor of an outhouse.

The buildings in the town were low and flat-roofed with sloped sides, almost like a mansard roof, but with no central peak.

I walked along an unpaved central street with telephone poles running along one side. Most of the civilians wore white, it seemed. The women wore dresses with the waistline just under the bosom, usually white or white with black skirts. I learned later they were called *hanbok* and were the traditional dress for Korean women. The men wore loose tunics and pants: they wore the traditional male *hanbok* only on ceremonial occasions. There were some men in Western dress, but those seemed to be Japanese, judging from their attitudes. There were men in Japanese military uniforms who treated the civilians with disregard bordering on contempt.

Fusan did not look like a pleasant place to stay, and I hoped it was not indicative of all of Korea. I was starting to wonder if I should just go back to America. Meyoung had said she loved me, but then she'd left, apparently willingly, with Nakamura. I still didn't understand why she'd done that and why he had seemed able to control her. Maybe this adventure was a fool's errand. I might find her only to learn she didn't love me but was, indeed, loyal to Nakamura. But why had she helped me on the docks of San Francisco until Nakamura stopped her? I hoped I could find her soon and at least get an answer to that question, one way or the other.

"Ah," I heard a voice say, interrupting my thoughts, "another expatriate."

I turned to see an older Caucasian gentleman dressed in a nearly worn-out black suit. He was smiling at me.

"American?" he asked.

"Yes," I replied, trying to sound as uninterested in talking to him as I actually was.

"Wonderful!" he cried out and took my hand, pumping it vigorously. "Carter Wagner, Boston."

"Joe Kader, San Francisco," I said, wondering if I should use a persuasion spell on him to get rid of him.

"First time in Chosun?" he asked, finally releasing my hand. He had a thick head of white hair and a white goatee and mustache. He was a thin man and his suit seemed almost too big for him.

"Yes," I replied.

"And what brings you to the Hermit Kingdom?" he inquired persistently.

I hadn't heard Chosun called that before. I wondered whether I could get some information from this man. "I'm a traveler," I said. "Out to see the world."

The man nodded knowingly. "I'm with the Brothers of Christ Missionaries, but please don't confuse us with the Christadelphians. We're Methodists, actually. I've been in Chosun for almost twenty years now."

We were standing on the street in the heat, and Brother Wagner was working up a sweat just talking.

"May I buy you something cool to drink?" I offered.

"Oh," Wagner laughed, "you'll be hard pressed to find cold drinks in Pusan—oh, dear, I shouldn't say that, the Japanese don't like it when I use Korean names. But," he continued without seeming to pause to breathe, "I can take you back to our church and offer you at least something wet and the company of fellow Americans."

"Thank you, I would like that," I said. Twenty years in Korea—maybe he could be helpful.

Wagner laughed and put his arm around me. "So, exploring the world, are we? Are you wealthy?"

"I get by," I said, trying to shrug his arm off my shoulders.

Wagner either took the hint or decided to stop on his own. He started walking westward, away from the docks. It wasn't long before we came to a neighborhood dominated by small squat houses surrounded by small gardens and occasionally a fence around part of them. Many of the fences were made of thin branches cut to nearly the same length, held together by horizontal but slightly thicker boughs. The houses seemed to be placed haphazardly, not in any order as they would be in America, where they would be lined up along both sides of the street. All the houses' fronts were pointed approximately south, which seemed to explain why they weren't in an orderly row. The dirt street, as it were, ran alongside clusters of homes.

The houses seemed to be made of adobe-like material and wood with paper windows. They either had straw or tile roofs. The houses with tile roofs were apparently owned by those with more money, judging by the size and repair of the houses.

As we walked along, Wagner pointed out the small gardens of the Koreans.

"The Rose of Sharon, or *mugunghwa* as they call it, is a symbol of Chosun," he explained, indicating a small tree, almost a bush, with big white or pink flowers, that was in most of the yards. "The Koreans grow them in defiance of the Japanese colonial government."

I wasn't really listening, but was trying to feel for other adepts as we walked. The closer I was, the more luck I would have sensing them—inverse square law—but Fusan seemed as devoid of them as Grand Forks was when I was growing up. I was also trying to get glimpses of the Korean women's faces, I suppose in the vain hope I'd stumble across Meyoung. Of course, I didn't.

The church, built on the outskirts of town, was a whitewashed clapboard box that wouldn't look out of place on the American prairie, including the spire in front. There were Koreans working around it, doing gardening and maintenance. They greeted Wagner in Korean with a bow and he answered in the same language, bowing also but not as low. Instead of entering the church, we went into a small house beside it.

"I share this with Brother Eckert and his mother," Wagner explained. "A God-fearing woman, Mrs. Eckert," he added admiringly.

Inside, the house appeared almost like a normal American home from the Grand Forks of my childhood, except some of the furnishings and rugs were obviously Oriental. A Korean woman approached and bowed. Wagner bowed and talked to her, and she bowed again and walked away. Then Wagner led me to a simple parlor with simple uncovered furniture and pointed to a chair.

"Do you speak any Korean, Mr. Kader?"

I shook my head. "None. I picked up some Japanese when I visited there. I was hoping they were similar." I wasn't going to explain to him about translation spells.

Wagner shook his head, laughing again. "Oh, no. They are nothing alike except for the use of Chinese characters. Fascinating language…has verbs for nearly everything, including what are adjectives in English. For example: to be tall, to be short, to be green."

I wasn't sure how that would help me. Before Wagner could assail me with more irrelevant facts, the Korean woman returned with a tray that she set on a low table. She poured water from a simple tin pitcher into glasses. She picked one up with both hands and walked to me, and held it out, her eyes cast downward. I took the glass, remembering to use both hands, and almost said, "*Arigato*" but decided against it. "Thank you," I said, hoping she'd understand.

She smiled slightly as if to acknowledge my gesture, bowed low, then turned and handed a glass to Wagner, who spoke to her in Korean. She bowed to both of us and left.

Wagner looked at me as if trying to determine who I was. "Very unusual," he finally said, "for a man to come to Chosun for no reason. Interested in Oriental cultures?"

"No, not really." I wanted to find Meyoung and go home, but I wasn't going to tell him that.

"Then why go to all the trouble of coming here?"

"I have a reason," I explained.

"And what is that?"

"To see it. It's not…" I thought quickly, "…Oklahoma."

He looked at me dubiously. "I thought you said you were from San Francisco."

I nodded, realizing he'd caught me in a lie. "San Francisco was where I lived before leaving for the Orient. I was born and raised in Oklahoma." And with luck he knew no one from there.

Then he asked, "Do you understand the political situation here?"

"I know Korea, or Chosun as I've heard it called, is a colony of Japan," I replied.

Wagner nodded. "That is correct. Do you think that was the Koreans' choice?"

"Frankly, I don't know."

Wagner took a deep breath, indicating he was getting ready to pontificate. "The Chosun peninsula is a land bridge between two ancient enemies, China and Japan. So it was in both countries' interest to dominate it. There has been very little time in history when Chosun wasn't under Chinese or Japanese domination—usually Chinese—but the Chinese allowed the Koreans a large amount of autonomy, asking mostly for tribute and passage for its armies to attack Japan. Japan has dominated Chosun since the Sino-Japanese war ended in 1895 when Japan defeated China here, in Chosun."

"Then they made it a colony?" I asked.

Wagner shook his head, making his white hair undulate. "No. They even signed treaties stipulating Chosun should remain free."

"What changed?" I asked, interested despite myself.

"The war with Russia," he said simply. "Western powers such as the United States and Great Britain feared Russian hegemony in East Asia more than they feared the rising power of Imperial Japan. The Treaty of Portsmouth— that's Portsmouth, New Hampshire—ending that war gave Japan virtual control of Chosun, if not outright control. And they never removed their army after the defeat of Russia. Still, they waited five more years, until 1910, to formalize it by compelling the Korean Prime Minister with force of arms into a 'Treaty of Annexation.' The Japanese knew that the highest caste in Chosun were not warriors as in Japan, but scholars, and that Korea had almost no army.

"Since then the Japanese have run Chosun with varying degrees of severity," Wagner continued. "I have been here nearly twenty years and I have seen nationalist movements arise only to be brutally suppressed. I've seen Governor-Generals who were tolerant, and those that were tyrants."

He stopped to look at me, to assure himself I was still listening. "Go on," I said. I hoped he'd say something about the situation with the local adept guilds and the *Omi Uji.*

"Things were looking better until this war started. The new Governor-General, Kazushige, has been turning Chosun into a war machine to feed the Japanese army."

By "war" I assumed he meant the Japanese occupation of Manchuria.

"The Japanese," he continued, "will point out they have built roads and hospitals, brought electricity, railroads, and schools. They'll point to the lower infant mortality rate and the rise in literacy. The Koreans will say they are not free and that the Japanese are trying to destroy their culture.

"And I tell you," he continued, his anger building, "they do not like Christians. I have seen Japanese soldiers come across Christian Korean girls and treat them most shamefully."

I looked at him. I knew what he meant, but it was hard to believe such a thing was possible. I realized that in America, we have no idea how brutal the world is beyond our shores.

There was a knock on the door that interrupted my thoughts. I noticed Wagner didn't move, but instead the Korean woman who had served us scurried to answer the door. A few minutes later she came into the parlor and spoke to him in Korean. I didn't bother to work up a translation spell. At the end of their conversation she nodded, bowed and walked away.

"You'll have to excuse me for a moment," Wagner explained. "There is a peasant man here who insists on speaking to me and since we are here to serve…"

I nodded, smiled, and said I understood.

By then the Korean servant had returned with the peasant. He was in the white tunic and loose pants I'd seen most of the men in town wearing. By now I had a translation spell going. The peasant bowed to Wagner and spoke rapidly.

"Sir, I have overheard that the Japanese are planning a raid on this very church for they suspect you of harboring new body meeting sympathizers."

Wagner looked at him hard. "This is not true. We are not political. Whom do they suspect?"

"Someone named Ee."

Wagner looked dubiously at the Korean. "There are several Ee's here. Do you have more information?"

The man shook his head. "I am sorry, no."

"Wait," Wagner said. He turned to me and switched to English. "This man is saying the colonial government suspects a Korean named Lee is part of the *Sin'ganhoee*—New Chosun Movement," he corrected himself, "a nationalist movement the government has been suppressing, especially since the start of the war. I'm sorry, we get these rumors and they need to be dealt with. Our relationship with the colonial government is precarious."

"The 'New Chosun Movement'?" I asked. I'd heard "new body meeting," but translation spells do tend to give literal translations.

"Oh," he replied, sounding exasperated, "yes. At least they aren't socialist like some of the nationalist movements.

"Please wait here, I'll return shortly," he said with strained courtesy, and turned to the peasant and said in Korean, "I will bring Mr. Eckert to talk to you, and he can help you."

The peasant bowed and said "Thank you, first born."

I was surprised at that, not knowing then that it is common in Korean culture to refer to an older person as "teacher," which literally translates as "first born."

Wagner walked out of the room and the peasant turned to me and said, "Mask," in the ancient language.

I looked at him, surprised.

"Mask!" he hissed, his eyes showing that this was no peasant farmer.

I touched my talisman and invoked the required spells.

"Meet me outside," he ordered.

I nodded my understanding just as the two missionaries returned. They spoke to the Korean and then Eckert took him away.

"Mr. Wagner," I asked, "where can an American stay here in Fusan? Is there a Western-style hotel?"

The missionary shook his head. "No, but there are hotels that cater to Japanese near the government offices; you'll find those are acceptable. Ask anyone where."

Yes, I knew about Japanese-style hotels: you sit on the floor, you sleep on the floor. No wonder they take their shoes off when they enter a house.

Since I was masking I couldn't use a persuasion spell on him, and ended up spending the better part of an hour listening to the man talk about his work in Asia. None of it was very useful, since it was mostly dealing with missionary work. He insisted I stay for dinner, but I told him I needed to go. It took a good ten minutes to convince him. Persuasion spells are so much easier.

I left the house and looked for the Korean man. I didn't see him, but the Koreans tended to dress alike and with similar black hair they tended to look the same unless one was looking directly at their faces...and sometimes even then. I decided to walk back toward town in search of a hotel.

The Korean adept somehow managed to sidle right up to me. I turned to talk to him and he said, "Keep walking, don't look at me," in the ancient language.

I obeyed. "Who are you?"

He didn't answer. "Nakamura is looking for you. He's heard of the *Migook Sarhom* asking about him in *Ilpone*." He was interspersing Korean words I didn't know with the ancient language. I assumed "*Migook Sarhom*" referred to me ("American"? "White man"?) and "*Ilpone*" probably meant Japan. The ancient language is lacking words for modern terms such as modern countries. And since I was masking, I couldn't run a translation spell.

"I assume that is you," he said.

"I am looking for Nakamura," I replied, also in the ancient language. "I assume he's looking for me. Is he in Korea-er, Chosun?"

"Yes."

"Why are you helping me?"

Again he didn't answer the question. "Follow me, discreetly, at a distance."

"Are we going to see Nakamura?"

"No." He said it with a finality that told me much. I suspected he was in a rival guild and given what Takada had told me, they were probably in a struggle to survive.

"Wait," I said forcefully.

He turned and looked at me.

"I need to talk to you," I said.

"Where we are going, we can talk," he replied.

He seemed anxious to get off the street and not be seen with me. But I wanted answers.

"Can Nakamura control other adepts?" I asked. I was thinking of Meyoung on the gangplank of that ship.

He looked at me, somewhat questioningly. "Yes, if he knows their names," he answered.

"Of course," I said. That was true of any adept, assuming they were more powerful than the adept they were trying to control, and knowing their name would almost automatically make them more powerful.

"But Nakamura seemed to be controlling Mey…" I decided not to say her name "…an adept."

"In his guild?" he asked.

"Yes."

Again the Korean gave me a questioning look. "Does not the head of your guild know your name?"

I felt horrified at the thought. I'd probably be dead if so; Newmark would not have hesitated to kill me if he'd known my name.

"No," I said. "We protect our names."

The Korean shook his head. "It's different here. When you join a guild, you give the head your name to prove your loyalty to him."

I was frankly shocked. While it would generate great loyalty, no Western adept I knew would agree to it. You'd be a virtual slave to the head of the guild.

"When the *Omi Uji* took over some Chosun guilds, the heads of those guilds bought their lives with the list of names."

I almost felt weak-kneed. Nakamura knew Meyoung's real name! That was how he'd controlled her in San Francisco. She had no choice! She did love me, but he knew her name. I was happy and angry simultaneously.

A thought occurred to me. "Nakamura doesn't have your name?"

"I was the leader of my *kye*—my guild. Now my followers and I hide from Nakamura. Now you follow me and no more questions until we are safe."

He started walking. I waited, pretending to be very interested in a Rose of Sharon bush, and then followed at a distance. I followed him through the town noticing he tended to walk with his head down. I noticed all of the Koreans seemed to be doing the same thing. When he came upon some Japanese, identifiable by being either soldiers in uniform or men in business suits, he would not make eye contact and would get out of their way. Hell of a way for an adept to behave, I decided. But if he had to mask to hide from Nakamura and the *Omi Uji*, then he had no power to deal with lessers.

We entered a residential neighborhood that was not much different from the one Wagner had led me through earlier that day, with the scattered small houses made of what appeared to be baked mud. My guide was walking toward a house with a tile roof. He glanced back at me and then looked toward the house. I got the message: follow me.

The house was different. It seemed in better repair than the others did. And there were no Rose of Sharon bushes. I hesitated. Looking around, I could see it was the only house close-by without the bushes. It might not mean anything; not every house I'd seen in Fusan had them. But the house also looked better, in better repair and with more plants in the garden.

The Korean knocked on the wooden door and waited. I stayed away, justifying it by thinking I didn't want to rush up on the house but would follow discretely later.

The door opened to a dark interior and the Korean went inside. The door was left open. I kept looking at that black hole in the side of the gray abode. I was starting to feel very nervous.

An elderly Korean woman was walking down the street in the classic white dress with the high waistline. She stared at me for a long time as she approached; then, as I looked at her, she broke eye contact. But she glanced at the open portal into the house before looking away. I caught the emotion on her face: fear.

Fear of adepts? But if they were masking and not using their powers in order to hide, then would she know they were adepts?

I turned and started walking in the other direction. I wanted to use a translation spell and, if needed, a persuasion spell on the old woman to find out what she was afraid of. But I didn't dare, for if she were only afraid of the adepts, I could reveal myself to the *Omi Uji*.

There was a yell from behind me. I turned to look. My guide was in the door, glaring at me. He held out his hand, palm down, and moved his fingers as if scratching an itch. It took me a second to realize this must be the local version of a crooked finger to indicate one should follow.

I looked at him. He was angry and scared. Why would he be scared?

I turned and ran away.

The man yelled, not at me, but back into the house.

I turned and looked just as three samurai emerged. They looked a lot like the ones I had faced on the Embarcadero, dressed in gray or black robes and carrying long thin swords with shorter ones in scabbards tucked into a sash around their waist.

And my guide stopped masking.

I wrapped my finger around the button in my pocket and pointed at the nearest warrior. An airbolt knocked him back and he hit the ground hard, dust billowing up around him. He didn't jump up immediately, so I hoped he was no longer a problem.

But by then the other two samurai had reached me as they moved at speeds that seemed almost impossible. They were screaming and holding their swords over their heads. I jumped aside as the nearest brought the sword down and grabbed his shoulder. He dropped to the ground unconscious. The times I'd fought samurai in Japan I'd learned how to defeat them more easily than the first time when I faced them in San Francisco.

Then the airbolt hit me. The pain was immense, and for a moment my vision turned gray. I was slammed into the wall of a house and the adobe-like material cracked under the impact. Part of the straw roof fell on me, leaving some hanging. I looked and saw my Korean guide pointing at me. He'd fired the airbolt.

The last samurai was running toward me; the first one had recovered from my airbolt and was standing, although somewhat wobbly.

I hit the samurai charging me with a persuasion spell and a fear spell. He stopped in his tracks and looked at me, bewildered. I turned up the power and watched as he swayed like a tree in a hurricane between attack and retreat.

But lightning hit the wall next to me. It set the straw hanging from the roof on fire. I don't know whether the Korean adept had planned that or had just missed me.

I jumped away from the house as the straw burned quickly. I wondered how many years that roof had been on the structure.

The distraction of the lightning and the fire had caused me to ignore the samurai, who sprang at me, swinging his sword, which hummed in the air. I gripped the button hard in my fist and reached for him, but he managed to duck my grasp.

Korean lessers were running screaming from the burning house when the Korean adept somehow sucked the fire off the roof and directed it at me. I've never seen that trick before, I thought (although I saw something like it years later in Norway). I stopped the flames inches from my body with a cool mist.

But the two conscious samurai, who wouldn't be stopped by a mist, were closing in. I had to stop the adept first, even though the samurai would be easier to kill.

Because of the flames, the warriors could attack from only one direction. They were very close together and I saw my opportunity. I dropped to the ground and ended the fire-stopping mist.

The flames I had been deflecting then shot over my body and blasted into the two samurai. They screamed and twisted away as their clothes and hair went up in flames.

The fire stopped streaming from the burning house as the Korean adept apparently tried to keep it from hitting the warriors.

I stood, ignored the agonized screams of the samurai, the yells and sobs of the poor peasants whose house had been turned into a weapon, and pointed a finger at the adept. Fire arced from my finger toward him.

He stopped it, as I expected, with a mist of his own. I stopped shooting fire, the last of it seeming to fly in slow-motion toward him, and I took his air away. The last of the fire rushed into the vacuum created, but was snuffed out due to lack of air. That did matter, because the adept passed out and fell to the ground.

I kept air away from him as I walked toward the burned samurai, who had scattered like injured animals. The adept was going to be dead soon, anyway, I knew, and I wanted to see whether the samurai were still a threat.

The one I'd rendered unconscious was in a growing puddle of blood, the red liquid turning brown in the dirt, his weapons missing. I hadn't stabbed him, but I noticed the Koreans were pointedly ignoring him. Most were forming a bucket brigade to put out the fire, lined up from the local well to the burning house, but to little effect. Some young men were eyeing the surviving two samurai and me. I could only guess that they'd killed the samurai with his own sword.

The other two samurai, knocked down by flame, had fallen closer to me—which had probably kept the peasants from killing them and therefore saved their lives—and were lying in the dirt, groaning in pain. I knew from experience how much burns hurt. I decided they weren't a threat, either. I walked toward the adept's body. As I did, the young men swarmed over one of the samurai. One took the short sword from its scabbard and cut his throat, and then they scurried away with both weapons, which somehow disappeared inside their white tunics and trousers.

I pointed at the sole surviving warrior. "Leave that one alive!" I called out, using a translation spell. The peasants seemed to cower at the sound of my voice.

I stopped the air movement spell and approached the Korean adept. His eyes were open, staring unblinkingly at the lowering sun.

I pried open his fist to find a flower petal. I could feel its power as a talisman.

I put it in my pocket along with the button.

I returned to the surviving samurai. The Korean men were watching him from a distance, as if he had a secure spell around him. He was lying on his back with his arm over his face. His clothes were not burning but appeared almost melted, which I found interesting. He smelled like burning hair, which was strange because his hair wasn't burned; I also knew what that locked like. His weapons were scattered around him as if he'd flung them away. I kicked them out of his reach and nudged him with my foot.

He moaned but didn't otherwise react.

I used a translation spell. "I won't kill you if you tell me what I want to know."

He didn't say anything.

I hit him with a fear spell combined with persuasion. If I could get him to talk, I'd hit him with a truth spell.

"Who are you?" I demanded, resting my foot on his chest. He winced in pain. The flames or heat must have reached there.

"My name is Hidehiko Yamamoto," he said, taking the arm from his face and glaring at me with black eyes. "I am a warrior for the *Omi Uji*."

I smiled grimly. I'd been right that it was a trap. If the house had looked more like the surrounding homes, if it had had Rose of Sharon bushes, I would probably be dead right now.

I switched to a truth spell, made even more powerful by my knowing his name.

"Where's Nakamura?"

He hesitated. I pressed down on his chest. His face showed the pain he was in, but he didn't cry out or ask for mercy.

"Where's Nakamura?" I asked again, keeping my voice softly threatening. I increased the power of the truth spell.

"Mukden," he said as if the syllables were being forcibly pulled from him.

"Where's that?" I asked.

"Manchukuo," he responded.

I was using a translation spell, but it was still as if he was speaking a foreign language.

I stood and looked around. The young men were hovering nearby. I walked away, being mostly ignored as the Koreans were too busy with their disaster. A young man with blood on his tunic looked at me with questioning eyes.

"I don't care about the samurai anymore," I told him.

He looked at me with a grimace, and then turned to the warrior. A group led by him swooped down on the samurai. I heard the pop as his throat was sliced open. I'd kept my promise: I didn't kill him.

\*\*\*

I masked again and wandered back to town. A horse-drawn fire engine, its bell clanging, leaving a trail of black smoke behind it, and with what looked like too many men hanging on its flanks, careened by me. This was followed shortly by a military truck full of soldiers. They ignored me just as I ignored them.

The sun was going down by the time I found the Japanese hotel Wagner had mentioned. I'd gotten used to the hotels in Japan, so there were no surprises.

In the morning I found Wagner's church again.

"Hello!" he said after the Korean woman showed me in.

"Hello," I replied.

"How are you finding Chosun?" he asked.

"Very interesting. Do you know where Mukden is?"

He frowned. "That's in Manchuria, or Manchukuo as the Japanese have now named it. You don't know of the Mukden Incident?"

"I've been traveling," I said. "Was that the incident that started the war in Manchuria?"

"Yes," he said, still acting surprised by my ignorance.

"Manchuria is China, correct?" I added.

"Yes; the Japanese are occupying a large part of it now. Why?"

"Could you do me a favor?" I was ready to use a persuasion spell to get what I wanted, if necessary.

"What's that?" he asked.

"Teach me everything you know about Korean culture."

He looked at me, surprised.

"And Chinese, too," I added. "And Japanese," I added again. I might have to go back to Japan and obviously would deal with Japanese in Korea and Manchuria.

"Why?" he asked.

"I have come to believe," I said, "that it will be helpful to me."

He furrowed his brow with thought. "What made you decide that?"

"A house without Rose of Sharon bushes."

# BOOK TWO
# KATANA
# 1943

# CHAPTER FOUR

From the window of my private sleeper berth, the American Southwest looked as if it were still stuck in the days of the westerns. I almost expected to see Tom Mix riding his "super-intelligent" horse, Tony, across the dry landscape. But no such luck; Tom Mix had been dead for three years, killed in a car accident. When the view along the railroad tracks wasn't of uninterrupted desert, it was of small dirty farms, small dirty towns, and small dirty people.

The Sunset Limited was slowing and passing more farms and roads, which indicated we were nearing a town. The occasional grimy vehicle passed on the highway paralleling the tracks. There was a knock on my door, which, thankfully, drew me away from the dismal scene. I took the few steps across the room and opened it to the smiling black face of a porter.

"Yuma, next stop, Mr. Kader," he said with more enthusiasm than I believed possible. He stood grinning at me in his blue jacket that seemed a bit small for him and black cap that was just a bit too large. I didn't, then, think that he also didn't look like the porter I had seen when we left San Francisco.

"Thank you," I said and started to close the door.

"I can take your bag, if you wish, Mr. Kader."

I smiled at him. "No thanks."

He looked disappointed, I thought at the time he was disappointed to lose the opportunity to earn a tip. "Fine, sir," he said and walked on as I closed the door.

And realized there was almost no air in the room. I reached for the door, but as my hand touched the metal of the knob, it jerked back in pain. There was a secure spell on the door, placed there by a very powerful adept. Damn, I swore at myself. Morgan had found allies.

I stumbled to the window, looking for a way to open it. The train was crossing a muddy river, the Colorado I was certain, on an iron bridge. The girders were mere inches away from the glass. But if I didn't act fast, I'd be dead soon. I could discontinuously traverse out of the room, but discontinuously traversing out of a moving train into the small gap separating the railcars and the bridge girders looked like suicide. The other choice was over the river, since it is not wise to discontinuously traverse where one can't see. If you materialize where something already is, the explosion will be spectacular and deadly. Going into the muddy river was my last choice, and I couldn't traverse into the corridor outside my room because I couldn't see out there and didn't have time to do a spell of far-seeing.

I picked up my valise and, using a strength spell, which right then might have made me as strong as normal, I swung it against the window. The glass exploded inward, cutting my face and hands. But air, sweet, wonderful air, poured in. I breathed deeply for a few moments, ignoring my bleeding, until my strength returned.

I didn't know what Morgan's next attack would be, but I knew if I stayed in this room I'd probably be dead very soon. The secure spell on the door was strong, so it took a few minutes for me to work a counter. While I was doing this, the train came to a stop at the depot. I could see the two-story building and maybe a dozen people waiting for the train, including some soldiers dressed in khaki uniforms. I debated diving out the window, but decided that would bring too much attention. Grabbing my hat and valise, I carefully opened the door and used every sense I had to survey the corridor. I could see that the other side of the train faced a dirt bank.

People were coming out of their suites, making it difficult to find any threat. The same porter was standing at the end of the corridor. And he was no longer masking. I mentally berated myself for the stupid assumption I had made. The Negro guilds were, in meta at least, as powerful as my own. But right here, in a corridor full of lessers, there wasn't much either of us could do except glare at one another and try to determine the strength of the other's meta.

Or, try to escape. I headed the opposite direction from him, looking for another exit from the Pullman. A woman looked at me and shrieked. I forgot that I must have looked macabre with blood streaming down my face, but I didn't have the time to do a healing spell and I wouldn't do one in front of lessers.

I moved into the car behind mine and there was a door to the outside. There was another porter standing there. I didn't know whether he was an adept, but I wasn't going to make the assumption he wasn't. He looked at me and the expression of shock on his face looked genuine.

He moved toward me. "Sir?" he called out. "Are you all right?"

I stepped down on the little wooden step and onto the concrete platform, even though the heat made me want to retreat inside again out of the sun. "I'm fine. I need a taxi, quick." I looked back at the door in the car I had been in. The adept/porter was coming out.

My porter was waving over a car. It was a Model A—even I recognized the formerly ubiquitous vehicles— inexpertly painted yellow. Well, there was a war on, and people were doing their best with limited resources.

"Sir, may I help you?" I turned to see a young soldier looking at me with concern.

"No, I'm fine," I said as I stepped into the taxi.

The soldier bent down to look in the window. I noticed the parallel silver bars on his shoulder. "Are you sure, sir?"

"Yes, I'm fine."

The soldier spoke to the driver. "Get this man to a doctor."

"Yes, sir," the driver said and the car oozed away, making an extraordinary amount of noise for something moving so slowly.

I looked out the hole in the rear where a window would be. The Negro adept was pulling off his blue jacket and signaling another car. It was newer than the jalopy I was riding in. The soldier was talking excitedly with his fellows. I did not need the attention of the U.S. Army at this point.

"I don't need a doctor," I told my driver. All I could see of him was the dilapidated hat on his head, his plaid shirt, and the tanned hands on the steering wheel. "Is there a hotel in this town?"

"If you're worried about the law, Doc Addleman's okay. He won't tell the cops."

"No," I said forcefully. "Just get me to a hotel."

The driver glanced back at me. "You know these folks?" he asked.

I looked out the back window again. The second car was following us. I could see the driver was a Negro, too, and the passenger was the porter/adept.

"No," I said, "and I'm not anxious to make their acquaintance."

"I could take you to the sheriff's."

"No!" I barked. This was turning into a fiasco. I did not want the attention of any government official, yet the Army knew of my presence, and if I wasn't careful the local John Law would be mixed up in this, too.

The other car was alongside us by then on the broad streets of the town. The adept grinned at me. Then I saw a rear-seat passenger pointing a revolver at my head. I slid away from the window, knowing that the car provided no protection, but hoping that if he couldn't see me at least he wouldn't shoot me.

"I'm sorry," the driver said as the car slowed. "I've got a wife and children." At least then I knew where the gun was pointed.

I started fingering my talisman and working a spell.

Seconds after the car stopped, the door was jerked open and the revolver was shoved in my face.

"Out!"

I slid out and stood, my hand still in my pocket, still on my talisman. We were still in town, but people were ignoring us. I looked at the covered sidewalks behind arched pillars—obviously designed to give much-needed shade to pedestrians—and saw the townsfolk were going about their business completely unaware of my situation. This was due to a spell the Negro adept was using, a kind of glamour on his warriors that disguised their weapons. The reason was obvious; we were far enough south that a Negro holding a gun on a white man would bring instant and unwanted notice from the locals, and we were far enough west that some of those locals were probably armed.

"Raise your hands," the Negro with the gun, the warrior, ordered. The driver had also exited the car and held a gun on me.

The adept remained in the car, looking out the rolled-down window. "Leave your talisman in your pocket," he added.

But it was too late. I pulled my hand out of my pocket and pointed at one of the tires on my pursuers' car. It exploded. Everyone but me flinched, the driver ducking behind the car and the man with the gun closest to me dropping to the ground. I kicked the gun out of his hand and placed a spell of holding on him. Then I pulled him into the taxi and yelled at the driver, "Go!"

By now the adept and his driver were starting to recover. I watched through the back window as the driver jumped in the car and started pursuit. It didn't last long as, with one tire shredded, the car couldn't go far.

I gave my captive a little fear spell and held him against the back of the seat. "Where's Morgan?" I put a little truth spell on him, too.

"Who?"

Okay, he didn't know the name. "Whom do you work for?"

"The guild," he answered.

"And why was the guild after me?"

"I don't know. I was told to help capture an adept from a rival guild, that's all I know."

I sighed in disgust and sat down. The Negro guilds were smart enough not to tell their warriors too much.

"Stop the car," I said.

The car stopped with a rattling jerk.

"Get out," I ordered. The warrior gladly did.

"Go," I told the driver. "Take me to a hotel. I need to rest." I added a small persuasion spell to make sure he didn't decide to swing by the sheriff's office. After running the spell to heat the air in the tire and doing what I had done to the warrior, I was unusually tired. Maybe it was the circle of hell-like temperatures. I had yet to run a healing spell on myself, and I was still just beat.

As the car approached the hotel, I could see both the Negro adept and his warrior standing on the sidewalk outside it. I realized my driver had had to circle back to get to the hotel, while our pursuers had only to walk a few blocks.

"Uh-oh," my driver said.

"Don't worry," I told him. "They won't try anything here."

The hotel had the same arched southwest style architecture as much of the town. The ground floor was recessed, making a covered sidewalk around its exterior. A neon sign on top read "Hotel Del Sol." It was on a corner lot and the entrance was part of a hexagonal structure. There, in the shade waited my adversary, leaning casually against the wall next to the door. His remaining warrior was standing erect and looking alert, as he should.

The taxi shuddered to a halt. "What do I owe you?" I asked the driver.

"Seventy-five cents, please," he said, seeming amazed that I could talk of such mundane things.

I gave him a five-dollar bill and stepped out with my valise. I tipped my hat to the adept. "Good day, sir." I wasn't positive he wouldn't try anything here, but guilds like to keep their matters private, and this was a very public place. If he tried to pull that glamour to disguise his warrior's weapons, I could simply walk away. He wouldn't shoot me here.

"Where my man?" he asked, barely concealing his rage.

"We dropped him off a few blocks back," I answered, and entered the hotel lobby. He didn't follow.

The clerk behind the reception desk gave me a startled look. "Sir, are you all right?"

"It looks worse than it is," I said offhandedly. "Just scratches, really."

The clerk looked at me as if he didn't believe me. I don't know why people didn't want to believe me; it hardly hurt anymore, and I'd stopped bleeding a long time ago. I continued, "I need a room, preferably on the third floor. Street noise keeps me awake."

"Uhm," the clerk hesitated, still not pulling his eyes off my face. "Sure."

After completing the formalities of signing the register I was given a key and the stairs were pointed out. I climbed them, found the room, entered it, and closed the door behind me.

I was tempted to fall on the bed and rest, but that would be tantamount to suicide. I put an alarm spell on the door. A secure spell would be better, but it needed to be maintained, and if I were asleep it would slowly dissipate. An alarm spell would last almost indefinitely and would warn me of intruders, even as I slept. I moved to the window. It looked out over the street, but I couldn't see my adversary. I closed the curtains and placed an alarm spell on the window, too. Then I went to the small bathroom and looked in the mirror.

My face was encrusted with blood that had also run down my neck and stained my shirt. A piece of glass was embedded just above my left eyebrow. If it'd hit a few inches lower, well, a healing spell on an eye is a powerful piece of meta. I could probably do it, but would most likely need a week of rest to recover from the strain. I had sometimes wished the guilds would have special adepts for healing alone. But how could you trust any adept with your real name, which he would need? I knew I could never trust someone else with my name, even to save my life. He'd own you afterwards.

I cleaned off the blood as best I could and painfully removed the pieces of glass (the one over my eye was only the largest of five or so), which caused the bleeding to start again.

I ran healing spells on the worst cuts, which stopped the bleeding, and then healed the lesser lacerations. By this time I was exhausted. I double-checked that the door was locked and collapsed on the bed. I barely remember hitting the mattress.

\*\*\*

Morgan had bought a ticket on the Sunset Limited to Yuma, Arizona. It didn't take much of a persuasion spell on the ticket clerk in San Francisco to learn that. I assumed this was a waypoint. From here Morgan would go somewhere else. But there didn't seem to be a lot of transportation options in Yuma. The Sunset Limited eastbound came through on Mondays and Wednesdays. The westbound hit town on Tuesdays, Thursdays, and in the summer, Saturdays. Before it had been dammed multiple times, there had been riverboats on the Colorado River, but now it was little more than a muddy trickle. There were roads out of Yuma, but that would mean getting a car and driver. So why Yuma? And why was a Negro guild doing Morgan's dirty work?

\*\*\*

I woke a few hours later and, hungry, sought out the hotel's restaurant. As I passed the reception desk, the clerk looked at me in shock. I smiled: "See, just scratches."

In the restaurant I was led to a table and chose to sit facing the door. There were soldiers dining at another table. I didn't recognize any of them from the train depot.

The menu was limited but included hearty fare with a touch of Mexican cuisine. Prices were outrageous, with a simple cube steak costing more than a dollar.

I felt her presence before I saw her. Then Morgan was standing at the door. I'd always appreciated the sight of her. Tall with long legs, long red hair and deep blue eyes; she walked as if bred for royalty. A woman like that hardly needed the skills of an adept. Seeing me, she smiled and glided over, sitting down in the chair opposite me. Her beauty was not a glamour spell; I would have seen through it, and she didn't need it. She was dressed immaculately, probably the best-dressed woman within a hundred miles, from her actual silk stockings to the cute hat on her head. The soldiers had gotten very quiet during her walk. She knew this was the perfect place to talk, being too public for any action on my part, or hers for that matter.

"Hello, Kader," she said, pulling out a cigarette and lighting it. She wasn't holding a lighter or match. I don't think anyone other than me noticed.

"Hello, Beverly."

She laughed musically. "Why are you here?"

"I assume you can guess." I worked a spell to make our words become inaudible mumbles a few feet from the table.

She frowned, which looked lovely on her. "Fitz ordered you to kill me?"

"He ordered me to stop you."

"Then you'll have to kill me," she said.

"If that's what it takes," I agreed.

She leaned forward conspiratorially. "This is bigger than this little dispute with Fitz. Really big. If you help me, I could make you number two in the guild."

"With you number one?" I asked, not bothering to hide my sarcasm. It wasn't that a woman had never been head of our guild, but I didn't think Morgan had what it took.

"Of course," she said as if it were obvious. She snaked her hand across the table and took mine. "And there could be other benefits."

I pulled my hand back. "I'm over you," I said forcefully. Too forcefully, for I felt two conflicting sensations as her soft hand touched mine. First the desire returned, if only momentarily. And for just a moment I felt fear, for I sensed her power. She was stronger than I'd ever known her to be. Perhaps something in this town had helped increase her abilities.

She almost pouted, which I knew was part of her act. Then she hardened her face. "I'm giving you an offer; join me and prosper, or go against me and die."

"Neither of those outcomes is certain."

Again she leaned across the table and whispered. "You can't know the power of what I'm working on. It's enough to rule the guild—all the guilds."

I made a little laugh of derision. "Tell me, little one," I said, using a sobriquet I normally reserved for the bedroom, "how did you know I would be on the Limited today?"

She smiled coyly. "Let a girl have a few secrets."

Which meant she had someone in San Francisco who knew Fitz had sent me after her and could use a persuasion spell on a ticket clerk as easily as I could, or obtain the information without meta. That left only two possibilities: Fitz's inner circle or one of his warriors.

"So why Yuma?"

"Only if I know you are with me."

I shook my head. "And the Negro guild?"

She leaned forward again. "I promised its leader the number two spot in our new combined guild."

"The same position you just offered me. Whom were you planning to betray?"

"Him, of course."

Or both of us, more likely, I thought. "Of course," I repeated sarcastically.

She continued, "I don't want niggers in my guild. But right now they are useful as the most powerful guild in this area, and he is oh-so receptive to my charms—as you once were."

Yes, before I'd learned what she was.

She continued. "I'm leaving tomorrow on the Limited—" which meant she was going west "—and you can either go with me as my partner or stay here, dead."

I had to admit, I was impressed with her bravado. Whatever she had planned, she expected it to bring her great power. Power enough to betray a guild, albeit a small one, and to rule ours, one of the most powerful guilds in North America.

"So," I said offhandedly. "Do you want to meet in the middle of this town's main street at high noon tomorrow, or would you rather have your errand boys ambush me in my sleep?"

She managed to look disappointed. "Goodbye, Francis." She stood and walked away which, if I were to die soon, would not be an unpleasant last sight.

The waitress approached about that time. "Is your lady-friend joining you?"

"No," I answered, and ordered the most expensive meal on the menu.

***

When I got back to my room I again placed an alarm spell on the window. Despite the heat, I didn't dare have it open. On the door, however, I placed a strong secure spell. I was going to stay awake to reinforce it. Then I picked up the candlestick-style telephone and put the earpiece to my ear.

"Hotel operator," a woman's voice said.

"This is Mr. Kader. I need to place a person-to-person trunk call to a Mr. Fitzgerald at the Huntington Hotel in San Francisco at Klondike-5-1326, room 1313."

"Yes, sir," she said. "I'll call your room when it goes through."

I planned to warn Fitzgerald that one of his two deputies or one of his personal guards was in league with Morgan. Using the telephone rather than meta kept my powers at full strength. I didn't know when Morgan or her minions would strike, but I did know it would be before the Limited would leave the next day.

"Oh, and do you know what time the Limited departs tomorrow?"

"Seven A.M., sir."

"Thank you." I hung up.

I surveyed the battlefield. The room was small, with one iron bed and a couple of small chairs and tables. Then there was the bathroom. I didn't know if Morgan would send warriors, adepts, or both. Or come herself. The secure spell would hold off warriors as long as I maintained it. An adept, however, could, depending on his power, break through eventually.

I was thinking so hard; I actually jumped when the phone rang. "Yes?"

"Your party, sir," the hotel operator said.

"Mr. Kader?" another female voice asked, and I realized it must be the long-distance operator.

"Yes."

"I have Mr. Fitzgerald on the line. Go ahead, sir."

There was a pause, then "Kader?" It was Fitz.

"Yes, Teacher."

56

"I'm glad you called. I need you back here as fast as you can get here."

"Teacher," I said, talking loudly over the noisy line. "I've tracked down Morgan. I've spoken with her. She has ambitious plans." He should understand that meant she was threatening him and the guild.

"Forget her for now. This is more important. How soon can you be here?"

It took me a moment to overcome my surprise. "I can be on the next Sunset Limited; it leaves here in the morning and arrives in San Francisco about twenty hours later."

"No. Use private transportation."

"Yes, Teacher. I think I can be in San Francisco by morning."

"Come to my place at four P.M.," Fitz ordered.

"I will, Teacher."

He must have hung up, for the line went dead.

I didn't know what could be more important than an adept who had stolen one of the guild's most powerful talismans, killing two warriors in the process, and had spoken openly about taking over the guild. But Fitz was the boss. And I could tell him in person about the spy in his inner circle.

"Private transportation" was a code for using a meta method. I looked at the bed. The bedspread looked sturdy enough.

First I placed enough money in the room to pay for the night's lodging, the meal, the phone call, and the bedspread, plus a little extra. Then I waited until dark. I reinforced the secure spell one last time. I opened the window and threw the bedspread out with one hand, clutching my talisman in the other. The cloth spread out flat and hung in the air. I climbed out the window and sat on it. Holding my talisman, I found the north star and directed my flying carpet spell (or, flying bedspread) toward it, getting out of town as soon as possible, crossing the Colorado River into California (at this point, the border between Arizona and California ran east-west, following the river). Then I went west until the railroad, paralleling Highway 8, came from the south to meet me. My plan was simple: follow the railroad to San Francisco.

I had to be careful. There was a new invention called RADAR and trigger-happy pilots in heavily armed planes flying around that made "private transportation" unusually dangerous.

In a way, though, I was relieved to be high-tailing it out of there. I knew I was powerful—one has to be in my job—but so was Morgan, and more so since coming here, apparently. I was not at all certain what the outcome of a battle between the two of us would be, especially with her new allies. And I was glad I didn't have to find out. However, tracing Morgan now would be more difficult, as she knew I was after her and the trail would grow colder as more time passed. I hoped Fitz knew what he was doing.

# CHAPTER FIVE

I was over the bay just as the sun was coming up, so I diverted from the city itself to south of town. I landed in an open area near a road, abandoned my "carpet," and hoped to find a ride into town. I got lucky and caught a taxi. The hack was just coming on duty, driving from his house into the city.

"Where to, mister?" he asked as I got in.

"The Drake-Wiltshire Hotel on Stockton, downtown. Know it?"

"Sure thing," he said. The car started to move.

"Wake me when we get there. And don't hurry." After a night of no sleep and expending all the energy needed to keep a flying bedspread in the sky, I was exhausted. I was going to need some sleep before seeing Fitz.

Too soon, about an hour later, he said, "Here we are." I got out and paid the fare along with a modest, forgettable tip and walked inside.

I stopped by the front desk to get messages—there were none—and then went to my room. I pulled down the blackout shades (using them to keep light out, rather than keep it in), wound up my alarm clock, set it for two, or about seven short hours later, and crawled into my bed. A small, easy spell ensured I slept soundly.

***

I had spent five years wandering Korea, Northern China, and Japan looking for Meyoung. I learned a bit of each language and how to read some Chinese characters, which all three languages used, but in slightly different ways and with different pronunciations. I also learned to read the Korean phonetic alphabet called *Hangul*. But I never, despite following many rumors and leads, found either Nakamura or Meyoung.

I did battle some members of the *Omi Uji* and their warriors. Some warriors were samurai: some, like Ito, carried modern weapons. But with each confrontation I survived, I became stronger, and the battles became more infrequent. I got the feeling Nakamura was hiding from me, which I found both amusing and frustrating.

I returned to San Francisco in 1937 to find Fitzgerald had deposed Newmark. I was told that the battle, which had been held south of the city for privacy, was spectacular. Newmark was dead and Fitzgerald was happy to have as powerful an adept as I back in the guild. Since Prohibition had ended, I celebrated with a drink.

***

59

The taxi stopped with squeaking brakes in front of the arched entrance to the Huntington Hotel as a cable car clanged by. I tipped the driver heavily because she was pretty, friendly, and oh-so-loyal to her husband, who was probably at that moment dying on some forsaken rock in the Pacific.

The elderly doorman opened the taxi door and I stepped onto the sidewalk and bounded up the few stairs, where another doorman opened the heavy oak door to the lobby. I walked in, removing my hat, and placed it under my left arm. There were two SPs smoking in the lobby, looking about as uncomfortable and out of place as a pterodactyl would in similar circumstances. They didn't give me a second look. I'd chosen a naval officer's uniform because these days a uniform was as good as an invisibility spell to the authorities. I also liked the Navy's uniforms because I look dashing in whites to the ladies.

The brunette elevator operator was chewing gum and looking bored but cute in her uniform. She was small, rather short, with beautiful blue eyes.

Another man tried to follow, but I gave him a look, reinforced by a quick anxiety spell, and he decided to wait for another elevator.

"Floor, please?" she asked, suddenly animated. She must have noticed the spell. Either that or it was the whites.

"Thirteen," I said after the doors closed.

"Yes, sir," she replied, smiling broadly.

"I'm completely in the dark here," I told her in a low voice. "I've been called in by the leadership. What's up there?"

She let out a low whistle. "It's Fitzgerald, a couple of aides, and a lesser."

Fitz (although I'd never call him that to his face) took a lesser to the thirteenth floor? I thought. This must be something strange. "Who?"

"Navy, admiral, I think."

That explained the SPs: the lesser had brought his own warriors. The elevator lurched to a stop and the girl opened the doors. "Good luck," she whispered after me. I looked back to smile at her and she returned a gaze to melt a winter day.

It was room 1313. I'd been in it before. It was a large suite, the biggest room on the floor, with windows facing the bay. The door opened as I approached. A large warrior holding a tommy gun with a large circular metal case attached underneath was standing along the back wall. Another warrior was just inside the door, with no obvious weapon, but he had a large bulge under his expensive suit jacket. He looked me over, apparently checking for weapons, as if I'd touch the vile things. It wasn't the usual, trusted warrior named Dennis that Fitzgerald usually used. Dennis would know me and know that I was safe.

"It's okay, Harold," Fitzgerald said from his chair. He was slouching in a leather wing chair, his suit wrinkled and worn, his rumpled hat in his lap, and his gray hair uncombed. He didn't look like one of the most powerful adepts in the 48 states. "Mr. Kader is well known to us."

"Teacher," I said in respectful greeting.

"Thank you for coming, Student. Please have a seat."

I placed my hat on a table, settled into a camelback leather sofa, and looked around the room as I did. The blackout shades were up and I could see both the new bridges: the Bay and the Golden Gate. Lessers were always trying something big, expensive, and ultimately doomed-to-failure to conquer nature. Fitzgerald's assistant, Marjory Reynolds, was walking back and forth behind his chair, impeccably dressed, her high heels clicking on the hardwood floor. She was an attractive woman in her late forties or early fifties. She was tall, even without heels, and had short dark hair. In another chair was Al Swartz—no, since the Japs had bombed Pearl Harbor at 8:00 A.M. on Saturday December 6th and the U.S. had declared war on the Empire of Japan, with Hitler returning the favor by declaring war on the U.S., he'd changed his alias to "Black." Both he and Fitz were old enough not to have to worry about the draft. Black was tending toward obesity in his old age, and with his hair mostly gone and his large, round face, in some ways he resembled an over-grown infant.

Finally, in a third chair was a lesser in a khaki Navy uniform. A slim, serious-looking man with a full head of white hair and a face eroded to a craggy countenance by too much time spent at sea facing either the hot sun or the cutting gale. To be honest, I immediately liked and respected him. He, however, looked at me angrily, and I wondered what I'd done to make him mad. There was something else in the room. A presence I could feel coming from the direction of the admiral. He couldn't be an adept, I mused. But it was definitely coming from him.

"This is Admiral Richards of the U.S. Navy," Fitzgerald explained. "He has brought disturbing news to us."

This was interesting. The official position of the U.S. government was that meta was smoke-and-mirrors illusions and adepts were charlatans at best, common confidence players most likely, thugs and criminals at worst. I looked at the sailor.

He cleared his throat. "Some of this you may know better than I do. We've long known that Hitler is obsessed with metas. We think he is a failed adept in one of the Germanic guilds. Since even before the war he's had agents all over the world gathering talismans, suspected talismans, mystical artifacts, anything he thinks will bring meta power to the Nazis. Now we have reason to believe Hitler has somehow gained the support of some guilds on the continent and is using their magic against us."

I ignored Richards' insults using the terms "metas" and "magic." Magic is all trickery and gimmicks. Erich Weiss was a magician and when he tried to be more than that, tried to disprove the abilities of adepts, well, he wasn't the first man whose death I'd arranged and I knew he wouldn't be the last. Someday, I might even tell his wife the ten words.

I looked at Fitzgerald and he just looked back at me. I turned back to Richards. "Why would the guilds get involved in lesser matters, especially this war of *yours*?"

"I was hoping you could tell me."

"I don't believe it," I stated flatly.

"Do you know," Swartz-Black interjected, "Hitler has tried to get the Norse Guilds to help him? Some say that's why he invaded Norway, to punish them. It wouldn't have mattered. We do not get involved in your petty disputes."

"It might have had more to do with Norway's rich iron ores," the admiral retorted. He picked up a briefcase that had been at his feet and pulled a manila envelope from the case and handed it to me. He had to stand to reach.

"Take a look at this."

The envelope had a small, heavy object in one corner. It was also the source of the power I'd felt. I unlooped the string that held the flap closed, tilted the bottom of the envelope up and let its contents drop into my hand.

I almost gasped as I saw it. It was a piece of a sword's blade, about three inches long. From the curve of the short segment I could tell it was cut from a samurai's weapon—a. That alone spoke of its power. It was made of *tamahagane*, a Japanese version of Damascus steel. The wrought iron had been layered with carbon to make a blade that was both beautiful and strong. I turned it over. There was writing on one side, scratched into the metal like some kind of antiquated vandalism.

"You've noticed the markings," Richards said. "We don't know what language it is."

"I'm sure you don't," I agreed. It was in the ancient tongue, and told of an adept who had defeated a powerful warrior. He had cut this remembrance from his enemy's weapon.

It was a very old and very powerful talisman. That it was of Japanese origin didn't surprise me. Talismans travel extensively between guilds and adepts. My own talisman that I'd obtained in Asia was of Black Sea origin.

"We believe it's a talisman," Richards said stupidly.

I nodded. "Yes, it's a talisman. Where did you get it?"

"Off an SS agent trying to board a ship for Buenos Aires. A sharp customs agent spotted his fake Swedish passport. Where would a Nazi spy get a talisman like that? And what good would it do him unless guilds, or at least some adepts, were helping Hitler?"

It was a good question. I turned the talisman over in my hand, feeling its strength flow into me.

"Student," Fitzgerald said with a warning tone.

I stood and took the talisman to my teacher. "Forgive me," I said, handing it to him. He took it as a dying man takes salvation.

I returned to the sofa and turned to Richards. "What happened to the man with the talisman?"

"We're holding him."

"Where did he say he got the talisman?"

Richards looked uncomfortable. "We haven't been able to get that information out of him."

"This is a very serious matter," Fitz said to the admiral. Fitz had a talent for understatement. If the European guilds were cooperating with the Nazis, it could be a power play on their part. Guilds weren't loyal to any country. It wasn't that we were above the nation-states; we transcended them Guilds were always fighting for supremacy among the adepts, but that was none of the admiral's, or any other lesser's, business. But guilds weren't above making alliances with lessers to achieve some means to an end. If the European guilds used Hitler to gain power it'd be hard to stop them. To counter the threat, our guild, the largest one on the West Coast, might have to join forces with the Negro, the native, and the Creole guilds. Hell, since the Civil War we'd been doing our best to keep those three guilds apart, getting the Creole to hate the Negroes, and everyone to hate the natives, so they couldn't threaten our power. To bring them together in an alliance under us would be arduous at best. And I for one certainly didn't want to bring those types into *our* guild.

"We'll look into this," Fitz told Richards. "This is a very serious matter and we'll let you know. Kader's the best man for the job."

"What will he do?" Richards asked.

"What he does best: solve problems."

I could tell Richards wasn't satisfied, but Fitz was hitting him with a persuasion spell strong enough to convince him to jump off a cliff.

"Fine," the admiral said, standing. "I'll be in touch. And you, sir," he looked at me, "do not belong in that uniform."

"I'll wear what I please," I answered smugly, just to make him madder.

"If you weren't—"

"If I weren't what?" I asked, standing and hitting him with a fear spell.

He looked straight at me. Must have taken all his courage.

I decided to break the tension. "There is," I said, "one thing you could do to help."

"What's that?" Richards asked.

"I need to talk to someone who might know where this talisman came from."

"Yes?"

"I don't know where he is."

"And why do you think I do?" Richards huffed.

"I don't know. It's your government that took him from his home and put him in an internment camp somewhere."

Richards rolled his eyes. "A Nisei?" But he took a notepad and pen from inside his briefcase. "What's the name? I'll see if I can find him."

"Takada. Kirozow Takada." At least I hoped that was the name he was using.

"When I locate him I'll let you know. He was taken—did he come from San Francisco?"

"Yes. And I might want to speak with this German spy."

"I can arrange that. I'll be in touch," Richards repeated and walked out the door, visibly relieved.

"See to it that he makes it to the street okay," Fitz ordered the warrior named Harold, who slipped out the door Richards had just slammed shut.

"We've got a problem," Black said.

"A huge problem," Marjory agreed, as if she were capable of any other reaction.

Fitz ignored her and looked at Black. "You have contacts in Europe." It was a statement.

"Yes, but communication's been difficult since the war."

I had to agree. The same things that had made my carpet ride the night before dangerous, RADAR and deadly warplanes, were even more of a threat in the actual theaters of the war. Traveling by pterodactyl, flying carpet, or floating cloud was very dangerous. The inter-guild message services were all but shut down, and adepts had to hold their noses and take public transportation such as the Sunset Limited.

Fitz looked at me intensely. "Can you find out what's going on in Europe?"

I looked at Black. "I can try." He looked skeptical.

"Try. We need to know. I don't want to be caught unprepared, but I don't want to challenge the continental guilds needlessly. I need information, and I need it fast."

I stood. "Yes, Teacher. If I may be excused, I have arrangements to make."

Fitzgerald waved a dismissive hand. "Of course."

When I didn't move, he looked at me. "Yes?"

"I need the talisman. I will return it, if possible, when finished."

I could see him debating. Was his lust for the talisman greater than his fear of the threat of the European guilds, and his trust in me?

"On my name, I will serve you faithfully," I said. Marjory gasped. It was the strongest promise an adept could make. I wrote my name, my real name, on a piece of hotel stationery, sealed it in an envelope, and handed it to Fitzgerald.

All adepts learn early how to protect themselves from spells; soon it becomes as natural as breathing. Well, they learn it or they don't survive long. But knowing a person's name, his real, given name, grants power over him. It is enough power that any protection an adept might have is nearly useless. And with a lesser, it makes one's spells that much more powerful. But lessers don't know enough to keep their real names secret.

Giving my name to Fitzgerald meant that if my service to him was at anytime unsatisfactory, he could open the envelope, learn my real name, and cast a spell to kill me while hardly lifting a finger. It also demonstrated my faith in his honor, something I knew the old man would appreciate.

The appropriate thing to do, the honorable thing, was to destroy the envelope in front of the person who gave it to you to demonstrate your faith in him. Fitz looked at it, then stuffed it in his jacket pocket before handing me the talisman.

"Go, Student. I trust you will do what is best for your guild."

What could I do? I turned and walked out the door. The elevator came when I punched the button. It was the same operator.

"Lobby, please," I mumbled, still shocked by Fitz's actions.

"What's wrong?" the operator asked as if genuinely concerned. I looked her over. I would see through a glamour spell, so she must have been as young, and beautiful, as she looked.

"Guild politics," I said, as if that explained everything.

"I hate politics," she said.

I nodded in agreement. Unfortunately for us both, the guilds invented palace intrigue before there were such things as palaces.

"Hey," she said, snapping her chewing gum, "I get off in half an hour. You wanna get a cup of coffee or something?"

Was it my imagination, or was the elevator moving slowly? "Do you know where Young Fat's is in Chinatown?"

"I can find it," she said with the confidence of youth.

"Meet me there—" I looked at my watch (yes, even adepts need them nowadays) "—at six. That's an hour from now." That'd give her time to get all dolled up.

"Okay," she said, smiling. "I'm Dorothy."

"Francis." The elevator stopped and the doors opened.

"Young Fat's," she said.

I stepped out into the lobby and called behind me. "It's on Grant Avenue; you can't miss it."

On the street one of the doormen asked, "Taxi, Commander?"

"No, thanks." I started walking east, down Nob Hill toward Chinatown. It was a beautiful day, with the sun sparkling off the water in the bay. I smiled at passers-by, who were universally friendly to a man in uniform. San Francisco still felt like a small town and the war had made everyone feel friendlier and closer than usual. But there was an underlying pessimism. The war was on everyone's mind, and while worries about an actual Japanese invasion had been relieved somewhat by American naval victories in the Pacific, there was still, just under the surface, a barely contained dread. And there was still the possibility of an air attack. It was a remote possibility, but still there.

As I walked I thought I could sense the *katana* talisman pulling me forward. If I had known then what that talisman was leading me to, I would have thrown it into the bay.

I was almost to Young Fat's when I realized I'd forgotten to tell Fitz about Morgan. Well, there would be time later.

\*\*\*

Young Fat served pressed duck with meta on the side. He had to leave China for some reason. His guild, made up of coolies in America, was inconsequential. His skills were not.

The restaurant was filling with the supper crowd. Young Fat greeted me at the door as I walked in. He must have felt me, or the talisman, coming.

"Mr. Kader, welcome back. What can I do for you today?" he asked, with a bow.

I bowed also, a habit from my travels in the Orient. "I want to show you something."

"Shall we go to my kitchen, then?"

"That'd be fine."

He led the way past booths and tables.

"Oh," I said, following, "I'm expecting a young lady to join me for dinner."

"I'll see to the matter," Young Fat said gleefully and spoke to a waitress in Mandarin. He must have assumed I'd used my charms on a lesser. I wasn't above that—no male adept was. But it was like self-abuse: too easily done and therefore wholly unsatisfying. Dorothy was an equal, an adept, albeit a young, inexperienced one. She would be much more pleasurable.

The kitchen was noisy with food flying, flames bursting, and cooks hustling everywhere. The smell of burning grease was very powerful and seemed to hang in the air like fog. Fat ignored the smells and sounds of the kitchen and led me to a small room with a table and chair. He sat, leaving me to stand.

"What do you hear from China these days?" I asked.

He frowned. "Don't hear much with war and all."

"Anything about the *Omi Uji*?"

"A little, in Manchuria, fighting my old friends."

The *Omi Uji*, a very old and powerful Japanese guild, was following the Jap Army into mainland Asia, expanding their power as Hirohito expanded his.

I handed him the talisman.

"What can you tell me about this?"

He said something in Chinese I didn't understand. "This is very powerful talisman. With this you become head of your guild." No wonder Fitz wanted it. And didn't burn that envelope. "Where you get this?"

"I can't say. Anything else?"

"This belonged to a very powerful adept. If he not leader of his guild he ready to challenge soon. Loss of this talisman a big loss to him, I think. You sell?"

"Not likely," I said. "What about this adept?"

Fat held the talisman in both hands and closed his eyes. "Woman. Dead."

"A woman, are you sure?"

"Yes. That may not be the original adept. But that woman last to have talisman a long time."

"Who was she?"

"Don't know. Powerful adept, though. This talisman inconsequential to her," he said. That was amazing. This was the most powerful talisman I'd ever known about, and the woman who owned it had had a stronger one?

"Guild?"

"Don't know. You want to return this talisman to them?" he said sarcastically.

"No. Can you tell me about its recent history?"

Fat held it longer, almost seeming to be in a trance. "There was a man waiting to board a ship. It's night, raining, everything wet. Water dripping off his hat." Fat was telling me everything he sensed, no matter how trivial. "He not adept. But evil man. His name is Daeubler, Jons Daeubler. He's nervous, has a gun under his coat. He in line, approach official, hands over papers. Name on passport is Nils Svenson. Swedish passport. Official looks at papers for long time. Man more nervous, touch gun under his coat. Official smiles and let him pass. Man feel better, see ship. Old rusty ship, he read the name *El Cielo de las Américas*. Someone speaks to him. He turns and there's a gun pointed at him. It's held by an SP. He reaches for his gun but is pushed down from behind. The SPs search him, find the talisman. They place in envelope. Another man approach, trench coat, hat. Says 'Navy Intelligence' and shows his ID. He take envelope and man away."

Fat stopped, bowed his head, and took a deep breath.

I gave him a moment to recover then asked, "Can you put a spell of tracing on it?"

Fat smiled wearily, showing crooked, yellow teeth. "Spell cost you. And I have to keep talisman while I do it."

"I have the resources of my guild behind me." I did. I had a Swiss bank account number, a letter of credit referencing that account, and I carried enough gold, disguised as checkers and poker chips, to buy and sell many small countries, all of it the guild's money.

"How much?"

"Two thousand dollars, in gold."

I chuckled. "Let's be more reasonable. Five hundred as a letter of credit."

I finally got him down to $1,100, half in gold, half by letter of credit. I also bought a powerful spell of protection for $200, all letter of credit. If Fitz was going to have my name in his pocket, the least the guild could do was buy me some protection.

A waiter interrupted us and spoke to Fat in Chinese.

"Your young lady awaits you," Fat explained.

I glanced at my watch; it was 6:15. Fashionably late, or playing not-too-hard to get.

"Come back this evening, after closing, with payment. The talisman and protection spell will be ready," Fat said.

Realizing how valuable that hunk of metal was, I decided I needed some insurance. "I want your name."

He didn't get angry but he did look hurt. "And do I need yours to secure payment?"

"You only need to finish the job to do that," I explained.

He shrugged his shoulders and turned his back to me while writing on a piece of paper. Out of habit, I suppose, he chopped it with his alias. Then he placed it in an envelope, lit a candle, and sealed it with wax, using a smaller version of his chop.

"Thank you, Teacher," I said bowing and taking the envelope.

"Come this evening. All will be ready. And bring payment." I could tell I'd really hurt him. It made me want to apologize but that would just cause him to lose more face.

I bowed and left the kitchen. Dorothy was looking lovely, and not quite so young, waiting for me in a booth. I slid in. "Any problems finding the place?"

"Nope." She smiled prettily.

# CHAPTER SIX

Dorothy and I had a nice dinner. I enjoy Chinese food (although what one gets in San Francisco bears little resemblance to what one gets in China), but it seemed new to her. She didn't share a lot of personal details about her life, which was normal for adepts. We keep our histories hidden because it might be possible to trace a person back to their origins, learn his or her real name, and knowing that, have power over the person to do most anything.

I escorted her to her apartment building, and in the dark beside the stairs we shared a tender kiss and embrace that turned passionate. Her nose was cold but her lips were warm.

A few minutes later I whispered, "Shall we go inside?"

She shook her head. "No men allowed."

"My place?"

"Yes," she breathed. "But I need to get something. I'll be right back."

I waited about ten minutes and then she returned, smiling demurely, wearing a light cloak against the night chill.

"Ready?"

"Yes."

It was a short walk to the Drake-Wiltshire: and besides, I think we floated.

\*\*\*

Dorothy was sleeping soundly in my bed. She had been a little too eager, I thought. Perhaps my position in the guild was what attracted her. If so, I was disappointed; how could a man in a position of power ever know if women were interested in him or just in his influence?

I dressed quietly, this time choosing a loose business suit and a large briefcase to carry the gold. I put a levitation spell on the gold (not for that reason alone it wasn't silver), so I had to carry only the weight of the case.

On the street I hiked up to Fat's place (nothing is too far from anything in San Francisco). Under "dimout" regulations, blackout shades had to be pulled lower than the lowest light source, neon lights had to be off, and streetlights were hooded, giving them a spotlight-like effect on the sidewalks. Restaurants and bars were closing in anticipation of curfew and there were almost no cars on the streets. All in all, it made what was once a lively, spirited town look dismal and drowsy.

As I got closer to Fat's I could tell something was wrong. I couldn't feel the talisman or Fat's presence. Finally, standing in front of his darkened restaurant, I was sure; the talisman was gone and so was Fat. I knocked on the door; maybe he'd left instructions as to where to meet him. No one answered. I swore an oath in the ancient tongue, I was so mad. I ripped open the envelope, shattering the wax seal, and unfolded the paper with his name on it. I had to step directly under a hooded streetlight to read it, thinking that when I had learned Fat's real name, I would trace him, kill him, and take back the talisman.

Under the light, I laughed bitterly. Fat had written his name in Chinese. I recognized his surname as the character for gold or metal, but the other two pictograms eluded me. I ran a quick translation spell. I learned something about Fat's name, not what I needed. Young Fat's real name meant "Little Dog," a name surely meant not to draw the attention of the followers of Yan Luo Wang (a very nasty, evil, and fortunately small guild), but did me no good because I needed the pronunciation. I almost threw the paper away when I realized I was in Chinatown. Someone here had to be able to read it and tell me how to pronounce Fat's real name. But at this time of night, who?

I heard the door to Fat's place open and returned to the threshold expecting, I hoped, an explanation.

"Get in here," someone stage-whispered angrily. The voice didn't sound Chinese. I didn't have time to think about it as strong arms grabbed me by the shoulder and jerked me inside. The door closed and the lights came on. It took a moment for my eyes to adjust (damn human frailties). Four severe-looking men were frowning at me while they surrounded me. If I was facing north, they were at my NW, SW, SE and NE positions. None were adepts unless they were masking. One at NW was holding a pistol, and it was pointed at me.

"Who the hell are you?" I asked, fingering my talisman in my pocket trying to think of the best spell to deal with these fools.

"Never mind that," the one with pistol said. "What do you want with Young Fat?"

"Any of you read Chinese?" I asked lightly. I held the paper up in my free hand. "Can anybody read this?"

Pistol snatched the paper from my hand and looked at it. "That's Fat's chop," he said to his colleague at NE. He looked at me. "What is this?"

"I don't know," I answered honestly.

Either SW or SE hit me in the back of the head with something hard. I nearly dropped to my knees. I again swore in the language of the ancients. I swore at them. I damned them all, except Pistol.

"What are you saying?" Pistol demanded.

The spell hit three of them simultaneously; I spared Pistol because he seemed most likely to answer a few questions. None were adepts, or I would have needed their real names to hit them with such a rune.

Pistol screamed in fright as his friends screamed in pain and horror. Must be quite a sight to see your skin melt, followed by muscles, and then bones. It started in the hands and feet and worked its way up. The screaming only stopped when the lungs went. Then they flopped on the floor in growing puddles of goo until the heart stopped supplying blood to the brain. The whole spell took about thirty seconds.

I pushed Pistol into a booth and removed his weapon from his slack hand, letting it drop to the floor. He didn't resist and to be honest, after that spell, I couldn't have fought him if he had. He just stared at what once was his gang, his mouth hanging open, although he'd long ago run out of scream. I went through his papers. He had a California driver's license, a 4-F card (he looked plenty healthy to me), and an American passport. He'd recently traveled to Argentina, according to the stamps in the back.

***

"Who are you?" I demanded.

He was still looking at the messy floor. I shook him, and made him look at me. I actually gave him a small fortification spell along with a truth spell.

"Who are you?" I repeated.

"Colonel Andenauer, SS," he finally said.

"Where's Young Fat?"

"We are holding him for interrogation." He said that a little too strongly, so I dropped the fortification spell.

"Why?"

"Berlin's orders."

"That's all?"

"That's all I know. Someone will arrive tonight to interrogate him."

"Who?"

"I don't know."

"Young Fat had a piece of metal, made of Damascus steel. Did he have it with him?"

"The talisman? Yes."

"Where is it now?"

"House in Cupertino. Where Fat is."

"You will take me there." Persuasion spell with a little reassurance thrown in.

"I can't. They'll kill me," Colonel Andenauer of the SS said like a frightened child.

"Who?"

"If Fat's not there when the person from Berlin arrives, I'm dead."

"The interrogator's coming from Berlin?"

"Yes. Oh Gott."

Who the hell, I wondered, could be coming from Berlin that would frighten an SS colonel?

"Who is coming from Berlin?"

"*Die Walküre*," Andenauer muttered. I knew he didn't mean the Wagner opera.

I felt a chill. No wonder Andenauer was afraid. But why would the Valkyries be interested in Fat? They couldn't have known about the talisman. This must be something else. Or was it? Swartz-Black was supposed to have contacts on the Continent. If the Valkyries were helping Hitler, then the information he had given us was either wrong or a lie. I didn't know he had it in him. If Black had gotten word to the Nazis about the talisman...but how did they know Fat had it? Unless...

"Dorothy."

She walked in, rather than riding through the air.

"Or should I say 'Brunhild'?"

"Please," she purred, "you flatter me." She floated over the mess on the floor and landed near-by. Before I could say anything, she said something angrily to Andenauer in German that made the poor man almost break down. Look at me, I thought, I'm feeling sorry for a member of the SS.

"You made a phone call from your apartment." It was a statement. "You knew I brought the talisman here; you probably felt it when you came here. And you knew I didn't leave with it." She just stood, not looking at me. "What do I call you?" I asked.

"Dorothy is just fine," she said flatly, looking up at me.

"I thought all Valkyries were blonde and I'd see through a glamour spell."

"It's a dye job," she snarled.

I had no idea what she was talking about. "Why are the Valkyries working for *Der Führer*?"

Dorothy looked me straight in the eye, "I don't have to justify my or my guild's actions to you."

"But Hitler," I protested. Getting involved with kings and princes was not unheard of, but it had a dismal record of success. Merlin had tried to unite Britain, stop the Saxons and the Vikings, and had failed because Morgana betrayed him. The pre-Columbian adepts in the Americas ran their societies through religion. Drunk on their power, they went so far as to sacrifice humans (necromancy being very powerful but dangerous meta). But their empires either crumbled under the weight of their own decay or were conquered by Europeans with superior technology. Governments, all governments, use power over their people. Some are worse than others. And Hitler? If half of what got out of the occupied countries was true, then Hitler's regime was the one of the most brutal in modern times. "How do you sleep at night?" I asked Dorothy.

"Quite well, thank you." She took a deep breath. "The colonel and I are leaving now. Please don't try to stop us or follow us." She pulled Andenauer to his feet.

"What do you want with Fat?" I tried. She ignored it and led the SS man toward the kitchen. They must have a car in the alley, I thought, although it was close to curfew and it would be hard to avoid the police, MP patrols, and the civil defense wardens.

"It can't be the talisman," I said, trying to sound casual. "The Valkyries have the Hammer of Thor." Suddenly it made sense, kind of. The talisman had been inconsequential to the woman who had owned it because she was a Valkyrie and the Valkyries have the Hammer of Thor, the strongest talisman in existence.

She turned and looked at me. Her eyes were bright with anger. "We had *Mjollnir*, the Hammer of Thor."

"Who has it now?" I asked, deeply shocked. The Hammer was what made the Valkyries a powerful and feared guild.

Dorothy stopped moving and looked at me. Her expression showed depths of sorrow that looked out of place on such a young face. She spoke in the ancient tongue: "You think you are so much better than the lessers. But if they wanted to, they could kill us all. Hitler sent divisions against Valhalla. That's 10,000 men, each. He wanted *Mjollnir*. We blasted his planes from the air, sent deadly miasmas over his troops, and still they came."

There were only about two-dozen Valkyrie, I remembered. "Berserkers?" I asked. There were maybe a hundred of them.

"They fought valiantly—as if they could do anything else—and we had the advantage of the mountainous terrain. It didn't matter. Have you ever heard the scream of a *Stuka*? It's like a wraith from the sky." She was rambling; I could tell the pain of the whole story was too great to tell. "Eventually," she continued, "only four of us escaped. One was killed in San Francisco and this talisman taken from her. Tonight I got it back."

"Killed by whom? The SS?"

She hesitated a moment. I think she was deciding whether to tell me. "A member of your guild who gave it to the SS."

"How do you know that?"

"The admiral had the talisman when I took him to the thirteenth floor. He didn't have it when he left. I used a truth spell in the elevator. He told me how he got it."

"No," I said emphatically. "How do you know it was a member of my guild?"

She looked frustrated. "This has gone on long enough; I have the talisman back."

"But this SS man is working for you?" I asked.

"We use persuasion spells on Hitler's spies to get them to do our bidding. They only think they are working for the *Führer*."

"The talisman?" I asked. "How powerful is it?"

"It united Japan."

I sat down in one of the booths. Who the hell needed the Hammer?

"What are you going to do when you get enough powerful talismans?"

"I don't have to tell you, Mr. Kader."

"Is Swartz-Black-involved in this?"

Dorothy laughed. "Black is a fool. I batted my eyes and got the elevator job."

"Can I help?" It was the only thing I could think of. I had to have that talisman back; Fitz had my name, after all.

"How?"

"Perhaps our guilds could unite against Hitler. This affects all guilds; we can't let a lesser attack on a guild stand."

"And your guild would keep the Hammer."

I nodded. It was probably true. "Okay, can I help? Just me, on my own— not my guild. If you can't keep the Hammer away from me—"

"Without your guild? How can you do that?"

"I am given a fair amount of autonomy. If Fitzgerald thinks I'm working on his problem, he'll leave me alone." And in a way I was. If Hitler had the Hammer of Thor, he might soon no longer be a failed adept and that would be a problem for the whole world, adepts and lessers. And it was still a problem for me as long as Fitz had my name.

"I don't think so, Mr. Kader. I can't trust you." She spoke a spell that was very powerful for one so young. The black and white tile floor between us started to burn. It wasn't burning the actual floor; just hot, angry flames shot up from the surface to the white painted ceiling, which remained unmarked. I had to step back from the heat. I was trapped by the fire, not able to leave the booth I had sought shelter in. Through the flames I saw Dorothy half-drag, half-lead Andenauer into the kitchen and as she did so, the entire room I was in filled with the flames, ensuring that I couldn't discontinuously traverse out except into a place I couldn't see, which ran the risk of my emerging inside a solid object. The flames didn't approach, so I didn't think Dorothy was trying to kill me.

I ran counter spells on the flames, but Dorothy's power made that a long process. Finally the flames were low enough and covered a small enough area that I could jump over them and run into the alley. It was empty, of course. I tried to sense Dorothy's presence. It was obvious she had been masking her clearly great power, and had done it so well that I never sensed her strength, despite the intimate contact we had. So she could easily mask enough to keep me from sensing her.

I went back into the dining room, recovered the paper with Fat's name, and contemplated my options. Cupertino was a small town but also comprised a lot of farm area. I could go there and try to sense the Japanese talisman and/or Young Fat. But getting there was a problem. There'd be no taxis after curfew. Maybe I should learn to drive, I thought bitterly. But even then I'd have to avoid the authorities. Wearing a uniform would help in that case, but I didn't have one on.

I sat down in a chair and toyed with the soy sauce bottle on the table. About the only thing left to do was talk to the SS agent that was caught with the talisman, Mr. Daeubler. See if I could find out where he got it and who had killed the Valkyrie. I hoped it wasn't someone in my guild or that would be another problem to solve and right then, I had more problems than I could tolerate.

Meanwhile, there was something else I wanted to do. I found Fat's phone and dialed a number.

"Hello."

"It's Kader."

"Yes, sir?"

"Get to Yuma, Arizona. Beverly Morgan, I had you watching her?" That's how I'd known she'd taken the train.

"Yes, sir?"

"She left Yuma this morning on the Sunset Limited westbound. Try to trace her to her final destination. Keep in touch; leave messages at the Drake-Wiltshire."

"Yes, sir. My usual fee?"

"Of course." And probably a little extra if I found out where Morgan went.

\*\*\*

Admiral Richards was not happy to see me. "How did you get in here?"

This day I was wearing khakis. I frowned at him. "You don't think I can convince a few SPs of my bona fides?"

"This part of Treasure Island is off-limits to civilians," Richards growled.

"Do I look like a civilian?"

"It's illegal for you to wear that uniform," he said, his voice seething with anger.

"Throw me in jail," I said.

Richard scowled. He must have known the jail hadn't been built that could hold an adept, unless maybe if it was constructed purely of silver.

"Why are you here?"

"You said you'd keep in touch. You haven't. I want to talk to the German who had the talisman."

Richards looked resigned. Angry, but resigned. "Fine." He picked up his phone and barked, "Bring my car around. And tell Smith to meet us at the brig."

He led me out to a civilian car painted Navy gray. We got in the back seat. "The brig," he ordered the young sailor behind the wheel.

"Yes, sir," the sailor snapped respectfully.

I looked at all the activity. The resources these lessers were expending were amazing. "All this for some petty dispute," I said.

"It's not some petty dispute," Richards snarled back. "They attacked us."

"And why?" I asked.

Richards sighed. "The Japanese army has brutally occupied Manchuria for about ten years now. That is why the United States embargoed oil sales to them. To replace that oil—they have none of their own—they needed to invade the oil-rich Dutch East Indies. But our bases in the Philippines and our Pacific Fleet threatened those plans. So they attacked Pearl Harbor and the Philippines, which is why we are in this war."

I barely listened. I didn't care. I still thought it was a stupid, petty affair that was interfering with my guild and my life. I should have been dealing with Morgan, not trying to find some talisman the Nazis wanted to use to fight this war.

The car stopped in front of a fenced-in area. Circular barbed wire, no doubt very sharp, covered the top of the fence. Inside was a small concrete building. There were two armed SPs outside the gate in the fence and two more by the door to the building. A big man in a gray, inexpensive suit waited. We got out of the car and Richards introduced the man in the suit as "Special Agent Smith, FBI." We shook hands and walked to the gate.

Richards spoke to one of the SPs. "I thought I ordered three strands of concertina wire," he said, pointing at the circular barbed wire.

"Yes, sir," the SP barked. "It has been ordered, sir. There are supply problems, as the admiral knows, sir." The man said "sir" as if he'd been punched in the gut as he spoke.

I thought "concertina wire" was a misleading name for something so obviously dangerous.

With Richards' rank, we had no problem seeing Jons Daeubler. The man, blond, blue-eyed, the very image of Aryan perfection, was wearing denim dungarees and handcuffs. His face was bruised and he sat passively, looking at the wooden table. Smith and I sat on the other side. Two SPs stood against the wall behind Daeubler and never took their eyes off him.

"He won't tell us anything," Smith said. "Even if we use aggressive interrogation techniques."

That explained the bruises.

"His name?" I asked Smith.

"Won't tell us except what was on his passport, Nils Svenson."

I looked at the Nazi. "How are you today, *Herr* Daeubler?"

Smith looked at me in surprise, then at the prisoner. Daeubler didn't react. I fingered my talisman and ran a strong truth spell over him.

"Daeubler is your name, isn't it? Jons Daeubler?"

"Yes," he said.

"Rank?" Smith demanded.

"*Sturmbannführer.*"

"SS rank equivalent to our major," Smith explained.

I didn't care; it wasn't germane.

"What is your relationship with a Colonel Andenauer?" I asked.

"He is my superior," Daeubler said slowly.

Smith pulled a small paper pad and a pen from his pocket and started taking notes, all the while looking amazed.

"How did you get the talisman you were captured with?" I asked.

"It was given to me."

"By whom?"

"I don't know her name."

A woman? "Valkyrie?"

"*Nein.*"

I tried anyway. "Brunette, blue eyes, petite?"

He shook his head. The truth spell was starting to hurt. They do for the strong-willed. "I didn't see her. It was a dead drop. We communicated by telephone."

I looked at Smith questioningly.

"A dead drop is where a package is left for someone else to pick up," he explained. "The parties rarely meet."

I looked at the *Sturmbannführer*. "If it was a dead drop, how do you know a woman gave it to you?"

"I spoke with a woman on the phone. I assumed she was the same operative using the dead drop."

"Damn," I said, realizing I'd hit a dead end. And his story did not jibe with Dorothy's. But I hadn't had a truth spell on her.

"What was the telephone number?" Smith asked. I was impressed—I hadn't thought to ask.

"I don't remember. It was on a piece of paper that I burned."

"Did you communicate in other ways?"

"Chalk marks on streetlight poles."

"Well that's a dead end," Smith said, finally agreeing with me. "His contact must have noticed that he's missing and gone into hiding."

"If you'd like to question him further, he should be very cooperative for about a half hour more," I said, standing.

"We could use someone like you at the Bureau," Smith said.

I ignored his statement and walked out, to learn that Richards had returned to his office. A car was brought for me, since I was, they thought, a commander who needed to go back to HQ.

Richards was again not happy to see me. "Now what?"

"Did you find my friend?"

"The Nip, Takada? Yes, he's in Tulelake."

"Where the hell is that?" I asked.

He told me.

I wasn't happy to learn.

\*\*\*

I went to Union Station and purchased tickets for Agent Smith—Richards insisted I take him along or I'd get no cooperation from the authorities—and myself on the Cascade Line of the Shasta Route to a town called Klamath Falls, in Oregon. It was my opinion that the Southern Pacific Railroad was getting too much of my guild's money lately. I'd much rather stay in town. I suspected Oregon would make Yuma look modern and cosmopolitan.

I stopped by Young Fat's and his head cook told me the old man had been released by his captors, but was resting at home and not available. I was glad to hear he was home safe.

I had one last chore to do before leaving town. I returned to the Huntington for a meeting with Fitzgerald. Dorothy was not operating the elevator, and the surly young adept who had taken her place was obviously unhappy about the job. But an adept was needed in that position because only members of the guild and the guild's warriors knew about the thirteenth floor, and only an adept could recognize some threats that could be used to get to the leadership of the guild.

I thanked him when we got to the thirteenth floor. He grumbled his reply.

In room 1313 Fitzgerald looked at me with watery gray eyes from behind his mahogany desk. The desk was mostly for show; running a guild was not a paper-pushing job. He was still in his rumpled suit, leaning back in his chair.

"Now, what's this about?" he asked.

When I had called I'd said I wanted a meeting alone and he reluctantly agreed, although Harold, the warrior, was just outside the door. Black and Reynolds both gave me looks that clearly communicated their displeasure as they exited the room.

I sat in one of the chairs facing the desk. "It's Morgan."

He seemed not to hear. "Yes? Have you made progress on the talisman?"

"No, Teacher," I answered. "I am working on it and need to travel to see my friend, Takada."

"Fine," Fitz said. "Now, what do you want?"

"Morgan," I repeated.

He leaned forward, resting his forearms on the desk. "Oh?"

"I learned that whatever she is up to, she thinks she can defeat you."

"I had deduced that," the old man said, leaning back into the leather of his chair. "Why else would she feel she could betray me?"

"Yes," I said. "I believe stopping her is important."

"As do I," Fitz mumbled. "But right now I believe this situation with Hitler and the European guilds is more pressing."

I didn't know if I agreed. "There is one thing you need to know, Teacher."

"Yes?" He looked bored, his eyes looking at a spot behind me.

"Morgan knew I was coming for her."

His gaze returned to me. "She may have assumed."

"Yes, but she knew the train I was on and my sleeper suite."

Fitz looked toward the window as he processed that information. "How do you know that?"

"I was attacked in that room."

Again, Fitz was quiet, staring at nothing.

I pressed on, speaking loudly to ensure I had his attention. 'That means someone in San Francisco who knew I was coming found out from someone at the railroad and sent the information to her. Now, who here, other than the two of us, knew I was going to Yuma, Arizona to find her?"

Fitz was silent for a moment. Then he breathed, "Black, Reynolds, and my personal warrior, Dennis."

"One of those three is working with Morgan. Where is Dennis. anyway?"

"Found out his brother was killed on Guadalcanal. Signed up to be a Marine."

"You believe that?" I was pressing him hard. I didn't need to anger Fitz, not with my name in his pocket, but I had to make him aware of the situation.

"Yes, he showed me his orders before he...left for wherever it is new Marines go. He was so proud."

"That leaves Black and Reynolds," I said.

Fitz nodded. "Yes. I suppose it does."

I waited for him to propose a course of action. But he again looked off, out the window. So I continued. "I have taken the liberty of using a resource of mine to try to track down Morgan. It'll cost the guild a small amount."

"Good," Fitz said, looking less unhappy.

The only thing I could do was offer some free advice. "Keep an eye on Black and Reynolds. I have no reason to suspect either of them over the other."

"Yes," Fitz agreed.

The conversation was apparently over.

"Good day, Teacher," I said, standing.

"Yes, good day," Fitz said laconically.

I left the room and Black and Reynolds rushed in like water trying to fill a space. I didn't know if Fitz's behavior was an act or if old age was catching up. If the latter was true, he wouldn't be the head of the guild much longer, and both Black and Reynolds were ambitious. As was I, to be honest.

# CHAPTER SEVEN

I met Smith at Union Station early the next morning for our journey north. The trip would be mildly pleasant, and short enough that sleeping wouldn't be necessary. Which was good since because of the war, sleeper cars were rare—I had been lucky to get one to Yuma—and the regular Pullmans were full. Signs at train stations, and in the trains, asked, "Is this trip necessary?" The train was at least half full of military personnel.

Smith and I kept to ourselves. The FBI agent had one fault: he talked too much. Not about anything important, but about inanities such as the weather, the little towns we passed or stopped in, and the war. I ignored him and stared out the window. The scenery was dull until we got in view of the Cascade Mountains and the train started climbing out of the San Joaquin Valley.

Smith was a big man. He looked somewhat like a prizefighter. But prizefighters are usually health nuts, and he smoked an occasional cigarette and attacked our meal in the dining car with gusto.

In the early evening the train stopped in Klamath Falls, which was just north of the Oregon-California state line. We stepped onto the wooden platform along with a few army men. Smith found an MP whose job seemed to be directing the army men getting off the train to a bus. Smith showed him his identification. The MP glanced at it and growled, "You can take the WRA bus," and he jerked his head at the dusty, old conveyance, "or wait and I can get a car for you, sir."

Smith looked at me. I looked at the bucolic scenery, smelled the fresh country air with just a tinge of manure. The heat, the dust, the smells, the complete *ruralness* of the landscape was enough to make a person run screaming back to the city. Any city. I wanted out of there, fast. "The bus," I said.

Smith shrugged his large shoulders and we queued up with the doughboys for the bus.

The bus headed south, back over the state line to the internment center. It was huge and surrounded by chain link fence topped by three strands of barbed wire. The posts holding the barbed wire leaned to the interior. There were guard towers, more than twenty, around the perimeter of the camp and adjacent farm. The interior was filled with tarpaper barracks.

The bus passed through a double gate and we were inside the fence. Stepping off the bus, I looked around. Now I could see that some of the barracks bore incongruous signs such as "Bank of America" and "Tri-State High School." Japanese people, including old men, pretty young girls, and mothers with children, were walking around in civilian clothes as if they were strolling the main street of any town.

I found the entire place depressing and focused my gaze outside the fence in lieu of the gloomy interior. There was an interesting rock formation not far away. Mount Shasta, visible in the distance, and the nearby lava beds gave a little mystical energy to the valley, as mountains and young land always do.

Smith led me to the War Relocation Authority administrative office, which was the nicest building inside the fence. Smith's ID got things moving quickly, and soon we were alone in a small office with a beat-up wooden table and uncomfortable chairs. Illumination came from a bare bulb hanging from the ceiling on a cord.

An MP brought in Takada. He smiled when he saw me, but, seeing Smith, didn't say anything. He was wearing what was probably his best suit. I didn't know his real name, of course, and I'd always called him Sam. I stood and took his hand, shaking it vigorously. "Sam, it's good to see you."

He smiled broadly and put his other hand on my shoulder. "You, too, Joe."

Then we sat, Smith and me on one side of the table, Sam on the other.

There was a moment of awkward silence. Smith was probably waiting for an introduction, but I planned to ignore him. This was adept business and he was there only because, for now, I planned to cooperate with the authorities.

"Joe Kader, to what do I owe the honor of this visit?" Sam asked, looking Smith over.

"I need your help, Sam."

"Anything for you, old friend."

I briefly described the lost talisman to him. As I spoke, his gaze grew steady upon me.

"You held this talisman?"

I stuck out my hand. "Right here."

Sam suddenly spoke in Japanese. "Do you know who this man is?"

"FBI," I said in English, not knowing the Japanese equivalent. I spoke passable Japanese as a result of my travels there. I used a translation spell to back me up, though.

Sam shook his head and switched back to English. "The Valkyrie took that talisman from the Tsar's mystics as punishment for some conflict that the Tsar obviously lost."

"How did the Russians get it?"

"From the Mongols, who got it from the Chinese, who got it from the Koreans, who got it from the Chinese, who originally stole it from the Japanese. It's been kicking around Asia for centuries. It's a very powerful talisman."

"Now Hitler's got it," Smith threw in.

"We don't know that, Smith," I said a little defensively. But I wondered how he knew. I hadn't told him or Richards about Dorothy and the SS man taking the talisman from Young Fat.

"But I need to find it," I said to Sam.

Takada looked at me intently. "His name is not what he claims it to be," he said in Japanese.

"What is it?" I asked in the same language.

"I believe it is Krupp. If it is, he's a dangerous man."

"A German? Dangerous to whom?"

"You, *sensei*."

I couldn't see it. Smith wasn't an adept, and as one myself I could kill him on a whim. Unless he was masking, and I'd been with him for most of a day, and that's a long time to mask.

"What are you two yakking about?" Smith/Krupp interrupted.

"Forgive me," Sam said, looking at the table. "There is a box that held the talisman for many years. It is a simple black lacquered box."

"Where do I find this box?"

"If you wait here, I will get it from my personal effects."

"You want us to believe you have this box and that you're just going to give it to him?" Smith demanded.

Sam stood. "I am grateful to have a day not working in the pig farm." He bowed slightly to me and went out of the office. He told the guard that he needed to retrieve something from his barracks and would return.

"What was he telling you?" Smith asked. He pulled out a cigarette and started looking in his pockets for matches.

"Guild business," I stated flatly. I reached over with my empty hand, opened it palm up, and held a little flame under the tip of the cigarette. It also gave me a chance to get my hand, at least, very close to Smith.

Smith lit his cigarette as if he used a flame in a man's hand every day, and the foul smell filled the room. "You really believe he is going to just give you this box?"

I pulled my hand back. I'd felt nothing. If he was masking, he was doing a superb job. "No. He'll want something for it, someday."

Smith took a drag and blew the smoke in my direction. "Do you trust him?"

"More than I trust you," I said blowing the smoke back at him with a small spell. It got no reaction.

We sat silently until Sam returned. He handed over, as promised, a simple black lacquered box. I stood to accept it with both hands.

"Where'd you get this box?" Smith asked.

Sam glared at him, still standing.

"Thank you," I said. I could feel the echo of the talisman from the box.

"I am glad to be of service," Sam said, bowing slightly.

"Why," I asked switching to Japanese, "do you stay here?"

"I could escape easily," Sam replied in English (he wanted Smith to hear this, apparently). "A glamour to make me look Occidental would be hard to maintain. And where would I go? Canada has interned their Japanese residents, just as has America. I have heard that Japanese living east of the Rockies have not been interned, but would I want to live where I was feared and despised?"

I knew what he meant. Adepts are ostracized by lessers everywhere. Mostly we don't care, but it does wear on one. Add to that being a hated foreigner, and I doubted I could stand it either.

"I can't go back to Japan," Sam continued, "and even if I could, I have a feeling the United States military will soon make it not safe to live there."

The room was silent a moment as Sam's words sank in. When it got too quiet to bear, I stood up and thanked Sam profusely. He smiled, bowed, and left. When Smith and I left the small office, I grabbed his arm. He looked at me, startled.

"I want you," I said looking intensely at him, "to make sure *they*—" and I was sure he knew who "they" were "—know that he is cooperating with an investigation, and not under any suspicion at all. Understand?"

Smith looked at my hand on his arm. I could tell he was debating how angry to get. He apparently chose to brush it off. He shrugged his shoulders and said, "Okay." He went to a secretary and asked to talk to the camp administrator.

I was impressed. I hadn't even used any meta on him. I would have, if it had been needed. But it wasn't.

Smith emerged from the camp administrator's office a few minutes later. "Taken care of. Happy?"

"I'll be happy when I'm back in San Francisco," I said, lying. I'd be happier, but I wouldn't be happy until Morgan was dead and the talisman was in my hands.

Stepping outside, we found that a car was waiting to take us back to Klamath Falls.

"How do you know," I asked Smith, "that the Nazis have the samurai sword talisman?"

For a moment fear flashed in his eyes, and he realized he'd said too much. "Intelligence reports. I can't tell you more than that."

I didn't believe him.

One interesting thing, though. Smith hadn't reacted to Sam's calling me "Joe." Perhaps it was because he realized adept names tend to be ephemeral, I thought at the time. But most lessers are surprised that we changed names as easily as they change socks. Their names—their real names—are so important to them.

\*\*\*

Smith and I spent the night in a motor lodge next to the highway in Klamath Falls. We had separate cabins. I slept fitfully; I had called my hotel and learned of no messages from my operative following Morgan. And that worried me.

The next day we took the train back to San Francisco. During the entire trip Smith never showed any sign of being an adept or anything other than a government lackey. Certainly, other than his mysterious knowledge of the fate of the samurai *katana* talisman, he'd been rather unremarkable. Once in the city he made some excuse and disappeared.

I caught a taxi back to the Drake-Wiltshire. I had a message waiting:

-Morgan. First and Last Chance Saloon, Oakland Docks. Hurry. Miles.-

Even though I wanted to take a shower and change my clothes, I went to my room only to put the lacquered box in my safe and to renew the secure spell on the safe, and then went back outside and caught a taxi. I paid the hack a fiver to get me there fast. Nevertheless, it was a long ride, over the Bay Bridge and down to the docks. It was dark by the time he dropped me in front of the bar.

The First and Last Chance Saloon was right on the docks, so close to the water it seemed you could reach out and touch passing ships. The docks were almost lifeless, as the longshoremen had long since gone home  A fog was starting to roll in from the west, obscuring the lights of San Francisco and giving an eerie feeling that the city was dissolving into the ocean.

The smells outside were unpleasant. A dirty water odor combined with dead fish and bunker fuel. Going through the dark door and into the saloon didn't improve things. Reeking of old stale smoke and beer gone bad, it was a small, dark place, heated only by a pot-bellied stove in the corner. There was money tacked to the wall. I wondered what that was about. Some of the bills radiated grief, unlike almost any inanimate object I'd ever encountered.

The place wasn't crowded; that'd only take maybe a dozen people. There were a couple of rough-looking fellows at a table in a corner. They eyed me as I came in, and I suddenly felt overdressed in my suit. I took them for merchant marines.

Miles was sitting at the very worn bar, sipping a beer. I sat next to him. Upon examination, I decided the bar was as old as the building, which looked very old indeed. There was a clock that wasn't running. It was stopped at 5:15. I wondered about that, too. The bartender, a man who managed to be fat and yet sickly-looking, approached, and I waved him off. He shrugged his shoulders and went back to reading a newspaper that apparently specialized in horse racing.

"Where you been?" Miles said as he put his beer glass on the bar.

"Out of the city; had an errand to run. Where's Morgan?"

He looked at me. He was a small, wiry man with a gravelly voice. He'd seen a lot of evil in his life, including the First World War and a stint in prison. "Nice-looking broad."

I took the hint and passed some greenbacks his way. He smiled as he picked them up and put them in his coat.

"We were lucky. One of the sheriff deputies for Yuma County's an old army buddy of mine. Got gassed together in Saint-Mihiel in the Seventh I.D. He owed me a favor, so he checked out the rail station. Learned she'd bought a ticket for right back here in San Francisco."

"How'd you know he had the right woman?"

He finished his beer and waved for another one. The bartender stood as if it pained him to move, and poured another glass.

Miles continued. "She's an attractive lady; people remember her."

"Fine," I said, hoping he was correct.

"In Frisco, she took a taxi to a hotel, didn't tip big but the driver remembered her legs. I stayed outside her hotel, watched her."

I imagined him asking every hack outside Union Station if they'd had an attractive, redheaded fare.

"That's why I never contacted you, I was watching her."

"And then what?" I was getting tired of this narrative.

"So today she gets in a taxi and comes here."

I looked around. "She came here?" The bar did not look like her kind of place.

"No," he shook his head and dove into his fresh beer. "The docks. I had a close eye on her. But she stepped into a shadow—the sun was getting low—and was gone."

"You sure?"

"Yeah, as sure as I'm sitting here."

Invisibility spell—no doubt about it. But what good this did me, I didn't know. "So you lost her?"

He smiled. "Yeah."

"And I just paid you for what?"

He sipped his beer and looked at me. "To tell you that she arranged to have her trunk loaded on a ship."

"Ship? What ship?"

"The *El Cielo de las Américas*. And it sails in…" he looked at the stopped clock, then pulled a pocket watch from his vest, snapped open the cover, and read it "…twenty minutes."

Same ship *Sturmbannführer* Daeubler was caught trying to board. I wondered if that was coincidence.

"Damn, where?"

"Down the wharf, you can't miss it. It's the rust bucket."

I stood and dropped a bill on the bar to pay for his drinks. "If this works out, look for a bonus in your mail."

"Yes, sir."

I left the bar and walked down the wharf through the thickening fog. The *El Cielo de las Américas* was docked against the pier, the gangplank running up at an angle from the wooden dock. The wharf was fenced off with chain link topped with barbed wire. It looked a lot like the fence around the internment camp. There was a line for customs, which was basically a wooden booth, painted white, with an official inside. A light hung over the whole operation, making a yellow cone in the fog. There were SPs in white Navy uniforms on both sides of the fence. They had wide white belts with holsters attached on one side and black, shiny billy clubs on the other. There was no doubt in my mind that they were armed.

Four people were lined up for customs. Since the war, passenger liners had been converted to troop transports. Often the only way to travel by ship was on freighters that usually had a few staterooms for some passengers. Of the people waiting for their passport check, three were men and one was an older, pudgy woman with black hair. I'd see through a glamour so I knew none of them was Morgan. However, if she was using an invisibility spell, she wouldn't need a glamour.

I found a dark place to stand and surveyed the scene without, I hoped, drawing attention from the SPs. Invisibility is a harder spell than discontinuously traversing. Doing both at the same time takes skill, which I have. I invoked the invisibility spell, then walked to the fence. The short traverse was no problem. I still wanted to stay out of the light. Strong enough light, especially sunlight, can cause you to cast a shadow when invisible.

I walked to the gangplank, avoiding puddles that I might splash in, and then slowly walked up it, trying not to make any noise on the boards. Two men stood at the top of the gangplank and I had to be careful not to brush against either as I passed, holding my breath. But I was on the ship. Now if Morgan was on it, too, I needed to find her, and fast.

The ship had a typical freighter layout. Ahead was the fo'c'sle that should have crew quarters below deck. The amidships was all decking, with the hold below. Toward the stern was the bridge house, which had, I presumed, officers' quarters, galley, bridge—of course—access to below decks and the engine compartment, and any staterooms the ship would have. I'd spent time on ships, from luxury liners to tramp steamers, in my travels.

Still invisible, I found a hatch and went inside the bridge house. In marked contrast to the exterior, inside the ship was immaculate, with shiny, brass brightwork, and clean painted walls. While working the invisibility spell, it was hard to concentrate. If I could simply be quiescent for a few moments, I should feel Morgan's presence. But I couldn't end the invisibility spell standing in this corridor. I looked at the floor. I was casting a faint shadow under the bright light.

I scanned the doors nearest and picked one. I opened it quickly, stepped inside, and closed the door behind me.

The room was dark. I listened for a moment and decided it was empty. I fumbled for a light switch, found one, turned it, and found I was in a storage closet.

I let the invisibility spell dissipate as I waited and sensed. Yes, there was power on this ship, and the odds of it not being Morgan were slim. She was above. I needed to find a companionway.

I knew that if she was paying attention, she'd feel me coming. And I didn't want to waste energy on an invisibility spell. If it was her on the ship, I'd need all my power.

I cracked open the door and peered into the corridor, keeping my ears open for the slightest sound of another human. Hearing none, I stepped out. A few steps toward the interior and I found a companionway leading up. I slowly ascended the steep stairs. Finally, on the next deck up, I was faced with six stateroom doors. I walked slowly down the hall, hoping to feel her before she felt me. I had my hand on my talisman and was mentally preparing for either a defensive spell, such as a shield, or an offensive one, such as throwing fire at her.

Just then the door to one of the rooms opened and there Morgan stood. She was dressed, as usual, impeccably in a dress suit. She hid well her surprise at seeing me.

"Congratulations," she said, smirking at me with perfectly painted red lips. "How'd you find me this time?"

I shook my head. "Let a man have some secrets."

She smiled at my little joke. "I was wondering why you sneaked out of Yuma. I thought maybe you had a change of heart and were going to let me go."

"Something came up." I was getting a little nervous talking in the corridor like this. If she had allies on this ship and they came across us, even lessers with guns, it would tip the balance in her favor.

We stood looking at each other for a moment, each deciding what to do. Since we were both adepts, a direct attack, such as I had made on the SS men in Young Fat's, wouldn't work. We had to use indirect methods.

I saw her hand move and ducked while bringing up my hand. The airbolt shot from her palm past my ear and hit the bulkhead behind me, denting it.

I pointed my finger at her and the air around her started glowing with the energy I was supplying it. She stepped back and steam rose from the hot air as she caused a cool mist to appear.

But that was okay, for that was only a distraction. I had my left hand on my talisman and my right hand facing her, palm up. The lightning arced from my palm and struck her mid-chest. Smoke rose from her suit coat and she staggered back, tripped, and fell backward against her trunk. She turned away from me, trying to open the trunk.

Before she could recover, or get the trunk open, I went in for the kill. I didn't want to make her suffer needlessly, so, in a version of the spell used on me in that sleeper berth in Yuma, I simply pulled the air away from her. She'd go to sleep and not wake up. I was surprised by how easily I defeated her, but I didn't have time to think about it.

"YOU!" a male voice called out.

I turned and saw a man was pulling out a pistol from under his coat. Damn, I swore to myself and, dropping the spell from Morgan, shifted my position so as to give him a moving target. He fired once and the bullet ricocheted off the metal walls but, miraculously, didn't hit anything important, such as my tender skin.

Out of the corner of my eye I could see Morgan opening her trunk with a sense of urgency. I went invisible, ran at the man with the gun, pushed him aside, and bounded down the companionway.

"Get him!" Morgan screamed.

"I can't see him."

"Look for his shadow on the floor, fool!"

On the deck below I headed for the exit. Another man came in the hatch I was planning to go out. He was carrying a gun that looked more like a pipe with a handle and a box underneath.

He was yelling in German: "*Was ist los?*"

Morgan was coming down the stairs with her pistol-wielding friend right behind her. She pointed at me. "Shoot him!"

The man with the strange gun said, "*Wer?*"

I ran into him with my shoulder and knocked him aside against the bulkhead. The man with the pistol said, "*Dummkopf!*" and shot at me. He hit the dummkopf instead.

Dummkopf fell backwards in front of me. I wasn't expecting that, and I fell over him. My head crashed into the bottom of the open hatchway. I remember it hurting a lot.

\*\*\*

I woke up tied to a chair in a dark room. The room was dark and seemed small. A little light was coming in from below the door. From the drone of the engines and the movement of the ship, I was fairly certain we were underway, probably outside San Francisco Bay and on open ocean.

I assumed they had taken my talisman—Morgan would have told them to—and the way I was tied, I couldn't reach my pocket if they hadn't. Not having my talisman severely limited what spells I could invoke. Discontinuously traversing was something I could do, but just barely.

I tried to move the chair and found it was connected to the decking either by riveting or, more likely, bolting. That meant I couldn't traverse because I was connected to the chair, the chair was connected to the ship, and the ship was far too much for me to move. And besides, I was inside it.

My head was throbbing, and without a talisman I wasn't going to be able to stop it. I was able to run a little spell that allowed me to see more of the room.

I suspected it was crew quarters from its small size and the hooks for hammocks. There were probably some surly crew members resenting me at that moment.

Since I was in a perfect position to do so, I tried to feel for Morgan and whatever else I could sense. I thought just maybe the *katana* talisman might be on the ship. Those crew members were speaking German, and this was the ship *Herr* Major Daeubler had been caught trying to board with the talisman. I didn't know what Morgan's connection was in all of this, but it seemed like too many coincidences. And I still wasn't sure Dorothy wasn't working with the Nazis instead of against them. Perhaps she was working with Morgan, too.

I closed my eyes and sat very still. There was Morgan, moving nearer. And her talisman, with her. My talisman (each talisman feels different) was not so close, and not moving. But there was something else. It wasn't the *katana* talisman, but there was definitely another talisman on board, and a powerful one. Why Morgan wouldn't be using it, I didn't know.

Morgan was very near. The door was flung open and the light turned on. It took a moment for my eyes to adjust— damn human frailties. Two severe-looking men were frowning at me. One was Colonel Andenauer, whom I hadn't seen since Dorothy dragged him out of Young Fat's. The other was a large man with a nose that looked as if it'd been broken a few times too many. And finally, Morgan was standing with them, looking very beautiful and very much out of place.

"Colonel," I said jovially. "Where's Dorothy?"

He just frowned at me. "Who's Dorothy?"

I drove on, "Where's my talisman?"

The German just looked at me in disbelief. "I haf no idea vhat you are talking about, und vee ask the questions, here, *Herr* Kader."

Under stress his accent wasn't as perfect, I noticed. God, I wondered, did Dorothy...?

"Okay," I said. "Just one more. Where were you born?"

Andenauer stared at me a moment, started to speak, and then stopped. He looked at Morgan for help, then he looked at me. "I don't remember," he said with amazement.

I shouldn't wonder. Maybe Dorothy was telling the truth about the Valkyries using persuasion spells to get SS men to do their bidding. And then she had used a spell to erase Andenauer's memory of it, apparently. But such spells are dangerous and imprecise. They often erase basic knowledge, such as one's birthplace. Inexpertly handled, they could make the subject a vegetable or even kill them. This actually made me happy. If Dorothy was willing to do this to a Nazi, maybe she wasn't in league with Hitler or Morgan.

"What are you smiling about?" Morgan demanded.

"Nothing. Just enjoying the ocean cruise. What's our destination?"

"You need not vorry about that," Andenauer said ominously. "You von't be on board then."

I kept going, thinking if I kept them talking I might find a way to escape. Or, at least, put off what the silent man was there for. "How's Dummkopf?"

Andenauer looked annoyed. "Who?"

"The man who was shot."

"Dead." The off-handed manner in which he said it scared me more than anything I'd yet seen on this boat. These people didn't seem to have a problem with death and killing. "Now, shut up. Vee ask the questions here. Ve're going to leave you a few moments mit *Oberschütze* Gmelin," he said, indicating his mute companion. "Then I'll return vhen you're feeling less inquisitive und more cooperative."

He stepped out and Morgan followed, glancing back at me momentarily.

Gmelin looked at me as if I were nothing but a piece of meat.

.

# CHAPTER EIGHT

I was, to be honest, pleasantly surprised. Apparently Beverly hadn't told them.

I felt nothing. The protection spell wasn't even a strong one, not that I could do a strong one without my talisman. *Oberschütze* Gmelin tried his best, but I'm sure his fists hurt him more than I ever did. I yelled, screamed, moaned, begged, pleaded, and used a glamour to make blood, bruises, and broken teeth appear. It was hard, especially without my talisman. I wondered briefly if that was Morgan's plan: to wear me out, then take me on herself.

A long time later Andenauer and Morgan came back in. I hung my head down and looked at them through supposedly swollen eyes.

Andenauer was smiling and Morgan was just looking at me.

"Ready to talk?" the Nazi asked.

I nodded my head.

"See," Andenauer said to Morgan, "even an adept is susceptible to the right kind of pressure."

"You ass!" Morgan yelled. "It's a spell. He's not hurt." Of course, she would see through a glamour. She said a bad word in the ancient language, then turned to me. "You have no talisman. It might take me a while, but I could kill you. You can't uphold a protection spell forever."

I let the glamour dissipate, which must have looked as if I were healing before their very eyes, for Andenauer and Gmelin watched, amazed. I saw fear in the eyes of the man who'd been beating me.

But I was also mad. "Then kill me and stop this game!" I yelled.

"We need to know," Andenauer told Morgan.

"Know what?" I demanded.

Andenauer looked at me. "Where is the samurai talisman?"

I have to admit, at that point, I was flummoxed. I looked at them in amazement. "What?"

Andenauer looked angrier. "The samurai talisman. American intelligence agents took it from one of our operatives. It was then given to your guild and you took it. A very thorough search of your hotel room did not turn it up. So where is it? Is it in the safe? We couldn't open it."

I bet they couldn't. Touching it should have hurt like hell, although that spell was slowly dissipating.

"You searched my room? When?" Even in this situation, that made me feel very uncomfortable.

"When you were out of town yesterday. Is it in the safe? How do we open it? What's the combination?"

I looked at him. "I'll tell you the truth, Colonel, but you won't like it."

He snarled at me. "Tell me."

"I gave it to a Chinaman named—" I stopped. "His name isn't important. You and three other Nazi agents kidnapped him and took the talisman. I don't know what you did with it, but I suspect you gave it to the Valkyries."

Andenauer spent a moment deciding if I was lying, then turned to glare at Morgan. "Can you make him talk?"

"I think so," she said.

"We need to know what happened to that talisman. I would think you'd be interested in knowing since you were the one—"

"Yes," Morgan said, cutting him off seemingly to just to shut him up. It was as if she didn't want Andenauer to say something in front of me.

"And then kill him. We'll weigh down the body and throw it overboard."

"Yes, fine," she said. "We need to be alone."

Andenauer again looked at me, then at Morgan. "We'll be outside the door."

The colonel and the proto-human stepped out and closed the door.

I looked at her. "Damn, how did I not see what you were when we were—?"

"You always were a sucker for a pretty face, Francis," she said almost kindly.

Maybe she had a point. She and Dorothy had both fooled me.

"Tell me what they want to know, and I'll kill you quick and easy," she said. "I remember in my stateroom. You were taking away my air. You could have lit me on fire."

"I'm not a sadist."

"Tell them," she whispered, moving her lovely face closer to mine.

"I already have," I said.

She stepped back, not so friendly looking. "That story about the Valkyrie?"

"It's the truth, Beverly. You noticed Andenauer doesn't know where he was born? The Valkyrie use persuasion spells to get Nazi spies to do their bidding, then erase their memories."

She looked at me, trying to decide whether to believe me.

"Ask him," I continued, "about the three men he lost in San Francisco. I killed them."

"He was very upset; three operatives never checked in."

"He was there when I killed them. His mind's been tinkered with."

There was a moment's silence.

"You know," I said, "you run with interesting crowds. First that Negro guild in Yuma, now Nazis. What the hell are you after?"

She smiled at me. "Power. And like the niggers, these krauts are just tools for what I want."

"Do they know that?"

"No, of course not."

"Then let me go, or do you think I can't convince Andenauer you're using him?"

"Nice try," she said. "I have Andenauer completely under my control."

And I knew what she meant the moment she said it. "God," I mumbled. "I can't believe I once cared for you, thought you cared for me."

She sneered. "You have a chivalry problem. You want to rescue all women you meet."

I actually had to think about that. There was a possibility that she was right. Why had I chased Meyoung for five years?

"But I do thank you for letting me into the guild's inner circle. It was very helpful in my plans."

I wondered what she meant by that.

"Are you going to be able to convince *Herr* Andenauer I don't know where the talisman is?" Our conversation had turned almost congenial.

"Yes, that won't be a problem."

"May I ask you a question?"

She nodded.

"Back in your stateroom, what were you trying to get out of your trunk?"

She thought a moment, then answered, "Something I picked up in Yuma."

Again there was an awkward silence. Hard to have a long discussion with a person planning to kill you, I suppose.

Beverly almost looked sad as she said, "Good-bye, Francis."

She took a step back and looked at me. Her face hardened. The air around me started getting thinner. My body automatically compensated by breathing harder.

Then the door crashed open. Andenauer came in. In the corridor outside someone yelled, "*Amerikanisch Kriegsmarine!*" Andenauer pulled a pistol, pointed it at my head, looked right at Morgan instead of me, and pulled the trigger.

I got the protection spell up in time. I had enough power without my talisman to stop one, maybe two bullets.

But Andenauer didn't fire again. Still just looking at Morgan, perhaps not wanting to see what a bullet fired at that range would do to a human head, he said, "We're being boarded," and rushed out.

Morgan followed, glancing back at me and giving me a sly little smile.

I heard shouts, gunshots, and some explosions. Footsteps came down the hall. I'd hear a door kicked in, an explosion, multiple gunshots, and then it'd happen again, closer. About the third time, which must have been next door, I realized what they were doing. A grenade thrown in my lap and a spray of machine-gun fire I couldn't survive.

I started yelling, "Hey, in here, I'm an American! Don't shoot."

A tommy gun (without the circular box underneath) came around the corner, followed by a helmeted head, and finally the U.S. Marine connected to them. He looked at me carefully, surveyed the room, and then stopped pointing the gun at me.

"Sir?" he said. "Are you all right?"

"I'm fine," I said.

A second marine looked in the door, then yelled back the way they'd come, "Hey, Sarge, we got a prisoner here."

"Good, the FBI will want to interrogate him."

"Uh, Sarge, it's their prisoner. An American."

From down the hall came a string of profanity to peel paint off the bulkheads. A larger, older man looked in at me. "Well, I'll be damned."

"Sergeant," I said calmly, "do you think you could have your men untie me?"

Walking on the deck, I was surprised to find it was daylight. The sky was a bright azure and the water was that wonderful hue of blue it only gets in the deep ocean.

The crew of the *El Cielo de las Américas* was lined up on their knees, hands behind their heads, with Marines standing behind them holding weapons. Not far away was a row of corpses, covered with a canvas tarp. Blood was running out the nearest scupper into the ocean. The ship was rocking gently in the medium swell. Two huge, gray warships were not far off. Smaller boats were passing between the American Navy ships and the freighter. When I saw Andenauer I walked up to him, smiled at him and said, "Missed me."

I thought he was going to faint.

My friend Agent Smith walked over to me. "What the hell are you doing here?"

"Long story." I put my hand to my head. It still hurt.

"Headache?" Smith asked.

"Yes," I said, tenderly rubbing my forehead.

"You have a nasty bruise."

"Great," I mumbled.

"So," Smith said, "how did you get on this ship?"

"I boarded in San Francisco. I was looking for Morgan."

"Who?"

"American woman, long red hair. Hard to miss."

Smith pointed at kneeling prisoners. "That's everyone we found on the ship alive." He pointed at the corpses. "And those were the ones that weren't smart enough to surrender. No females."

"Damn," I said. "Have you searched the staterooms?"

"Yes. We did find a trunk that looks as if it belonged to a woman."

"Find anything interesting in it?"

"Like what?"

I shrugged my shoulders. "Something one would pick up in Yuma, Arizona.

Smith looked at me as if I were nuts. "Nope. Just clothes and stuff."

"Mind if I look?"

"Yes, I do. It's evidence."

I turned to him. "There was a woman on board, American. Adept. Do you understand what I'm saying?"

It only took him a moment. "She might still be on board, hiding."

"Yes. Invisibility spell. Now if I can see her room, look at her things, I might be able to find her."

He thought about it for a moment. "Okay, let's go."

We returned to the bridge house and up the companionway to the deck with the staterooms. It wasn't so neat and tidy. There was blood on some of the bulkheads. Marines and civilians were everywhere. I assumed the civilians, like Smith, were G-men.

Outside Beverly's room, Smith talked to a civilian who looked at me suspiciously, but let me in the room.

I pulled open the trunk and, after looking through a few unmentionables, found one treasure: my talisman. I started to put it in my pocket.

"Hey," the other civilian said. "You can't take that."

With my talisman it was easy, and I was in no mood to futz around. "Yes, I can."

"Yes, you can," he repeated.

Smith didn't say a thing.

I put my hand to my head and healed the damage there, eliminating my headache.

But after a thorough search of Morgan's room, I didn't find a damn thing, especially something she might have found in Yuma.

"So?" Smith asked as I came out of the room.

"Got what I was looking for."

Smith looked angry. "And the woman?"

I held up my hand to quiet him. Then I concentrated. It took a few moments, not helped by Smith and the other civilian looking at me. And it's harder to prove a negative. "She's not here." And neither was the power source—the other talisman I had sensed—that she had in her trunk and that she had apparently found in Yuma.

"Where'd she go, then?" he asked.

"Probably did what I'd do: invisibility spell, discontinuously traverse off the ship, fall into the ocean, swim."

"We're a hundred miles off shore."

"That's not a problem for an adept." She wouldn't even have to swim the entire way, but I didn't need to tell Smith that.

"So," I said as I started walking toward the companionway, "how'd you find this ship?"

Smith followed. "Daeubler finally cracked."

I turned before going down the stairs. "What? That was three days ago."

"No," Smith said. "We didn't get much more out of him then. To be honest, we've suspected this ship for a while. But we didn't have enough on it when we picked up Daeubler so we let it sail. When I learned it was back in Oakland, I pressed Daeubler hard. He didn't want to talk, so we threatened to bring you back in if he didn't."

"And that worked?"

"You scared him, apparently."

I continued down the stairs. "When was this?"

"Late yesterday, after we got back from Klamath. But by the time we got to the docks, the ship had sailed and was out of the bay. It took us until this morning to find the damn thing. Spotted by a PBY patrol after the fog cleared."

I wasn't going to ask what a PBY was.

"Now," Smith said as we exited the companionway, "are you going to tell me what you were doing here and how they managed to tie up an adept?"

"I was looking for Morgan," I said. "And I had an accident." I looked; there were still bloodstains where Dummkopf had been shot.

That seemed to satisfy Smith for the time being.

\*\*\*

I found out what a PBY was shortly thereafter. A small boat took Smith, a couple of the other civilians, and me to an airplane that had landed on the water. It was funny-looking even by airplane standards. It appeared as if someone had taken a fair-sized boat and grafted wings and a tail onto it. The two propellers were on the high-mounted wing.

I considered offering to find my own way home. Trusting my life to that contraption seemed foolhardy. But Smith had insisted I return to San Francisco with him, and I didn't want to make a fuss around all these lessers. So we were loaded in and strapped down, and the airplane began skimming across the water with an ever-louder noise of the engines and the water slapping against the bottom. Was it called a "hull"? I didn't know. Just when I thought the waves were going to smash the little craft apart, it slowly ascended into the sky.

This wasn't, obviously, the first time I'd flown. But it was the first time I'd flown in one of these contraptions that lessers build. The noise was terrific and when the damn thing turned, it leaned. The tilting sensation was made worse by not being able to see out. The one bubble window was behind me.

A few miserable hours later we landed at Moffett Field, which is south of San Francisco. Apparently the plane could land on the ground, too. Getting out, I was tempted to kiss the Earth.

Cars were waiting for Smith and the others. Smith tacitly assumed I would be traveling with him back to the city. I needed a ride anyway, so I climbed into the back seat of one of the vehicles with him. A second G-man got in the front seat with the young driver.

"Treasure Island," Smith told the driver.

"You can drop me off in the city," I said. "Drake-Wiltshire Hotel, if you please."

Smith tried to look intimidating. "No, you'll come with us and answer a few questions." The agent in the front seat turned to look at me, also trying to appear tough.

"I don't have time," I said. "And frankly, I'd like to see you try."

Smith and the other agent exchanged a look of resignation.

"Fine, we'll drop you in the city."

"Thank you," I said sincerely.

As the car pulled out of the Navy base, I asked Smith, "What happens to the crew of the ship?"

"The crew is probably German Navy; they'll go to a POW camp. It's the SS men we're interested in. The ship is being towed back to Mare Island, where it will be dismantled. Depending on what we find, they will either be tried and convicted as spies or spend the rest of the war in a POW camp."

I nodded my understanding and watched the scenery pass by. I saw a huge building on the Navy facility. It was triangular in shape with a rounded top, but very long. There were clamshell doors on the end I could see that were open, revealing a very large space inside. I couldn't imagine what could be housed inside such a large structure. I was about to ask Smith about it when he interrupted my thoughts.

"Tell me about Morgan."

"Guild business," I answered.

"That's not good enough. If she's working with Hun spies, then the FBI needs to know what they are up to."

I turned in my seat to look at him. "Which is exactly what I was doing on that ship. And when I find her again—" *if* I find her, I thought; I was sure she'd cover her tracks better now and who knew where on the west coast she had come ashore? "—I will deal with it. It's a guild matter."

Smith didn't say anything, but by the way he was breathing I knew he was angry and frustrated. But what could he do? The lesser governments have no authority over the guilds. How could they have, when they can't put us in jail and they can't kill us, at least not before we can kill a lot more of them. All governments, even these precious "democracies," derive all their power by force. Do something the government doesn't want, like, say, cross the street against the light, refuse to submit to its authority, and it won't be long before they'll use some form of force, usually a weapon and the threat of death or injury, to compel you to comply. The only difference between Franklin Delano Roosevelt and Adolf Hitler was a matter of degree.

It was one reason I'd become an adept.

They actually did drop me at my hotel.

"We'll be in touch," Smith said as I got out of the car.

I just smiled at him condescendingly and went inside. There were no messages at the desk so I went to my room. Stepping in, I felt it. I hadn't had time before, but now I could. Someone who didn't belong had been here. I opened drawers and things had not been put back exactly right. I called the front desk and asked when the room had last been cleaned. Unfortunately, it had been that morning. I didn't know what I hoped to find: a long red hair, sand that only came from a beach in Argentina. But the fact that it had been cleaned made me feel better.

I took a shower and went to bed. The next day I had an unpleasant task ahead of me, which meant yet another trip to Union Station.

***

Yuma looked a lot like it did the last time I was there. Again a member of the Negro guild met me. He greeted me as I stepped on the platform.

"Kader?" he asked.

I nodded. I'd sent a telegram addressed to "Negro Guild, Yuma." Apparently they had received it.

"I have a car, Teacher."

"Good."

It was the same car that they had used to chase me around Yuma. I got in a little nervously. The back seat held two warriors. One was the one I had abducted briefly. I smiled at him. He glared back.

We were driven out of the town going east. The desolation was amazing. Desert, marked by gray-yellow sand, extended for miles in every direction. It was broken up only by the dots of vegetation, which surprised me. I could not understand how anything managed to live in this climate.

The road soon became dirt and then little more than a glorified trail. The car came to a dusty stop in front of a small house that would barely qualify as a hovel. It looked like the sharecropper shacks you would see in the newsreels from the days of the Dust Bowl.

I got out and looked around. There didn't seem to be another human within miles. If they wanted to kill someone, this was the place to do it.

"Inside, please," the adept said.

I crossed the rickety porch and went into the shack. In comparison to the outside, the interior was quite nice. It was old, but clean, with aging furniture and rugs. It was cooler than outside in the sun.

An elderly Negro man was sitting in a comfortable-looking overstuffed chair. A warrior stood behind him holding a pistol. The old adept was drinking what appeared to be iced tea. I didn't know where he got ice. There was obviously no electricity; the interior was lit by oil lamps. He must use meta: slow the atoms in the water down enough, and you get ice.

"Teacher," I said respectfully.

He was gruff in his reply. "Sit down, Mr. Kader."

I found a chair. "Thank you for agreeing to meet with me."

"Would you like some iced tea?"

"No thank you," I replied. "How may I address you, Teacher?"

"Call me Mr. Brooks."

I nodded and smiled. "Thank you, Mr. Brooks."

He didn't smile back. "You have about two minutes to peruse me that I shouldn't have you killed."

I think he meant "persuade" and I didn't doubt he would try to kill me. Between himself, the adept that had stayed outside, and the three warriors, it would be a neat trick for me to survive.

"We are not each other's enemies. Morgan set us against each other for her own gain."

He looked angry. "Who?"

"The redheaded woman. I knew her as Beverly Morgan."

Brooks nodded. "Yes, she called herself Beverly. Beverly Johnson."

"She offered you a position in her new, more powerful guild?"

"Yes." He looked embarrassed.

"Did you know she offered the same position to me?"

"No, but it doesn't surprise me now."

I leaned forward and looked into his dark eyes. "I am trying to find her and stop her. I need your help. I am not your enemy. My guild is not your enemy. Beverly Mor—Johnson is."

"We need to make an understanding. She has something; I want it back."

"What?"

The man looked uncomfortable for a moment. "She came to me, said she knew of a talisman of great power in the Yuma area."

"How?"

"She said it was found at the new U.S. Army base, dug up, when they started construction. It was something that belonged to the Indians. A ceremonial rattle."

"How would she know that?" I asked, thinking out loud.

He answered anyway. "I do not know. But she said with this talisman, me and her could rule your guild."

"But she betrayed you?"

"Yes. She took the rattle and disappeared."

I looked at him questioningly. "She took the train to San Francisco." Not a hard thing to stop for even a minor guild such as this.

"Impossible," he said. "We were watching the train."

"With adepts?"

"Yes. She couldn't have used a glamour."

I sat back and had to think. Miles had been able to track her because she had taken the train. But if she hadn't taken the train, how did Miles track her? But he did track her, because he traced her to the *El Cielo de las Américas.* Unless Miles was lying about how he traced her. And why would he do that?

"I need to talk to your sheriff," I said.

The old adept looked at me. "My boys can take you into town."

"Good."

"Assuming I let you go," he added. Then: "What will you do when you find her?"

"Kill her," I said dispassionately.

"My guild will get the rattle back." He said it as a statement.

"I will try."

He shook his head, then looked at me intently. "My guild will get the rattle back or you will not leave Yuma. We had plans to kill you last time you were here; we can impalement them now just as easily."

I think he meant "implement."

"It's not up to me," I explained. "My guild will want such a powerful talisman. And I don't think your guild could survive a conflict with mine."

"Doesn't matter, you'll still be dead."

"If I'm dead, Beverly keeps the rattle. I've found her twice; I can find her again." I hoped, but I wasn't going to tell him that.

"We also are looking for her."

I chuckled. "I wish you luck."

He glared at me, his black eyes reflecting the flame of an oil lamp.

"However," I continued before he became angry enough to kill me, "I will do everything I can to conceal the existence of the rattle from my guild and return it to you. You have my word on that."

It was his turn to chuckle. "What good is the word of an adept? You could deluge me as easily as Beverly did. Easier, in fact, since you will be outside my area of power."

I did not want to give him my name, even to stop me from deluding him. Unfortunately, he asked for it. This was getting to be a bad habit with me. To be honest, I wasn't sure how I was going to find the *katana* talisman, never mind Morgan and the rattle.

# CHAPTER NINE

The courthouse was a three-story white granite building with arched windows and palm trees in front. The Yuma County sheriff's office was little more than a room in the basement of the courthouse. Cells lined one wall, all three of them empty. An officer in a khaki uniform was behind a large wooden desk. He was balding and slightly overweight. His mustache extended to his jowls in the style cowboys wore them in old pictures. He stood up as I came in and smiled jovially.

"What can I do for you?" he asked.

"I need to see the sheriff," I answered.

"You've found him," he said, smiling, and pointed to a chair, then sat himself. "What can I do for you?"

I hesitated a moment. I wasn't sure exactly how to go about this. "I served with one of your deputies in the Seventh I.D. in France in the First World War. Thought since I was in town, I'd stop and say hello."

The sheriff looked at me quizzically. "I don't think so. I have two deputies and neither served in World War One."

"Really?" I asked, trying to sound surprised.

He nodded. "I'm positive. George was right here in Yuma, deferment for being a peace officer, and Mitch is too young, being he was born in 1910."

I stood up. "Well, I must have been misinformed." I started walking toward the door.

"Now, hold on there, mister," the man said in a forceful voice. "I think maybe you should tell me what this is about. I don't like no one coming around asking 'bout my deputies."

I turned to look at him. His hand was on the gun in his holster.

I smiled and slipped my hand in my pocket where my talisman was.

It was like in the movies; he had his gun out so fast I hardly saw it leave its holster. "Just keep your hands in plain sight, there, now."

I extended my arms away from my body, but I wasn't going to do something as stupid as put my hands up. And I could still work spells, just not as powerful ones.

"Just a mistake, sheriff," I said.

"A mistake," he repeated, trying to believe it.

"Yes, I was in the wrong county. Isn't this California?"

"No, Arizona. When you cross the Colorado, you're in Arizona."

"See, there's my mistake."

"Mistake," he repeated.

I smiled at him. "Good day, sheriff."

"Yes," he said. "Same to you."

I turned around and left. The car the Negro guild had provided was waiting. I climbed into the back seat.

"Where now?" the driver/warrior asked.

I thought for a moment. "Is there a museum in town?"

My driver looked at me in the rearview mirror as he talked. "No, not really. Except maybe ol' Doc Addleman's place. He collects all sort of junk."

"Let's go see Doc Addleman."

It wasn't a long drive to the doctor's house. The front yard was full of artifacts, making it look like a somewhat less crowded junkyard. I opened the fence gate and walked the clear path to the front door. A small, hand-printed sign tacked on the door read, "Walk in."

So I did. The living room of the house had been converted to a waiting room. The walls were plastered with old pictures, more artifacts, a couple of Indian blankets used almost like tapestries, and over the door leading further into the house, a rusty horseshoe, pointing up, of course. There were a couple of people sitting around on couches and chairs. Both, I noticed, were Indians. Behind a desk was a middle-aged woman. I approached her.

"I need to see Dr. Addleman."

She looked at me, perhaps trying to assess my health.

"If you don't have an appointment, you'll have to wait," she said, pointing the pencil in her hand at the chairs. "Doctor's with a patient right now."

"I need to see the doctor now," I said, smiling at her benevolently. She wasn't aware of the light spell I was casting on her.

She nodded. "I'll get him." She stood and walked into the next room of the house, under the horseshoe.

I waited for a few moments, and a man emerged wearing a white coat. The woman followed and pointed me out. "This is the gentleman."

Dr. Addleman looked me up and down; again I felt as if I was being judged somehow. "What can I do for you?"

"I was wondering if you knew anything about some Indian artifacts dug up at the Army base." I had my hand in my pocket, on my talisman, in case he got antsy.

He glanced furtively at the Indians sitting, waiting, then said, "Come with me," and walked back through the door he'd come through.

I walked under the horseshoe to follow. "That doesn't work, you know," I said.

"What?" he asked as he walked into a small office. The front part of the house was apparently for the doctor's practice and the rear part the living quarters. An examination room and his office had been carved cut of what I decided was probably the dining room, since the kitchen was the next room in.

"Horseshoes. They aren't good luck."

He sat at a desk covered with papers, folders, and the ubiquitous antiques. "Why do you say that?"

"There's no such thing as luck," I said.

He smiled at me, deciding I was one of *those*, although what his idea of "those" was, I didn't know. "What can I do for you?" he asked.

"I was wondering if you knew what happened to some Indian artifacts dug up at the new Army base."

He again looked uncomfortable. "Who are you?"

I don't know who or what he feared. I didn't answer his question. "I heard that some artifacts were found during some construction at the new Army base outside of town."

"Most the buildings out there are Bureau of Reclamation buildings converted over to wartime use."

The truth spell I ran was mild. "Yes, I understand that. But what about the artifacts?"

"They didn't know what to do with them. So they called me. I'm sort of the local Indian lore expert. I've been collecting antiques since I arrived in Yuma almost 20 years ago."

"And?" I prodded.

"They had some arrowheads—" he rummaged on his desk for a moment and picked up a stone arrowhead "—this is one—and some other items. Not very interesting, really."

"Was there a rattle?"

He looked at me, surprised. "Yes," he answered despite himself.

"What happened to it?"

He didn't say anything for a moment. Finally he spoke, looking at me. "I want to live quietly. I can help some people. I'm tired of the guilds."

Now I was surprised. "You're an adept?"

He nodded.

"But my truth spell."

"I felt it, didn't block it."

"The rattle?"

"Powerful talisman. Probably a thousand years old." Yes, could be. Talismans are ageless: metal doesn't rust, stone doesn't wear, and organic doesn't rot.

"What did you do with it?"

He took a few moments to answer. "The local guild, I don't trust its leader."

"The Negro, Brooks?"

"Yes. First I don't want him to know I'm an adept—he'd probably try to kill me, and as old and tired as I am, he'd probably succeed. Second, he's a power-hungry fool."

"A lot of guild leaders are," I threw out.

"Yes. What is your guild?"

"West Coast."

He looked impressed. "That's a powerful guild."

"Yes," I said simply. "But what of the rattle?"

"It was stolen from me."

"By whom?"

"Two warriors and an adept from the local guild."

"Negro?"

"Yes. They came in as we were closing. I didn't have a chance. They took the talisman."

I believed him.

"Who knew you had it?"

"The commander of the Army base, a few construction workers."

I had a feeling that wasn't the entire list. "Anyone else?"

He looked at the floor. "I should have destroyed it."

"Takes powerful meta," I said.

"Yes," he said.

"Beyond your abilities."

"Yes." It was almost a whisper.

"So you didn't."

He looked at me with pain in his eyes. "No," he hesitated for a moment. "I'm not a doctor, but I try to help people. Indians, poor white people, Negroes, coolies, anyone who can't get help otherwise. I use my slight powers mostly to determine what exactly is wrong. I'm not powerful enough to heal, not without a powerful talisman. But I've learned. Some local herbs, Indian lore mostly, some stuff from the pharmacy. Or in Mexico I can buy what I need. They pay what they can. I like helping them. I thought with the rattle I could help them more. I thought with that power, I could help more people."

"You used it to heal people?"

"Yes."

"And they saw it."

"Yes."

"So a lot of people—"

"Poor, powerless people," he interjected.

"Yes, poor, powerless people knew you had it."

"Yes, but they wouldn't know what it was."

"Maybe they talked to someone who did."

"Maybe," he said softly, not looking at me.

That still didn't answer how Morgan had found out about it.

This man was a surprise. Or perhaps not. Someone this giving and apparently guileless would have a hard time surviving in the Machiavellian atmosphere of a guild. Hell, at that moment, I was having trouble with the usual guild politics, machinations, and calumny.

"What would this rattle look like?" I asked.

"Just a second." Addleman turned in his chair and opened a filing cabinet. He rummaged around for a while before pulling out a worn artifact. "This one's missing its beads, so it no longer rattles."

I looked at it. It looked like a gourd stuck on top of a wooden stick. There had once been a pattern carved into the gourd, and it looked as if some color had been added.

"The talisman," Addleman explained, "was like new."

I thanked "Doc" Addleman and went back outside to where the car was waiting. The driver was leaning against the hood smoking a cigarette.

"Where to now?" he asked slowly before dragging on his smoke.

"Hotel Del Sol," I said. "You can drop me there and thank your guild for the help."

He seemed glad to be rid of me.

Walking into the lobby of the Del Sol, I saw a knot of people in the corner gathered around the large console radio. I couldn't help but hear the speaker:

"...the ship flew an Argentinean flag and had a false Argentinean registry. But in reality, it was a German navy vessel used for spying on American soil."

That got my attention, so I moved closer.

"Brave agents of the Federal Bureau of Investigation," the speaker continued, "assisted by the U.S. Navy, Coast Guard, and the Marines, captured the ship, named deceptively *El Cielo de las Américas*, which is Spanish for 'The Sky of the Americas,' off the coast of California. The crew, and as many as five Nazi spies, were captured."

"But most disturbing was evidence found on board the ship that the Nazi spies are being assisted by members of the meta guilds. Evidence of at least one adept was found on board."

I had to stop myself from saying something very bad.

"The adept or adepts unfortunately escaped," the speaker continued. "This is yet another example of enemy collusion on U.S. soil. We must remain ever vigilant, ever strong, against threats to our American way of life, both foreign and domestic. Thank you and good night."

There was a short pause, then, "Ladies and gentlemen, you've been listening to a report from Federal Bureau of Investigation Director J. Edgar Hoover. Stay tuned for 'Nick Carter, Master Detective,' staring Lon Clark, Helen Chaote..."

I stopped listening and tried to wander away inconspicuously. I tried to think of a course of action. About the only thing I could think to do was confront Smith when I got back to San Francisco. But I doubted that would do much good. The government never liked the guilds, and Hoover especially didn't like us.

I realized I was at the desk and the clerk was looking at me. "Sir, may I help you?"

I rented a room under another name, thinking they might be sore about how I'd left last time I was in town. The return train to San Francisco left at seven the next morning and I wanted to get some sleep.

\*\*\*

Even with meta power, one can't always get what one wants. There were no sleeper suites available on the train, for there were no sleeper cars. The train was packed with soldiers out of Fort Bliss, Texas, heading for the West Coast to ship out, one would presume, to the Pacific. I was crammed in a seat next to an eager, pimply private. I had to use a spell on him to shut him up so I could think.

I now knew that Miles had lied to me about the "friend" in the sheriff's office. Why would Miles lie? Maybe Morgan didn't hide her surprise at seeing me on the ship because she expected me to be there. Miles had set me up and Morgan had paid him, either with money or other enticements. Andenauer knew I had the talisman, that Admiral Richards had given it to our guild. Who in that room told him? I wondered. Had to be Black or Reynolds or maybe Fitz. But I doubted it was Fitz. It didn't make sense for him to be working with Nazis. But little about what was happening made sense.

Andenauer also said they had searched my room to find the *katana* talisman, but of course didn't find it because Dorothy had it. Maybe they thought if they lured me on the ship either I'd have it with me or they could get its location out of me. And Morgan had thanked me for getting her into the inner circle of the guild because it helped her plans. Was she working with someone else in the guild? Fitz, or Black, or Reynolds? Black was the logical choice. He'd drooled over her since the first time he met her, and Morgan could use her charms on him, easily. And he was German. Maybe he had loyalties to Hitler.

Thinking about it made my head hurt and made me angry and frustrated. So I watched the desert go by out my window and ignored the massed humanity around me.

\*\*\*

As I walked into the lobby of the Drake-Wiltshire, the night desk clerk tried, but failed, to point me out subtly. Two men, who had been watching him, stood up and came toward me. By the inexpensive clothes, comfortable shoes, and general air of authority given but not necessarily earned, I could tell they were cops. Also, cops don't take off their hats indoors in order to keep their hands free.

"Mr. Kader?" one asked.

"Yes." I casually put my hand in my pocket and grasped my talisman.

They both reached into their coats and pulled out wallets with badges, as if I needed to see them. "I'm Lieutenant Halloran; this is Detective-sergeant O'Reilly. San Francisco Police Department."

"Yes, gentlemen?" I asked.

"Could you come with us, please, sir?" O'Reilly said.

"It's four in the morning," I said. "What's this about?"

"We'll explain that, soon. If you don't mind?" His polite words were in contrast to his commanding tone. He stepped forward and forcefully grabbed my upper arm. I looked at them. Both were big Irishmen, and Halloran had a red nose from drinking too much. But I wasn't going to go with them without knowing why.

"Gentlemen," I said, trying to keep the anger out of my voice, "I just returned from a long train trip. I would like to go to my room and rest. I can call you in the morning and we can talk then."

Halloran looked amused. O'Reilly pulled on my arm. "That's not acceptable."

At that I got angry. I looked O'Reilly in the eye and hit him with a small fear spell. "Remove your hand from my person."

His face registered his confusion. This was apparently a man not used to being afraid of much. He pulled out a pair of handcuffs and held them in front of me. "Don't make this more unpleasant than it has to be," he said, still politely but with an ominous undertone. As if those could hold me.

And Halloran grabbed my other arm. That pulled my hand out of my pocket, but I managed to hold on to my talisman.

The lobby was deserted except for minimal hotel staff. However, if I wasn't careful, the management might ask me to move out if they decided I was an undesirable guest. I could use spells to convince them otherwise, but they'd have to be maintained and that would be a bother.

"Fine," I said, "I'll come."

They led me outside, each one holding an arm, Halloran so tightly I was sure he would leave a bruise. It was just turning light in the east and clouds made the sky darker than usual. On the sidewalk, I used a spell on both of them. They let go of me and moved backward. I grabbed Halloran and pushed him against a wall while using a spell to keep O'Reilly out of the action.

The night doorman for the Drake-Wiltshire looked at me, his eyes wide. "Mr. Kader, do you require assistance?"

"No, everything's fine."

"Yes, sir," he said and ignored us.

I looked at Halloran. "You need to learn some manners, sonny," I growled, holding him against the granite.

"Yes, sir," he said. The spell was making him very receptive to new ideas.

"Now, what's this about?"

"A body."

"What body?"

"Someone found a body, at the bottom of Jackson Street. No identification, just your name and hotel." He reached in his pocket and pulled out a scrap of paper on which someone had scribbled "Kader—Drake-Wiltshire."

"What did the body look like?"

"Caucasian male, small, wiry."

I let go of him. "Where's the body now?"

"The morgue."

"Let's go," I said as I released O'Reilly's spell, allowing him to move again. He stepped forward like a drunk and looked as if he wasn't sure what was going on.

They led me to an older car and asked politely if I would get in back. I did and they got in front and we drove.

"Are you an adept?" Halloran asked. There was fear in his voice that he was trying to mask.

"Yes." I assumed they were smart enough to figure that out.

"We're really sorry, sir. If we'd known."

I waved my hand dismissively. Yeah, you wouldn't have treated me like you treat all civilians, I thought ruefully.

The car stopped in front of a government building. The cops took me inside and into the basement.

"These guys who work the morgue at night give me the willies," O'Reilly said to no one.

We went past double-doors with a sign that read "Morgue." Three walls of the room were covered in green tiles. The fourth wall was full of large drawers. A couple of white-coated men were floating about.

Halloran spoke to one of them. "John Doe number 43, Fred."

Fred glided over and smiled with small, crooked teeth.

"Yes," he said, drawing out the "s" sound. "John Doe number 43." He consulted a clipboard hanging from a nail on the wall, and then, after consulting the numbers on the drawers, pulled one open. A white sheet covered what was obviously a body. "Here we are, gentlemen."

Fred pulled the white sheet off the body.

"His name is Miles Archer," I said, looking at the naked corpse. "I have his phone number and address, if that's helpful to you."

Halloran nodded and O'Reilly was taking notes, so I told him the information.

Halloran continued the narrative. "He was found this morning—apparently shot last night."

"Five times," Fred added quietly, as if he were afraid he'd wake the dead.

"At close range," Halloran added, "judging from the powder burns on his clothes."

"We found an intact slug," Fred whispered sibilantly. "A .455 caliber. I believe a Webley-Fosbery Mark II."

O'Reilly nodded. "Six-shot automatic revolver. They don't make them anymore."

I ignored that bit of useless information.

"Thanks, Fred," Halloran said. I allowed him to lead me away, not unhappy to leave Fred and the late Miles Archer behind. I heard the drawer close as we walked away. We stopped just outside the door to the morgue, where I think Halloran and O'Reilly were more comfortable talking. Halloran looked at me.

"Where were you last night?" he asked.

"Yuma, Arizona," I answered. They looked doubtful. "Check with the Southern Pacific and the Del Sol Hotel  Except I checked in under the name 'Eric Overfield.'"

"Why?" Halloran asked looking exasperated.

"My own reasons," I replied in a manner that indicated that was all I would say.

O'Reilly was still taking notes.

Halloran tried to sound tough. "Don't you adepts have other ways to travel?"

I looked him in the eye. "Not that it's any of your business, but yes."

"Then," he continued bravely, "you could have killed this poor sap, then used some magic way to get to Yuma."

"I took the train to Yuma Tuesday, arriving late yesterday afternoon."

"Fast trip," Halloran stated.

"I took care of my business and left. Believe me, Yuma is not a place where I need or want to spend much time."

"And what is that business?"

I glared at Halloran. "None of yours."

"Then you could have had time," O'Reilly said, "to travel back to Frisco and then go back to Yuma."

I was getting tired of this game. "I didn't kill Miles. I had no reason to. And if I did, I wouldn't use a gun. I have other ways of killing a man and I wouldn't touch one of those vile things."

"What?" Halloran said. "A gun?"

"Yes."

The two flatfoots just looked at me.

"Take me back to my hotel," I ordered, using a persuasion spell.

"Yes, sir," O'Reilly said.

We returned to the car by the way we had come.

Alone in the car, before they drove away, I hit Halloran with a powerful truth spell and put O'Reilly to sleep.

"What else do you know about Miles' murder?"

He answered like an automaton. "Body found by men going to work at 6:00 A.M. No witnesses found yet, probably won't be with the curfew. Only thing found on the body was a slip of paper with your name and hotel, and two-hundred dollars cash."

"Anything else?"

"Probably knew the shooter; he was shot at near point-blank range, so he allowed the person to get close. Might have been a woman."

"Why do you think that?"

"A man will let a woman closer than a man, generally."

"Take me home," I said.

"Yes, sir."

Eventually, I got in my bed and slept.

# CHAPTER TEN

I wanted to talk to Smith about what J. Edgar Hoover had said. I realized I'd never gotten ahold of him before. So, the next day, after my morning toilet, I looked in the phone book, and right there was a listing for the Federal Bureau of Investigations. I dialed the number and a woman answered, "Federal Bureau of Investigation, how may I direct your call?"

"Agent Smith, please," I said.

There was hesitation. "Which Agent Smith are you looking for, sir?"

Oh, damn, I thought. I had no idea what his first name was. "The one working on the *El Cielo de las Américas* case."

Again there was hesitation. Then she said, "Just a moment, sir"

I waited, wondering what the problem was, and vowing to get Smith's first name.

A long time later another voice came on the phone. "Who is this?" he demanded and he didn't sound like Smith.

"Who is this?" I asked.

"This is Special Agent Heston. Who are you?"

"Where's Smith?" I asked.

"That's what I'd like to know," Special Agent Heston said angrily.

"What do you mean?"

"Who are you?" Heston demanded again.

This was going nowhere. "My name is Francis Kader. I was on the *El Cielo de las Américas* when it was captured."

"Are you the adept who was a prisoner of the Nazis?"

"Yes," I said, embarrassed.

"I need to talk to you, now. Where are you?"

While I didn't like his attitude, cooperating seemed the best way to get information out of him. At least until I was close enough to run a truth spell on him. "The Drake-Wiltshire."

"Stay there," he said as if it were an order.

I went to the lobby to wait, taking my coat with me; it had started to rain.

It didn't take long. I spotted Heston when he walked in. G-men have a look. Like cops, but more self-important.

"You Heston?" I said, approaching him.

"Yes, you Kader?" He was tall with the requisite trench coat and snap-brim hat. Rainwater dripped off the brim.

"Yes."

He looked around. "We can't talk here."

"Why?" I was loving this terse conversation. Why was he so serious? I wondered.

"Classified information. I need you to come with me."

"Where?"

"My office."

I shrugged my shoulders. "Fine, but I'll need a ride back. I don't drive and I don't want to look for a taxi in the rain."

He looked at me as if he didn't believe me. He apparently didn't know about the disdain adepts have for technology. For the same reason I wouldn't use a gun to kill Miles, I also had never learned to drive.

Outside he ushered me into a car. He sat in the back with me and a younger man drove. I was surprised when we went to an office building.

"The FBI has nearly doubled in size since the war," Heston explained. "We've had to rent space where we can find it."

Inside we took an elevator to the fourth floor, then we walked to an office with frosted glass doors. Painted on them was "Universal Exports, Ltd." I looked at Heston and he smiled. "Sign was there when we moved in; we never got around to replacing it. Doesn't hurt to have a little misdirection, also."

I shrugged and followed him inside. The interior was filled with metal desks. Men and women were running purposefully around the room. The sound of typing crescendoed until my ears got used to the assault.

Heston took me to a small room. It had no windows and only one of those new fluorescent lights buzzing overhead. One of the ubiquitous metal desks was in there along with three metal chairs with green plastic seat cushions.

"Wait here," Heston ordered and left.

I sat in one of the chairs, spent about thirty seconds examining the room in minute detail, and waited.

By my watch, it took Heston almost an hour to return. I was not happy. I had, after about half an hour, decided to go find him, only to learn I was locked in. I was so angry I seriously considered discontinuously traversing out.

"Is there a reason you locked me in this room for an hour?" I demanded, standing as he came in.

Heston ignored me. "Sit down."

A second, younger man followed Heston in and sat in one of the chairs. Heston sat behind the desk and placed some papers on it.

I remained standing, glaring at him.

"Sit down, please," he said. "I apologize for the wait. It took longer than I expected. This is Agent Shaw."

I sat down. "Where's Smith?" I asked, trying to sound calm.

"That's what we were hoping to ask you," Heston said. "He's disappeared."

I looked at him, wondering if he thought I had anything to do with it. "What do you mean?"

"I mean," Heston said, sounding frustrated, "that no one can find him. Also, when we informed Washington, we were told that they have no record of that 'Agent Smith' ever being with the FBI."

The look on my face probably registered my surprise. "Really?" I said.

"Yes. We suspect he's an adept. There are spells to deceive people, correct?"

I nodded. "Yes, there are such spells, but I assure you, he's no adept."

He leaned forward. "How do you know?"

I took a breath before deciding how much to tell him. "Adepts can spot each other pretty easily."

"Then he could have been in league with an adept, perhaps?"

"Perhaps," I said.

Heston was quiet a moment, then said, "Look at this." Agent Shaw, who up until then had been as quiescent as a statue, handed me a paper. The first thing I noticed was that it was singed around the edges, as if someone had tried to burn it. Then I looked at the text. It read:

WACUW KQWEQ UYDGD CSAEB LMJCX ZXCMU YAPXG

The whole page was filled with similar five-letter groups of seemingly random letters.

"Can you read it?" Heston asked.

"No," I said.

"Don't you have translation spells?"

"This isn't a language," I said handing the paper to Heston. "At least none I know of."

Heston looked at it briefly and set it aside. "Actually, it's encrypted. We were hoping you could decode it. The ship, the *El Cielo de las Américas,* was full of these. The Huns managed to burn a lot of them but we rescued some, including that."

"Let me see it again," I said. I studied it. "This is in German when decoded?" I asked.

Heston nodded. "Yes."

I tried a translation spell, tried a spell to discern the original writer's meaning, combined the two, and soon the letters made sense, at least in German:

UNSER SPION INYUM AWIEV ONALL GEMEI NENAU FTRAG

I pulled out my talisman and ran a second translation spell, German to English, and started reading: "Our agent in Yuma," I read slowly, working all the spells simultaneously and trying to read the five-letter groups as words, then translate them, "as required by general orders, reports the discovery of a talisman at the U.S. Army base where he is working as a laborer. Instruct the adept spy, through her handler, Daeubler, to recover talisman for the leader's collection. A local doctor name Addleman possesses it. No known German sympathies so likely need to take by force." I looked up. "That's it."

The younger agent whistled. "They could use him at Bletchley Park."

Heston glared at him. I think Shaw said something he shouldn't have.

"'The leader's collection'?" Shaw asked, as if trying to change the subject.

"*Führer* is German for 'leader,'" Heston explained.

"What is this?" I asked.

"A dispatch from Berlin, we think, probably directly from the *Reichssicherheitshauptam*, to Colonel Andenauer who was apparently the head of the spy cell here in San Francisco."

Both men looked at me. Finally Heston said, "I have some good news. I talked to Halloran and O'Reilly. They don't suspect you in Archer's death. Your alibi checks out."

"Good," I said, wondering where this was going.

"But that means," Heston continued, "that we know you've been to Yuma. Now what business would you have in Yuma? And you know we can find out if you were there before."

Oh, that was where it was going. "I am not the adept spy mentioned in this dispatch, if that's what you're hinting at."

"We don't think you are, since that spy is female."

I realized then that either Heston was a fast thinker, which I doubted, or they had already decoded the dispatch.

"But look at it from our point of view," he continued. "You were found on the *El Cielo de las Américas* when it was boarded—"

"I was a prisoner," I interrupted.

"Yes, and how does one capture an adept?"

"It's possible," I said. "With luck and cunning." I did not want to explain my own bad luck and clumsiness to these lessers. "And they were waiting for me. I was lured onto that ship."

"Why?"

"They thought I had something they wanted."

"What?" Heston was boring in on me. I resented it.

"A talisman. I didn't have it."

"Why?"

I was getting angry and spoke a little too loudly and a little too fast. "None of your business. I came here today to find out about Smith, and what the hell Hoover was doing accusing the guilds of working with the Nazis." I realized I was leaning over the table, talking directly to Heston. I sat down.

Heston smiled. "The Boss loves publicity," he said casually. "Look what he did with the George Dasch incident. That convinced Roosevelt to give Hoover more discretion in counter-intelligence operations."

I looked at him, trying to decide if that was the entire story. It made sense, in a way. No lesser trusts the guilds, and lessers fear what they cannot control or understand. I, personally, thought it was a mistake for the guilds to reveal their presence and power back during American President William Jennings Bryan's first term. Even before we revealed ourselves adepts did not, apart from the occasional fairy godmother, have a good reputation among lessers. Sure, people suspected our presence and a few innocent lessers got burned at the stake as a result; a true adept would have many options to prevent this, something that never seemed to enter the thick skulls of the lessers with the torches.

So if Hoover could make us the enemy, people would clamor for him to have more power to control any Nazi spies and us. And it wouldn't pass through their craniums that even the vaunted J. Edgar Hoover couldn't control guilds. I'm sure Hoover knew that too, but it didn't matter to his plans.

I hadn't realized up until that point that lessers sometimes worked the same backhanded deals so common in the guilds. Lessers desired power, the same as adepts. They just had other means to achieve it. Usually, I had observed, through the edge of a sword or, more recently, the barrel of a gun.

Heston spoke, interrupting my thoughts. "We know an adept was helping the Nazis, so perhaps Hoover's right."

"One adept is working for Hitler—" and also Black or Reynolds making it two adepts, but I wasn't going to tell him that "—and, not that it's any of your business, but I went on that ship to find her and kill her."

"Why?" Heston asked.

I sat back and looked at him. "None of your business."

"We could help you find her," Heston said.

"I doubt it."

Heston just looked at me and I looked at him. Shaw might as well not have been in the room.

"I'm going now," I said. "Bring me a car."

"Take a cab," Heston said, not hiding his anger.

I looked directly at him. "I can make you, personally, drive me back to my hotel. I can make you do it in your skivvies, if I wish. You won't like it, but you'll do it. Do you believe me?"

Heston took a long time to answer. This was a man not used to being bullied. Then he turned to Shaw. "Take him home," he ordered gruffly.

"Yes, sir," Shaw said, not looking very happy about it.

* * *

Outside the rain had stopped, leaving wet streets and sidewalks. "Take me to the Huntington Hotel on California," I told Shaw as we got into the car. "Do you know it?"

"Yes," he said, a little too emphatically. He knew it and knew it was the headquarters of my guild, I decided.

Fitz welcomed me happily. Black and Reynolds were less enthusiastic.

"Teacher," I said, "we need to discuss the matter we spoke of before. Alone."

Fitz looked at his assistants and the new warrior, Harold. Harold, wearing an expensive suit that didn't go very well with his large frame and the machine gun he was holding, stood quietly against the wall by the door.

Then Fitz looked at Reynolds again and they exchanged a look. I looked at Reynolds and studied her for a moment. She was not young, but to Fitz she was probably young enough. She was attractive, although her dark hair was too short for my taste.

"Whatever you have to say," Fitz said, finally taking his eyes off his apparent paramour, "you can say in front of these others."

I debated a moment, then, with my hand on my talisman—the guilty party might attack me, I feared—spoke. "Morgan was working with German spies. Apparently the Nazis have a 'general order' for spies to recover talismans. This explains why the Americans found the samurai *katana* talisman on an SS agent trying to leave the country. The Nazis ordered Morgan to recover a talisman in Yuma. That's why she went there."

"That's very interesting," Fitz said. "Have you found her yet?"

"Yes," I said, "but she escaped with help from her Nazi spy friends."

"Perhaps you are not as powerful as you once were, Student," Fitz said, glancing at Reynolds as he said this. Was she trying for my job and undermining my credibility with Fitz during pillow talk?

"That's not the problem. I encountered situations I did not expect. Specifically, an adept working with lessers."

I hesitated, wondering what spell I'd have to use: a protection spell, or just discontinuously traverse out of the room. "The Nazis knew that Admiral Richards gave the *katana* talisman to our guild and that I had it."

I was watching Reynolds and Black. Neither seemed to react to that statement, so I continued. "Only the people in this room—"

Fitz cut me off. "Speaking of the samurai talisman, where is it?"

"It is safe," I said. I kept talking before he could ask more questions. "Only the people in this room—you, me, Black, Reynolds, and Harold—knew that. And I think we can eliminate Harold, because he didn't know I was going to Yuma and couldn't have warned Morgan. I know I'm not working with the Germans and I'm fairly confident you aren't either, Teacher. Which leaves only Black and Reynolds. So which one told the Nazis?" I watched Black and Reynolds carefully, especially Black.

"And Richards," Black said.

"Excuse me?"

"Richards knew," Black explained.

I had to admit that was a possibility I hadn't considered, but I dismissed it immediately. "He could have simply turned it over to the Nazis if he were working for them."

Fitz thought about that, looked at Reynolds, then at Black, and finally at me.

"Who do you think?" Fitz asked.

"I have no idea," I said. I looked at Black, who was sweating a little too much for a cool, rainy day.

"So," Marjory interjected, "what you are saying is Morgan is working with the Germans and either Black is or I am working with Morgan and therefore also working with the Germans?"

"Yes," I said.

Reynolds looked at Fitz, got his attention with her green eyes, and then looked at Black. Fitz followed her eyes to look at the man.

"Teacher," I said before this silent condemnation of Black could go too far, "I have no proof either way."

"Black admitted he has contacts on the Continent," Reynolds said, her gazed fixed on him.

Fitz stood up, a long process somewhat reminiscent of unfolding a beach chair. He pointed a finger at Black.

"Teacher," Black pleaded in a high voice.

Reynolds also pointed at him.

"Teacher," I said somewhat loudly. "We don't *know*."

Fitz just glanced back at me. "Thank you for bringing this to my attention. I assume you have things to do in order to find Morgan."

He was dismissing me. I looked at Black. His hand was in his pocket on his talisman and his lips were moving slightly, indicating he was preparing a spell. Reynolds and Fitz were doing the same thing.

Flame raced from Fitz's finger, across the room, and into Black. The fire spread away from Black; he'd had his spell up in time.

Reynolds added her fire. Harold, who up until then had been as active as a piece of furniture, approached the center of the room and pointed his machine gun at Black.

Black should have discontinuously traversed out, but it was too late. He couldn't while using a protection spell, but as he tired, the protection spell would dissipate and fire or bullets or both would kill him.

I ran between Fitz and Reynolds while preparing my own protection spell.

"Kader!" Fitz yelled, seeing what I was doing. I stood in front of Black, putting my body and my skills as an adept between Black and certain death. The flames hit me, but my spell dispersed them.

"Stop!" I ordered.

Fitz and Reynolds both ended their attacks. Harold still pointed the amazingly large open end of the gun at me.

"What are you doing, Kader?" Reynolds demanded.

To be honest, I wasn't sure. I suspected Black, but there was something about the conspiratorial looks Fitz and Reynolds had been exchanging that worried me. More was going on here than I knew about, beyond Fitz and Reynolds sharing a bed.

"Teacher," I said forcefully, "We don't know." It was the best argument I could think of.

Fitz looked at me and, thankfully, not Reynolds. "You are right, Student."

"Wait," I said. "I'll find proof, either way." I looked at Reynolds. "I suspect when I find Morgan, I'll find the proof." I returned my gaze to Fitz and held it.

"Then go, find her."

"And Black?"

"We'll take no action, for now."

I found that "we'll" very interesting.

"Thank you, Teacher," I breathed.

Reynolds looked mad. Black looked relieved. Harold looked disappointed.

"I have things to do," I said and walked toward the door. I half expected an attack from the rear. From whom, I didn't know.

Outside the room in the corridor, I leaned against a wall to breathe and ponder. I still wasn't sure why I had saved Black.

\*\*\*

Back on the street, I asked the doorman to get me a taxi. The rain had returned as a light mist and it was growing dark. Some of the hooded streetlights had come on and in the mist they made cones of light. I took the taxi to my hotel and told the driver to wait while I ran to my room and got the box that Sam had given me. Then I had the taxi take me to Chinatown.

It was positively black out by the time we arrived, and the mist had become oppressive in the darkness. The taxi dropped me off in front of Young Fat's and I gladly entered the well-lit interior. A waiter recognized me and took me to the kitchen. Fat was sitting in a chair in his small office. He looked older and more tired than I remembered him ever looking before.

"Kader, so you return," he said stoically.

"Yes," I said bowing. "I apologize for placing you in danger. Had I known—"

He cut me off with a wave. "I apologize for losing the talisman."

"What happened?"

"They caught me unawares; knew I am adept so kept me attached to something at all times. Your girlfriend comes, takes the talisman, orders my release. They bring me back here. I find big mess on floor out front."

"She's not my girlfriend," I said, the anger in my voice obvious. "She used me to find you."

"Yes, women are a blind spot for you."

I looked at him. Both he and Morgan had said something to that effect. Was it that obvious? In order to change the subject, I took the envelope with his name inside and destroyed it in front of him by making it burn. If he noticed the broken wax seal, he didn't say. He probably knew I couldn't read it anyway.

"Thank you," he said. "Now, what is this box you're holding?"

"This box held the talisman for years," I said, holding it out.

Fat smiled, showing his few yellow teeth. "If there are enough traces left, we could."

"How much?"

"I owe you. Free, this time. Close the door."

I pulled the door shut and Fat turned off the lone bulb by pulling the string hanging from the fixture. He began speaking in the ancient tongue and running his hands around the box. The spell was powerful, and green light emerged from the space between his constantly moving hands until the light coalesced into a sphere; in the sphere there was a scene. By the porthole in the background, I could tell it was on a ship. By the rust I could tell it wasn't a very nice ship. It was rocking back and forth as if it was in rough seas. Dorothy was there and another woman, blonde, buxom. You almost expected her to wear a helmet with horns and carry a spear. They were speaking in a language I didn't understand. I knew Fat was busy, so I ran a translation spell:

Dorothy: "...before she was killed she traced *Mjollnir* to Berlin. We'll never make it to Berlin."

Other Woman: "We don't have to go to Berlin, Student. On the new moon after the next, Hitler's crony adepts will be meeting in Paris in an attempt to read the minds of the Supreme Allied Command [these last three words were in English] to determine when and where the invasion of Europe will be. Needless to say, they will have *Mjollnir* with them."

Dorothy: "But Brunhild, how will we get to Paris?"

Brunhild: "This ship docks in Lisbon. From there we'll go across Spain, cross the Pyrenees into France. We will have to be careful in both Vichy, France and especially in occupied Europe. Hitler's agents will be looking for us and Vichy is independent from Germany in name only. The Vichy *Milice* cooperates with the Nazis, enforcing their rule. Hitler still fears us and will be hunting us."

Dorothy: "But with only two of us left—"

A male voice said, "And me."

Brunhild: "I admit, young one, it will not be easy, but..."

Brunhild let her voice trail off on that sentence; then she spoke a word in the ancient language of the guilds. It was a very, very obscene word. The vision collapsed and I heard Fat gasp. I fumbled for the string on the light and, finding it, jerked on it, bathing the room in its harsh incandescent glow. Fat was very pale as he held the lacquered box. The lid on the box was broken as if something hard had slammed into it.

"Are you hurt?" I asked.

In a moment he answered. "No. But she is very powerful."

I looked at a calendar on the wall of the office, with its pictures of girls in swimsuits on a beach wearing incongruous amounts of makeup, far too fancy coiffeurs, and shoes that were not very practical for walking in sand. The next new moon would be in two weeks, on the first of the next month. The one after that would be on the thirtieth of the same month. I knew Dorothy and Brunhild would be in Paris then with the *katana* talisman. I had to be there, too.

Walking into Fortress Europe would not be easy. I was going to need help.

# CHAPTER ELEVEN

The rain the day before had cleaned the air, and it was a beautiful sunny day. I took a taxi to Treasure Island and, because I was wearing a uniform and was able to convince the SPs at the gate that I belonged there. I was soon standing before Admiral Richards' civilian secretary. She was reluctant to let me in to see her boss.

"The admiral is very busy, Commander," she said, assuming from my Navy uniform I was part of the club.

"He'll want to see me," I told her.

She looked dubious, but used the intercom to contact Richards.

"A Commander Kader, sir. He insists on seeing you."

"Send him in," Richards said with a growl.

"Yes, sir."

I again entered Richards' office. He was sitting behind his large wooden desk. It was covered with maps of the Pacific Ocean and some island I'd never heard of called Tarawa. Noticing I had seen the map, Richards turned it over.

"I trust you found your Jap friend?" he said, none too friendly

"Yes," I said. "I trust you heard about Smith?"

Richards looked embarrassed. "The FBI informed me. I assume he was one of yours."

I sat in one of the chairs facing the desk and crossed my legs casually. "If by that you mean an adept, I can assure you, he wasn't." Richards was glaring at me, as if sitting without his permission was *verboten*. Perhaps it was; the military had a lot of idiotic rules.

"How do you know?" Richards demanded.

I chuckled. "I know."

"The FBI assumed he bewitched us into thinking he was an agent."

I almost laughed at the word "bewitched." "He didn't," I said. "He couldn't. He was not an adept."

Richards just looked at me. If Smith hadn't "bewitched" him, then he had been fooled, and he didn't like that idea, I could tell.

"What do you want?" he asked impatiently.

"I need to be in Paris next month. On the thirtieth, to be exact."

Richards stared at me as if I'd asked for my own personal battleship. "Not possible," he said.

"Why not?" I demanded.

"I can't send you into occupied France. First of all, it's not my department."

"Then pull some strings."

Richards looked at me with that disgusted look. "Can't you just take a cloud over or something?"

"And risk getting shot down by some fly-boy just off the farm? No thanks!"

"And if I get you into France, how will you get to Paris? Walk?"

"What do you mean?"

Richards was looking happier. Here was something he knew that I didn't. "You'll have to be dropped off on the coast by submarine or perhaps parachute in. In any case, it won't be anywhere near Paris." He smiled when he saw my horrified reaction to the prospect of parachuting.

"Then I'll need help," I said. "The Resistance, I suppose."

"You're out of your mind," he said. "Why should I help you? Why should the French Resistance help you?"

I thought for a moment. "Three reasons."

"Yes?" he said skeptically.

"One," I started, counting off on my fingers, "you asked my guild to find out what Hitler was doing with guilds in Europe and with talismans. I can tell you that Germans spies have something called a 'general order' to gather talismans."

Richards suddenly looked interested. "For what reason?"

"I don't know, but I can probably find out in Paris."

He nodded. "Okay, go on."

"Second," I said switching fingers, "I have reason to believe that Hitler is planning to use the talismans he's gathered to try to learn the timing and location of the Allied invasion of Europe."

Richard's jaw dropped to unprecedented depths. "How do you know that?"

"I can't tell you that. But if I can get to Europe, I might be able to stop it." If, I didn't add, I decide I really want to.

"Okay, and number three?" I really had Richards interested.

"Number three, if you don't, I'll simply 'bewitch' you so you will."

That brought him back to reality. "Fine," he said. "But I will want you to tell everything you learn to our intelligence people. And everything you know before you go into France, in case you don't make it back out."

"No problem," I agreed.

"I need to call the Pentagon. To get you to Europe that fast you'll have to fly, and that means the Army Air Corps and the Air Transport Command."

He smiled when he saw the look of dread on my face.

"Don't worry," he said, grinning. "It's a hell of a lot safer than going into occupied France."

\*\*\*

The young Navy officer met me in the lobby of the Drake-Wiltshire. A few days had passed, during which I'd waited impatiently and tried to c ean up some loose ends, but failed miserably. The police had no idea who had killed Miles, but they were pretty sure it wasn't me, although I think Halloran still had me on the top of his personal suspect list. I thought it must have been Morgan or a German spy working for her.

Black was still alive and well, but Fitz and Reynolds had basically shut him out of the guild leadership. Fitz promised me he would take no action until I returned. But I didn't know if his patience would last that long, or if Reynolds would allow it to last that long. And of course, I had no idea where Morgan was. Plus, Smith was a complete mystery. Was he a German, as Sam had suggested, or something else?

I paid my room fee for the next two months. The manager assured me, when I told him I was going on a long trip and wasn't sure when I'd return, that they would store my belongings if my rent ran out. I'd been a good tenant for a long time.

"Sir," the kid in the Navy uniform said, "I have a car waiting."

"Thank you," I replied, actually surprised by his polite demeanor.

On the sidewalk I said goodbye to the day doorman, Sebastian, and handed him my valise. With the help of an enlisted man, the driver I assumed, he put the valise in the car's trunk, then came and opened my door.

"Good-bye, sir," he said, smiling at me before closing the door. "Good luck." I wondered what he thought I was doing. Probably the entire hotel staff knew I was leaving for an extended time, and soon all would know I had left with the Navy. Maybe they thought I was going to war, and I suppose I was.

"Thank you," I said.

The officer sat next to me in the back. The enlisted man, who was older than the officer, got behind the wheel. "Sir?" he asked.

"Moffett Field, petty officer."

"Yes, sir."

As the car pulled away from the curb the officer spoke. "Have you been briefed, sir?"

"No," I said, watching the city pass by. It was very early in the morning and the purple glow of the just lightening sky made my San Francisco look almost magical. I realized how much I didn't want to leave.

"From Moffett you'll take a C-117 to the North Island NAS near San Diego," the officer explained.

"NAS?" I asked.

"Naval Air Station."

"And what's a C-117?"

"A gooney bird for bigwigs," the driver interjected.

"A transport plane," the young officer explained, ignoring the driver. "There will be a car waiting at North Island to take you to Lindbergh Field.

There you'll join a ferry crew taking a B-24 to Wichita. In Wichita the plane's actual crew will take over, and you'll go with them over to England."

"Yeah," the driver said, looking in his rearview mirror at me, "the fly-boys are taking heavy losses with this 'precision daylight bombing.' Makes me glad to be a swab."

"Petty officer, please," the young officer said, almost whining.

The driver shrugged his shoulders.

"What happens when I get to England?" I asked.

"I don't know, sir," the young man said. "I suppose you'll be met. I wasn't briefed on that part of your mission. I assume it's classified."

The drive to Moffett Field took about an hour. We passed out of San Francisco and through some small towns such as Daly City, and went past a lot of farms and open fields. The two Navy men were quiet, leaving me with my thoughts, which clashed with the peaceful-looking farmland we were passing through. I wasn't sure what I'd do when, or if, I found Dorothy and Brunhild. I doubted I could overpower them both. By definition, Brunhild is the name of the leader of the Valkyries, which would make her a dangerous foe. But also, I had to admit, a powerful ally.

As we got closer to Moffett, I again saw the huge triangular building. The clamshell doors were closed.

"What in the world is that?" I asked.

The driver glanced over. "Poopie bag hangar. It's so big clouds form inside and it sometimes rains."

I looked at the officer for help.

"Blimp hangar," he explained. "We use blimps for ASW."

Before I could get the question out he said, "Anti-submarine warfare."

I looked back at the building. I'd seen blimps and they looked even more fragile than airplanes. I could see why they'd want them to be protected inside. But to build such a structure for that purpose alone struck me as either madness or desperation. Or perhaps a resilient determination to do whatever it took to survive.

We passed easily through the gate, the SPs reading a piece of paper the officer handed them, then waving us through with amazing urgency. The driver parked the car next to an airplane with a low wing and two engines. It was unpainted except for a white star inside a blue circle with a white horizontal stripe and a red border, and some seemingly random numbers and other markings. Its aluminum skin flashed in the morning sunlight. The airplane's body was at an angle because the back wheel was smaller than the front two. There was a rounded door near the rear. I got out of the car and the driver handed me my valise. The officer walked me to the door.

"Good luck, sir," he said and held out his hand. I took it and shook it, wondering what he thought I was. Perhaps he thought I was a spy going off on a dangerous mission for the United States. I guess, in a way, I was. He handed me the paper he'd shown the SPs. "Your orders, sir."

I looked at it.

"You'll need these, sir."

"Thanks," I mumbled and took the paper, jamming it into the pocket of my suit.

I had to duck to enter the airplane. The interior looked comfortable, nothing like the PBY, but more like a nice car. There were chairs lined up on both sides of the interior. Two were occupied, as Admiral Richards was there along with a second man I didn't recognize. A young man in an Army uniform politely took my valise.

"Kader," Richards said. "Take a seat; we're taking off as soon as you're ready."

I had to climb uphill to move forward. I chose a seat and then Richards told the Army man we were ready.

The propellers on one engine begin turning very slowly. Then, with a loud noise and a burst of black smoke, the engine started. It made a horrible noise, but not as bad as the engines on the PBY.

The second engine started and the plane traveled on the ground to the runway. I watched out the window, ignoring Richards and his friend. The airplane built up speed and the back end came up, making the interior level, which made me happy, as I didn't want to spend the entire trip tilted back at that angle. Then the plane ascended. It passed over the bay before turning left (and tilting in the process) and then heading south.

Richards spoke over the noise of the engines, getting my attention. "It's about a three-hour flight to San Diego."

I looked at him. "Who's he?" I asked.

"Lieutenant Commander Sillman, Naval Intelligence," the other man said, introducing himself.

"We want to know everything you know about Smith, that Nazi ship, the..."

"*El Cielo de las Américas*," Sillman filled in for him.

"Yes," Richards confirmed, "and Nazi spy activity in the Bay Area."

I looked at Richards. "You know everything I know about Smith. I didn't see that much of the ship, and I know nothing about Nazi spy activity anywhere."

Both Richards and Sillman looked skeptical. I let out a heavy sigh, realizing the three-hour trip would be much longer in some ways.

They stopped pestering me after about two hours. I think they realized I wasn't lying to them or was very good at resisting their queries. They tried to bully me, plead with me, appeal to my non-existent patriotism, and finally just scowled at me. I looked out the window and enjoyed the scenery. While I'd flown plenty of times using "private transportation," I had never flown during the day.

The plane engines got quieter and for a moment I wondered if something was wrong, but none of the others acted concerned. I realized the plane was going lower, as more detail on the ground was visible. We passed over an area with houses spaced far apart, but each house a rectangular box almost identical to all the others. The streets were laid out in broad sweeping curves rather than square blocks. The curvature of the streets looked like a feeble attempt to distract from the ugliness of each little house. It looked like a miserable way to live.

"What is that?" I asked.

Sillman looked out the window. "Tract housing for defense workers, probably at Consolidated."

I again looked at the houses, like little hives set out in some pattern, but each with a green lawn surrounding it like a verdant moat. I almost shuddered involuntarily.

The airplane landed, which looked to be a precarious operation as it seemed to fly just a few scant feet over the concrete runway, then dropped down and almost bounced back up again. The military men seemed unfazed by this.

Stepping out of the airplane, I was shocked by how warm it was. As promised, a car was waiting.

Richards got off the plane and took my arm before I could get in the car. "One thing, Kader. No magic, at least not until you get to France. This mission is classified at the highest level; if you go pulling your tricks, word will get out."

Sillman poked his head out the door and looked at me, trying to look very serious.

"I'll try to avoid it," I said.

Richards and Sillman looked reluctant to let me go, but apparently they were taking the same plane back to Moffett. I got into the car, and they returned to the plane. I relaxed during the drive, another enlisted man behind the wheel of another gray car. We had to pass a security gate to leave the naval air station and another one when we entered Lindbergh Field. I knew who Lindbergh was, but had no idea why they'd named this particular airfield after him. I was dropped in front of a building that looked brand new and smelled of fresh paint, yet had apparently been built in such haste it looked dilapidated. A stenciled sign read "AIR TRANSPORT COMMAND, LINDBERGH FIELD."

The inside was not much better than the exterior. About ten feet in was a large metal desk with a large, angry-looking man behind it in an army uniform. He was shuffling through a stack of papers, glancing at them, and having an emotional reaction to each one:

"You've got to be joking!"

"What the deuce?"

"They are out of their minds!"

"And if my grandmother had wheels she'd be a wagon!"

Beyond him, filling the small building, were multiple desks, each with an unhappy-looking man looking through papers, typing on an Underwood, or talking loudly on the phone.

"Excuse me," I said stepping up.

The angry man looked up at me and growled, "Yeah?"

I realized suddenly that I had no idea what to say. "I'm supposed to take a plane to England," I tried.

He just looked at me as if he were trying to decide whether to laugh or just get really mad.

"What?" he finally asked in disbelief.

"England," I said forcefully. "I'm supposed to go to England."

He decided to get mad, apparently, because he nearly yelled when he said, "This ain't no passenger service. What do you think this is?"

I was getting angry now, but I wanted to remain calm. I needed these people's help. That was not something I was used to.

"Sir," I said, "I was told—"

That set him off. He stood up and pointed to his arm. "Do you see that? Those are chevrons, mister. I am a sergeant in this man's army. I ain't no 'sir.' I work for a living." He glared at me, as if daring me to contradict him.

"Sergeant," I said in a calm voice, my hand on my talisman just in case, despite Richard's warning, "I was told I would be taken to England by plane from this spot."

The sergeant sat behind his desk again. "Who told ya?"

"A Navy officer."

Again he just looked at me. Then: "Does this look like the Navy?"

Before I could reply he waved his hands dismissively. "Never mind. What was his name?"

"I didn't catch it."

"You're going to have to do better than that," he growled. Then, as if I weren't there, he went back to his papers: "Oh, that's funny."

I think he was talking about the paper and not me.

And that reminded me. I let go of my talisman and pulled from my suit pocket the paper the young Navy officer had given me. And I remembered the reaction of the SPs at Moffett.

"Sergeant, these are my orders."

He looked up at me, took the paper, and started reading it. As he read, his eyes grew wide and the perpetual scowl on his face melted. He picked up the phone receiver on his desk.

"Uh, sir, I think you should come out here."

He hung up. "Just a moment, please," he said with measured courtesy. I decided I was going to have to read that paper that seemed almost as strong as a good talisman.

A few minutes later a harried-looking, young Army officer (one silver bar on each shoulder) came out. "What is it, sergeant?"

Silently the sergeant handed him the paper. The officer had the same reaction, occasionally glancing up at me as if to confirm I was still there and not an apparition.

"Sir," he said to me, handing back the paper, "are you Francis Kader?"

"Yes," I acknowledged.

"Thank you, sir. Please have a seat." And he rushed back to wherever it was he'd come from.

There were some wooden chairs against the wall. I sat in one and read the paper.

In too many words and with a lot of unneeded military jargon, it basically said, "Get Mr. Francis Kader to England." It was signed by a General George C. Marshall, Chief of Staff.

I noticed the sergeant was also looking at me as if I weren't quite real. I wondered what power this General Marshall had.

About half an hour later the officer emerged and approached me. "Sir, someone will be coming to pick you up soon."

"Thank you," I said.

"And the sergeant will get you anything you need."

"Thank you," I said again and smiled at the sergeant.

The wait was closer to two hours. The sergeant made some phone calls, apparently trying to speed things up, but that didn't work. I suspected he wanted me out of his domain. The building grew steadily hotter as the day wore on. Sweat was trickling down my back and I was stretched out, trying to relax and get comfortable in that hard chair. I heard the front door open, as it had many times, and saw between almost shut eyelids a blue uniform walk by.

"There's your man," the sergeant said.

I looked up to see a man in a blue uniform, wearing a leather helmet. He turned and looked at me while taking off the helmet. Long curly blonde hair fell out of the helmet to the shoulders. The pilot was a woman.

"You our passenger?" she asked. I noticed she had pretty green eyes.

I stood. "Yes."

"Come on, daylight's a-wastin'."

I picked up my valise from where I'd dropped it and followed her to a jeep. Another woman, dressed identically except with a blue hat that matched the uniform, was in the driver's seat.

"Skipper," the woman with me said, "this is our passenger."

The skipper looked me over, then hooked a thumb over her shoulder indicating the back of the vehicle. "Climb in."

So I did. The blonde woman took the lone passenger seat.

"I'm Captain Hewitt," the driver said, "and this is Lieutenant Doyle."

"Nice to meet you," I said, thinking of nothing else to say.

The jeep started with a lurch across the wide concrete toward a group of identical-looking planes.

"You have any winter gear?" Hewitt asked.

"A coat," I said. It was in my valise.

"You'd better get some before you fly over the pond."

She drove to one of the planes and stopped the jeep beside it. This one had high wings with four engines. There were two tails on the back.

"There she is," the driver said as the jeep stopped. "A 'D' fresh out of the box."

"No," the other woman said, "it's the box it came in."

They both laughed. I didn't get the joke. I was looking for the door. The women picked up canvas bags and carried them under the plane. They opened a small door on the bottom, threw their bags up inside, and climbed in. I handed up my valise, which barely fit, and climbed inside.

The interior of the plane was not built for comfort. The spars and ribs of the body were exposed, and I assumed the metal I was looking at was the inside of the metal on the exterior. A third woman came out of a small opening toward the front of the plane.

"Course to Wichita set, ma'am," she said to Hewitt.

"Good. Another popcorn run. You must have the route memorized by now, Kate."

"Yes, ma'am. You must too, by now. You can navigate and I'll just take a nap."

Hewitt laughed. Then she turned to me. "The B24D normally has a crew of ten. We're flying with three. So there'll be lots of room for you. Just stay off the flight deck. Kate will show you where to plug into the intercom system."

Hewitt and Doyle moved forward. The space was so small they had to turn sideways.

"You can sit at the radio operator's position, on the starboard side," Kate said. "It has a window. If you want to come forward and see me, take the catwalk through the bomb bay. If you do come up I'll show you the bombardier's window or the front turret—there's a nice view up there. But stay away from the front gear. The doors are spring-tension closed and will open if you step or fall on them, and that first step is a doozy."

Although I'd understood only about a third of that, I found the radio operator's position, made obvious by the large radio below a metal table, and sat on the utilitarian seat. Kate showed me where to plug in a set of headphones, put a throat microphone on me, and showed me how to activate it so I could be heard—"But don't unless the captain tells you to"—and then went through the same narrow opening from which she'd emerged.

I could hear Hewitt and Doyle talking to each other on the flight deck over the intercom. A few moments later, Kate reported that she and I were ready.

As before with the PBY and the C-117, the engines started up one at a time, adding their din to the growing racket. The plane started moving slowly. The noise was terrific, worse than the PBY. Once again the plane took to the sky.

"Now the fun begins," Hewitt said, almost laughing.

I tried to smile but couldn't.

# CHAPTER TWELVE

We arrived in Wichita, which is somewhere in the middle of the United States, seven hours later. The land was as flat as a calm sea, but was cut up into squares, each growing something. There were different shades of green in nearly every square. As the plane dropped lower for landing, I could see that most of it was corn.

I was surprised by how breezy it was inside the plane. Wind seemed to leak in nearly everywhere. I got quite cold in just my suit and coat.

The sun was going down as we climbed out of the plane, and I was directed to a "BOQ" to spend the night. I ate supper in the Officer s Club…"O-Club" they called it. Kate wasn't allowed in for some reason, but Hewitt and Doyle were, and they were curious about me. Hewitt wasn't as cute as Doyle, but she was the more talkative of the two. She explained how they ferried the bombers from San Diego to here, then took the train back or sometimes got lucky and could take a plane back. I asked what they meant by "ferrying." Hewitt explained that when they flew the planes from one place to another, just to get them to the new destination, it was called "ferrying."

We shared a nice meal and then I went to the male BOQ and they went to the female version, I presumed. Yes, I was tempted.

The next morning at an ungodly early hour—somebody called it "oh-dark-thirty"—I met the crew that would take the plane to England. There were only four, as this, too, was a "ferry job," the pilot explained. The rest of the crew had gone over by ship. This time there was a radio operator, so I couldn't sit in that seat. That left the bombardier's position, which was really a couch where the bombardier lay prone, or one of the "waist gunner" spots. The crew warned me to stay out of the turrets. I was also given a winter suit and shown how to plug it into outlets on the wall to warm it electrically.

The next leg of the trip was about eight hours long, and we landed near New York City. Then we flew to Newfoundland and a dreary place called Harmon Air Force Base. That took almost seven hours, and again it was growing dark as we landed. I ended up putting on the winter suit about halfway there, but I didn't need to plug it in.

Harmon Air Force Base was mostly tents and a few buildings; luckily, one of them was the BOQ. It was chilly there, and when the sun went down, it got colder. Falling from the gray sky was mist that made the cold seem to seep into your bones. The crew of the plane insisted we eat "off-base" at a nearby civilian restaurant and have the local delicacy, which suited me after the food served in Wichita and New York. It was hearty but plain. I thought perhaps a restaurant would have better food.

I was sadly mistaken. The restaurant was little more than a wooden shack with long tables and benches. Most of the patrons were American airmen. Entrees included cod tongues and cod cheeks. Apparently there was an abundance of cod in the waters around Newfoundland. The local delicacy was called "scruncheons", which were pencil-eraser-sized chunks of deep-fat-fried fat. They made the cod tongues almost palatable.

The next morning, again at a time when only farmers and their roosters should be awake, the five of us climbed back into the plane for the next jump, to Iceland. We were all wearing winter gear, and the reason became obvious as we passed over icebergs.

Later I was glad for the electric warmer in the suit. There was a knob on the wall plug; supposedly to regulate the heat, but it seemed to vary between too hot and too cold with no setting being just right. But it was better than freezing.

It was amazingly clear, with sunlight sparkling off the blue water below. We passed within sight of icy Greenland and then landed in Iceland about 9:00 P.M. local time. We weren't allowed off the base, so it was back to the same simple but filling food the Army Air Corps served and another night in another BOQ. The BOQ's had been degenerating as the trip progressed. In Wichita there were private rooms with an actual metal-framed bed, a chair, and the bathroom not too far down the hall. The dark green wool blanket was scratchy, though. In Newfoundland it was still metal-framed beds, but four to a room and the same scratchy green blanket. In Iceland the BOQ was a large room filled with cots covered with scratchy green blankets. A potbellied stove was the only source of heat, and during the night the poor sap sleeping next to it had to get up and add wood from a pile on the floor. I couldn't wait to see the accommodations in Scotland. I was sure; however, there'd be a scratchy green blanket.

Iceland had a power I could feel. The land is very young there. Even lessers must have sensed it. To me it felt as if I'd had just a touch too much to drink, except I was in full control of my faculties. I was sad to leave the next day; one could get used to that intoxicating level of power.

Although it was before dawn when we left Iceland, it was growing dark when we reached Scotland. I didn't know how the pilots navigated in the dark. I did it by the stars, or used spells that can keep you oriented to direction. But we flew in clouds the entire way from Iceland to Scotland. And while I thought the mist was cold on Newfoundland, this time we were in it for hours, with a breeze blowing through the plane and the temperature below zero. I was glad to have the electrically warmed suit.

After several interminable hours, the pilot's voice came over the intercom.

"Listen up, Macmerry's socked in. We'll have to land at Skaebrae in the Orkney Islands. Now that's an RAF fighter base, so we'll have to get it right."

I unplugged my heater and intercom and walked up to the radio operator.

"What's wrong with Skaebrae?" I yelled over the noise.

The radioman looked at me. "Short runway."

I could feel the tension in the plane building. Everyone was nervous. I looked out the small window just ahead of the waist gunner's station and tried to peer through the dusk.

The plane was approaching a cliff with a very short-looking runway at the top. The bomber touched down almost at the cliff's edge. Then I could see that the runway dropped down a hill. The pilot must have put on the breaks hard—the plane shuddered as it slowed, going down that slope. I could see why the pilot was anxious to stop. At the end of the runway was a four-foot berm. The runway became level again for a short distance and then started climbing toward that bank. Going uphill seemed to help us slow down. I didn't know what would happen if we hit the berm. I didn't have to find out. The plane slowed enough that the pilot was able to turn before hitting the berm. But I think he did it on one wheel.

We ended up staying overnight in Skaebrae. The lodgings were acceptable, but crowded, since they hadn't expected us. The next morning we made a short hop to Macmerry in the north of Scotland.

Upon landing on the British mainland, the crew invited me to a pub for a beer. Apparently this is a tradition. The pub's interior was brightly lit, paneled in what appeared to be very old oak, and had a fire going strong in a fireplace. We found a table to hold the five of us. A waitress came to take our orders. No one could understand her, even though I think she was speaking English. I actually ran a translation spell, subtly, to interpret.

* * *

The accommodations in Scotland were quite nice, except the buildings were a lot like the Air Transport Command building in San Diego. They had that same brand-new yet dilapidated look of hastily built buildings that weren't quite finished. And of course, the ubiquitous scratchy wool blanket was on the bed.

The next day I was driven to a train station for the trip to London. The Isle of Britain appeared to be almost one huge military camp, but the scenery was pleasant to look at.

I was met by what I thought was a civilian. He drove me to downtown London in an unmarked civilian car. After asking if I was Mr. Kader, he never spoke a word unless needed, which was damn seldom. We passed bombed out blocks on the way. I was amazed to see people going about their business as if nothing were going on. Yes, most of the windows had Xs of tape on them and some buildings had sandbags piled up in front. But the stoic way the general population simply lived with this horror amazed me. If it weren't for the troops, the bomb damage, and the taped windows and sandbags, it would be impossible to tell that this was a city that had been under siege from the air for months. That had ended a couple of years ago, but there were still the occasional German bombing raids.

We stopped before a nondescript building on a busy commercial street. Inside the building, after getting past armed MPs who checked my escort's identification very carefully and eyed me suspiciously, I was taken to a large, ornate office. The man occupying it wore a suit. As we walked in, he stood and talked to my escort.

"This the adept?"

"Yes, sir," my escort said and without another word, he turned and left.

"Quiet fellow," I said.

"Have a seat," the man said, pointing to a leather chair, not appreciating my humor.

I looked him over. He was a tall man with broad shoulders. His hair was cut short and swept back. It was darker on top and gray on the sides.

"I'm William Donovan," he said, sitting again. "I'm the Director of the OSS. Do you know what that is?"

I had to admit I didn't.

He looked at me across his desk. "It's not important that you do know. In fact, in my opinion, it's important that you do not know."

I remained quiet.

"I flew here from Washington to meet you," he continued. I was sure he hadn't flown in a noisy, drafty, cold, uncomfortable metal contraption. "I have been ordered to get you into occupied France and provide you with any assistance you need, including a Resistance group to get you into Paris by the thirtieth."

"Yes?" I didn't know where this was going.

He leaned on his elbows on the desk, still looking at me. "I don't like metas. I don't trust you and I don't believe you."

"You don't have to trust me or believe me," I said. He was making me angry.

"Do you know," he said as if changing the subject, "how hard it is to establish, maintain, and support contact with the French Resistance?"

"I have no idea."

He stood up and walked to the window behind him, which was covered with heavy blackout curtains. "It's very difficult. Often it means sending over a person, an operative, to work with them. I have lost good men and women in France. All were killed. Those captured alive were tortured for information before facing a firing squad."

He turned and looked at me. "You'll never be captured, I know, so you don't have to worry about that. But I am supposed to 'lend' you a Resistance group of brave men and possibly women to help you. And what do you care if they are captured, tortured, and executed?"

I just looked at him, surprised. He was right; I hadn't given it a second thought.

"I just want to let you know," Donovan continued, "if you cause the needless death of one member of the Resistance, meta or not, I will have you killed."

He glared at me, apparently waiting for me to respond. I didn't.

He sat down and changed his tone. "I don't suppose you know how to parachute?"

"Uhm, no."

He looked annoyed. "Great. Normally we'd parachute you in on one of the Carpetbaggers' special B-24's."

"I really don't want to spend more time in a B-24," I said with more emphasis than I meant.

"Don't worry. We'll have to use a Grasshopper and land you."

"Grasshopper?" I asked.

"You'll see. Now, what were you going to wear in France, certainly not that suit?"

Actually, the thought had never occurred to me. "Why not?"

Donovan looked annoyed again. "We're going to be dropping you off in northwest France and from there you'll walk to Paris. You're going to need some fatigues and good boots." He picked up the telephone on the desk. "This is Donovan. I need someone to take Mr. Kader to Station 179. And get him some appropriate clothes." He hung up and talked to me again.

"When they get you some boots, wear them to break them in. We'll need to make contact with a Resistance group. Once we do, you may need to leave in a hurry. So you'll have to wait at Station 179. From there you'll be flown into France."

He just looked at me for a few moments, perhaps expecting me to say something.

"You can go now," he finally said, flicking his finger in the direction of the door behind me.

***

The same silent man drove me out of London to a small, ramshackle airstrip in the country. If the scenery weren't different, I'd have thought I was back at the base in Scotland. They must have knocked these bases up like those houses around San Diego: fast and cheap and all the same.

I was introduced to the base commander, who grumbled and ordered a corporal to show me to the BOQ.

The clothes arrived, mostly the same green (I learned it's called "olive drab") as the uniforms and, as ordered, I wore the boots.

I waited three days. The military men ignored me for the most part. I didn't know if they resented me or if they were just naturally quiet. I was in the "O-Club" eating dinner when the same corporal found me.

"There you are, sir. The base commander wants to see you—now."

"Now?"

"Yes, sir."

I paid my bill and followed the corporal back to the headquarters building. I walked into the commander's office. There was another man present, slouching in a chair.

"This the Joe?" he asked.

"Yes," the commander replied.

"Ordinary Joe?"

"Not hardly," the commander said. To me he said, "Sit down."

I took the other chair, wondering what a "Joe" was.

"This is Lieutenant Gilmore; he's going to be your pilot. You leave tonight at nineteen-hundred hours. You'll land near Amiens, about 70 miles north of Paris, and meet up with a Resistance cell. They have orders to take you into Paris. Get to your room and pack only what you need and get back to the flight line. You have…" he looked at his watch "…about twenty minutes."

"Fine," I said, standing. I was becoming alarmed by how docilely I was acting with lessers lately. That's the problem with needing people's help.

"We told the Resistance your name is Thomas. Here, you'll need this." He threw me a package. I opened it. It was a map of France printed on a silk cloth. It folded up into a very small package.

I went to my room at the BOQ. The corporal showed up, and I handed him my valise with all my civilian clothes in it. "Could you have this sent to the Drake-Wiltshire Hotel in San Francisco?"

"Sure," he said unenthusiastically. I gave him the address and he wrote it down on a notepad.

I walked out to the flight line, where the planes sat on the tarmac waiting. There were B-24s, C-47s, which were identical to the C-117 except painted black and I doubted the interior was as nice, and other two-engined planes I had learned were called A-26s (why they called everything by a letter and a number, I didn't know). But there was another type of plane, the smallest one there. It had a single engine in the nose, a high wing over the greenhouse-like cockpit, and two wheels that were at the end of triangular spars. Gilmore was standing beside it.

"Ready to go?" he asked me.

"In that?" I said, pointing at the metal contraption.

Gilmore looked insulted. "This is a great little ship. An L-6 Grasshopper. We fly low and slow. Don't attract attention that way. The Limeys are doing a big bombing run tonight on Berlin or something and that'll keep the Kraut radar and interceptors busy and we'll just slip in unnoticed."

I wasn't convinced. The Grasshopper made a B-24 look safe and roomy. There were two seats, one behind the other; neither had much room. I had to duck under the wing to approach it. I could see cables running up the spar

138

holding up the wing, running around a metal pulley, and going into the wing. I was hoping they didn't have anything to do with controlling the aircraft, as it looked primitive.

"Climb in," Gilmore said with a grin. I think he was enjoying my trepidation.

\*\*\*

We flew low—"below their radar," Gilmore told me. The moon was a waning crescent and the sky was nearly pitch black by the time we came to the Channel. We crossed the coastal defenses so low I thought I could see the faces of German soldiers looking up at us. That didn't seem to worry Gilmore. He just brought the plane lower. I'd swear that at times the trees were brushing the wheels. Then Gilmore flew down a river, below the trees on each side. He turned and grinned at me. "This is the great thing about flying; you're not limited to two dimensions. I can fly lower than the trees or higher than the mountains."

I decided he was slightly crazy.

Gilmore had told me during the comparatively calm part of the flight, while we were still over Britain, that we would land on an improvised landing strip and that he would stay there just long enough for me to jump out.

Still flying over the river, he yelled, "Get ready!" over the noise of the engine. The plane seemed to leap up, slipped over the trees, and dropped into a meadow. There were two small fires ahead. Gilmore put the craft down between them. When the plane stopped I pushed the window open and crawled out under the wing, setting foot in Nazi-occupied Europe for the first time. Nothing happened for a long period that lasted maybe ten seconds. Then the window on the plane opened again and Gilmore screamed at me, "Get away from the damn plane!"

Not knowing what to do, I walked away. As soon as I cleared the wing, the plane pivoted and headed back toward the two fires. From the sound, I could tell the plane was climbing. I looked into the sky, trying to catch a glimpse of it, and as I did the fires went out. Then someone tackled me. A hand was clamped over my mouth. I was about to use a very powerful spell on whomever was on top of me when he hissed into my ear, "Are you Monsieur Thomas?"

I nodded in lieu of trying to speak through the hand held tightly over my mouth. The man said something in French that sounded roughly like "idiot" and stood up, jerking me to my feet. "Do you want us all to be hung from the gallows?" he whispered. It seemed a rhetorical question, so I ignored it. He pulled me into a hedgerow and only then did he release his grip on my mouth.

"You have a map?" he asked, still in English.

"Yes," I whispered, handing over the silk.

He unfolded it and smiled. "*Bon.*"

Meanwhile I'd stuck my hand in my pocket and fingered my talisman. I called up a translation spell. I heard voices speaking in low whispers but couldn't see faces.

"This is our pick-up?" one said in French. "He doesn't look like a spy."

"Nor does he act like one. You keep an eye on him; make sure he doesn't give us away."

"Me?"

"Yes, you. Now let's move out." I presumed this was the leader of the group.

Someone grabbed my arm. "Come on," he said in heavily accented English. "And be quiet."

# CHAPTER THIRTEEN

We hiked for what seemed like miles. By the stars I could tell we were going mostly south. We walked mainly in ditches (with cold water and mud in the bottom; I silently thanked Donovan for the boots) and between tree lines or hedgerows. It was obvious we were traveling in such a manner to avoid being seen by anyone.

At one point we came to a road. The leader stopped us all about fifty feet back from the pavement. He sent one man across. Then, on a softly whistled signal that could have been a birdcall, we each went across in turn, running and bent over. I went just before my escort, who was second to last; the leader crossed last. As the sky lightened in the east, we stopped at an old farmhouse. It was constructed of rock and had a thatched roof. The surrounding farm didn't look very well-maintained. There was a damaged, barn-like structure, but I didn't see any animals. By now I could see I was with four men, all dressed like peasants. Two carried rifles; one had a pistol in a holster, and the other carried a club like a small baseball bat, but bigger than the billy clubs the SPs carried back home in San Francisco. The leader knocked on the door of the farmhouse. There was something strange about the house. I could feel it. Words I couldn't hear were exchanged and the door opened. We slipped inside silently.

There was no light inside and the windows were covered. Once the door was closed, it was pitch black. Then an oil lamp was uncovered. Our host was an older man who looked about nervously.

"Why do you bring him here?" the man asked in angry French. He obviously meant me. Even though he was trying to mask, I could tell he was an adept. His powers were diminished with age.

"Orders," the leader said. "From London."

The old man looked at me. "What is your business here?" he asked in English.

"I can't discuss that," I said.

"At least he knows enough to keep his mouth shut," the old man muttered in French. He turned to our group's leader. "I will help downed pilots escape, but I will not get involved in other operations again. Is that understood?" He stopped masking and was running an anxiety spell on our fearless leader.

"*Oui*." He looked as if he were going to crumble. The spell wasn't that strong. He actually feared the old adept.

"You will sleep in the cellar," the old man instructed. "It is dark and cool. I have some old blankets down there. If you hear anything, don't come up. I will come to get you. Now help me."

Two of our group helped him move a massive-looking wardrobe. Then the man pulled up the floorboards. I was hit in the face with the smell of wet dirt. The cellar was about three feet high. We all lay down on the old blankets as the man replaced the boards. The resemblance to being buried alive was eerie and unsettling. Finally the darkness was nearly complete. As my eyes adjusted I could see a little light coming between the boards, but not enough to see by. We heard the old man move the wardrobe back over our hiding place, cutting off the light, and then he left the house. I fell asleep.

***

Our leader woke me. "Have a good sleep?" he asked in French, not bothering to hide his sarcasm. I smelled something cooking and was suddenly hungry, despite years of disciplining my body. I crawled out of the hole and brushed the dirt off of me. The old man was serving eggs and cheese and wine. I almost fell over at the sight of an adept serving lessers.

"What are you doing?" I asked in the ancient language.

He looked up at me. "Do you want some food or don't you?" He spoke French.

I stuck with the old tongue. "Then let them make it. We don't serve them."

The man stopped cooking to look at me. "I thought because you were here that maybe the American guilds realized that they, too, have a stake in this war. And that we all have to work together, adepts, lessers, Frenchmen, Englishmen, Americans, Russian, right-thinking Germans, everyone who values freedom, to stop what is happening here—" he pointed at the ground "—from spreading. So I will cook for these brave men, and you will respect me and them." As he spoke he stopped masking altogether; and that he had still been masking and I hadn't realized it spoke to his power. His blue eyes blazed, and even the lessers could feel his power. They looked at us as if we were coiled snakes ready to strike at one another.

I bowed my head. "Forgive me, Teacher." I didn't know about this fighting together, but if I angered this powerful adept I'd have more problems to deal with, and I didn't need that right now.

"Now, come and eat. I will be outside having a smoke."

"Yes, Teacher."

The man handed me a tin plate with eggs and cheese and a piece of black bread. He then went outside and pulled the door closed behind him.

The leader of our group came to life. "In the morning we enter Paris." He was talking to me; apparently the others knew the plan already. "Once it is daylight we cannot carry rifles and clubs in Paris, so the pistol will be our only weapon. Where exactly in Paris do you want to go?"

"Once I'm there, I'll know."

"How will you know?"

"I will know." I gave him a little confidence spell.

"Okay," he said using the one English word everyone knows. "The closer we get to Paris the more dangerous it will become. There will be more patrols and checkpoints. You will have to be very quiet, and very exact in following my instructions. We leave in ten minutes. *Bon appetit*."

Coming out of the farmhouse with the men, I saw that it was dusk. I had expected it to be morning. The old adept was leaning against the wall, smoking a pipe.

"Why are you here?" he asked in the ancient tongue.

"I cannot tell you, Teacher. But it is guild business. I thank you for your help."

"Will it help liberate these lands from the darkness that has overtaken them?"

"Yes," I said. "That's why the Americans and the Resistance agreed to help me." "Americans" and "Resistance" were in spell-translated French.

"There are evil forces at work here. Adepts are helping Hitler."

"I know. That's why I'm here."

"And that is why I hid here, in this house. I am glad there are adepts helping the Americans."

"So far there is only me," I said. "And it is only because I needed their help."

He looked at me hard, his blue eyes piercing. "The American guilds need to help their country."

"I don't understand. Aren't most governments corrupt and power-hungry?"

The adept laughed. "You haven't seen corrupt and power-hungry until you've seen Nazis. And I fear the Russians may be worse." He became very serious. "No government of man is perfect. The guilds are more corrupt than most governments, and yet you are part of that system. It's time to choose sides, Student. We cannot let the likes of the Nazis win, or the adepts who support them."

I was quiet while I thought about what he said.

"Let's go," the resistance leader ordered, walking away.

"Thank you, Teacher," I said quickly. And I meant it.

\*\*\*

Again we hiked through the night. We stuck to trees, hedgerows, and ditches again. We had to avoid towns and German checkpoints and bases, so we couldn't just go straight into Paris. We crossed a couple of roads the same way as the night before. There were more farms and houses, and it was getting harder to avoid them. The leader decided we should cross a road again to avoid a farm. The first man went across. Then the youngest man, the one with the club, went. A light from down the road hit him in the face and he stood in the road, paralyzed in fear. A truck had been parked on the road and had turned its lights on. In the pitch-blackness, even the slits of the blackout lights were like Klieg lights. We could hear men running before we saw them. German soldiers were jumping out of the back of the truck and sprinting toward the man on the road. The leader whispered a very nasty oath and pushed us away from the road. "Our only hope is to escape."

"What about them?" I asked, flailing an arm at the road. I stood my ground.

"That's a squad of German soldiers. We can't worry about our friends, now." He pushed on my chest.

"Can't you save them?" I asked.

"If I had a platoon, maybe."

"What's a platoon?" I asked.

"About thirty men."

"Armed?"

"Of course, armed."

"With what?"

"Rifles, machine guns, grenades."

"Wait," I commanded, loudly enough that some of the soldiers (who by now had reached our comrade and had him on the ground and were searching him) turned toward us.

I closed my eyes and reached into my pocket, where my talisman was. The Germans were entering the trees by the road now. I muttered words in the ancient language. A shot rang out. It came from down the road. The Germans shouted and started firing in the direction the shot had come from.

"Tell me, quick," I asked our leader, "what would a platoon do?"

He looked at the Germans, now shooting down the road at nothing, and then at me.

"Tell me!" I demanded.

"They'd shoot off a parachute flare, for light, then the machine guns would open up."

"How many?"

"Four, one per squad."

A flare arced through the black sky before settling into a slow descent, rocking in the breeze. Next, a steady staccato of machine-gun fire filled the night. German soldiers were falling over, dead. The unsteady light source made shadows move on their immobile bodies, giving them a ghostly appearance. The rest of the Nazis were shooting. They had forgotten about their prisoner and us.

As more Germans fell, they started to retreat.

"As they retreat the platoon would move forward, by squads," the leader kept up the narration. "Two squads fire while the other two maneuver ahead about five meters."

The shooting grew closer. The Germans were in a full panic retreat, running from the enemy. Some stumbled backwards, got up, and ran. Some fell, not to move again.

"Once they get close enough for a grenade they'd take out the vehicle," the leader said.

"No," I stated. "I have plans."

Every German was either dead or had run away in a few moments. My platoon ran after them. As they passed the truck lights, you could see they were translucent.

"Are the Germans gone?" I asked.

"*Oui.*"

"The truck," I managed to say before collapsing from exhaustion.

"There's no blood," was the next thing I heard.

"They weren't shot," I said, sitting up. They had apparently dragged me to the road and laid me down. My head still hurt.

"Then why did they die?" our leader asked.

"They thought they were shot, so they died."

"What did you say about the truck?"

"With these uniforms and the truck, could we drive to Paris? It would save time, and I'm sure these rifles and uniforms would help your cause."

The leader looked at me with a grin on this face. Then he shook his head. "No, too dangerous."

"You've seen what I can do. I don't think it'll be that dangerous."

"But we need papers for the checkpoints."

"Look for a leader," I suggested. "Someone must have had papers on him. Once I've seen what they look like, I can fake up papers that'll get us into Berlin."

The leader looked skeptical. "We need to leave. Those Germans that escaped will eventually report an enemy platoon here and the Nazis will respond in force."

"The truck will be faster," I said.

The leader turned to his men. "Find a uniform that fits you and pick up the weapons."

The men, who had been standing around nervously, jumped to their task. I picked out a uniform of a leader, marked by having more superfluous decorations, found his papers, and, using a translation spell, read them.

It didn't take long and we were soon driving south down the road wearing German uniforms. The leader was driving, I was in the passenger seat, and the three other men were in the back.

It also didn't take long to reach a checkpoint. A sandbagged machine gun nest was set up on the side of the road. There was a wooden arm painted with red and white diagonal stripes stretched across the pavement with the word "HALT" painted on it. Four Germans manned the checkpoint. Two were at the machine gun, one appeared to operate the wooden arm, and one stood with his hand out, indicating that we should stop.

I ran a glamour spell to make these malnourished Frenchmen look like healthy Aryans.

When the truck stopped, the German standing in front of the gate approached my window. "Papers, sir?"

I handed over the orders I had found in the uniform and started running a persuasion spell on him. He looked them over, seeing what I wanted him to see. I could tell my *camarades* were nervous. The leader was fondling a pistol he'd found.

The German handed back the papers. "Thank you, sir," he said and signaled for the arm to be lifted. "*Heil Hitler.*"

I returned the salute and we drove through.

"See?" I said.

He smiled at me, but I could tell he still wasn't convinced. "You're an officer, they are sergeants. You outrank them. Act a little arrogant; they'll expect it."

I did, and we got through checkpoints even faster. They got more numerous and more heavily manned as we approached Paris. But we got to Paris close to midnight, rather than in the morning as originally planned.

Rattling down the streets in the German truck, the leader asked "Where to?"

I could feel the power of the talismans. Probably never since the sinking of Atlantis had so many powerful talismans been gathered in one place. I pointed. "That way."

I could understand the need for that many talismans and the power they would provide. Mind reading is difficult enough if the subject is standing before you and you don't care if the person knows you have peered into his soul. Usually it's easier to just run a truth spell and have the person tell you what you want to know. Doing that with the leaders of the Supreme Allied Command would be worthless because, if they knew the Germans knew their plans, they would change them. However, mind reading subtly, without the subject knowing, is possible. It takes skill and strong meta. Also, due to the inverse square rule, the distance from Paris to London made it harder still. Why they hadn't done this in Calais, I didn't know.

Since Paris's streets tend to run in circles, it was not easy to follow my directions. And the truck was getting low on fuel. Damn these technological limitations, I thought.

We passed a checkpoint with ease and got closer and closer. As the sky was growing light in the east, I knew we were close. I pointed down a street. Our leader steered the truck in that direction and then stopped short. He said a very nasty word.

At the end of the road was a hotel. I counted the stories: thirteen. But between the building and us were at least a hundred German soldiers. The street was full of Nazis. There were barricades with sandbagged machine gun nests. Concertina wire was strung around like deadly Christmas garlands. There were armored cars with more machine guns and bigger weapons. And worst of all, a German officer in a handsome black uniform was walking straight toward us.

"SS!" the Resistance leader whispered.

"What's his rank?" I hissed.

"*Sturmbannführer*."

"What am I?" I asked.

"*Oberleutnant*."

"Do I outrank him?"

The leader laughed in a way I took to mean, "Not even close." He said, "He outranks you. Ensure you salute him first."

By then the Nazi was at the window; I noticed he had a small metal skull on his cap. "What is this, Lieutenant?" he asked me.

I went into my most military posture; I've seen movies. "Sir, we have orders to inspect the premises for listening devices." I looked at the Resistance leader, who silently handed over our "orders."

The Nazi gave the papers a glance and said, "We have already swept the area and I have never heard of this 'Major Shultz' who signed these orders."

I worked an anxiety spell. "You've never heard of Major Shultz of the *Führer's* general staff?" I looked very serious while working the spell. "My men have special skills and our orders come directly from Berlin." I turned up the anxiety to a level that would make most men wet their pants.

The Nazi handed the orders back to us as if they were causing him pain. "Park your truck over there and be quick about whatever you are going to do."

"Thank you, sir," I said with a smile and raised my right hand. "*Heil Hitler*." It left a bad taste in my mouth.

The Nazi clicked his heels together and threw his arm into the Nazi salute. "*Heil Hitler*."

"You heard him," I said to the Resistance leader (in German). "Park over there." I made a motion with my hand that could only mean, "Drive forward." Once the German couldn't hear, us I pointed and said in French, "Park over there." These translation spells work wonders.

"What are we to do?"

"What do you want to do?"

"Get the hell away from here."

"Okay, park the truck. I'm going inside the hotel. Then you're on your own. Can you escape?"

"I think so." He stopped the truck between two armored cars.

"Okay. Thank you and good luck."

"Bon chance," the leader repeated.

I exited from the truck and walked toward the hotel, trying to use the purposeful stride the *Sturmbannführer* had used. I returned a lot of straight-arm salutes like the one the SS officer had given. Two SS soldiers (black uniforms, skulls on their hats) guarded the entrance to the hotel. They both held the same sub machine gun the Nazi on the *El Cielo de las Américas*, Dummkopf, was carrying. I flipped the guards a "*Heil Hitler*," expecting to walk right by.

One said, "Halt!" and stepped in front of me.

I glared angrily at him. "What is the meaning of this?"

"No one gets in without direct orders from *Sturmbannführer* Schroder."

I was so close the power of the talismans was making my nerves sing like high-tension wires. I had no patience left for these most petty of all lessers' concerns and, with all the meta in the atmosphere, I had the power to do something about it.

"Let me pass," I said simply. The man stepped aside. He had no choice. I could have ordered him to shoot his own son and he would have. I walked in.

What was at one time a luxury hotel had been turned into a military outpost. There were uniforms everywhere, which meant I blended in perfectly and no one gave me a second glance. The talismans were above me, so I looked for the elevator. I pressed the button, half expecting Dorothy to be the operator. Instead it was an armed soldier.

"Floor, sir?" he asked as I stepped in.

"Thirteen."

"Sir?"

"Thirteen." I had counted the floor from outside.

"Sir, there are only 12 floors."

I forgot. In Europe it is different. They call the ground floor the ground floor and then start at "one," what Americans would call the "second floor."

"Twelfth floor," I said. "My mistake."

"Sir, that floor is restricted…" You can imagine it didn't take me long to convince him.

I stepped off the elevator. The talismans were so close I couldn't locate them more precisely. I would have to go room to room. I had started for the end of the hall when a small German soldier came out of one of the rooms—except it wasn't. It was a woman using a glamour to look male. I saw through it, of course. I almost didn't recognize her with blonde hair.

"Dorothy," I said simply.

She turned and looked at me, and looked very surprised. "Francis?"

# CHAPTER FOURTEEN

Dorothy looked at me for a second and then her eyes grew wide. "How did you…?"

I pushed her back into the room she'd come out of and closed the door behind us. She had the *katana* talisman on her. I could tell. "Give it to me."

There was no debate about what "it" was.

"It's made me very powerful. Do you want to take it from me?" She spoke with a confidence and, yes, power that hadn't been there before, even that night in Fat's. "Also, Brunhild will start looking for me soon. Do you want to fight her?"

No, I didn't. "My guild's leader is holding my name on the return of that talisman. If I don't return it to him…" There was no need to finish.

"I'm sorry, but we need it."

"What if I help you?"

"Why would you help us?"

"In exchange for the talisman. All you want is the Hammer."

She thought a second. "I'd have to talk to Brunhild. Can we have your name on it?"

I really did not like all the copies of my name floating around. "If I can have your name on it."

A larger (although not fat, just healthy) blonde woman came into the room. She, too, was wearing a German uniform and using a glamour. It didn't hide her power. She still wasn't wearing a helmet with horns.

"Dagmar, who is this?" She spoke the ancient language.

"I'm the rightful owner of the samurai *katana* talisman," I tried.

"Ahh, Mr. Kader," Brunhild replied, turning to me. "We have held that talisman for decades. Your short possession is inconsequential."

"Not when my name is riding on it."

"That is not my concern."

Then a man walked into the room, also wearing a German officer's uniform but not using a glamour. It was Smith.

He looked at me. "I was afraid of this."

"What?" I asked.

"You got here somehow."

"Why, Smith, or should I say '*Herr* Krupp'?"

"Neither one is my name, so it doesn't matter."

"You led him here?" Brunhild demanded.

"The box," Smith said. "I told you he got the box from that Nip."

"We knew someone heard us talking on the ship," Dorothy/Dagmar added.

"So, what's his involvement?" I asked, indicating Smith.

"He's a Berserker," Dagmar said. "The last survivor. He infiltrated the American intelligence organization for us. One of our members, dead now, killed by an adept from your guild, used persuasion spells on key people to get him in. We used him to keep an eye on Nazi spies in America in order to locate our samurai talisman."

"Killed by a member of my guild?"

"Yes," Smith said. "A woman that was working with the Nazis."

"Morgan," I said.

"Maybe," Smith agreed. "Remember Daeubler's contact, the one he got the samurai talisman from, was a woman."

"Oh, yes, that's when you were supposedly an FBI agent," I said sarcastically. I was, like Admiral Richards, rather annoyed that Smith had fooled me. It was rather brilliant of the Valkyrie to use a Berserker. I would detect an adept, eventually. But a Berserker is just a highly skilled and powerful warrior.

"And now you're supposedly a Nazi, apparently." I looked at Smith again. "I thought Berserkers were bigger?"

"I'm a runt," Smith sneered at me.

"So what do we do now?" I asked.

"Kill him," Smith said.

"You might find that difficult," I replied with a blast of meta power.

Smith stood his ground. "I've killed more powerful adepts than you," he said, and it seemed that he was getting bigger.

"We don't have time for this," Brunhild said with impatience. "After we get *Mjollnir* you two can kill each other in peace. But first we have to get *Mjollnir*."

"I can help you, but in exchange for the *katana* talisman."

Brunhild sighed, her massive bosom moving up and down.

"Think of it as payment."

"We don't need him," Smith said.

"We might," Dagmar added. "An extra adept would be a help."

"And what will happen if you have the samurai talisman?" Brunhild asked.

"I have to turn it over to my teacher; he has my name on it."

Brunhild shook her head. "No. That would make your guild too powerful."

"And if you have it your guild isn't too powerful?" I asked.

"I do not trust your guild, Mr. Kader."

"And we are supposed to trust your guild?"

"No member of our guild killed a member of yours."

"She's a rogue. I'm under orders to kill her." My voice was getting louder.

"How do I know that?" Brunhild demanded. She and I were glaring at each other. I didn't know about her, but I had my hand on my talisman ready to defend or attack.

"Wait," Dagmar said.

We both looked at her.

"Teacher," she said to Brunhild, "we need his help. And I think we can trust him. I'm sure he had nothing to do with Bente's death."

"But what about his guild?"

"Can you trust me?" I asked. "With that talisman I could rule my guild."

Brunhild thought for a moment. "Will you sign a treaty?"

"Will you?"

"We don't have time for this," Smith hissed.

Brunhild nodded toward me, almost smiling. Dagmar found some hotel stationery while Brunhild and I allowed truth spells to be cast on each by the other. We both wrote our names, our real names, on separate pieces of paper under the written sentence, "Our guilds are at peace." Each paper was sealed in an envelope and given to the other adept. Finally, spells were put on them. If the envelope was ever opened, both signers would know and they would probably kill each other simultaneously. If the holder of an envelope died from other causes, the paper would burn so no one else could use the name inside. It was a mutual suicide pact, but it worked. Usually.

Smith looked disgusted.

I put my envelope in one of the many pockets in my uniform.

"If you don't become leader of your guild," Brunhild said, "this treaty is void and we will exchange envelopes and destroy them in each other's presence."

"Agreed," I said.

There was a quiet moment when it hit me. "This is her room."

"Whose?" Brunhild asked.

"Morgan," I said. As close and intimate as I'd been with her, I was surprised it took me that long. I went to the wardrobe and opened it. I rummaged through the clothes, some of which I recognized, which meant she'd been back to San Francisco after escaping from the ship. I pulled out a heart-shaped locket. That was a strange thing, I thought, especially for such an unfeeling bitch. I opened it, looking at the picture inside. It wasn't me, which didn't surprise me. Whose picture it was did surprise me a lot. Then I closed it and pocketed it. I searched the rest of the room, but found nothing interesting. The others watched me with some bemusement. Unfortunately, I did not find the rattle talisman. I assumed she had it with her.

Finished, I turned to Brunhild. "Okay, what do we do?"

Brunhild lined out a plan. The talismans were in a room down the hall. The adepts loyal to Hitler, and Morgan I assumed, were gathering in that room to attempt to read the minds of the Supreme Allied Command leadership in

England to find out when and where the invasion of Europe that everyone was expecting any day now would happen. They would be using the Hammer of Thor, along with some German talismans, to increase their power. I didn't mention the rattle, since they didn't seem to know about it.

Before they all arrived, we would storm the room, using meta to protect us, steal back the Hammer and any other talismans present, and discontinuously traverse to the nearest building, an apartment building where Smith had a room. They drew a diagram showing me the physical distance between the apartment and the hotel room. I didn't want to miss and materialize in a wall. Then they'd change clothes—I was stuck in the uniform but could use a glamor—and traverse to the street, where we could make our escape.

It seemed too simple. Especially when we heard, and felt, three adepts walk by the room and go down the hall.

"I told you we didn't have time," Smith remarked.

"Shut up," Dagmar spat.

"Now what?" I asked.

"We fight them for it," Brunhild said.

"Are you nuts?" Smith said. "They have *Mjollnir*."

Brunhild said something to Smith in some language I didn't understand. He turned pale. Then he bucked up and said, "I'm not dying in this uniform." He stripped off the Nazi garb and Brunhild produced out of the air a breastplate of steel, chain mail, a shield, a helmet, and a battle axe that glowed greenish-gold with meta power. As he put them on, he then looked like a Berserker.

I looked at Dagmar/Dorothy and smiled. "I have an idea."

\*\*\*

Dagmar and I walked out into the hall. She was using a glamour not to look like a man but to look as if she were wearing a maid's uniform. The corridor was full of Nazis in those black uniforms. One stopped me.

"Where are you going, *Oberleutnant*?"

I roughly grabbed Dagmar's arm. "I believe this woman is a spy," I replied with a spell of convincing. "I must take her to the adepts. They can interrogate her properly."

"Right this way, sir." He took us to the very room. I could feel Dagmar building up her power, like winding up a spring. I was doing the same.

The Nazi knocked on the door. It opened a crack.

"Who dares interrupt—"

I pushed hard against the door and Dagmar and I burst into the room, the Nazi clumsily following. The woman holding the door fell into the room on the rug. Dagmar made a sound and the rug wrapped around her and became form-fitting. I touched the Nazi's head and he dropped to the floor, near death; it was hard not to over-spell with all the power present.

Then I quickly surveyed the room. There were four adepts, the woman on the floor in the rug, two men, and Morgan. She saw me and jumped to her feet.

"Kader, how?"

I shot an air bolt at her and she slammed into the wall, cracking the plaster. She crumbled to the floor, apparently unconscious.

The woman on the floor was trying to move, but the rug wouldn't give an inch. There was a commotion in the hall and for the first time I heard a Berserker scream. I suspected it could kill weak men at thirty yards. The sound of rapid machine-gun fire couldn't compete with Smith's scream. I imagined him hacking through the Nazis, the bullets of their machine guns bouncing harmlessly off his shield and breastplate.

But I had little time to reflect, for I felt flames about my head. One of the Nazi adepts, standing by a table, was shooting fire at me. He was a little effete-looking guy dressed in a tan suit. I cooled the flame with a mist and looked for an attack. Dagmar was busy keeping the woman on the floor in her rug cocoon and the other male adept, an older man wearing an SS uniform, was attacking her by dropping big, venomous bugs from the ceiling.

I blasted the flame back at the little guy shooting it at me. To keep from being fried, he had to go to a protection spell. That gave me time to create a wind to blow the bugs away from Dagmar. The SS adept stopped his attack on Dagmar and pointed to the floor at my feet. The wood reached up, grabbed my feet, and started to pull me down; to where, I didn't know— perhaps the floor below. If so, it was awfully hot down there.

Brunhild entered the room and immediately helped Dagmar, taking over the woman on the floor. She also reached out a hand to me. I touched it and was immediately on solid hardwood again. Smith crashed through the wall. He was covered in gore and the white plaster stuck to the blood, making him look ghost-like. He cleaved the woman on the floor in half, but the two men attacked him directly. He blew away like a pile of leaves facing a strong wind, his scream fading to nothing. Smith, or whatever his name was, was gone, except for the axe. With the woman on the floor no longer a worry and Morgan still unconscious, the Valkyries concentrated on the survivors. I checked the hall. It was a gully of blood and body parts. Additional soldiers were pouring out of the stairwell. The gore caused them to stop quickly, and I hit them with a fear spell. The stampede down the stairs probably trampled the slower ones.

Suddenly, I couldn't breathe. The little man had used my distraction to attack. The air around me was gone. As my vision started going dark, signaling that I was about to pass out, I moved to my left and felt air on my face again, and took a deep breath. I shot lightning at my adversary. It missed, but I had wanted to scare him. He tried the flame thing again, but I easily deflected it. Then he jumped for the Hammer. It was lying on a table and about three times bigger than a normal sledgehammer should be but had a very short handle. I dove for Smith's axe and brought it up just in time to parry the little man's Hammer blow. I lit his pants on fire and when he jumped away, I swung the axe again. His head bounced off the wall.

I turned to see the women watching me, their opponent apparently dispatched. All that was left was a smoldering SS uniform. I smiled at Brunhild and Dagmar, breathing hard. The women started to smile, but something stopped them.

It hit me from the rear and knocked me to the floor, face down. I turned. Morgan had the Hammer in her hands. There was blood on the head. I assumed it was mine, from the pain in my head.

I shot fire at her, but she ducked it. Brunhild used an ice attack, but she melted it. Dagmar tried to take her air away, but instead Morgan took her air. Dagmar collapsed.

"It's *Mjollnir*," Brunhild screamed. "It has made her powerful!"

I could feel it. Her blue eyes were blazing. I put a hand to the back of my head and, ignoring the feeling of wetness, invoked a small healing spell. Then I pulled Dagmar to where I knew there was air. She gasped and started breathing.

"We have to work together," I said as Morgan sprayed small balls of flame at us. I covered Dagmar and myself with a mist that cooled them, but they still hurt when they hit.

"How?" Brunhild asked, using a protection spell to keep herself safe.

From the floor, Dagmar said, "The *skodde*."

"No," Brunhild said, "it requires at least three. He can't know the secret."

Morgan stopped the flaming balls attack, realizing it wasn't working. She stood on the other side of the room, holding the Hammer. I swear her red hair was aflame. She'd never looked more beautiful.

"Damn it, Kader," she growled.

"You have to trust me," I told Brunhild, ignoring Morgan.

Brunhild looked at Dagmar, who nodded.

"I'll kill all of you," Morgan screamed. She was, it seemed, going mad with power.

Brunhild pulled me near her and whispered in my ear. Dagmar stood and guarded us for the few moments it took to explain the *skodde*. Morgan glared at us, probably preparing her next attack.

Brunhild took my hand and I took Dagmar's. All three of us were holding our talismans, Dagmar using the *katana*. A mist formed around us. Morgan tried to send a wind, but the mist was as unmoving as a brick wall.

We walked forward, stepping together. Morgan threw fire, ice, spiders, and airbolts, but nothing penetrated. Then, when Brunhild said, "*Na*," the mist shot forward and crashed into Morgan. It encased her and turned solid. She fell over like a statue.

"Is she alive?" I asked.

"No," Dagmar said grimly.

The *skodde* was starting to dissolve, revealing the corpse inside. I bent down and tenderly closed her eyes when they were clear. I didn't understand why she did what she did, except maybe for the reason she had told me on the *El*

*Cielo de las Américas*: power. But I think I understood her actions. She'd been told by the Nazis to recover the rattle talisman for Hitler. She'd held it in Yuma; that was the power I'd felt in the restaurant there. But she didn't use it after that, in order to deliver it fresh to Hitler. It must have been in her trunk on the ship when I attacked her. That's why she had been scrambling to open it during our fight, and she'd told me later that she was getting in the trunk for something she'd found in Yuma. Plus, I was sure that she was the one who had turned the *katana* talisman over to Daeubler in the "dead drop."

I stood and pointed to Morgan's prone figure. "That's who killed Bente."

"No it's not," Brunhild said.

"What? How do you know?"

"I was using far-sight; I saw it. It was not she."

I reached in my pocket and took out the locket, opened it, and showed it to Brunhild. "Is that the one?"

*"Ja."*

I pocketed the locket.

Brunhild picked up the Hammer. She looked as if it gave her physical pleasure to touch it. Dagmar also took the handle in her hands.

I checked the hall. Soldiers were advancing slowly. I tried the fear spell, but there was something downstairs they feared even more. So I put a fire spell up in front of them. A secure spell on the door would have worked too, but the hole in the wall Smith had come through couldn't be secured.

"Time to go," I said. We couldn't stop bullets from that many guns simultaneously.

There were about ten talismans scattered around the room. I found the rattle near Morgan's body. It was a gourd on a stick with a pictograph of some sort carved into it. It looked brand new. Brunhild and Dagmar picked up three or four talismans and then, both holding the Hammer; they winked out, the air clapping in to fill the void they left. I took three of the remaining talismans, chosen more for their ability to fit in my uniform's pockets than anything else. I heard the Germans approaching. One looked through the hole Smith had made and pointed his machine gun at me. I made the jump, landing dangerously close to a wall.

"Now," I said holding out my hand, "my talisman."

Dagmar started to hand it to me, stopped, and looked at Brunhild. The old woman nodded and Dagmar placed it in my palm.

"We need to go," Brunhild said. "First thing they'll do is search the area for us."

"Yes, and fast," I agreed.

I looked out the window to check for approaching soldiers. I could see the entrance to the hotel. My stolen army truck was still there and the Resistance members were lined up alongside it. Two soldiers holding machine guns were watching them. They'd been caught.

"Let's go," Brunhild said.

I shook my head. "There's something I have to take care of first. Wait for me."

"We can't wait long. They'll start searching these apartments."

"I'll be back soon." I couldn't let the brave men that had helped get me here be executed, even if they were lessers.

I traversed to a spot near the truck. Luckily I had plenty of power, so all this meta expenditure wasn't tiring me. I walked to the nearest soldier.

"What is this?" I demanded in German.

"Sir, we have captured Resistance fighters. They obviously were planning to attack the adepts."

"Oh. Good work. What's happening inside?" I touched both men.

"I don't know—" The men collapsed. It was too easy. I picked up the machine guns and handed them to the leader of the Resistance. I realized then I didn't even know his name.

"Get out of here while they're distracted."

The leader just looked at me, then smiled. The men ran behind the hotel, but not before I put a spell of invisibility on them. It should have lasted long enough to get them out of the city. I traversed back.

"What was that about?" Brunhild asked.

"Those brave men helped me."

"They were lessers. You risk your life for them?"

"They did for me."

She harrumphed her disapproval, but Dagmar gave me a smile.

156

# CHAPTER FIFTEEN

Our escape was fairly easy, as we used both discontinuously traversing and invisibility. Brunhild said I might as well come with them. They had a German staff car waiting for them in another part of town, with an actual German driver.

"Persuasion spells," Dagmar explained when I looked amazed. "He thinks we're a general and his aides."

"Who's the general?" I asked.

"Brunhild, of course."

"Of course," I replied. "Glamours?"

"Yes," Brunhild said. "But you're fine, *Oberleutnant*."

"*Jawohl, mein General*."

The staff car took us out of Paris and south. It dropped us at a villa near the border to Vichy France. The villa was empty, but civilian clothes were stashed there. Clothes meant for Smith were a little large for me, but serviceable. We waited until night to cross the border, invisible.

Brunhild was indeed the general of our expedition. In Vichy she'd arranged for bicycles to be hidden near the border. We rode them into a village and there caught a train to a town near the Spanish frontier. Brunhild had hidden a car there, and Dagmar amazed me by knowing how to drive it.

We drove up into the Pyrenees and crossed over into Spain, again at night, on foot, and invisible. Once in Spain, travel was easier, mostly by train, and we were soon in Lisbon, Portugal. Money was no problem; there was a casino there. They politely asked us never to return, as if they could stop us.

I found a freighter that would take me to New York via the Canary Islands. It was Portuguese flagged, so I hoped it would be safe from attack from German U-boats.

There was a little restaurant overlooking the Lisbon harbor. The sun was setting over the Atlantic as Dagmar and I ate a meal there together the night before my ship sailed. The fare was heavy on seafood.

"Come with me," I said, looking into her blue eyes. I still wasn't used to her as a blonde.

"I can't," she said. "We're going to have to rebuild our guild. Brunhild and I are all that's left of the Valkyrie. The man you knew as Smith was our last Berserker. Even with *Mjollnir* it will be difficult."

I reached across the table to take her hand. "You could join my guild."

"No," she said. "Stop tempting me."

"Tempting you?"

She nodded. "I used you. I didn't trust anybody, least of all you. I knew someone from your guild had killed Bente. I assumed it was with the guild's knowledge and approval."

"It wasn't, I assure you." However, if it suited Fitz, he wouldn't have hesitated to order it.

"But since then," she said, "I've come to think you're the kind of man I could …" she let her voice trail off.

I decided to change the subject. "This is quite a change from Young Fat's."

She smiled, her eyes sparkling like the water in the bay. "Yes."

\*\*\*

The next day I boarded the ship to New York. I had the rattle and my old talisman secured in my newly purchased trunk, and the *katana* talisman was in my pocket as Brunhild's payment. It was almost as nice as Dagmar's "thank you" had been the night before. It's a good thing, I mused, watching Lisbon's harbor recede, the legends about the Valkyrie aren't true.

It took nearly two weeks to get to New York. The other passengers were mostly refugees from France or North Africa.

In New York I had to use some strong meta to get off the boat, since I had no passport and no visa and no identification of any kind. I would have simply discontinuously traversed past, but I couldn't do that carrying my trunk.

From there, it was a train ride to Chicago, then to El Paso, then to Yuma, Arizona again.

\*\*\*

Getting off the train, and after securing my trunk in the stationmaster's office, I spotted a Model A painted yellow.

"Taxi, sir?" the driver asked without looking at me.

I got in. "Head east, out of town. I'll show the way."

He turned and looked at me. "Oh, no!"

I smiled at him. "Oh, yes."

"Git outta my car now, mister."

"Hang on," I said. "I like the way you handled yourself last time. Take me where I want to go and I'll kick in a fiver."

He shook his head. "Ain't worth it."

"This won't be dangerous, I promise."

"Yeah, I know what's east of town: the darky metas. People don't go out there, not for no reason."

"I've got a reason. A ten-spot."

"No!"

I got out of the car. "Okay. I guess I'll walk. I hoped to have a good man like you at my back." I started walking toward the street. I heard the old car pull up behind me. The driver spoke through the window.

"Okay, for twenty dollars."

I smiled and got in the back. "You know the way?"

"I know where people say not to go."

"Good, I can get you the rest of the way there."

I settled in the backseat and realized I hadn't taken the easy route of using a persuasion spell. I was out of the habit of using lessers, I supposed.

\*\*\*

Outside the dilapidated house were two warriors. The driver of the taxi stopped it about a hundred feet away. "This is as far as I go, sir."

"Wait for me," I said, getting out onto the dusty ground. I was carrying a small leather bag I'd bought in New York. The rattle talisman was too big to fit in a pocket; I'd carried it in my hand over a large part of Western Europe. "This won't take long."

"I hope not. But just in case, can I have that twenty now?"

I gave him a ten.

The house's porch looked as if it were about to fall down under the weight of the air on it. But two warriors were sitting in wicker chairs in the shade. They eyed me as I walked closer.

"You have business with the guild?" one asked, standing and meeting me at the step to the porch. He was wearing an expensive linen suit that jarred with the rustic landscape. The large bulge under his arm meant he had a very big gun.

I looked him in the eye as if he didn't intimidate me, because he didn't. "Tell your leader that Mister Kader is here to see him."

He looked dubious, but jerked his head in the direction of the door. The other warrior, smaller and dressed more appropriately in khaki, stood as if it were the hardest thing he'd done all day and went inside. He emerged a few moments later. The two exchanged a look and linen suit said, "Go on in."

"Thank you," I said, trying to step past him onto the porch.

He blocked the way. "What's in the bag?"

I opened it, making sure it wasn't in the shadow of the porch, and let him look inside. I was counting on the dark interior of the bag and the bright sunshine to keep me from having to use a spell to fool him.

"What is that?"

I pulled out the rattle and held it up, taking his eyes out of the bag. "The reason I'm here."

He looked at it for a moment as if trying to determine its possible threat, and deciding there was none, stepped out of the way.

I walked across the squeaky boards on the porch, pushed the door open, and slipped inside. It was dark, and after the bright sunshine it took me a few moments to clearly make out the room.

There was the leader of the guild, Mr. Brooks, in the same comfortable-looking overstuffed chair. There was the same warrior behind him, holding a pistol. A young adept, the one who had posed as a railroad porter and chased me all over town during my first trip to Yuma, was leaning against the wall, smoking a cigarette. And an attractive young Negro woman, her stylish dress just a bit too tight across her ample bosom and wide hips, was sitting on the floor on a pillow at the feet of the leader. She smiled at me as I came in.

"Darling," Brooks said, "would you please fetch me some iced tea?"

She stood up, an interesting exercise in contortion as she managed to alight on her high-heeled shoes while remaining in that dress. "Sure thing, hun." She turned to me. "Would you like anything, sir?"

I smiled at her. "No, thanks."

"Sure thing," she said and walked toward the back of the house, which was distracting.

The leader of the guild looked at me. "I believe you owe me something."

I opened the bag and pulled out the rattle. Brooks' eyes lit up at the sight. He held out his hand.

I held it away from him. "My name?"

Brooks smiled in a way that worried me. "What about it?"

"My name for the rattle. That was the deal."

Brooks reached into his suit jacket and pulled out the envelope. It had been ripped open.

I invoked the protection spell fast, but not fast enough. I was slammed painfully against the wall and held there. I couldn't move. The rattle and the bag lay on the floor where I'd dropped them.

"Teacher," the younger adept said, "this ain't no good thing. His guild be powerful."

Brooks just sneered at him. "This is my business, Student," he said as a warning.

I didn't say anything; I couldn't. My eyes were the only things I could move voluntarily. I saw the girl start to come back carrying a tray with a glass of iced tea. She saw me, looked scared, and turned around and walked the other way.

"Search him, and bring me that rattle," Brooks told his warrior.

The warrior walked over, picked up the rattle, and handed it to Brooks. He grinned at it greedily.

The warrior searched my clothes. I could do nothing about it; my arms were flayed out from my body. He took my talisman, my wallet containing my cash and my train ticket for the next day, and nothing else. He handed them both to Brooks. Brooks opened my wallet and, as a final degradation, took the money and placed it in his pocket.

"Teacher," the young adept said warily. He was standing, having snuffed out his cigarette.

Brooks just glanced at him as if he were an annoying bug. "With this talisman, we need not fear his guild anymore."

He stood and walked close to me, still holding the rattle. "Now, tell me, where's Johnson?"

It took me a second to remember he meant Morgan. And he must have released my mouth, for I could speak, but it was difficult. "Dead. I killed her."

"Good," he said. "That's one reason not to kill you." He walked back and sat in his chair. "Where is that damn girl and my iced tea?" he said in a loud voice.

The girl scurried out, holding the tray. "I'm sorry, sir, coming," she called, and I realized she feared him, too.

"Teacher," the other adept started.

"Be quiet, Louis," Brooks snapped.

I watched Louis. He was angry, but he, too, was afraid of Brooks.

The girl brought the tray over and Brooks took the glass from it, setting down the talisman to do so. "Thank you, dear," he said in tones almost loving.

"You're welcome, sir," she said. "May I go now?"

"Of course, dear."

I could tell she was glad to leave. Not once did she look at me.

Brooks took a sip of his tea and I fell to the floor. Brooks had released me, but not expecting it, I fell like a rag doll. I fell near the bag.

"Without a talisman, I think you're safe," Brooks said, pausing once to sip. "Any attack you can make without it won't be determinal."

I nodded, as if I agreed my attacks wouldn't be detrimental, while letting my muscles get used to being used again.

"What you gonna do now?" Louis asked worriedly.

"Kill him," Brooks answered. "Unless you'd like to, Student."

"I doesn't know his name," Louis answered, apparently glad to have an excuse.

"Oh, it's—"

While they were talking, I quickly reached into the bag and pulled out the flat *katana* talisman I had taped to the side of the container where it would be damn near impossible to see, especially in a dark bag in bright sunshine. I wanted to run a protection spell, but I had to shut up Brooks.

Brooks noticed my movement and pointed at me. He dropped his iced tea to the floor, splashing the brown liquid over the wooden planks, and grabbed for the rattle. I felt my insides start to boil, but I dove for the rattle, too. I didn't reach it, but I managed to knock it out of Brooks' reach. I put up a protection spell, which only slowed his assault, and healed myself slightly. That all took maybe five seconds. Then I attacked Brooks. The molecules in the air around him slowed and ice formed on his body, but not fast enough or thick enough. The spell should have formed a thick ice coat that would immobilize and suffocate him, but instead he just had a frosty patina, like a car window on a cold morning. I had forgotten that in this dry atmosphere there wasn't enough water in the air. I had needed that attack to be devastating to Brooks, and it didn't work.

He easily countered my spell, but his direct attacks on me were blunted somewhat by my protection spell. So he went indirect and shot fire at me. Even with the *katana* talisman, I was straining my ability to invoke more spells. My counter, a cool mist, only managed to boil and spray hot water back on me. And my protection spell was weakening, because I was expending too much energy stopping the fire as best I could. But I was keeping him busy and he couldn't get the rattle, now on the floor beside his chair.

"Louis," I called out, feeling Brooks' attacks penetrate. "Help me!"

Louis looked at me and looked at his leader.

"Why should I?" he asked. I could tell he wanted to.

I was weakening. "My guild," I said before my protection spell failed. Louis picked up the rattle just as my sight went dim. Even then, I could see Louis' lightning jump across the room.

Brooks was thrown out of his chair by the unexpected attack. I crumpled to the floor, and with the last bit of power left to me, healed myself. It wasn't enough, but I was still alive, for now.

Louis walked over and looked at me.

"Brooks?" I rasped.

"Dead."

I knew I was losing consciousness. "Envelope, name, Addleman," I breathed. I didn't hear him reply.

***

I blinked. There was a bare bulb above my eyes.

"Oh, you're awake," I heard. The voice sounded tired.

I turned my head toward the sound. "Addleman?"

"You're a lucky fellow," Addleman said. "Too much longer and you'd have been dead. Internal bleeding."

"Name?" I asked.

Addleman held up the paper with my name on it. "Yes, I used it. Couldn't have saved you, otherwise."

"Trust you," I breathed.

"I know. Thank you." He picked up a Zippo lighter and burned the paper.

"Louis?"

"The young Negro? I don't know. You'll have to ask him."

"Talisman?" I said. These one-word sentences were a lot of work.

He held up the rattle. "Louis let me use it to heal you."

"Thank you," I said. "Mine?"

He handed me the *katana*, placing it carefully in my hand. "This is actually more powerful than the rattle, but I didn't have your permission so I didn't use it."

I did. After the healing spell I fell asleep again. I don't know for how long, but Addleman was still there when I woke up.

"Feeling better?"

I sat up, realizing I was lying on an examination table. "Yes, thank you."

"The young Negro and your driver are waiting for you."

"How long?" I looked at my watch, but realized I had no idea when I'd arrived.

"A little more than an hour."

I stood up, becoming aware that I was still a little weak.

"He'll want this," Addleman said, handing me the rattle.

"Yes," I said.

Addleman showed me to the waiting room. Louis was there, and the taxi driver. "Thank you," I said to Louis.

"You're welcome," he replied, looking a little embarrassed.

I noticed a rip in the sleeve of his jacket. "What happened?"

"Brooks' warrior shoot me after I killed Brooks. So I killed him."

"Excuse me," the taxi driver said. "I think you owe me something."

I looked at him quizzically.

"Ten dollars," he reminded me.

"Oh, yes." I reached for my wallet but it wasn't there. I remembered Brooks had taken it. Louis handed it to me. I quickly checked it. All the money and my train ticket were there. I paid the driver. "Thank you for bringing me here."

"I didn't bring you here, he..." he nodded at Louis "...flew you here on a rug. He told me where to find you."

I looked at Louis. "Thank you, again." Addleman had said any longer and I'd have been dead. If he hadn't flown me here, I'd have died in the back of that taxi.

The driver, happy, said, "If you won't be needing any more of my services, I'm late for my dinner."

"I gots a car," Louis said.

I dismissed the driver, who left happy.

Louis and I walked outside. The sun was low and it was starting to cool off. "Can you take me to my hotel?" I asked.

"Sure, where?"

"Hotel Del Sol."

"Get on in."

We both got in the back. The warrior in the linen suit was driving. "Where to, sir?"

"Hotel Del Sol," Louis said.

After a few minutes of riding, I said, "You're the head of your guild now."

"Yes," he said. "'Cause of you. He was fighting so hard to get through yous protection spell, my spell hurt him bad."

There was a long silence. Then I asked, "My name?"

I felt him tense. "I didn't look," he said. "Addleman did, but I didn't."

"Okay," I said.

He visibly relaxed. "Okay?"

"Yes, I believe you. I have no reason not to."

He looked at me as if I'd just admitted to paying income taxes. "Okay," he said again, still not sure what to think.

"Listen," I said. "You're now head of this guild. But I plan to be head of my guild as soon as I return to San Francisco. I could use men like you in my guild."

He didn't answer while, I think, he debated whether I was serious.

"You would have a high position in my guild. And your guild could become part of it," I explained.

He looked out the window a moment.

"Cans I think about it?"

"Sure," I said. "You can contact me at the Drake-Wiltshire Hotel, San Francisco. I'm leaving on the Sunset Limited in the morning, if you change your mind by then."

"Okay," he said, with a genuine smile.

He spoke a few moments later. "Why you staying at the Hotel Del Sol?"

"Why not?"

"The San Carlos a lot nice, even though they has a gas station on the bottom floor."

I smiled. "Well, take me there, please."

And it was nicer.

***

Louis met me at the train station in the morning. I smiled at him.

"Good morning," I said.

He looked at me. "I just wanted to know if you was serious."

"About what, Student?"

"Me joining your guild. Our guilds combining."

I nodded. "Yes. I think it would make both our guilds stronger."

Louis smiled as if he'd been told a joke. "Never been no white guild and no Negro guild together."

"No," I said, "that's true. Doesn't mean we can't."

He looked at me as if to ensure I was serious. "I'll think about it, Teacher."

"Good," I said and held out my right hand.

He took it and shook it with a broad smile on his face.

The train's whistle blew, letting out a white plume of steam, and the conductor leaned out a door and cried, "All aboard!"

I boarded the train and found my sleeper suite. I had made advance reservations and made sure my schedule included a train with a sleeper car. The porter took my trunk to the baggage car after I removed a few items I needed for the trip.

Which wasn't much, because most of what I did in my sleeper suite was sleep. The porter acted scandalized when I asked him to let down the bed shortly after lunch. But the battle the day before, and healing, had left me extremely weary. Just moving was hard, as if gravity had increased. Sleeping also made the trip go by much faster.

In San Francisco I took a taxi to the Drake-Wiltshire. Sebastian grinned broadly as I opened the door and stepped onto the sidewalk.

"Welcome back, sir!" he said.

"I have a trunk in the back," I said.

"Yes, sir," he said. "And good to have you back, sir."

"Thank you," I said.

Sebastian got the bell captain to take my trunk to my room.

The desk clerk was also happy to see me. I somehow got the feeling they hadn't expected me back. "A package arrived for you from England," he said. "It's in your room."

"Thank you."

"And you have multiple messages from a Lieutenant Halloran. Says he needs to speak with you."

He probably still thought I had something to do with Miles' death.

When I got to my room—oh, it felt good to be home—I dialed Klondike-5-1326.

"Hello?"

"Teacher, it's Kader. I'm back in San Francisco and I have good news."

"Good," he said. "Come over and see me in the morning." Technically, it was already morning.

"Afternoon is better for me," I said. "And Black and Reynolds need to be there."

There was a hefty pause. I wondered if he was consulting with Reynolds. Then: "Fine, about five?"

"Yes, Teacher. I'll be there."

# CHAPTER SIXTEEN

I was out of the Drake by mid-morning. It was a bright, sunny, late-summer day and I wanted to enjoy it. I walked around the city, and lunched at Original Joe's; I wanted something as American as I could get, and a steakhouse fit the bill.

In the late summer, in the late afternoon, fog is the prevalent condition in San Francisco. By the time I arrived at the Huntington, fog was rolling in from the Pacific like an invading army occupying the city. It settled into the cracks between the buildings and hung there, enveloping all denizens of the city with its cold and gloom. It matched my mood as I entered the lobby.

On the thirteenth floor I walked to suite 1313. There was a warrior outside holding a tommy gun. Seeing me, he opened the door.

I walked into the room and looked around. It looked much the same except for the addition of wall-to-wall carpeting, an extravagance in these austere times.

Outside the window I could barely see the nearest building. This was a thick fog for a summer afternoon. Fitz was sitting behind his desk. Reynolds was there sitting in another chair, her legs crossed; Black was missing. Reynolds smiled at me as I walked in. It was not a pleasant smile. Harold was also there, against the wall, also holding a tommy gun casually in his right hand, the barrel pointing down. This one didn't have the circular container underneath but was like the one the Marine had had on the ship. It seemed like an awful lot of firepower for this little meeting.

"Welcome home, Student," Fitz said.

"Thank you, Teacher," I replied.

"Where did you go?" Reynolds asked.

"You wouldn't believe me," I said with a smile.

She just looked annoyed.

"Teacher," I said, "I have the *katana*—the samurai talisman; and I have killed Morgan."

Fitz smiled at the news. Reynolds didn't react.

"Very good, student," Fitz said. "May I have it?"

"My name?"

Fitz turned to the warrior. "Harold?"

Harold walked to the wall and, propping the machine gun against the wainscoting, removed a painting, setting it on the floor near the gun. Behind the painting was a safe. He spent a few minutes twisting the dial; then he opened it and stepped away. The safe was little protection from an able adept, but it would slow one down. And it kept the warriors out, who might be tempted by the large amounts of cash usually kept there. Harold, of course, would be paid enough that there'd be no temptation.

Fitz stood, slowly and carefully, and walked to the safe. He pulled out the envelope with my name in it and shut the metal door. He walked back, sat down in a manner that managed to make it look hard to do, and placed the envelope on the table. I could see it was still sealed. I ran a special spell. There was a modified far-seeing spell to see the contents of an envelope. The spell I ran determined if anyone had used any meta on the paper. It was clean. And I was pretty sure I wouldn't be alive if Fitz or Reynolds knew my name.

Harold had meantime spun the tumbler on the safe, replaced the painting, and resumed his usual post against the wall holding the tommy gun.

I placed the talisman on the desk. Both Fitz's and Reynolds' eyes lit up at the sight of it.

"Where's Black?" I asked, attempting to break its hold on them.

"He'll be here soon," Fitz said. He pushed the envelope toward me. "Take it," he said.

I picked up the envelope and it burst into flames.

Fitz and Reynolds were looking at the *katana* talisman as if neither one was ready to pick it up. I wondered what deal they'd made. Or what she had talked him into.

"Teacher," I said in a rather loud voice.

"Yes," Fitz said, barely looking up.

"Do you recall the matter we spoke of? Morgan's accomplice who told the Nazis I had that talisman?"

He looked up at that. "Yes." I had his full attention.

I removed the locket from my vest pocket and dangled it in front of his eyes. He stared at it for a moment. Reynolds looked perplexed.

"What is this?" Fitz said, squinting at it.

"Sorry I'm late," Black said, coming into the room. His overcoat was damp and the remaining hairs on his head were pasted down to his skull. "Couldn't get a taxi in this weather."

Reynolds took the opportunity of the distraction to grab the locket from my hand. "Let me see that," she said.

"I think Fitz should look at it," I said. Even though it was metal, I was sure she could destroy it. Even as she held it, she might have been heating it up enough to burn the picture in the locket.

"I found that on Morgan," I said, not bothering with the complete story. "I believe it holds the picture of her accomplice. And lover."

"How do you know?" Reynolds demanded.

I was holding out my hand, indicating I'd like the locket back. She ignored it and pretended to examine the locket in minute detail. She did not open it.

"What is that?" Black said.

"It's a locket," I explained. "It has a picture of Morgan's accomplice in it."

"You think it does," Reynolds said.

"I have other reasons to believe that. Now, may I have the locket back?"

Reynolds looked at it a moment, then handed it back. It didn't feel warm. I opened it. The picture inside was fine. I looked at Reynolds; it would have been so easy. I wondered why she hadn't destroyed it.

"Teacher," I said, handing the open locket to Fitz, "the person pictured in here was, I believe, Morgan's lover."

"I thought you were Morgan's lover," Reynolds said.

"Apparently," I replied, "she had round heels." I almost kept the hurt out of my voice.

Fitz looked at the picture, then at Reynolds, then at me. "This proves nothing."

"Except Brunhild, the head of the Valkyrie, identified the person in that picture as the adept who killed a member of her guild to take the *katana* talisman. That talisman ended up in the hands of Nazi spies. Luckily, the American government stopped the spy before he could escape with it. They gave it to us and someone, someone in this room, told the Nazis that we—actually, that I—had it."

Fitz looked at the locket carefully. Then he turned to Reynolds.

She must have been building up the spell as I was talking. The airbolt hit Fitz in the chest and knocked him off his chair. He slammed into the wall and crumpled to the floor. From the angle of his neck, it was obvious he was dead.

I scrambled for the *katana* talisman, still on the desk. But Reynolds beat me to it, scooping it up and then stumbling backward on her high heels.

Sounding like a rain of exploding steel onto sheet metal, the machine gun fired and a line of red stains appeared on Reynolds' white blouse as she was knocked backward against the wall. Most people would have crumbled under the assault; she stood straighter and pointed at Harold, and he dropped the tommy gun and curled up in a ball.

I'd seen that spell only once before, but I still recognized it. I didn't want to watch.

Reynolds touched herself and the stains stopped growing. Black and I attacked her simultaneously. Fire made a bright orange rainbow across the room and hit her full on the chest. It had no effect; her protection spell was strong, helped, no doubt, by using the *katana* talisman.

The warrior from the hall burst in at that moment and pointed his weapon at Black and me. "Stop!" he yelled.

"Shoot them, fool," Reynolds screamed.

Harold squawked, a sound to shatter small trees it seemed, and came across the room, his talons cutting the carpet. He was a six-foot black bird with large eyes and obsidian talons and a yellow hooked beak. Reynolds had turned him into a rukhkh. It would have been more merciful to kill him. Harold jumped, talons out as he sailed through the air.

"NOOOO!" Reynolds wailed and pointed at Harold/rukhkh.

But it was too late; Harold landed on the other warrior. Blood sprayed from the poor guy's chest and the talons cut deep. Harold's huge wings beat rapidly as he carved the warrior's flesh, filling the room with a tornado of black feathers.

I stopped watching. Harold must have thought the other warrior was threatening his mistress. How he missed Black's and my attacks I don't know. Perhaps in what was left of his mind, a gun was more of a threat than anything else.

Reynolds' plan became clear. She tore off her skirt, leaving her in girdle, stockings, and high heels only from the waist down. She put her hands against the outer wall and it fell away. Her blouse was darkening as her protection spell weakened.

Harold dropped the string of bowels in his beak, squawked even louder, ran across the room shredding more carpet, and jumped out the opening. Just then Reynolds' blouse caught fire and she jumped out the gaping hole herself. A few moments later, with Reynolds straddling his back and her blouse simply missing, Harold flew down the street, quickly being obscured by the fog.

I said a very bad oath in the ancient language. "I need a rukhkh!" I called out needlessly. And the warrior, who was dead in a very large puddle of blood, was the last lesser I could use.

"No," Black said, "you don't."

"What do you mean?" I asked, looking at him. Was this a trick?

He bent down and started pulling up the ripped carpet. "Look in Harold's clothes; he might have had a knife," Black said.

Harold's suit was a pile of shredded cloth where he'd been transmogrified. I dug through them and pulled out a pocketknife. "Here." I tossed it to Black.

He caught the knife, opened it, and started cutting. "Get Fitz's talisman; you'll need a strong one. I saw what the samurai talisman can do."

I went to Fitz's body and pulled a pebble out of his pocket. It had scratches in it that looked as if they'd been made five minutes ago. But by the spelling and grammar I could tell it had been written before or just after Atlantis sank. It was very powerful. Almost a match for the *katana*.

By then Black had a large enough piece of carpet cut for me to sit on. He even elevated it off the floor. I jumped on it.

"I thought it was you," I said, sitting on the ripped and bloody floating carpet. "I'm sorry."

Black pointed out the hole in the wall: "Get her!"

I flew the carpet out the hole and went in the general direction Reynolds had gone. But I realized that was foolish. I decided I had only one hope of finding her. I went up and broke through the fog.

The sky above the fog was crystal clear blue, and the fog was an intense white; the brilliance dazzled me. I surveyed the white horizon. It almost looked like a flat snowy plain from my childhood home. North, I could see the orange tops of the towers on the Golden Gate Bridge. The Bay Bridge towers were nubbins in the distance to the east. The Russ Building and the Pacific Telephone Building were just poking out of the fog, the mist swirling around their tops. To the south were Mount Sutro, Mount Davidson, and the hill for Buena Vista Park. I didn't know whether it had a name.

I had expected to see Reynolds as a speck in the distance, fleeing for her life. But I didn't see her at all, meaning she was still under the fog bank. I moved slowly in the last direction I had seen her go. I could see the tops of buildings under the fog, but not the street.

Off to my right, not very far away, I saw the fog flowing over an obstacle. I thought it was a building just under the surface, but the object moved. I came in closer and, just as I could tell it was a rukhkh perched on a building, I jerked the carpet away as Harold and Reynolds shot out of the fog. While trying to avoid the bird's talons and beak, I also managed to miss Reynolds' lightning bolt.

I swung the carpet around in time to see Reynolds duck into the fog again. I chased her, diving into the cold mist. I could still see her. She looked over her shoulder and sprayed fire at me that seemed to sizzle as it cut through the fog. I swerved the carpet to miss it and heard small explosions behind me as the fire hit buildings.

The advantage I had over Reynolds was that the carpet didn't get tired, as the rukhkh eventually would. However, as I tired, I wouldn't be able to keep the carpet going. So the more spells I shot at her, the faster I'd lose my ability to chase her. However, she could spell so much she'd pass out, and Harold would keep flying until he tuckered out.

I had to decide how I was going to fight her.

Reynolds was cutting around buildings, trying to lose me. I saw people on the street pointing up at us as we flew overhead. I decided Reynolds must be uncomfortably cold with her shoulders and arms bare, and legs protected only by thin silk stockings.

Reynolds ducked around the Russ Building. I followed, going too fast. Harold was hovering there and facing me. His talons cut painfully into my chest and knocked me off the carpet. I hung for a long, agonizing moment from those claws. Then, as my flesh ripped, I fell, watching my blood drip from the black hooks after me.

I tried to work a protection spell fast, before I hit whatever was below me. I'd been told it doesn't work, but it was the only thing I had left.

Something grabbed me, slowed me down, and stopped me, just a few feet above the sidewalk.

It was Black on another piece of carpet. "Got you!" he said. He lowered me to the ground. Lessers watched with wide eyes as I landed on the concrete. I touched myself and healed, but my shirt was covered in blood.

My carpet was fluttering to the surface. I chased it down and climbed on it, floating up to where Black was waiting.

"Where's Reynolds?" I yelled across the gap between us.

"Don't know."

"I'll go above the fog," I said. "You look up and down the streets."

"What do I do if I see her?"

I shrugged my shoulders. "Hell, I don't know, send up a flare," I yelled and sped away above the fog. The day was still bright, and I searched for movement that might be Reynolds and her rukhkh. I turned around in circles, looking in all directions. I didn't see her. About the third time around I saw balls of fire shooting up like, well, a flare. I flew toward them, dropping below the fog as I approached. Reynolds was diving down a canyon between buildings with Black behind her. Reynolds shot a lightning bolt at him that missed but hit a building, knocking off part of its brick outer wall. The debris crashed to the ground, nearly hitting a pedestrian.

The rukhkh was getting tired, I thought, as Black was gaining on her. I looked around. This was my city. I knew the shortcuts. I went right, found Market Street, and raced down it, then cut left at Bush. I was right in front of her.

Seeing me and panicking, Reynolds tried to go left, but a building blocked her. She smashed into the façade in a cloud of black feathers and rukhkh shrieks. Somehow she managed to stay on the great bird's back as it tumbled down the wall, then twisted itself around, spread its wings, and flew off again, although slower and, it seemed, with just a slight stiffness in its left wing.

I gave chase and Black was beside me, to my left. I could see Reynolds' bare back had a large red scrape on the left shoulder. She didn't bother to heal it.

The rukhkh was definitely going slower. Black and I caught up to it, but the narrow streets meant we couldn't get beside Reynolds.

And then it hit me: we were flying. I wasn't limited to two dimensions. As with the trees on the river in France, I dropped down between the buildings and under the rukhkh, ignoring the hurricane its wings were blasting down. I pointed up and shot flame at the bird's belly.

When the feathers ignited, the beast jerked spasmodically and stopped flying. Its shriek shattered glass in nearby buildings. I was nearly crushed under its fall, but managed to duck out of the way. Reynolds was holding on to the bird's neck with both arms. But the beast, apparently sensing its own imminent death, gained control and landed softly. It tried to rub the fire out by scraping its belly along the pavement of the street. It didn't see the trolley and neither did Reynolds, who was simply holding on.

The trolley hit what was left of Harold with a deep yet moist basso profundo sound. The bird bounced off the front of the trolley and landed a few feet in front of it, with Reynolds managing to still cling to its neck. I landed and Black dropped his carpet near me. I ran to the bird, looking for Reynolds. She was no longer on it.

"Where's Reynolds?" Black said, catching up, pushing through the crowd that had gathered close, but not too close.

"I don't know."

Harold let out a rattling, squeaking breath and died.

"Damn, where did she go?" Black said, looking around.

"A half-dressed woman shouldn't be too hard to find," I said. "Should cause quite a ruckus."

"Glamour," Black said. "Only we'll see she's undressed."

"What the deuce!" I looked around. "She couldn't have gone far."

The attack came from above and behind. Flames hit both Black and me as Reynolds flew over us on one of our carpets. Neither of us was prepared, but Black took the brunt of it. My clothes caught on fire but I was able to extinguish the flames quickly. Black fell to the ground, burning. I put out the flames with a spell that drew water out of the foggy air by cooling it (a less powerful version of the one I had tried to use against Brooks in Arizona). But Black was unconscious and couldn't heal himself and, of course, neither could I.

I yelled to the crowd, "This man needs a doctor, now!"

I heard sirens in the distance, their wails muted by the fog, it seemed.

A man stepped forward. "I'm a doctor."

"Take care of him," I pleaded, placing my hand on his upper arm.

"Don't worry, I will."

"Thank you."

The crowd parted for me as I ran to the remaining carpet. As I approached, it started to hover about a foot off the ground. I jumped on, lying flat on it, and it bounced into the gray sky.

Again I went high, over the fog, and the bright sunshine blinded me momentarily.

But I saw Reynolds. This time she was fleeing, going east. I chased after her. Now it was a question of who had the most power to keep a flying carpet going. She had the *katana* talisman; I had Fitz's ancient one. She'd been making more attacks, but hadn't been using a carpet up until now. So we were probably fairly evenly matched. The problem was, I needed to speed up to catch her. I didn't know why it was so, but every adept with any experience with flying carpets knows that if you double your speed, your energy seems to drain at least four times as fast. I supposed I could simply follow her until fatigue forced her to land, but we might be over Iowa by then. And I might tire first.

I flew faster.

As I got closer, I got hit in the face with a piece of carpet. Then I noticed her rug was shredding in the wind, leaving a trail of fibers floating down. The fog was packed right up against the Berkeley Hills, their green tops poking out. Reynolds started going higher to pass over them. I was very close. I didn't know whether she was aware that her carpet was disintegrating. From its shape, I could tell it was the one I had been using before.

I came up behind her. She glanced over her shoulder, and seeing me so close, sped up. This only increased the tearing of the fabric.

I decided to help it. I shot an airbolt at the carpet. Not at her, but at the rug she was on. She tried to duck the shot, not realizing I was aiming at her carpet and not her. She looked relieved when the attack hit only the carpet.

But her relief turned to panic as the carpet tore itself in half. She held on, but it was no longer capable of supporting her. She turned over in the air and fell toward the hills in an arc. The carpet pieces dropped toward the ground like falling leaves. Reynolds screamed until she hit. I didn't see her hit because of the trees, but I heard it. The sound of soft flesh impacting and breaking wood was as unpleasant a sound as any other I'd heard that day.

I won't describe what her body looked like as I searched the area for the *katana* talisman. It was about twenty feet east of the body.

***

I found the dead rukhkh on the street; one could hardly miss it. Black, however, was missing. A policeman in his blue uniform was trying to make the crowd disperse as I flew in on the carpet.

"Are you responsible for this?" he demanded, his anger making him forget that he had no power over me.

"No," I said, giving him a look he probably wouldn't mistake for friendly. "There was a man here, burned."

"They took him to Saint Francis, sir," he said, suddenly remembering what I was.

"Was he alive?"

"I think so."

"Good." If the lesser doctors could keep him alive, as soon as he gained consciousness, he'd heal himself and be fine. Because he had a talisman, he wouldn't have to go through what I did eleven years ago when I was burned.

I walked through the crowd that once again moved aside like water in front of a large ship. I found a taxi and got in.

"Where to, bub?" The driver was a cute woman.

"Huntington Hotel, up California Street," I breathed, slouching in the back seat.

"Nice," she said. "Classy place."

I waved my hand in agreement. The fatigue hit as my adrenaline wore off.

California Street was full of police cars and fire trucks. The part of the building Reynolds had blown out was in the street in pieces. The taxi had to drop me a block away.

Entering suite 1313, I bumped into Lieutenant Halloran.

"You responsible for this disaster?" he asked, indicating the wall, the carpet, and the corpse of the dead warrior that his partner, O'Reilly, was searching.

"No," I said.

"What happened to him?" Halloran asked, pointing at the body.

"Rukhkh attack."

"What's that?"

"A very big black bird," I said.

"We got a report of a big black bird hit by a trolley down near Chinatown."

"Same bird," I replied.

He pointed at my torn, bloody shirt. "What the hell happened to you?"

"Long story," I said with a weariness in my voice I think let him know I wasn't going to tell him.

"Hey, Sean, look at this," O'Reilly said, holding up a strange-looking pistol with his finger in the loop of metal around the trigger. Even as covered in blood as it was, I could tell it was unlike any pistol I'd ever seen.

"I'll be damned," Halloran said.

"What?" I asked.

"A Webley-Fosbery automatic revolver, four-four-five, too, I'm betting."

"Meaning what?"

"That's very likely the gun that killed Miles Archer," Halloran said to me. "Have the lab boys check it out," he said to his partner.

I looked at the body of the warrior. I didn't know his name, but he'd obviously been working with Reynolds and, yes, probably had killed Miles for her. Reynolds must have wanted to shut Miles up because she probably was the one who had paid him to send me on the *El Cielo de las Américas* to get captured or killed by Morgan and their Nazi friends.

Halloran broke my reverie by pointing. "Who does that pile of shredded clothes over there belong to?"

"He's on the corner of California and Montgomery. A cable car hit him."

Halloran looked at me. "The rukhkh? It was human?"

I nodded. "Yes, once."

"And that skirt? Who's that belong to?"

"She's in the Berkeley hills, dead."

Halloran shook his head. "How you people live with yourselves, I'll never know."

**1946**

Louis and Black were sitting in the chairs before my desk in the repaired suite 1313 of the Huntington. I'd moved there from the Drake, somewhat reluctantly.

"Have you contacted the coolie guild?" I asked.

Louis rolled his eyes. "Those people are worse than the whites that I left the South to get away from."

"And they don't want to talk to me, either," Black said. He hadn't gone back to "Swartz," although the stigma of being German was less now that Hitler was dead and Nazi Germany was crushed and divided among the victors.

"Okay," I said, "I'll talk to Young Fat again. Maybe they'll talk to me." Given that I was the head of what was quickly becoming the most powerful guild in the world, they'd better. "Anything else?"

"My contacts back in 'Bama ain't sure they can trust you, Teacher," Louis said.

"Aren't," I corrected. His education at some separate but wholly unequal school in the deepest, darkest South didn't bother with niceties such as grammar. Plus he'd told me that at age twelve he'd "lit outta there" and gone to find a Negro adept to apprentice with up in the hills. But he was intelligent; he had to be to be an adept, and he was learning fast.

"Sorry, Teacher."

"You're learning, Student," and I smiled to let him know I thought it was fine.

"Thank you, Teacher."

There was a moment of silence. Then I spoke. "Let's not worry about the Southern Negro guilds for now."

"There's talk," Black said, "that they are getting with the Creole, the coolies, and the Indians to form their own guild to counter ours."

"Then it's even more important to bring the Chinamen into ours."

The door to the suite opened and Sam Takada came in, smiling. "Greetings, *sensei*."

"Sam," I said, standing to shake his hand. "How are talks with your guild going?"

"They are going well," Takada said. "They can see your vision of one guild for America. They are, however, not happy about losing what small power they have."

"I had an idea 'bout that, Teacher," Louis said. "We could have regional sections, with their own leadership. All under your leadership, of course. Some may even increase their power."

I smiled. "That's a good idea. We'll have to bring that up with the Southern Negroes and the Japanese. Anything else?"

Black spoke. "We received a telegram from Brunhild." The inter-guild messenger services were just starting to rebuild after the war. "She agrees to an extension of the peace treaty between our guilds and would like to meet you in Lisbon to formalize it."

I smiled. First I'd had to get used to calling Dorothy "Dagmar" and now "Brunhild." But I was glad she said "Lisbon." I was sure that was only to send me a message.

"Send a telegram back saying New York or St. Johns would be more convenient for both of us, and propose the next new moon or the one after that."

"Yes, Teacher," he said.

"Okay, you have jobs to do, let's go."

"Yes, Teacher," they both said and stood. They left me with my personal warrior, a newly returned veteran named Larsen. I walked to the window and looked out. It was a bright, sunny day. With the war over, the city was returning to normal and I could almost feel the optimism shining off the street.

It reflected my mood. The Nazis were gone and I'd had a small part in helping with that. The bitter fighting between guilds was being diminished as they joined my guild, which I'd renamed the American Meta Association. And I was going to see Dagmar in a few weeks.

Yes, it was a good time for optimism.

# Book Three
# Mjollnir
# 1950

# CHAPTER SEVENTEEN

Dagmar rolled over and draped her small, nude body around mine. I put my arm around her back and pulled her close. I didn't know what time it was—the sun had yet to set since I'd arrived.

"Awake?" she asked.

I moaned in the affirmative.

"Worried?"

"A little," I said. Actually that wasn't the truth; I was more than a little worried. There were always unknowns, and I hate surprises. But I was the second most powerful adept in the world, as far as I knew, and the most powerful was lying in my arms. I possessed the second-most-powerful talisman known—the piece of a *katana* that had been used to unite all the Japanese guilds into one—and in the six years I'd possessed it, I had felt it grow stronger as I used its power to unite the American guilds. So I was rather certain I could handle almost any surprise. Still I worried. But I didn't want to worry her.

Dagmar snuggled in closer. The bed was a bit smaller than I was used to, but it made for more skin contact, which was enjoyable.

"Trouble sleeping?" she whispered against my neck.

"I think it's the time difference." I'd flown to Oslo, Norway on American Overseas Airline rather than take a ship. The trip took just under 24 hours with stops in New York and Reykjavik, Iceland (the second time I'd ever been to Iceland and I'd seen even less this time than the first), which didn't give me much time to adjust to the ten-hour time difference from San Francisco. From Oslo I had taken Norway's national airline, *Det Norske Luftfartselskap's* "Flying Coastal Steamer," which was a huge flying boat—like the ones that used to fly out of San Francisco for the Far East before the war—that stopped at the towns along the coast, landing in fjords or bays at each one. Tromsø was the last stop; we'd arrived around 11:00 P.M. It hadn't felt like nearly midnight though, as it was still as light out as at midday and people were still walking the streets or working in their gardens. I'd even seen some children playing as Larsen drove me in my armored car to Dagmar's house from the flying boat pier.

The quick trip didn't give my circadian rhythm the chance to get coordinated with the local time. "That," I added with a smile, "and maybe the perpetual daylight. What time is it?"

Dagmar looked at the window covered with heavy curtains, which couldn't totally keep out what looked to me like late morning overcast. "Maybe seven."

I turned my head to look at the alarm clock on the nightstand and let out a long sigh. I was enjoying what I was doing at the time. Also, I knew the room would be chilly, and snuggling next to warm, soft skin was much more pleasurable than getting up. "Guess we'd better get started." According to the clock, it was indeed a little before seven.

I slipped out of the bed and Dagmar followed. I looked at her nude, petite form as she moved to pull on a robe. When I'd first met her I'd known her as Dorothy. She'd had dark hair then. Shortly after that she returned to her natural blonde state and her usual name of Dagmar. When she inherited the leadership of her guild, the Valkyrie, she changed to Brunhild, as is the tradition among the blonde female adepts. I stuck with calling her "Dagmar."

I was dressed quickly and ready when there was a knock on the small house's door.

"Sir?" Larsen's voice called through the thick wood.

"Ready," I called out. I looked at Dagmar, our eyes locking for a moment.

"Are you sure you wish to do this alone?" she asked, concern making her words soft and slow.

I looked at her; she was the one person I could trust to say this to: "I have to do it alone. To ask for help would be a sign of weakness. I'm holding together this guild by the force of my power and my reputation. Showing weakness would undermine both." And, I didn't add, if the guild falls apart, then we return to the days when America had many guilds fighting for dominance. I'd unified most of the guilds in the U.S. into the American Meta Association. Only the North American Guild—a conglomeration of guilds in the Southeast U.S., Latin America, and parts of the Caribbean—had remained independent because they, too, had merged into one guild to oppose me.

Dagmar looked at me with sadness in her eyes. "I see," she stated flatly. "You do not even trust Louis?"

"I trust Louis; it is others' reactions I cannot trust."

I reached for her, and she slid into my arms. I kissed her, but felt her worry.

"Be careful, Frank," she whispered after our lips parted.

"I will, but don't worry. I'll have no problem with this." I was hoping she'd believe it.

"Let me know where the meeting is; I'll have help close-by and ready, if you need it."

I debated telling her not to, but decided since it was her doing, it would be fine. I wouldn't use the help, anyway, unless something unexpected happened. "Okay, I'll let you know."

I pulled on my trench coat and put on my hat; then I stepped out the door. It was chilly outside, with a low gray, overcast sky that was dropping a fine misty rain on everything. The middle of July and temperatures might reach the sixties. Larsen was standing there waiting patiently in front of Dagmar's small house, water dripping from the brim of his hat. Even though he was all-American, he looked as if he could have grown up around these parts, with blond hair and blue eyes. He was tall and had the shoulders of a football player, which filled out his trench coat.

"Ready?" I asked him, looking up at him.

"Yes, sir!" he said with determination.

Nils was there, also. He was larger than Larsen, probably larger than most human males, both taller and broader of shoulders, but he shared Larsen's Nordic features. Nils was dressed in a breastplate, chain mail, gauntlets, and a steel helm. He carried a large broadax, and at his hip was a pistol in a holster. One change Dagmar had made after World War II was to require her Berserkers to carry modern weapons in addition to their traditional arms. I looked at Nils and he returned a gaze devoid of all emotion except resolve to protect his mistress. I sometimes wondered if he still didn't trust me.

"Let's go," I said to Larsen.

"Yes, sir."

We walked to the car. I'd had it shipped over from America at Larsen's insistence. It and Larsen were waiting for me in Tromsø, Larsen having come up the coast on the ferry that runs from Bergen. In fact, I'd bought the damn thing at Larsen's insistence, even though it looked to me like a hoodlum's car. It was armored under the metal skin and the windows were made of bulletproof glass. The only difference I noticed from a regular car was the windows that couldn't be rolled down and were about three inches thick.

Larsen opened the back door and I slid in, sitting on the cold leather. My warrior got into the driver's position and started it up. The engine was quiet and I barely noticed it. Larsen drove through the small town. It was on an island, part of a group of islands on Norway's western coast. We were about 450 miles north of the Arctic Circle. Until I started traveling to visit Dagmar in Valhalla, the Arctic Circle was just a line on a map or globe to me. But I had learned here in Norway that north of the Circle there will be at least one day when the sun would not set in June and one day when it would not rise in December. This far north, it was from the end of May to almost the end of July that there was what they called a "midnight sun." Dagmar confirmed that there were also nearly two months in winter when the sun did not rise. I didn't visit then. I shuddered at the thought of sixty days without sun.

The houses of the town were low and squat, with multi-colored sloped roofs and small windows. I wondered briefly how much the climate affected the architecture. Tromsø was one of the lucky cities the Nazis didn't burn as they were forced from Norway at the end of the war, so most of the houses and other buildings were very old, in some cases centuries old.

Larsen drove to the ferry terminal on the east side of the village. We'd been instructed to take the 8:00 A.M. ferry to Tromsdalen on the mainland. If the ferry hadn't been such a public place, I would have worried about being vulnerable there.

The ferry was a flat-topped boat with a small cabin on the port side. At least it would be the port side if the bow faced the direction we were facing. In all my time on ships I'd never considered where the bow was on a ferry that traveled in two directions. We ended up parked on the starboard side. I stayed in the car, but Larsen got out to look around and smoke a cigarette. As the ferry pulled away from the dock, I watched the gray water slide by and wished the clouds weren't quite so low. It would be nice to see the mountains.

A soft tapping on the glass startled me. I turned to see a young boy, about twelve, looking at me with intensely blue eyes that his blond hair was just about covering. He was talking but I couldn't hear him, and tapping hard on the glass, but I could barely hear that. I opened the door, forcing him to step back a bit.

"Kader?" he asked.

"Yes." When he looked confused I said, *"Ja."*

He said something in Norwegian—I hadn't bothered with a translation spell—and handed me a folded piece of paper.

*"Takk,"* I said.

He smiled and walked away, then turned back and said excitedly, *"Cadillac, göd!"*

*"Ja, göd!"* I answered back perfunctorily, wondering why a Norwegian boy would be excited about an American car.

The boy turned and ran off, slipping between two other vehicles and thus passing from my sight. I closed the door, unfolded the paper, and frowned as I looked at the numbers and letters. It made no sense to me.

Larsen opened the driver's door and slid in. "No sign of a tail," he said. "I don't know when they are going to contact us."

"They already have," I said, and handed him the paper. "Does that make sense to you?"

Larsen looked at it, surprised, then read it. "Yes, sir. It's latitude and longitude: degrees, minutes, seconds."

"Can you find the place?"

He pulled a large map from off the seat next to him and placed it against the steering wheel. I watched, mystified, as he followed lines on the map. He took a pen and drew a dot on the map. "There, approximately. Close enough, anyway. Probably up the road that seems to be in a valley."

"Where'd you learn to read a map like that, Larsen?"

"France, about six years ago."

"The war?"

"Yes, sir."

I thought about that. It worried me that they apparently knew that Larsen could read a map; that is, that he was a veteran. Then again, most men his age were veterans. But how many veterans could read a map and translate those numbers into a location? I didn't know.

"Larsen?"

"Yes, sir?"

"What did you do in the war?"

He looked at me in the rearview mirror, seeming surprised. I'd never expressed any interest in his history before. Adept habit: don't talk or ask about the past. "I was an artillery forward observer, sir. Used maps and lat-long coordinates all the time."

"Lat-long?"

"Sorry, sir, latitude and longitude."

"So this was a specialized skill?"

He shrugged. "Somewhat."

I stopped questioning him and watched the low clouds press up against the mountains. Maybe a back-up is a good idea, I thought.

"Hand me the map," I told Larsen.

He passed it back.

I'm no good at reading maps, but I could see where his dot was. I started a spell. It took a few moments, but I could see Dagmar's face. She looked at me with concern.

"It's a valley," I told her, "north of Kroken." I tried to pronounce it: "Movikdaelen."

"I know the place," Dagmar said.

"About a kilometer west off the main road," Larsen added.

I repeated that to Dagmar, as she wouldn't hear Larsen.

She nodded. "Yes, a swampy area." She didn't speak for a moment. "Be careful, dear."

"I will." I stopped the spell before it turned into a scene I didn't want to play out in front of Larsen, even if he would only hear one half.

The ferry docked and we headed north on the main road, which followed along the side of the sea channel that separated the mainland from Kvaløya Island. Tromsø was on an island in that channel.

We could tell it was the main road because it was wide and graveled. The drive wasn't long. There were a few houses and farms beside the road, although I wondered what could possibly grow this far north. There were wildflowers sprinkled everywhere and when the sun was shining, they were quite pretty. Today they just looked morose.

We turned off the road onto what was little more than a trail, twin dirt ruts with grass growing between them at normal spacing for a wagon or car's wheels. This part was slow; Larsen seemed to be proceeding carefully. Our destination was not hard to find. The exact spot was marked by a hatless man in a long black coat standing before a copse of pine trees that ran along the side of the road.

He was alone as required, I saw, except for a warrior standing beside him with no obvious weapons. They had apparently driven to the appointment using a roundish-shaped car I'd seen a lot of here called a "Volvo" that was parked off the side of the road.

I looked around. Across the road from the trees was a meadow with tufts of grass and the ubiquitous wildflowers. I saw standing water and thought the meadow was probably quite boggy. I saw no one else, so there were apparently no adepts near unless they were invisible. But if they were invisible they couldn't mask, and I'd sense their presence and could, with a little work, see them. Since I could neither see nor feel other adepts, I was reasonably sure the man had met the agreed conditions of being alone except for, of course, a warrior to drive the car. I smiled; this might not be as difficult as I'd feared.

The narrow valley was a bit claustrophobic, especially for one raised on the northern plains. There were mountains to the east, north, and south. To the west was open water and then Kvaløya Island with yet more mountains.

Larsen stopped the car near the other men and got out. He walked around and opened the door for me. This was more to make sure he was next to me when I exited the car than courtesy. I looked at him—his expression was grim— and turned to walk closer to the other men, knowing Larsen was right beside me without looking.

"Are you Francis Kader?" the hatless man asked.

I looked at him. His thick, dark hair, wet from the falling mist, was combed straight back, leaving a high, pale forehead over one long thick eyebrow. He had a black beard that dripped with rainwater.

"Yes, I'm Kader," I replied. My hand was in my pocket on the *katana* talisman. The touch of the cold metal was reassuring and I felt its power. I had learned to be careful when I touched it. The cutting edge was like a perpetually sharp razor. More than once I'd cut my fingers on it, requiring a little healing spell.

The man—the adept—looked at me angrily, causing his deep-set black eyes to become slits and that one eyebrow to bend into an inverted chevron. "Where's Brunhild? She was to be here to negotiate her guild's surrender to mine of the talisman known as the 'Hammer of Thor.'"

I smiled as if I found this amusing. "Brunhild does not cow that easily."

"So where is she?" he demanded. "Let her fight for her guild's honor. When I agreed to this meeting, I agreed to allow you here to ensure I dealt with the Valkyrie fairly, that is all. Not to fight for her."

"Her guild and mine are allies," I stated. "And I'm sure you know the power of my guild."

"This matter does not concern you, Kader," he spat.

"As I said," I retorted, "we are allies."

He glared at me for a long moment. His guild was powerful, and I could feel that he was, also. The Transylvanian Guild had a history, going back to

Vlad Dracul's dabbling with necromancy in the fifteenth century and his aggression against other guilds. When the Soviet Union annexed Eastern Europe after the war, the Transylvanians had moved west. But the Western European guilds didn't like having them in their territory, and there had been power struggles and outright inter-guild wars. The Hammer would give this man the power he needed to win those wars and carve out a new homeland for his guild. The Valkyrie had been terribly weakened by their conflict with Nazi Germany, so they were vulnerable. Dagmar as Brunhild had been able to ward off other, less powerful guilds' attempts to take the Hammer, the most powerful talisman known. But this guild had a chance of succeeding. And its head, the man standing in front of me, knew it.

"Do you wish to fight my guild?" he demanded.

"No," I said. "But I will to honor my guild's commitment to the Valkyrie. And I will win." It wasn't much of a bluff. I was sure I could beat him in a fair fight.

I expected the man to grow very angry. He had to know he'd lost. And not getting the Hammer probably meant he'd lose his ongoing struggles with the other European guilds and could mean the end of his guild. But he didn't get angry; instead, he became very calm.

"That's the way you want it?" he asked.

"That's the way it is," I told him.

"You know," he said, glancing at his warrior whom I'd ignored up until then, "we learned some tricks fighting the fascists."

I didn't know why he was saying that.

He again looked at his warrior and said softly, "*Acum*."

I had no idea what that meant, but I didn't have time to worry about it. The warrior put a silver whistle in his mouth and blew a short blast followed by a long one. The sound seemed to cut through the wet, heavy air.

Larsen spat, "Damn!" and reached into his coat. The other warrior did the same, and in seconds both men were pointing at each other with pistols. Neither fired.

At about that moment I started to doubt my sanity, for men who were invisible were suddenly coming out of the woods, emerging from the grasses behind us, or seeming to metamorph from small grass-covered mounds into humans. All were wearing mottled clothing, and most had vegetation in the hats they wore or fastened somehow to their jackets. And the skin on their hands and faces was painted green and brown, giving them an almost inhuman look. All had weapons that were wrapped in greenish or brown cloth. The weapons reminded me of one I had seen on a German spy ship during the war with a short barrel and body, and a grip like a pistol, and a long box underneath to hold the bullets. Even I knew that was a type of hand-held machine gun and very deadly.

I still hadn't sensed any adepts other than the Transylvanian, but these men's ability to hide seemed almost like meta.

"Camouflage," Larsen whispered angrily. "The partisans were experts at it."

"Warriors?" I asked, to make sure I hadn't lost all my senses.

"Yes," he said. "And those are German MP-40 sub machine guns."

I assumed he meant the guns. By then I'd decided there were at least thirty of the warriors, all pointing their "MP-40s" at us.

The other adept interrupted our talk. "I'm giving you thirty seconds to tell me where I can find Brunhild," he said, "before I kill you."

He didn't have to explain how. I could use a protection spell, but it wouldn't last long under the onslaught of thirty machine guns. I could teleport away, but I'd risk emerging in a solid object unless I could see where I was going, and everywhere I could see, one of his warriors stood ready to shoot me. And both those options left Larsen to die, and I wasn't going to sacrifice him.

"Teleport to the car, sir," Larsen whispered. "It'll protect you." I noticed he'd moved the aim of his pistol to the nearest man holding a machine gun.

"They'll kill you," I said back, also keeping my voice low.

"They can try," he whispered. I don't think even he believed that boast. Plus, teleporting from a standing position into a car was damn near an invitation to leave a body part inside the roof, floor, or door. If losing the body part didn't kill you, the explosion as two objects tried to occupy the same space probably would.

We must have been getting low on time. "Listen," I said. "When I touch you, run away from the car. Don't fight, just run."

"I won't leave you, sir," he protested, still whispering.

"Just do it," I commanded.

"But, sir…"

"I don't have time to run a persuasion spell on you, Larsen," I hissed. "So just follow my damn orders. Understand?"

"Yes, sir."

"When you can, go back to the car, start the engine, and wait for me."

"Yes, sir." He didn't sound very convinced that this was going to work.

I wanted to surprise the enemy, so I acted immediately. I touched Larsen, and he went invisible from my spell. Simultaneously, I teleported. I went straight up about fifty feet.

It probably appeared to the multitude of warriors that both Larsen and I had disappeared.

"*Foc!*" the adept yelled loudly.

Most, if not all of the weapons fired at the spot where Larsen and I had been. Assuming he'd run away, he should have been unharmed, I hoped (I didn't have time to work a counter to my own invisibility spell). The sound of the guns filled the valley, crashing off the mountain walls to pound our ears.

"*Cu auto!*" the adept screamed, assuming we were running for the car.

I was falling, so I knew I only had fractions of a second to act. I shot fire at the adept. He wasn't ready for it and it knocked him to the ground, his clothes and hair on fire.

The warriors who had been shooting at the car swung their aim up toward me. I teleported to just inches above the ground, keeping my knees bent to absorb the impact, since I would fall to the surface with all the speed I'd built up falling before I teleported. I ended up in a crouch, my buttocks almost on my heels. I pointed to my right and shot fire, then swept my hand around to the left, leaving a trail of flame everywhere I pointed. I put all my power, and the power of my talisman, into that arc of flame. Trees, grass, and most importantly, warriors were on fire. The adept was standing shakily, steam rising from his burned coat. Some of his hair and beard were gone. His burned, red skin seemed to blaze in the mist. His fortitude surprised me. My attack should have killed him, I thought.

I went invisible and ran for the car. I pulled the door open and jumped in, slamming the door shut behind me. I heard gunshots and felt the impacts on the car. I was surprised to see that bulletproof glass didn't repel bullets without damage. All the car's windows contained constellations of white, shattered glass circles. But touching them on the inside, I found that the glass was smooth and undamaged.

The front passenger door opened and then closed. I peered between the pockmarks and saw the Transylvanian adept still standing, barking orders at his warriors.

"Larsen?" I asked the air.

"Yes," came his voice from the front seat as the car started. "Thank you, sir."

"Get us out of here," I yelled.

The car backed with a lurch and turned. I could see the controls moving, seemingly on their own. The car bounced forward, heading back the way we had come. A burning warrior, running blindly in what must have been excruciating pain, cut across the road in front of the car. Larsen didn't hesitate. The car hit the poor bastard, the force causing him to fly over the hood and smash into the windshield. He then bounced off, flying through the air like a flaming comet, to land beside the road.

Larsen swore loudly.

I pulled my talisman out of my pocket and started another spell. Louis' dark face appeared before mine.

"Where are you?" I asked, hoping Dagmar had told him where we were.

"Close, Teacher. What happened?"

"It was an ambush," I growled, adrenaline feeding my anger. "Meet us at the gravel road. This bastard has seen his last day on Earth."

"Yes, Teacher."

The car bounced down the dirt trail. I got the feeling Larsen was having trouble driving while invisible, unable to see his hands. Or maybe it was just that the windshield was also covered in white circles where the bullets had hit and white steam was coming out of the front. I looked out the back window but couldn't see any pursuit. I guessed I'd killed about half the warriors. Unfortunately, the adept was still alive.

The car turned sharply and stopped. The sound under the tires had gone from a hiss to a growl, and I knew we were on the gravel road. I stepped out and looked south.

Three flying carpets were hovering about five feet off the ground, Louis on the lead one, two of my adepts on others. Two Valkyrie, beautiful blonde women, were sitting bareback on white horses next to the road. Louis dropped a rolled-up carpet to the ground. Larsen, who was almost visible again, had exited the car and picked up the carpet and unrolled it. I ran the spell and it started to float about two feet off the surface.

"Wait here for me," I told Larsen. "And don't let that adept's car leave."

"Yes, sir." He walked to the back of the car, opened the damaged trunk, and pulled out a large weapon I'd heard him call a "B.A.R." I had no idea why.

I looked at my car. I hadn't had time before to see the damage. Almost all the metal had bullet holes in it, and the front was hissing and venting off steam. But it had just saved my life. I developed an appreciation at that moment for having an armored car.

"Let's go," I said, and my carpet bounced into gray sky. "You take care of his warriors. I'm going to kill the adept." I knew I could handle the Transylvanian alone, but he'd ambushed me. Thirty warriors with machine guns was too much for even me. Louis and the others would know that. Asking for help was not a sign of weakness when one's opponent cheated.

The other adepts followed, Louis and mine on carpets, the Valkyrie on their horses, which rose into the sky before the Valkyrie turned them to follow the carpets. I glanced back to see Larsen taking his weapon behind the car, using it for protection, and watching up the valley. I was sure he'd let nothing get by him.

The six of us flew up that valley. Not far from the main road, the glow from burning trees and vegetation guided us to our target. The Valkyrie swung wide in opposite directions and sped up, the horses' hooves a blur in the air. Apparently they were going to swing around and come in from the east. I went high and Louis went low, about treetop level. The other two stayed maybe fifty feet up, but also separated from each other. Bunched up, we would make too juicy a target.

The scene of carnage was worse. There were burning and smoldering bodies lying about. Other warriors were looking around, seeming dazed by the sudden violence they'd witnessed. The adept was leaning against his car.

Louis shot flame at a clump of warriors. They screamed as they went up in flames. Some ran away in a panic, while others dropped to the ground and rolled, which seemed to smother the flames.

The adept looked up and saw us. I could see him holding his talisman in both hands, I assumed for a healing spell. But he pointed at the burning trees instead. I wondered why, but had other things to worry about.

Louis and my other adepts shot airbolts or lightning at lone warriors, picking them off one by one. But this was slow and there were still standing, healthy warriors who fired at us. I started to come lower to join the fight when one of the adepts slipped from his carpet and fell to the ground with a loud, wet smack.

I aimed for the warrior who had shot him and he blew apart like so much mist before a fire. That's how angry I was.

Just then the Valkyrie arrived from the other direction, their blonde hair flowing behind them. They attacked the warriors with lightning and runes. Soon all the warriors were dead or dying but, in any case, no longer a threat. I turned my attention to the Transylvanian.

He was still pointing at the trees. I followed his finger.

"Oh, damn!" Louis yelled.

A tornado of flame was coming right at us, seemingly burning a hole in the damp air. We scattered. A Valkyrie turned her horse too late, and both woman and beast were sucked into the blazing vortex. Their screams lasted far too long. The tornado left their charred bodies in its wake as it moved on. I could smell charred flesh even at this height and almost vomited.

This wasn't a random weather event: the Transylvanian was directing the tornado. It headed for Louis, the next closest person. Louis turned his carpet, but I could tell he was not going to escape as the swirling flames seemed to speed up.

I swooped down, heading straight for the Transylvanian. I pointed my finger at him and fired lightning. It hit him in the chest and he was knocked back against the grille of the car. I looked over my shoulder. The tornado, no longer under control, had turned, missing Louis.

I flew past the adept, turned, and came back. He was standing up again, and the flames again pursued Louis. The remaining Valkyrie drove her horse over to Louis, yelling his name. He looked up as she reached down. He extended his arm and she grabbed it, pulling him off the carpet, which was almost immediately sucked into the flames. The faster horse pulled them both to safety.

But then the tornado turned and headed for me. I was amazed by how fast it moved, leaving a black, smoldering trail on the ground wherever it went, steam hissing where it hit the standing water of the bog or a dead body. I turned my carpet. I was in little danger then of its reaching me, but it was between the Transylvanian and me, stopping me from attacking him. I flew away from the orange funnel and tried to circle back at the same time. That was a mistake. The tornado, having to cover less distance by going straight where I was going in a circle, caught up to me. Now I was in the same situation as Louis. The heat from the tornado was almost unbearable. But I was close to the adept. I saw one chance for survival. I jumped from my carpet and teleported to where I was just above the Transylvanian. I screamed like a Berserker as I fell, landing on top of him, knocking him to the ground, and alighting on top of his chest. His eyes were aflame with anger or hate or both. I pointed my finger at him. For a moment I thought about offering him a chance to live, but then decided I wanted him dead. The lightning bolt cut through his brain and he went limp, his eyes staring at the gray sky, the black of them fading to match that color.

The tornado dissipated shortly after his death.

I found his right hand and pried open the fingers, pulling out a leather string that must have come from an ancient bow: a new talisman for my guild.

I stood up and looked down on his body. A few minutes later, I realized Louis was standing next to me.

"Are you okay, Teacher?" he asked.

I only nodded. I was feeling as if I were about to pass out.

"Henderson is dead," he said angrily.

I realized that up until that moment I hadn't known the name that he went by. "Damn," I whispered.

"And the Valkyrie," Louis added needlessly.

I nodded again. This had been more expensive than I had planned.

I looked around, surprised at how hard I was breathing. The grass was burning in places, but the forest was becoming a conflagration. I looked angrily at the warriors and the weapons. The Transylvanian had used technology to ambush me. I shook my head. My other adept and the surviving Valkyrie were pulling water from the air to douse the grass enough so that we weren't in any danger.

"Let's get the hell out of here," I said.

Louis nodded. "Yes, sir."

"Bring his body," the Valkyrie ordered, pointing at Henderson. "He will be honored by the Daughters of Thor."

# CHAPTER EIGHTEEN

We were sitting around a table made of thick wood planks. Dagmar was to my left, her right hand laid over my left as it rested on the table. Louis was to my right and Larsen across the table from me. Nils was a towering hulk in the corner. A fire in a stone hearth made the room warmer than the fifty-degree weather outside. Larsen had joked that except for the sun never setting, summer in Tromsø was not much different from summer in San Francisco.

"I need to return to Valhalla," Dagmar said softly. "We have dead to mourn and honor. In addition, apprentices need training, as do Berserkers."

I looked at her, noticing the sorrow and worry in her eyes. Hitler's soldiers and spies and, unfortunately, renegade adepts from my guild, had managed during the war to kill all their warriors, that they call Berserkers, and almost all the Valkyrie. All because of Hitler's quest for the Hammer of Thor. By VE-Day, only Dagmar and the head of the guild survived, and no Berserkers. While there are normally only a couple dozen Valkyrie and a few hundred Berserkers, for centuries this had been adequate to protect Valhalla and hold on to the Hammer.

Not long after the war, the oldest Valkyrie died of natural causes, leaving Dagmar as the head of her guild with the title Brunhild. Building a guild from almost nothing had taxed her abilities, I knew. I'd helped whenever I could. But the Hammer was a tempting target for any guild that thought they could take it by force. The Valkyrie's numbers were still low, and one had just died protecting their treasure.

"We'll leave in the morning," she said, looking at me and then Nils, who nodded his understanding. Valhalla was somewhere east of here, in the mountains between the sea and the Swedish border. I'd been there, but to me one incredibly beautiful mountain looked pretty much like the others around here. Tromsø was the nearest city and therefore was the Valkyrie's base of operations in civilization.

"Louis," I said turning to him, "I need you to get back to San Francisco and keep an eye on the affairs of the guild."

"Yes, Teacher," he replied, smiling. He'd become an invaluable member of my inner circle: the few adepts I could trust completely. His intelligence and creativity made him a good candidate to replace me. In most guilds, that would make him a threat. But I was trying, and I thought succeeding, to make the AMA different by replacing intrigue and calumny with openness and respect.

We still fought internal battles, sometimes literally, but I was hoping to forge a guild more on the model of what Atlantis was supposed to have been.

"Stop in Boston," I continued, "and see what that Houser fellow is complaining about now."

"Yes, Teacher," Louis replied again, but I could tell from his expression he didn't like Houser. I didn't either, but he commanded respect among members of the guild in the Northeast U.S. "What will you do?" Louis asked.

"I need to find what's left of the Transylvanian Guild leadership and convince them they don't want to try to seek revenge on either the AMA or the Valkyrie."

"Sounds dangerous," Larsen said, his voice tense.

I nodded. "It could be." I said it as dismissively as possible for Dagmar's sake.

Dagmar squeezed my hand, indicating it hadn't worked.

"I'd like to get the car fixed first, sir," Larsen continued.

"What will that take?"

"All the windows need replacing and most of the sheet metal. The engine's damaged, also. There's a company in Stuttgart, West Germany that can do the work, but…" He let his voice trail off.

"But what?" I asked.

"North Korea invaded South Korea about three weeks ago. Some think that might be a prelude to an attack on West Germany by East Germany and the Russians. I wouldn't want the car caught behind communist lines."

I nodded. "I agree." I had a sudden affection for that machine, a novel emotion for me.

"I'll arrange to have it sent home, then, sir," Larsen said.

"Fine," I replied. "We're going to England."

"England?" Louis asked.

"Yes, London. That's where the communications from the Transylvanian originated. Larsen, make the arrangements. I want to leave tomorrow." Because Larsen would be going with me, it would have to be by mundane transportation methods: that is, airplane or ship. I could take him and all our luggage on a carpet, but it would be a very unpleasant and tiring trip. Plus, I wasn't in that much of a hurry.

"Steamer or flying boat to Oslo?" he asked.

I thought a minute. The scenery from the flying boat had been wonderful, and I wondered what it would look like from the surface. And, as I said, I wasn't in a hurry. "Steamer."

"Fly to London from Oslo or sail from Bergen, sir?"

"Might as well fly." I was getting more used to those lesser contraptions, and more trusting of them. That, too, was new for me.

"Yes, sir."

"Then that's it," I stated.

"Sir," Larsen said, "I need to speak with you in private."

"Sure," I said, looking at Dagmar. "Let's go into the bedroom."

Larsen followed me in and I shut the door. "We have no secrets from the Valkyrie," I said, knowing that wasn't completely true, but Larsen wouldn't know that.

"I understand, sir. I just wanted to give you this." He handed me a silver-colored metal cylinder about six inches long with ribs about three quarters of the way up one end. That same end had a rounded protrusion.

"What is it?" I asked.

"The barrel of the pistol the Transylvanian's warrior used. You killed him; it's your trophy."

"I killed him?" I asked. I wasn't sure; I'd sprayed flames rather indiscriminately.

"Yes, I saw your fire hit him."

"A new talisman," I whispered, looking at the object. Peering down the middle, I could see spiral grooves.

"Yes," Larsen said. "We have more, us and the Valkyrie: parts of the guns of the warriors killed in that battle."

"Good," I mumbled, not paying attention. I wrapped my fist around the barrel and could feel its new, emergent power. Talismans have power because of their origins. They gain power as they age and as they are used. "Thank you."

"You're welcome, sir."

***

"Daughters of Thor?" Dagmar asked.

"Yes." I was threading my fingers through her long hair, smiling at her in the dim light. Heavy curtains kept the room almost dark.

"She shouldn't have said that in front of you."

"I'll pretend I didn't hear it," I said softly. This didn't surprise me, as most guilds have secrets. The Valkyrie have that making-horses-fly bit. The Transylvanians apparently can work with weather or fire, or both. Flying carpets and rukhkh originated in Arabian guilds, but most guilds knew those secrets. European guilds tended to use broomsticks but if you'd ever tried to sit on a broomstick for a few hours, you'd know why carpets are much more popular. The Arabians had managed to keep secret the ability to control jinni. The AMA, being an agglomeration of many smaller guilds, didn't have many secrets. We were one of the few guilds able to use invisibility, however.

I didn't ask any more about the phrase "Daughters of Thor." I was curious, of course, but Dagmar had identified it as a secret. I used my other hand on the small of her back to press her body against mine.

We were quiet for a long time, our skin doing most of the communicating. Then she said, "Thank you, Frank."

I nodded and kissed her.

***

195

The car was one of those local Volvo things. Larsen looked at it with disdain. The driver/Berserker almost looked hurt.

"It's a short ride to the quay," I said, trying to make Larsen feel better. Larsen had actually decided to take the ferry back down the coast because it left sooner than a steamer.

We boarded the ferry, without the car, and traveled south, stopping at about a dozen towns along the way to pick up passengers and mail. Not long after we'd left Tromsø the sun actually set, although it didn't get dark but more like dusk. By the time we got to Bergen at about 10:00 P.M. the sun was setting, but was rising at 3:00 A.M.; I learned this by accidentally leaving the curtains open in my stateroom and being wakened by the rising sun. I was glad I'd chosen this route; the scenery was wondrous as the ship passed through fjords and narrow inner channels marked by granite cliffs, snow-capped mountains, waterfalls, and grassy hills. We had a view of Torghatten Mountain, which has a hole that runs through it caused either by erosion or by a knight shooting an arrow through a troll's hat, depending on whom you ask. The land felt young and wild here, and I drank in the power from the deck of the ferry.

In Bergen, Larsen and I took a taxi to Fornebu Airport outside Oslo and there caught a Scandinavian Airlines System—which was starting to go by the initials SAS—flight to London's Heathrow. The airplane was, to my astonishment, a version of the craft the U.S. Navy had used to fly me from Moffett Field to San Diego during the war. This one, like that military version, was tilted while on the ground and one had to walk uphill from the door to one's seat. There was a rail in the aisle between the wings that one was required to step over. Larsen knew that it was called a "DC-3" and informed me it was a "tail dragger."

I'd expected London to still be recovering from the war, as was Norway and, I supposed, most of Europe, but was still surprised when the passenger facilities at the airport were temporary canvas tent-like things. Permanent facilities at Heathrow were still in the process of being built. There was not one finished building at the airport, as far as I could see.

Getting through customs was easy with a few persuasion spells to ease transfer. The inspector didn't even notice the weapons in Larsen's case. Stepping outside we saw there were three black taxis waiting under a clear blue sky.

"Rained most the time I was in England," Larsen said.

"When was that?" I asked.

"Before D-Day."

Before I could ask another question, I realized an adept was near. I felt him before I saw him, naturally. "Kader?" a male voice sounded from my right.

I turned to see a familiar face. "Drake."

He was standing in a black suit and bowler, smiling at me. Next to him was a larger man also in a suit but hatless. Drake was the leader of the Round Table, the oldest and largest guild in Britain. They claimed Merlin had founded it and no one had yet disproved the assertion.

"May I give you a lift?" Drake asked, looking at me with his gray eyes.

"We hadn't decided where we are going," I answered truthfully.

"I could probably recommend a very nice hotel," Drake said, continuing to smile.

"That would be nice," I replied. "Where's your car?"

"Not far."

And it wasn't. Even I recognized a Rolls Royce. The car looked brand new, yet was styled like something built in the thirties. Drake's man opened the back right door for him and then ran around and did the same for me with the left, curbside door. I noticed then that the glass looked about three inches thick. The car, like my Cadillac, was armored. Getting in and sitting on the very comfortable leather seat, I started to wonder whether adepts were going to be replaced by technology; something I'd heard called "obsolescence." Becoming an adept takes years of training in addition to talent, ambition, intelligence, and determination. And with that you can manipulate humans and animals, bend some of the forces of nature to your will, and protect and heal yourself. To kill an adept use to require another adept or a heavily trained warrior. Such training also took years, and their weapons were very expensive. Swords were one-off items that could be made only by skilled craftsmen. Archers could kill at a distance but the training needed was no less arduous, and good bows were as expensive and rare as swords. Arrows were hand-made one at a time and often were damaged upon use.

But with technology, a fifty-dollar gun firing ten-cent bullets could kill at a hundred yards or more, by a man with only a few months' training. Hitler had overwhelmed the Valkyrie with numbers—thousands of men—and technology—aircraft dropping bombs. Hitler had thousands of men to throw at the two-dozen most powerful adepts because of how cheaply he could train and arm them. Two hundred years ago, or even just one hundred, such an attack would have been unthinkable. Until what was called "mass production" had made killing cheap, it wasn't worthwhile trying to attack a guild. I was afraid Hitler's attempt would be only the first.

The Transylvanian had had his thirty warriors for the same reason: cheap, powerful weapons that were easy to master.

So we had to fight back with technology. We used cars, and airplanes and ships, rather than carpets or brooms or rukhkh. We armored our cars. We used telephones or telegraphs rather than far-seeing spells. We armed our warriors with machine guns and pistols. In a race between technology and meta, I was afraid technology might be winning.

While I was ruminating, the warrior had again gone to the right side of the car and had gotten behind the wheel. Larsen opened the front left door and sat next to Drake's warrior. I watched as Larsen and the driver looked at each other, apparently sizing each other up. The Englishman was bigger, but Larsen wasn't driving. I relaxed, some. If Drake wanted to threaten me, he wouldn't have his warrior occupied with driving.

The car started and moved away from the curb with a silkiness I'd never experienced in a motor vehicle before. But I was distracted as it seemed the driver was suicidally trying to drive in the left lane. I was about to protest when I noticed all the other cars were driving in the same direction; of course, in England they drive on the left side of the road. It's amazing how one assumes certain things in the world and when those assumptions are violated, the effect is shocking.

"So," I said, recovered from my scare, "do you have sources in my guild, or are you having me followed?"

Drake looked ahead as if he were watching traffic. "The latter is more correct than the former."

The way he said it, I doubted I'd get more information out of him.

"Why are you here?" he asked.

I thought about saying "guild business" but that was insultingly obvious. I decided to be honest with him. "I'm here to visit the Transylvanian Guild."

"Oh?" he commented knowingly.

"I was wondering," I asked casually, "why you allow them in England?"

"Until very recently, they were too strong for my guild to be assured victory."

"Recently?"

"Yes, Nikolai's death has weakened them substantially."

"Nikolai? Was that the name he used?" I wondered if he'd been watching the Transylvanian and that was how he had known about my movements.

"Yes," Drake said matter-of-factly.

"Why don't you form an alliance with the Scots and the Welsh guilds to eliminate the Transylvanians, or at least get them out of Britain?"

"Not as simple as all that," Drake replied, finally turning to look at me. "There are hatreds going back centuries. Plus, I think they hoped that a conflict between us and the Transylvanians would weaken both of us to the point that one of them could become the dominant guild in Britain."

Guild politics, I thought ruefully. There was a time, supposedly, when it was said adepts lived in peace, at least among themselves. There was the outside threat of barbarians, but no fighting between adepts and therefore, no need for guilds.

"But now," I said, "you can handle the Transylvanians?"

"Yes," Drake said, "and we should still be strong enough to survive a challenge from the Scots or the Welsh."

I wondered what would happen if the Scots and the Welsh teamed up to attack him.

"There is talk," Drake said, "among the European guilds that they should merge to form one guild to counter the power of the AMA."

I laughed. "If you can't make an alliance with the Welsh and the Scots, how do you expect to merge with the French or the Germans?" Hatreds there only went back five years and had heightened when it was learned that some of the Germanic guilds had backed Hitler.

"I know," Drake said, sounding discouraged. "It's not likely."

"Where are we going?" I asked.

"The Great Western Hotel."

He offered no more information, so I looked out the car's window. When I'd been there in '43 the Nazi bombing had mostly stopped, but there were still bombed-out sections. Other than a lot of construction going on, there wasn't much evidence that there had been a major war only five years previously.

The car stopped along the left-hand curb, which again startled me before I stopped to think about it, and Drake pointed to a large, luxurious-looking hotel across the street. It looked only about six stories tall, but seemed to occupy an entire block. "That's where they are staying— booked one wing of the fifth floor." Which would be what Americans call the sixth floor, I remembered.

"Where are they getting their money?" I asked.

Drake shrugged. "Haven't the foggiest. Nazi gold, for all I know."

I couldn't suppress a chuckle and Drake smiled at his own joke, "Nazi gold" having taken on a mythology all its own since the end of the war.

"Thanks for the ride," I said. "Do you happen to know the name of Nikolai's lieutenant?"

"Anica. She uses no last name that I know of."

"A woman?" I asked stupidly.

"Yes."

It wasn't unusual for a woman to be a leader in a guild; it just seemed more common in Western guilds than in Eastern and Eastern European guilds.

"It would help," Drake was saying, "if you killed her."

"I won't, unless it's unavoidable," I said, opening the door and stepping out.

He didn't look disappointed or surprised. "I understand." My business wasn't his business.

Larsen got out of the car and stood on the sidewalk waiting for me.

"I would," Drake continued before I shut the door, "suggest being out of there in less than an hour." He gave me a grim smile.

"I understand," it was my turn to say, and I shut the heavy door.

"Nice car," Larsen said. "Did you notice…?"

"Yes," I cut him off. I had once—hell, often—questioned the need for an armored car.

I looked left, didn't see any cars coming, and started to cross the street. Larsen grabbed my arm and pulled me back just as a truck coming from the right nearly flattened me.

"Damn," I breathed.

"Look right, not left," Larsen explained. "Don't worry, sir, I nearly got run over a few times during the war before I figured it out."

My previous visit had been too short and spent mostly on American air bases.

We crossed the street without incident and entered the large hotel. The lobby was ornate, with a railroad theme. Not railroads such as in America with steam locomotives and train robbers and Indians, but English railroads with comfortable coaches and fast electric trains.

I saw the two men from across the lobby, sitting in chairs watching the entrance. One was an adept and the other a warrior: the same arrangement I used in the lobby of the Huntington back home. The adept looked at me with knowing eyes. The warrior, following his gaze, looked at both Larsen and me.

I walked over and stopped in front of the adept as he stood. The warrior also stood, and he and Larsen had locked eyes.

"I need to see Anica," I said to the adept in the ancient language.

"And who are you?" he demanded in thickly accented English.

"I call myself Francis Kader."

There was a flicker of recognition and fear in his eyes, but he stood his ground. "Your warrior stays here."

I smiled in a manner I didn't think he would mistake for friendly. "You don't want to argue with me," I said simply.

"No weapons," the warrior growled.

Larsen snorted contemptuously.

"Where can I find her?" I asked the adept.

"No weapons," he repeated like an automaton.

I glared at him. "Do you want to have this out here, now? You do know who I am."

He looked at me, then said softly, "Fifth floor, room 513."

"Thank you," I replied, keeping all sincerity out of my voice. I turned my back on him and walked to the elevator.

"He's going to the house phone," Larsen reported, looking over his shoulder.

"Fine," I said. I expected that.

The elevator operator was also an adept, a young male who, apparently sensing my power, didn't ask questions when I said, "Fifth floor."

The door opened to two more warriors openly holding weapons like those in the field in Norway.

"Your warrior must leave his weapons here," the larger of the two said.

I looked at the operator, who seemed to try to shrink into a corner of the car, and then back at the warriors. "No."

The warriors looked frustrated for a moment, but realized I'd just called their bluff. They stepped back, allowing Larsen and me into the hall.

"Where?" I asked one.

He pointed down the hall.

"Thank you," I said dismissively.

Larsen and I walked abreast toward the door. The two warriors followed and Larsen chuckled.

"It seems your reputation precedes you."

"Yes," I said. My hand was on the piece of samurai sword that is my talisman. I wasn't worried about the warriors. They could, I supposed, shoot me in the back and bring the entire wrath of the AMA down on this guild. But Anica, apparently the second-most-powerful adept in a reasonably powerful guild, was an unknown. Nikolai had been more powerful than I'd expected, so I wouldn't make any assumptions about her. It might have been smarter to bring Louis with me. But if word got out in my guild that I'd needed help, it would undermine my authority. And if that happened, the result could be a bloody intra-guild war.

As we approached the door it opened, held by yet another warrior. I stepped into the room and Larsen followed. Two men were sitting in chairs. They were both adepts. But standing, facing me, was a beautiful, young, female adept. She had long dark hair and black eyes so deeply expressive I felt I could fall into them. Her lips were full and painted a stylish red. She was tall, yet curvy with long legs. Her dress was tight yet demure, and her high heels clicked on the hardwood floor as she took a few steps toward me.

"Are you Kader?" she asked in the ancient language.

"Yes," I replied. "Anica?" She must have been; I could feel her power. It was a great deal for anyone so young.

"Yes," she said softly. "Where is Nikolai?"

"Dead. I killed him."

The pain that crossed her visage told me a great deal about their relationship. The two other adepts looked angry. One, the older with gray in his hair and beard, swore in the ancient tongue.

"Why are you here?" she finally asked, grief laced through her voice.

"Simply this," I replied matter-of-factly. "My guild has no quarrel with yours. I killed Nikolai in fair combat. He called for the battle when he attacked my guild's ally, the Valkyrie. I will not seek vengeance with you or your guild for the death of my adept that Nikolai killed." Well, his warrior, but that wasn't an important distinction. "If you wish your guild to survive, I strongly suggest you do not seek vengeance for Nikolai's death with me, my guild, or the Valkyrie."

She didn't reply for a while, simply looking at me with her eyes shiny with tears. "I told him the Hammer of Thor was a fool's quest," she finally whispered.

"And it got him killed," I concluded for her.

She blinked back her tears and looked directly at me. "Neither I, nor any member of my guild, will seek vengeance for the death of Nikolai."

"What?" the older, male adept exclaimed, standing and pointing at me. "He killed the leader of this guild. That is an act of aggression we cannot allow to stand."

She turned on him, throwing her words at the man in such a way it seemed to drive him back into his chair. "What would you have me do? Attack this man and have the most powerful guild in the world hound us to the ends of the Earth?"

I was impressed by her power. I was glad I didn't have to fight her. Nikolai must have trained her well.

"I will offer you this," I interrupted, "in way of a peace offering."

She turned sharply to look at me. "What is that?"

I hesitated. I wasn't sure why I was doing this. I had no loyalty to Drake, but also no reason to help her. I wondered briefly whether I was allowing a woman's looks to sway my judgment again. "The Round Table Guild is going to attack within the hour. I think you have bigger things than me to worry about."

She looked at me, stunned. "Are you sure?"

I nodded. "Yes."

The older adept looked at me as if he didn't trust me. But I was sure he could think of no reason I'd lie about such a thing.

"I have to go," I said. "Good luck."

"Thank you," she replied softly.

"You're welcome." I hoped I wouldn't regret this. Drake would be a troublesome enemy.

I turned and left. Larsen and I made our way to the street and he hailed a cab.

"Damn," I whispered as one of the ubiquitous black cars stopped in front of us.

"What?" Larsen asked.

"I told her."

We got inside. After the door closed Larsen said, "Told her what?" He wouldn't have been able to follow the conversation in the ancient language.

"That Drake is going to attack."

Larsen stared at me with wide eyes. "Why'd you do it, sir?" he asked.

"I'm a sucker for a pretty face," I said sourly, hoping that wasn't the only reason.

"Where to, governor?" the driver asked.

"I know a good place," Larsen said.

\*\*\*

The taxi took us to a small luxury hotel near the airport. I was planning to leave in the morning on the first flight back to the States. Apparently, the hotel, overlooking the Thames, had been one of Sir Christopher Wren's houses, we were informed as we booked our rooms. I'd never heard of him. I just cared that the bed was comfortable and I didn't have to share a bathroom.

As we ate dinner in a restaurant near the hotel, Larsen asked, "What now, sir?"

"I see no reason not to return to the States."

My warrior looked glum. "The car won't be back in the U.S. for weeks."

"Maybe I should have a backup," I said. "An armored car, if it's doing its job, is going to get damaged. It wouldn't hurt to have two."

Larsen perked up at that.

I felt him approach. I worried for a moment that it was Drake angry that I had warned the Transylvanians, but I turned to look and it wasn't. It was an Oriental man in a western business suit, which to my eye always was somehow jarring. He was an adept but not powerfully so.

He bowed. "*Kader sunsang nim e'shim ne ga?*"

I blinked. It took a moment to realize he was speaking Korean.

"*Nay,*" I replied, reaching into my pocket to touch my talisman. I brought up a translation spell. I felt lucky I'd remembered how to say "yes." I hadn't been in Korea since before the war, when it was a Japanese colony.

"Are you Joe Kader, Teacher?" he repeated, still in Korean.

"Yes, that's me," I replied, letting the translation spell convert it to his tongue.

"This is for you," he said, holding out a small box with both his hands. It was black, lacquered, with an intricate dragon design inlaid in different-colored woods. I noted the dragon had four toes.

I took the box with both hands and a slight bow. He bowed lower and released it.

"Thank you," I said.

"Thank you, Teacher," he replied, backing away, then finally turning.

I watched him go. He left the restaurant through the front door.

"What language was that?" Larsen asked. I noticed he had his hand under his jacket where his gun was.

"Korean," I said.

"Did he call you 'Joe'?"

"Yes," I said. I was impressed he'd picked that up listening to a foreign language. But I just continued to look at the box. I could tell from examining it that it was very old. And I could feel it, too.

"The box?" Larsen asked.

"Let's see." I pulled off the top and glanced inside. Resting on a blue velvet cloth was a blue crystal about the size of a walnut with white veins running through it.

"What is it?" Larsen asked, trying to see into the box.

"A message," I whispered, wondering who in Korea would be trying to contact me.

"A message?" Larsen asked, still trying to peer into the box. "Can you..." he didn't seem to know the proper verb.

I put the lid on. "Yes, but not here."

***

I set the box on the bed in my room. I'd sent Larsen to his own room. He didn't look happy about that. I knew he'd prefer to sit in my room watching me all night, but I knew he'd need some sleep.

I pulled out the crystal and looked at it. To the untrained eye it could be simply be a chunk of sodalite—and, in some ways, it was. I started the spell, working slowly, taking my time. This was not a form of meta I had used often.

The crystal glowed faintly, starting with blue then weaving in multiple colors as I spoke in the ancient tongue. The light grew to an almost unbearable level. I closed my eyes and held the crystal.

"Joe," she whispered.

I knew that voice, even after…my god, had it been eighteen years?

"Meyoung," I replied.

"Joe," she repeated, as if unsure.

"It's me," I tried to assure her.

"Joe," she said, more strongly. And I could see her, hair straight and black as night, seemingly with blue highlights, eyes nearly as dark, almond-shaped, yet large and expressive. She was wearing the same two-tone western dress she'd had on when I'd last seen her. I wasn't seeing her as she looked now, but as I remembered her when I had last seen her in San Francisco on the Embarcadero.

"Joe," she was saying, "I need you."

"What's wrong, Meyoung?"

"War," she replied. "I need your help."

War? I thought. The Red invasion of South Korea? Is that what she means? Korea being in the news had stirred up old memories of her, even though I didn't know for certain that she was in Korea, or even alive.

"What can I do?" I asked.

"Seoul," she replied. "Come to Seoul."

"Seoul?" I asked.

"I need you," she said. "Help me, please."

She faded away as I called her name again and again.

I put the crystal back in the box and shut the lid, and realized with surprise that tears were running down my face.

# Chapter Nineteen

"Where?" Dagmar asked, her face scrunched up with concern.

Her image floated in front of me. There was no phone service to Valhalla. "Korea," I repeated.

"Korea?" she exclaimed. "Is there a place on the Earth you could go that's farther away?"

I shrugged. "I doubt it," I said. Maybe Australia, I thought.

"Why?" she asked softly.

I hesitated. "You remember I traveled extensively in the Orient before the war?"

She nodded.

"I visited Korea. An old friend who lives there contacted me. They need my help." It was all true, if a half-truth can be called the truth.

"They asked for help?" Her voice indicated her disbelief.

"As I said, an old friend. This isn't a guild matter; it's personal."

I could tell she was debating asking, "How personal?" Instead she frowned. "Isn't there a war there?"

"Yes, I believe there is," I said lightly.

She didn't look happy but said, "Be careful, Frank."

"I will."

"I love you," she added.

I smiled and felt like a heel. "I love you, too, Dagmar."

The image faded. I picked up my suitcase, with the appropriate spell added to make it nearly weightless, and walked out of the room into the hall. Larsen was waiting, leaning against a wall and smoking a cigarette.

"Where are we going, again?" he asked, standing straight and taking my suitcase.

"Korea."

He stopped walking, forcing me to turn and look at him. "You know there's a war on? The Communist North invaded the South last month."

"I know," I grumbled. That was big enough news even I couldn't ignore it, although up until last night, it hadn't concerned me in the least.

I stepped out of the hotel and Drake was standing there with his warrior who had driven the Rolls the day before.

"Good morning, Kader," he said by way of greeting.

"Drake," I replied, surprised. "Good morning to you. To what do I owe the pleasure of seeing you again?" I slid my free hand into my pocket to wrap my fingers around the *katana* talisman.

Larsen set down our bags as if he were tired of holding them, thus freeing his hands. I knew he was keeping an eye on Drake's warrior.

Drake looked at me without a hint of mirth on his face. "I just wanted to ask you what you told the Transylvanians."

I watched Larsen out of the corner of my eye. His arms were crossed across his chest. I'd seen this before. One hand was under his jacket on the butt of a pistol. "Why?"

"When we got there," Drake explained, "they were gone, except Anica."

"Except Anica?" I asked.

"Yes. She told me her guild was leaving Britain and wouldn't come back."

I smiled. "I simply told her it might be a good idea to leave before the local guilds got tired of their presence."

"Then how," Drake asked, "did she know I was coming?"

He had me there.

"I warned her you might attack," I said slowly, watching his reaction.

If Drake was angry, he didn't show it. "Well, it probably saved an unnecessary battle," he finally said.

The four of us were quiet, although I knew Larsen was probably as tense as a mountain lion about to spring upon a rabbit, ready to act if needed.

"By the way, Kader, when are *you* leaving?"

I had the feeling he wanted me gone.

"Going to the airport now."

He gave me a smile. "That's very nice. If you ever come back to England, be sure to look me up."

"I will," I said.

And he turned and left, his warrior following.

"That was lucky," Larsen said, looking at me. I saw him relax, his shoulders and chest slumping.

"What do you mean?" I asked.

"If Anica had set up an ambush, you might have made a new enemy. As it is, I think you've made two new friends."

He was right, but I wasn't going to admit that. "Let's get a taxi."

***

"I'm sorry, sir, there are no flights to Korea." The girl was a toothsome English blonde with that English bulb of a nose, and she was very sincere in her apology. "The closest I can get you is Hong Kong." She was looking through her B.O.A.C schedule book. "With stops in Cairo and Calcutta, the trip takes just over thirty hours."

I looked at Larsen and he shrugged.

"Are there any airlines that fly from Hong Kong to Korea?" I asked.

"I wouldn't know, sir," she replied. "But I doubt there are any flights into Korea. There's a war on, you know."

"I know," I grumbled.

"I'd be glad to book you through to Hong Kong."

I was worried about being stuck there. With China having gone Communist—and making noises about reclaiming Hong Kong—and the war in Korea, I didn't know how easy it would be to travel in the Far East.

"Do you have flights to the U.S.?" I asked her.

"Yes, sir!" she answered, seeming happy to be able to help. "Daily flights to Idlewild. Seventeen hours, non-stop. It's pressurized and has a bar and a lounge." She was trying to make it sound like a nice trip, and to be honest, it did sound rather pleasant.

I knew that from New York I could get to San Francisco, and from there maybe I could find a way into Korea. At least I'd be home. "When's the next flight?"

"This afternoon, sir."

"Give me two tickets," I said, looking at Larsen, who pulled a roll of bills out of his pocket.

"Will that be a return ticket, sir?"

"No," I said emphatically.

\*\*\*

Idlewild is south of the part of New York City that's on Long Island called "Queens." I'd spent most of my life trying to escape small towns such as the one I'd grown up in in North Dakota. But even for me, New York was too huge, too dense, too populated, and too dirty. Larsen and I took a taxi to a hotel, slept, returned to Idlewild, and caught a Constellation—Larsen called it a "Connie"—back to San Francisco. If Larsen was unhappy that the armored car was en route, he didn't say anything. But he didn't seem to relax until we were ensconced in the Huntington with two of the guild's warriors outside the door.

"What now, sir?" he asked as I sat in the leather chair facing the window. When I'd had this room rebuilt I'd had plenty of windows installed so I could look over the bay. It was a sunny summer day and, as of yet, no fog had invaded the city, as it often does on summer afternoons.

"Find a way to Korea," I said.

Larsen looked disappointed, perhaps hoping I'd given up on that quest.

"How, sir?"

I shrugged my shoulders. "I'm not sure."

Larsen didn't respond

At that moment the door opened and Louis entered, looking handsome in a business suit.

"Teacher," he said as a greeting.

"Student," I replied. "What did you learn from Houser?"

Louis sat on the leather couch I had inherited from Fitzgerald. "Nothing. Claimed he had no problems, is happy as a clam."

I looked at Louis to see if he was joking. "He's up to something," I speculated.

"Yes," Louis agreed. "But what, I don't know."

"We'll have to keep an eye on him," I said.

"Yes," Louis agreed. "Any idea how?"

"Find someone in his territory loyal to us," I said.

Louis nodded. "Quietly."

"Of course." I smiled and he grinned back.

Then I had a thought. "Richards!"

"What?" Louis and Larsen asked simultaneously.

"Admiral Richards," I repeated.

"Oh," Louis said, realizing who I meant.

"Who?" Larsen asked.

"I need a phone book," I stated.

Larsen handed me the thick, heavy book. I don't know, I guess I thought under UNITED STATES GOVERNMENT NAVY, DEPT OF I'd find a listing for Admiral Richards.

I closed the book in frustration.

"Who is this?" Larsen asked.

"Admiral Richards. He was..." I hesitated, not knowing the correct term, "in charge of Treasure Island during the war—or at least he worked there."

Larsen looked at me as if trying to determine whether I was serious. "That was a long time ago. Surely he's been transferred or maybe even retired."

I was taken aback by that. I hadn't even considered it.

"Let me see what I can find out," Larsen said.

"You have connections in the Navy?" Louis asked him.

"No," Larsen said, grinning. "But if I can't con a swab into telling me..."

He didn't finish his sentence.

"What was his first name?" Larsen finally asked.

I looked at Louis and he looked at me. Finally I looked at Larsen. "I have no idea."

My warrior looked a little frustrated, but smiled. "I'll see what I can do."

"How soon?" I asked.

Larsen looked out the window. "It's Sunday, so tomorrow at the earliest, maybe Tuesday."

"Thank you," I said. It was part of Larsen's job to help me with lesser matters.

\*\*\*

"The base commander's name is Rear Admiral Boyer," Larsen was saying as he pulled one of the guild's cars—unarmored—up to the gate at Moffett Field Tuesday morning. I'd been here before and recognized the large hanger blimp.

"James Boyer," Larson continued. "Has a reputation for being a stickler for going 'by the book.'"

"What does that mean?" I asked.

"He follows the rules."

I was about to ask another question when a screaming wail came from the heavens. I looked out the car's window in time to see a white plane with orange markings streak across the sky. The strange thing was how fast it moved and that it had no propellers.

"They're testing jets here," Larsen said.

I shook my head. I barely understood how an airplane managed to fly, but a propeller made some sense, like the propeller on a boat, allowing the airplane to move. But jets were a complete mystery. Technology, I thought again. I didn't understand radio and now there's television. The last war had ended with two atomic bombs being dropped on Hiroshima and Kobe, Japan. It had come as quite a shock last year when the U.S.S.R. announced that they, too, had atomic bombs, and had exploded one to prove it. If an atomic war happened there was only one way to survive: not be where they dropped the bombs. All the armored cars, armed warriors, and meta wouldn't save you.

"We're at war," Larsen was saying. "They'll have stepped up security."

A man in a khaki uniform with a white policeman-type hat was waving at us, indicating we should pull over. Larsen stopped the car and rolled down the window.

"Can I help you, sir?" The man spoke as if he really didn't want to help at all.

"This is Mr. Francis Kader," Larsen said, jerking his thumb over his shoulder at me in the back seat. "He has an appointment with Admiral Boyer."

"Just a moment, please, sir," the man answered crisply and returned to a small building by the road.

"Marines," Larsen said under his breath exasperatedly.

The man, apparently a Marine, returned with a clipboard and said in the same crisp, clipped voice, "I'm sorry, sir, Mr. Kader is not on the list."

I pointed at him. "Admiral Boyer wishes to see me," I said.

The marine looked at me and blinked as if thinking about it. "Yes, Mr. Kader." And he gave us directions to the base headquarters before waving us through.

"Marines," Larsen said again, this time with a chuckle.

There was a naval officer—a "Lieutenant J.G."—as well as a much more formidable civilian secretary to get through before I was standing in front of Admiral Boyer's large desk. The admiral was a man with a round face and only a fringe of gray hair around his pate.

He looked up at me from his chair with squinting gray eyes. "Who the hell are you and how did you get past Mrs. Riddell?"

He was reaching for the intercom button when I said, "My name is Francis Kader and I'm the head of the American Meta Association. Perhaps you've heard of it."

Boyer stopped his hand and continued squinting at me. "You're a meta?" He had a southern accent that made him sound as if he'd walked off a farm someplace.

"Adept," I clarified. "I'm the chief adept for most of the United States."

Boyer blinked and stood up, as if to take a closer look. "That doesn't answer my question. How did you get in here?"

"I can make people believe things, such as that you desperately want to talk to me."

Boyer sat down heavily and I could see his face becoming crimson. "This is just great. We're at war and you can just waltz right in here. What if you were a commie spy?"

"Believe me," I said, sitting in one of the chairs facing the desk, "no adept is going to worry about your war and who wins it."

"Why not?" he demanded in a loud voice.

"Because we don't care," I explained patiently. I didn't add, "As long as no one does something stupid such as dropping atomic bombs on San Francisco." Sure, I didn't want to live in a communist country with the poverty and the constant bother with over-zealous government officials. But the whole world couldn't go Communist, I was sure.

The admiral looked at me as if trying to decide whether to believe me. "Then why the hell are you here?"

"I need to go to Korea."

Boyer actually smiled at that. "Did you say Korea?"

"Yes."

Boyer was chuckling. "Just to satisfy my curiosity, why do you need to go to Korea?"

"That's my business."

"What part of Korea?" Boyer asked, as if still simply curious.

"Seoul," I stated.

Boyer laughed aloud for a long time as I watched. Then he looked at me, still chuckling. "Seoul fell to the NKPA three days after the war started."

"NKPA?" I asked.

"'North Korean People's Army': The Commies."

I looked at Boyer. "During World War II I was able to get into Nazi-occupied France. Admiral Richards arranged it."

Boyer leaned forward. "Richards, that old spook? He got you into France?"

"Spook?" I asked, ignoring his question.

"Naval Intelligence," Boyer explained.

I thought about commenting that so far I hadn't seen a lot of intelligence in my dealings with the Navy. "Can you get me to Seoul?" I pressed.

Boyer shook his head. "Even if I were in the least bit inclined to help you get into Communist-held Korea, it's impossible."

"I got into France," I stated.

"That was a whole 'nother situation. We had resistance networks, operatives, signals intelligence, the whole kit and caboodle. In Korea we have zero assets in the Communist-held areas. We're falling back, hoping to hang onto Pusan. That's a port city in southeastern Korea."

"Yes, I know," I said. "I've been there."

That stopped him for a moment. He looked at me, perhaps to see if I was serious. Deciding I was, he went on. "Don't believe what you read in the papers," he continued.

"Don't worry, I don't," I said, since I rarely bothered to read them, anyway.

Boyer looked at me again as if trying to determine if I was serious. "The Army's gotten its ass handed to them by the Commies. The Koreans are almost no help; they fight bravely enough, but most of the ROK army was destroyed in the first few days after the North invaded."

"Rock army?" I asked, remembering how the military loved their jargon, although I had an interesting vision of an army throwing rocks at their enemy.

"Republic of Korea," Boyer explained with exaggerated patience. "We are shipping men and supplies into Pusan as fast as we can. It has to hold; otherwise we'll lose the entire peninsula and have to do a D-Day-type invasion on Korea's coast.

"And if we lose Korea," he said almost to himself, "then Japan holds by a thread. And if we lose Japan, we'll be right back where we were after Pearl Harbor, except this time the enemy will be the Soviets and Red China, and we can't do to them what we did to Japan and Germany; Hitler learned the folly of a land war in Asia. There'd be no way to stop them short of atomic war."

I ignored all that. "Fine," I said. "Get me to Pusan and I'll get to Seoul on my own."

Boyer chuckled again. "What makes you think I want to do such a thing, even if I could?"

I leaned forward in my chair. "I can make you want to."

"Didn't you hear me? I can't. CINCPACFLT will have my ass."

"Sink pack fleet?" I asked, annoyed again at his use of jargon.

"'Commander-in-chief Pacific Fleet,' my CO."

That explanation didn't help much.

"But," Boyer continued, "I know someone who can probably help you."

"Who?"

"Richards," he said.

"Admiral Richards?" I asked. "Where do I find him?"

"Yokosuka."

I didn't say anything for a moment, trying to think how to get to Japan.

"That's in Japan."

"I know," I said. "I've been there." Actually, I hadn't been to Yokosuka, but I knew where it was, southwest of Tokyo at the entrance to Tokyo Bay. And I had been to Tokyo. "I need to know how to contact Richards once I get there."

Boyer looked at me. "You're serious about this."

"Yes."

"Well, it's your funeral."

"Can you give me more information on how to find Richards?" I asked.

Boyer shrugged. "His first name is Riley and he'll have his fingers in something covert, believe me. He's probably bucking for a job at the CIA."

"The what?" I asked.

Boyer started to speak, but I held up my hand. "Never mind," I said. I decided I didn't really care. "Thank you," I said perfunctorily and stood and left.

"Good riddance," Boyer said after me under his breath. I decided to ignore it.

Larsen was waiting in the car parked in front of the white building. "Where now, sir?"

"Japan," I said.

Larsen didn't say anything, and I could tell he wasn't happy. But I knew I could get Richards to get me into Korea; I just needed to be within spell distance.

\*\*\*

I retired to my apartment on the thirteenth floor, down the hall from the suite where I conducted business. Larsen had a room adjoining the suite and would enter at the least sign of trouble, even for something as minor as a dropped glass. I swore he slept with one eye and one ear open.

I sat on the floor next to the bed and folded the bedspread back, revealing my personal safe. I ended the alarm spell—the secure spell I'd put on it, even on such a small space, hadn't lasted as long as my trip to Europe had taken—and dialed in the combination.

Inside I found my personal collection of talismans, mostly taken from adepts or warriors I'd defeated; a black lacquer box with a broken lid; some gold and cash; and, toward the back, so hidden I had to remove most of the contents to reach it, an envelope. I opened it gently and slipped the folded paper from it. The paper had yellowed in the nearly twenty years since she'd written the note. The ink was slightly faded as well. The creases where I had clutched it, the folds where I'd placed it in my shirt pocket in the taxi, and the singed part where flames had briefly touched it, were all still evident.

Up until five nights ago in London, I hadn't even known she was alive.

I replaced the paper in the envelope and put the envelope in my attaché case. Then I returned all the items to the safe, closed it, and spun the tumbler to lock it. Finally, I placed alarm and secure spells on it, and pulled the bedspread down over it.

"Larsen!" I called out, standing.

He entered the room a few moments later. "Yes, sir?"

I handed him my attaché case. "Put this with the luggage; then get some sleep."

"Yes, sir."

"Good night, Larsen."

"Good night, sir."

\*\*\*

From San Francisco, we flew to Honolulu in the Hawaiian Islands. It was the same kind of plane, with the double deck and the lounge downstairs, that we'd flown in from London to New York even though it was a different airline. The trip took just under nine hours. After staying overnight in a hotel next to a beautiful white beach, we left for Tokyo early in the morning on a different plane. This leg took more than thirteen hours and we arrived in the early afternoon of the next day due to having crossed the International Date Line.

In the plane's lounge, I was enjoying a vodka martini and looking over the expanse of ocean through the small window. I'd often observed the sea from the deck of a ship, but at the altitude at which the plane was flying (and I had no idea what that was) the ocean looked entirely different. Waves that could move a huge ship were ripples, and the sun seemingly reflected off half the surface. Instead of being deep blue it was almost gunmetal gray. I wondered why that was.

While I was enjoying the view, a tall American, aged about fifty I guessed, with receding dark hair and wire-frame glasses, sat next to me.

"Going to Japan?" he asked.

"Yes," I replied, hoping to sound uninterested in talking. It seemed a dumb question, since that was where the plane was headed, but I knew it was just to open a conversation.

Larsen, in a seat not far away, was carefully observing my visitor.

"First time?" the man asked.

"No," I said, "I was there before the war."

He looked at me, surprised. Then, as if to recover, he said, "I'm Edward Deming." He held out his hand.

I shook it perfunctorily. "Francis Kader."

"Businessman, Mr. Kader?" Deming asked.

"No, I'm retired." He apparently was not going to take the hint that I didn't want to talk. I started preparing a small spell to convince him to leave.

"I see," he said softly and I thought for a moment he'd given up. "Going to Japan for pleasure?"

"Yes," I stated, thinking he was about to leave.

"I'm going at the invitation of the occupation government."

I stopped preparing my spell. I might learn something from him, assuming I was going to be dealing with the occupation government.

"Really, why?" I asked.

"I've been asked to teach Japanese industry the basics of quality control, including the use of statistics in quality."

I blinked. I had no idea what he was talking about. He could have been speaking Saami for all I understood, but I didn't think a translation spell would help.

He continued without my prompting. "U.S. industry is forgetting the lessons of the war. They don't have any competition, yet. They are over-confident. They don't think anyone can compete with them, and for now, they are right. But the Japanese are building their industries from scratch after they were destroyed in the war, and they are not over-confident. They are using all the tools available to them, including the principles of quality control the U.S. developed for war industries."

I started preparing the spell again. I wasn't looking for a lecture on...whatever he was talking about.

"Give the Japanese twenty years and they will probably be competing with, and in some cases beating, major U.S. industries."

Someone sitting nearby chuckled. A man turned and looked at Deming. "You think by 1970 the Nips will be competing with U.S. industries?" he asked, not hiding his amusement.

"Yes," Deming responded forcefully.

The man laughed derisively.

I walked away without having learned anything meaningful, and not wanting to get dragged into the lessers' arguments.

I sat next to Larsen.

"What was that about?" he asked with a smile.

"I have no idea," I said truthfully.

The two men continued talking. At one point I heard Deming say, "You must drive out fear."

The other man laughed. "If my employees don't fear me, I'm doing something wrong."

"So you want them to be too afraid to ask for help before they cause you reject or rework?"

The man didn't have an answer, I observed.

\*\*\*

The airport was on what appeared to be an artificial island in Tokyo Bay, south of the city. The plane circled, approaching the airport from the north. Looking out the window, I was surprised not to recognize a thing. I'd arrived by ship the last time I was there, but still, I had expected to see more things I recognized. It seemed only the Imperial Palace was untouched by the war. The city looked as if it'd been attacked by some great monster and the rebuilding was hardly started. There were cars and buses on the streets, more than in 1932, but less than there would be in a large U.S. city.

Japan was still occupied by U.S. military forces. The airport was actually Haneda Air Force Base and we were greeted by Air Force SPs; I didn't think that stood for "Shore Patrol" as it had in the Navy. The customs official was an American MP. We were given our luggage to take through inspection. A few judicious spells got us through customs without incident. I didn't know what the occupation forces' opinion was of civilians with weapons, but neither Larson nor I wanted him to be unarmed.

In a makeshift lobby, I saw Deming being greeted by uniformed Americans and Japanese in business suits. So he truly was dealing with the occupation government. I should have hit him with a truth spell, just to shut him up, and then asked him questions.

Larsen and I stepped outside, looking for a taxi. A group of Japanese rushed up, offering to carry our bags. I got the feeling the only English they spoke was, "Carry your bags, Joe?" Larsen looked nervous, so I shooed them away.

There were American cars lined up with Japanese drivers leaning against them smoking cigarettes. Some of the cars were even yellow, looking a lot like taxis one would find in San Francisco.

Larsen picked one and approached the driver.

"Where to, Mac?" the driver asked in reasonable English, speaking around the cigarette in his mouth.

"Yokosuka U.S. Navy Base," Larsen replied.

The driver's eyes lit up, knowing he had just gotten an expensive fare.

"Don't hire him," a voice said. "He'll steal you blind."

I turned toward the voice. Admiral Richards was standing a few feet away in a khaki uniform. Standing a few steps behind him was a man in a white sailor suit, with the funny hat and the pants with the wide bottoms.

I looked at Richards. He hardly seemed to have aged since I'd last seen him during the war. The last war, I corrected myself.

"I can't believe this is a coincidence," I said, keeping my voice flat to hide my surprise.

Richards shrugged. "It isn't."

"So," I asked, "are you having me watched or do you have an informant in my operation?" Must be a warrior if he does, I decided.

"I make it my business to know who's coming to Japan," he stated. Then he smiled. "Plus, Boyer warned me."

We stood looking at each other for a long time; then he said, "Let me buy you a drink. My car's this way."

His car was an American sedan painted Navy gray. Richards and I got in the back seat; Larsen sat up front with the sailor who was also the driver. I didn't see any overt weapons on Richard's driver, so I doubted he was armed.

We drove into Tokyo. From the ground the devastation looked worse. The war had ended almost five years before and although there was a great deal of rebuilding going on, most of the buildings looked to be haphazard, temporary structures made of wood. And there was bomb damage that had yet to be fixed. The worst seemed to be in public spaces, such as parks and government buildings. Most of the people were wearing Western-style clothes. Many women wore dresses one could expect to see in San Francisco, albeit not as fancy or as stylish. The men wore suits with hats, although ivy hats, or newsboy caps I've heard them called, seemed more popular here than in the U.S. Some men wore tattered remains of their military uniforms. I wondered how desperate they had to be to wear them.

"What's this about Korea?" Richard asked, interrupting my thoughts.

I looked at him, deciding Boyer must have told him that, too. Boyer's supposed ignorance of Richards must have been a ruse. Should have hit him with a truth spell, I decided.

"I need to go to Korea," I stated flatly.

"Why?"

"My business." I left it at that.

"You realize there's a war on?" He was looking at me, I think, to gauge my reaction.

"I think it's because of the war that I need to go." Although I couldn't imagine Meyoung, or any adept, being bothered much by a war; except, of course, an atomic one.

"This war's a bad situation," Richards said, looking out the car's window. "A total screw-up from the beginning."

He turned and looked at me. "But I remember your attitude; you didn't think World War II was a big deal."

"I had changed my mind by the time the war ended."

"I'd hope so," Richard said sarcastically. "Hell, we don't know if this is the beginning of World War III. This could be a diversion from an attack on Europe by the Soviets, or for Mao attacking Taiwan. We've interrogated North Korean POWs. They said they were trained by Russians to kill Caucasians."

I didn't say anything. I hadn't thought about this being a Russia-versus-U.S. thing; I'd thought of it as more like a civil war.

"Stalin knows what he's doing," Richards went on. "Kim Il Sung was a nothing guerilla leader during the Japanese colonial period. Stalin took him to Moscow and trained him and then installed him as the leader of North Korea after the war. He's fighting with Soviet equipment, Soviet training, and Stalin's personal go-ahead, I guaran-damn-tee you. And he's attacking with a cadre of experienced Korean fighters who fought the Japanese and then the Chinese Nationalists.

"The ROK army didn't have a chance," he continued. I decided to let him continue, as I might learn something I could use in Korea. "Some incompetent in the ROK government ordered bridges over the Han River to be blown while civilian refugees were crossing them and before the ROK Army had gotten over them. Killed hundreds of civilians and trapped most of the ROKs north of the Han to be wiped out by the NKPA."

He seemed to be ranting. Maybe I was the only person he dared vent in front of.

I watched the scenery go by. Houses had been rebuilt, but were little more than ramshackle shacks. I thought about Deming's assertion that the Japanese might be beating the Americans in twenty years. If so, they had a long way to go just to catch up.

"I've read it's bad, sir," Larsen stated. I noticed his tone had a level of respectfulness I'd heard him use only with me.

Richards sighed sadly. "In the five weeks since the invasion, we've been in full retreat the entire time. We're averaging a thousand casualties a week—just the Americans. Field officers, generals even, are being killed because they have to fight on the front lines due to a terrible shortage of combat-ready troops."

Larsen had been listening intently and looked shocked at that statement.

"The ROK losses are even worse," Richards continued. "We weren't ready for this. Old Louis Johnson thought the next war would be atomic and cut ground forces as 'fat.' And those cookie pushers at State! They were so worried that the South Koreans might attack North Korea, which might make the Soviets think we weren't interested in 'peaceful coexistence,' that they kept the ROK army as small as possible. Hell, they were using our left-over World War II equipment, and not much of that."

He was turning red as he spoke. "And then Secretary of State Acheson says in public in January that South Korea is not in our 'defense parameter.'" I thought he was going to stomp on the car's floor. "Might as well invite them in." He fumed for a few more minutes in silence.

"We're learning an expensive lesson here," he finally said.

We had entered an area of booths and open markets, like a bazaar. The car had to creep along through the thick crowds of people; like tall grass, they parted as we moved through them, aided by the driver's blasts on the horn.

"What's this?" Larsen asked, looking over the crowd.

"The black market," Richards explained. "Everything's rationed, everything is in short supply. Just to survive, most of the civilians are cheating the system. A local cop told me that the only people not breaking the law are those in jail." Richards snorted, "We probably should have handled this better. A rice ration card can buy you a lot of things. And it's been a boon for the Yakuza."

The car stopped in front of a bar. A hand-painted sign read "Happi Go-Go Luck Bar."

"Here we are," Richards said.

"You're kidding," I replied.

He answered by opening the door and stepping out.

# CHAPTER TWENTY

I followed Richards out of the car and Larsen jumped out of the front looking around nervously at the crowded streets.

I glanced around but sensed no threats. Larsen and I exchanged a look of confusion, and then followed Richards into the Happi Go-Go Luck Bar. His driver stayed in the car.

Richards opened a squeaking screen door and led us inside. The place was full of Japanese and Caucasians, most of the latter in uniform. The noise level dropped for a moment, I assumed in recognition of Richard's rank. But when Richards simply walked in, the cacophony returned to its previous level.

The admiral picked out a primitive-looking table with benches and sat down. I sat opposite him and Larsen sat next to me on the end so that he could move quickly if necessary.

The place looked like everything else I'd seen in Tokyo: ramshackle, slapped together using any material available. An old woman came over, bowed and smiled, but didn't say anything—just looked at us.

Richards held up his hand with three fingers extended. "Beer," he said slowly and loudly, as if that would help her understand.

The woman bowed and said, "*Hai, biiru!*" before scurrying off.

I wondered what we'd get. My thoughts were interrupted by something soft touching my back. I turned to see a very pretty Japanese girl in a too-small Western-style dress smiling at me as her small, delicate hand brushed my shoulders. She looked to be about twelve, but I was sure—I hoped—she must be older. She looked at me in a way I couldn't mistake.

"Wave her off," Richards said. "Unless you want to," he added with a sneer.

I smiled at her and shook my head.

She frowned angrily, which made her much less pretty, and stormed away.

I turned to Richards. "Why are we here?"

"I can't get you into Korea," Richards replied.

Before I could say anything he continued, "I know you can make me want to get you into Korea, but I can't. I don't think anyone could except MacArthur. And I don't recommend you try to see him."

"Then why are we here?" I repeated, getting frustrated.

"I know someone who can get you to Korea."

"Who?"

"The Yakuza."

I looked at him to make sure he was serious. He looked to be.

"What's the Yakuza," Larsen asked.

"Organized crime," Richards, replied. "Japanese Mafia. They still have their fingers in Korea from the colonial days. I know they can get you to Pusan, maybe even Seoul."

"Admiral Richards," a new voice with a Japanese accent said.

I turned and looked at the speaker. It was a Japanese man in a flamboyant Western-style suit that was mostly white, except for his striped vest. His white fedora was set back on his head. The suit looked as if it would cost a hundred dollars in San Francisco back when it was in style before the war. I couldn't imagine what it would cost here.

"This is the man you're here to see," Richards said. He stood and spoke closely and softly to the man, but by the time I got the spell up to hear what they said, he'd stopped speaking.

"Nice to see you again," Richards said to me. "Good luck; you're going to need it."

He walked out of the bar and the new man, a Yakuza I supposed, sat down.

"I presume you have American dollars," he said by way of introduction.

\*\*\*

The train was coal powered, judging from the sharp smell of its smoke. Everything in occupied Japan seemed about twenty years out of date. Or maybe the American air corps had bombed them back to the thirties.

A payment of five hundred dollars to the Yakuza in Tokyo got us a promise that we would be helped in Fukuoka, a port city across the Korean Strait from Korea, to get a boat or ship to take us to Pusan, which at last report was still held by American and South Korean forces. But Fukuoka was about 650 miles south of Tokyo and the train seemed the easiest way to get there.

Larsen amazed me by being able to sleep in the cramped wood and cloth seat. At least it had a high back, but was not adequately padded for me. But there were no other seats available; the entire train was made up of seemingly antique passenger cars. And it was crowded and slow. It seemed the whole country was trying to go somewhere by train. We weren't the only Americans on board, as GIs and sailors were traveling also. All the Japanese were fanning themselves, seeming to do it as thoughtlessly as I breathed. I imagined it helped; the train was mercilessly hot, despite the open windows that let the coal smoke in.

I was reminded of how mountainous Japan was, as the railroad cut across Honshu to wind its way to Fukuoka. The train passed south of Mount Fuji, giving us a wonderful view. I think even Larsen was impressed, although he tried to act as if he wasn't. "I did OCS at Fort Lewis; Mount Rainier's got that beat," he said. I think he said it more out of national pride than as a matter of fact.

What did impress him was Kobe, which we passed through on the second day. He kept looking out the window and shaking his head. I, too, was impressed by the destruction one atomic bomb had created. The heart of the city was nothing more than skeletons of destroyed buildings.

Larsen turned from the window to look at me, pain evident in his eyes. "I was in Europe, after VE-Day. They told us we were going to be redeployed to the Pacific for the invasion of Japan."

He stopped to look out the window for a few minutes, and then turned back. This time he couldn't meet my eyes, but just looked ahead. "I knew I'd die in that invasion; I figured I'd used up my share of luck in Europe."

He paused, not seeming to look at anything. "Combat was bad enough and I had a lot of close calls. But just when I was starting to feel safe, a Nazi insurgent—we called them Werewolves—sniped our unit. This was after Doenitz signed Germany's surrender and we'd pretty much relaxed for the first time since D-Day. My friend's head exploded as we waited for chow. He'd been standing right next to me, talking about looking forward to the end of the war and seeing his wife again. Sure, I hit the dirt and we chased the Werewolf off…never caught them, but found their shell-casings at the bottom of a tree."

I listened; this was the first time he'd ever talked about the war.

"And I got to wondering why him and not me. I decided I'd drained my reserve of luck that day. So I knew I'd die in the invasion of Japan."

For a moment he turned to meet my eyes; then he looked away.

"The intelligence guys were saying every man, woman, and child in Japan would fight us to the end with whatever they could find. The Japanese would never surrender but would have to be driven out of their holes and killed, like on Iwo Jima. Or if they lost, they'd commit suicide like they did on Saipan. Casualty estimates were a million-plus, for each side."

He finally looked at me, his face tight with barely controlled emotion. "When we heard the Japanese had surrendered, we all broke down and cried. Men who had fought on covered in the blood of their friends were crying like children. The bombs, the atomic bombs, they stopped the war. They saved our lives. They saved a lot of lives."

I just nodded. I had nothing to say. All I thought about was whether the guilds would survive lesser technologies. If there were an atomic war, being an adept would not help you survive. I wondered whether we should start paying more attention to lesser affairs, and perhaps even taking a role.

The train sped up once we were past Kobe, and Larsen seemed his normal self again. He turned to me and started speaking in a professorial tone: "Another thing the bombs did was get Japan to surrender fast. Stalin and FDR made a deal for Russia to declare war on Japan. If there'd been an invasion, we might have a Communist-occupied North Japan and U.S.-occupied South Japan, just as we have North and South Korea and East and West Germany. And since Stalin broke his promises to Roosevelt to hold free elections in Poland and Korea, we could be sure he'd break any kind of similar promise in Japan, and this war in Korea might be happening here, instead.

"As it is, the Soviets are occupying some northern islands, but that's all."

This time I listened, thinking maybe I'd learn something important. Pretty much what I got was, "Don't trust Stalin."

***

We crossed under the Kanmon Strait between Honshu and Kyushu Islands in a railroad tunnel.

We arrived in Fukuoka in the evening on the third day, feeling dirty and tired.

As we stepped off the train onto the wooden platform, we were greeted by a young Japanese man—almost a boy, really. He was dressed like an American gangster, right down to the pinstriped suit and the fedora.

"You must be," he said with a deep bow, "honorable Mr. Kader and Mr. Larsen." He was speaking English.

"Yes," I said, bowing also, but not as deeply.

"My name Kyoji. I take you to hotel. In morning we go to the ship. You bring money?"

"Yes," I said.

"Good, you need money."

We walked to the hotel, only a few blocks from the train station. It was an attempt at a Western-style inn, but the beds were too low and the mattresses too thin. And the bathroom—shared, of course—could hardly be called that. I thought about trying to find a Japanese bathhouse, but, ironically, I felt too dirty to use one.

Larsen and I found a restaurant near the hotel. The food was very good and surprisingly included many Korean dishes. I tried to introduce Larsen to *kimchi* but he wasn't interested after I described how it was made.

The next morning Kyoji met us in the hotel's lobby. "All is arranged. I will pick you up at six tonight."

We were in front of the hotel at a quarter to. Kyoji drove up in a car: a dirty, small, black toy of a vehicle that obviously pre-dated the war. It looked like a Ford Model A that had been squished from both ends and the sides, so it was very short and narrow, but tall. It did not actually have room for three people, especially if two of them were Westerners with luggage, but we squeezed in. I felt guilty when Larsen put his suitcase in.

Kyoji ground the gears on the old car, causing it to protest in metallic groans before he got the contraption moving down the dirt road. Like the English, the Japanese drive on the left side of the road, but Kyoji didn't seem to be aware of this, driving wherever it suited him.

"How far to the ship?" Larsen asked.

"Not far," Kyoji responded, leaning over the large steering wheel. "Not far. We go to Hakata Bay. There you see ship."

From the position of the sun I could tell we were heading east, parallel to the bay. The remains of the bomb damage from the war were worse here than in Tokyo. We passed by a stone wall, about six feet high in places, crumbling in others. I could feel its antiquity and wondered what it was.

Eventually, and none too soon in terms of getting out of that car, we stopped at a wharf. I looked for the ship, but saw only small fishing vessels and junks.

"Where's the ship?" Larsen asked, echoing my thoughts.

Before Kyoji could answer, another man stepped off a dirty, ancient-looking fishing boat. He greeted Kyoji with barely concealed contempt and spoke to him in Japanese. I started a translation spell.

"Pusan is too dangerous," the man was saying, "too many American patrols. But I'll get them close." I had the feeling that wasn't entirely the truth; there was some other reason he didn't want to go to Pusan.

"That is acceptable," Kyoji said. He turned and bowed and switched to English. "This is honorable Captain Han."

"Is that the 'ship'?" I asked, pointing at Han's tub.

Kyoji bowed. "Yes, that the ship. Need money now. One thousand American dollars, please."

Larsen guffawed. "That hunk of junk?"

"Yes," Kyoji said, ignoring the insult. "You pay money, now."

Larsen started, "If you think we're going to pay—"

I cut him off. "Pay him," I said.

Larsen looked at me, surprised. "Sir?"

"Pay him," I repeated.

"Yes, sir," Larsen said incredulously. He opened his suitcase so the others couldn't see, messed around inside—I knew he was opening the hidden compartment—and pulled out ten one-hundred-dollar bills and handed them to Kyoji. The Japanese man counted them and smiled, then shoved them inside his tunic.

"This pays my debt?" Han asked Kyoji in Japanese.

Kyoji looked at him with malice in his dark eyes. "It's a start."

Han looked at him angrily and for a moment I thought he was going to attack the little Japanese man. But he calmed himself and turned to Larsen and me. "Come with me, please." He still was speaking Japanese

"Thank you," Kyoji said to me with a bow. He started walking back to the car.

"Wait," I called out.

He turned and looked at me questioningly.

I turned to Larsen. "Go back to Tokyo and wait for me."

"What?" he asked, sounding hurt.

"You can't come with me," I said. "The way I'm going to have to travel once I get to Korea, I can't take you. You'd be a burden, you'd slow me down. It will only be more dangerous."

Larsen just looked at me, the hurt rimming his eyes. "Sir, I survived…"

"Yes, I know, the European war, Normandy, Battle of the Bulge, and all that. But you're not an adept."

Larsen just stared at me, looking a bit like a lost little boy. Finally he said, softly, "Yes, sir."

I gently kicked my suitcase with my foot. "Take that with you; I won't need it, either."

"Yes, sir," Larsen stated more confidently as he accepted that I wouldn't take him.

"There's a hotel near the Imperial Palace on the rail line," I said. "If it's open, stay there. If not, ask where all the Americans stay. I'll find you."

"Yes, sir," he repeated, his shoulders back and his head held high.

I turned to Captain Han. "Let's go."

I'd forgotten to switch to Japanese but he apparently understood. He bowed and walked wordlessly to his boat. I followed. The ship's name was painted on the bow in *Hangul*—the Korean phonetic alphabet:

천년 송골매

Han climbed aboard and I followed. I expected it to smell like fish, but instead I smelled only diesel and wet wood. Han introduced me to another man—younger, more muscular, and in desperate need of a haircut—whom he called "Choi." Choi pointed me to the cabin, which was small and in need of repair, but clean. Han climbed up to the bridge and Choi followed him.

When the engines started, I decided this was no fishing boat. The entire vessel throbbed with their power.

\*\*\*

Five hours later Choi came to the cabin and signaled with his hand that I should follow him. It was close to midnight and very dark out, except the low moon was at about three-quarters full.

Choi led me to the very modern-looking bridge with lighted instruments providing the only illumination. Han was there, holding the wheel and looking out the window, then at his chart and his compass.

"*Hankookmal haseayo*?" he asked, noticing me.

I whipped up a quick translation spell.

"Yes, I can speak Korean."

He looked at me, surprised. "Good, I hate speaking Japanese."

"What about English?"

"Hello, Joe!" he said in English, apparently demonstrating his entire knowledge of my native language.

224

I laughed and he smiled, showing a mouth full of gold teeth. When he noticed my noticing them, he said, "Japanese soldiers knocked them out when I was a boy."

At that point Choi left without a word.

"Where's he going?" I asked.

"To get ready," Han replied, as if it were obvious.

I had nothing to say so I looked out the windows. It was black out and all I could see was our green phosphorescent trail in the water. "Where are we?"

"Almost to Tongyoung Island," he said. "I'll be dropping you off near Chinhae. That's west of Pusan."

"I know," I said.

Again he looked surprised.

"Are you Yakuza?" I asked.

He shook his head vigorously. "They will allow me to do some work for them, but I cannot be Yakuza, even if I wished."

"Because you're Korean"

"Yes. I don't care; their money is money."

"How much longer?" I asked to change the subject.

"Half an hour, maybe more. We have to proceed carefully We have to avoid American patrols." He scowled at the moon. "I wish we had some fog; that would be good cover."

I took my talisman out of my pocket and held it in both hands. Han watched, his face looking confused in the glow from the instruments.

But fog appeared around the boat, and he looked almost frightened.

When I was finished I put my talisman away, although I kept one hand on it to maintain the spell, and smiled at him in what I hoped was a reassuring manner.

"Why do you need a boat?" he asked, trying to sound brave.

"It's easier than swimming."

He thought for a moment, and then laughed.

"What about radar?" I asked. I had extended the fog as far as I could, thinking a boat-sized fog bank on a clear night might be a little too obvious. But I was fairly certain radar would penetrate fog, and I could do nothing about that. Technology again!

"There is no need to worry about radar," Han said confidently.

"Why is that?"

"We can't do anything about it, so there is no need to worry."

This time I had to think for a moment before laughing. He joined in.

Our merriment was cut off by a bright light cutting through the fog.

"STOP YOUR ENGINES AND PREPARE TO BE BOARDED!" a disembodied voice commanded in English, with the boom of an electrically amplified sound.

Han spat, "*Sshiboul*!" and shoved the two chrome engine throttles forward.

I just had time to grab a handhold before the "fishing boat" leapt forward. I wondered if fish ever touched the deck of this vessel.

My thoughts were interrupted by gunshots, first rapid and small, then slow and big. Water splashed around the boat where bullets and shells landed, and I wrapped my fingers around the talisman and made sure there was plenty of fog to throw off the gunners' aim. Even then I ducked when I heard bullets hitting wood. Han stayed at the wheel, peering ahead. He turned the boat wildly right and then left, as if trying to miss something, and I hoped he knew what he was doing. The coastline near Pusan is a lot like northern California, with rocky shores and cliffs, and I didn't want to think about what would happen if we collided with a submerged boulder.

"Don't worry," he said, as if he knew what I was thinking, "I grew up in these waters."

Despite the fog, I could see we were very close to a shoreline, going parallel to it very fast.

"Tongyoung Island," Han called out. "They won't come this close to shore."

The shots tapered off and Han looked at me. "Can you make this fog stay put and not follow us?"

"Yes," I said, and simply ended the spell. The fog would stop and slowly dissipate.

Han cut the ship right and we were in the clear. I could now see waves pounding the coast and the rocks. But I didn't see what I assumed to be a U.S. Navy patrol boat.

"We lost them," Han said, smiling.

"Good," I replied, not as sure as he was.

But we didn't see the American ship again, and about half an hour later Han stopped the boat near a sandy beach. He picked up a flashlight and pointed it toward shore, turning it on and off twice. A light on the beach responded.

"This is the dangerous part," he said and he produced a pistol from under the instrument panel. He set it on the panel and then looked through binoculars. "Looks like two men—good. They're coming."

Choi returned then. "Ready," was all he said. He was carrying a nasty-looking gun with a long box to the side that I assumed was the magazine. Larsen would know what it was, and for a moment I missed my personal warrior.

"Go with Choi," Han ordered. "And good luck." He was working the throttles and wheel, trying to keep the ship steady in the currents.

I followed Choi to the deck. I saw a bullet hole in the gunwale and realized how close we'd come to disaster.

Choi was watching the shore with binoculars.

"How do I get to shore?" I asked. I could get there on my own, wouldn't even get my feet wet, but if they had some other plans, I thought I'd let them carry them through. And I wondered who was coming; someone to take me to shore? I kept my hand on my talisman.

"Be quiet," Choi ordered.

Apparently he thought the fog bank had appeared by luck.

A few minutes later I heard splashing, and a rubber raft, bouncing up and down on the waves, came alongside the boat. Choi threw out a rope with one hand, holding the gun with the other. A person in the raft caught the rope and Choi pulled them in. Choi opened a hinged section of gunwale and seawater slopped in, but now the deck was accessible and nearly at the same level as the top of the raft.

I hung over the low gunwale and reached out my hand. A cold but small and soft hand grasped mine, and I pulled aboard a lovely Korean woman in a man's pea coat. Next came an Oriental male. "*Arigato*," he said, identifying himself as Japanese.

Choi held onto the raft and spoke to the man while pointing the weapon in his general direction. "Do you have the money?" he asked in Japanese.

So this was why Han hadn't want to go to Pusan, I realized; he was doing another job on the side.

The man handed him a roll of American bills. Choi looked it over and, apparently judging it adequate said, "Okay," in English, and then he looked at me.

"Take the raft back to shore; then cut it open and bury it." He was back to speaking Korean.

"Hurry," the woman said. "There are shore patrols."

I looked at her. She was absolutely gorgeous, maybe in her late twenties, which made her old enough to remember the Japanese Colonial days. The man was older, more like in his fifties. But she was dressed expensively, except for the aberration of the pea coat, and he obviously had financial resources. And he clearly didn't want to be in Korea if the Communists took over.

I nodded to Choi and got into the raft carefully. The bottom was moving on top of the waves and the whole thing was unsteady, but I managed to get in without falling into the ocean.

"Remember," Choi said as he used his foot to push me away from the boat, "bury it."

I found a wooden oar in the bottom and started paddling for shore. I heard the boat turn and race off, and its wake bounced me up and down. I looked back. Han was running without lights and the ship was almost impossible to see once it got a few hundred yards away. Han had himself a profitable smuggling operation. He didn't have weapons and those powerful engines for catching fish. I supposed at that time there were a lot of people trying to get out of Korea, afraid the whole peninsula was going to go Communist. And those that could afford it were leaving any way they could.

And when there weren't people to smuggle, I was sure there were other commodities to keep Han in business.

I paddled toward the shore and when I got close enough I teleported to the beach, landing on the dry sand. I turned and could see the raft was drifting out to sea. It would probably come to shore somewhere, but nowhere near where I was.

I used a spell to see in the dark. The beach was between the ocean and a rocky cliff. A trail zigzagged up the cliff, and I followed it to the forest above. It was calm and peaceful under the pine trees; it was hard to believe I was in a land at war. But I wasn't sure exactly where I was, or if I was in Communist-held or U.S.-controlled territory. A map would be handy, I realized. I searched the sky for the North Star, but ruddy clouds made it hard to find. I found a long pine needle on the ground and invoked a spell. The tip bent northward. That helped. But I thought I'd like to find some outpost of civilization where I could get food, water, and maybe a map. Han had said I was near Chinhae, but I had no idea in which direction it lay, except that it was on the coast. So was I, so should I go east or west? I didn't know.

My thoughts were interrupted by voices in the distance. They were coming closer, and soon I could understand them.

"Sarge," one said, "why is we out here again?"

"El-tee said the Navy said there was suspicious activity out here," another voice said.

"Oh, those squids think everything's suspicious," the first voice said.

"We're less than twenty clicks from the front," the second voice replied, "and we've had reports of commie infiltrators."

By then I could see them, about ten men in uniforms and steel helmets, each carrying a rifle, most slung over their shoulders with a cloth strap. The one identified as "Sarge" was leading the pack. He had an unlit cigarette dangling from his mouth.

I went invisible and watched them approach.

Sarge walked to the cliff's edge, passing so close to me I could see the patch on his upper arm that looked like a leaf with a lightning bolt, and for a few minutes looked over the beach I'd just left; and then Sarge grumbled and took a pair of binoculars from a pouch on his belt.

"Can't see a damn thing," he said, and he looked up at the moon and seemed to scowl at it for not providing enough light. "Johnson!"

A man ran up breathlessly. "Yes, Sergeant?"

"Shoot an illumination flare over that beach."

"Yes, Sergeant!"

Johnson took a paper tube from the pack on his back, pointed it up and toward the ocean, and pulled something on the bottom. There was a whistle accompanied by an orange flash of light, followed seconds later by a pop over our heads. An actinic bright light appeared in the sky and it dropped slowly, apparently attached to a parachute. I'd seen this before, in France. The light cast crazy wobbling shadows, and I stepped under a tree fearing my shadow would draw their attention.

"Damn!" Sarge said looking through the binoculars again. 'There's two, maybe three sets of fresh tracks in the sand." He moved the binoculars around. "And a rubber raft in the surf."

Damn, I thought, so much for it going back out to sea.

"Looks like the Navy was right," Sarge continued. "We gotta call this in."

I thought that was a bad idea. I didn't need a group of soldiers out here looking for communist spies and instead finding me. Already this group was acting nervous; some had taken their guns from their shoulders and were holding them with both hands, diagonally across their abdomens and chests, looking around for enemies.

I ended the invisibility spell and stepped out of the trees.

"Sergeant," I said softly.

The guns were instantly pointed at me. I raised my hands to shoulder height, which, unfortunately, made it so I couldn't touch my talisman.

"No reason for the guns," I said, trying to keep my voice calm.

"Who the hell are you?" the sergeant asked, his rifle pointed at my chest.

I had to think fast. "Joe Kader, Navy Intelligence."

The sergeant peered at me and I suddenly wished that I were wearing something other than a business suit, or that I had used a glamour before becoming visible.

"What are you doing here, Kader?" the sergeant demanded.

"Helping two people who would find it unhealthy to be captured by the Communists," I said, using as strong a persuasion spell as I could without my talisman.

"Don't they know we stopped the Commies at the Naktong River?" Johnson asked.

That's good to know, I thought, although I wasn't sure where that river was. "Is there any guarantee that will hold?" I asked.

"How do we know he's not a Commie?" Johnson asked. "We've had NPKA disguise themselves as peasant farmers."

I looked at Johnson. "Do I look Korean?"

"You could be a Ruskie," he retorted.

The sergeant gave Johnson a look that shut him up. "Who did you help leave?" the sergeant asked.

"May I please put my arms down? I assure you that I'm unarmed."

"Why," the sergeant asked, "would you be unarmed in a combat zone?"

Oops, I thought. "We're twenty clicks from the front," I said. "I don't need weapons here and they made my"—I thought for a moment—"charges nervous." Unfortunately, I didn't know if a "click" was a yard or a mile or something in between.

Along with the persuasion spell, that must have convinced them. The guns were lowered and the sergeant motioned that I could lower my arms. I put my hand in my pocket. "You don't need to call this in," I said. "In fact, it would be best if you just forgot about it."

"Wait," the sergeant said. "If you're Naval Intelligence, why did the Navy send us out here to check on suspicious activity?"

"Do you know everything your intelligence guys do?" I hoped the Army had intelligence guys.

The sergeant snorted. "No."

"It's the same in the Navy. Only my superiors know of my mission. The regular sailors know nothing."

The persuasion spell, diluted by having to be used on all ten of them, was working a little. The sergeant nodded. "So, you need us to forget this ever happened?"

"Please," I said. "It would be the best for your country and the war effort."

The sergeant thought for a moment, and I concentrated my spell on him, and eventually said, "Okay."

I smiled. "You don't happen to have a map I could borrow?"

\*\*\*

A different kind of spell made a cloud I could sit on. I went high; as long as it was dark I could avoid being seen and shot at. When it got light, I'd land and look for a place to rest. There was also "radar," but I had no idea whether I would be detected by that.

My realization that I was going to have to travel this way in Korea was what had made me decide to take a boat to Korea. I was rested when I arrived. That, and leaving Larsen behind, had been last-minute decisions.

When I got high enough, I could see the front lines. Even in the dark it was obvious. Angry orange sheets of flame washed over the hills like waves of death. As I got closer, I could see propeller-driven airplanes dropping bombs from which the flames were sprouting. They were being dropped on masses of soldiers rushing for the American lines. The flames even stopped the small North Korean tanks that had made it across the river. The battle was where a river, identified on the map as the Naktong, curved around a bulge. From my perspective, it was obvious that the Americans—the soldiers west of the advancing troops trying to hold the line and protect a small town the map identified as Kang-ni—were outnumbered, and the flames were the only thing holding back the Communists.

I swung around the battle, not wanting to collide with one of the planes dropping the deadly bombs, and headed for the city of Taejon, even though it was slightly east of a direct line to Seoul. I thought I could find some food and water there. I passed over burned and burning towns and villages and hundreds of corpses; most in uniform, some not. I remembered what Johnson had said about the North Korean soldiers disguising themselves as peasants. But some of the bodies were obviously those of women and children, and I doubted that they were disguised communist soldiers. It was impossible to know who had killed the civilians. I tried not to look and continued on toward Taejon.

# CHAPTER TWENTY-ONE

I landed on the outskirts of Taejon as the sun was rising. I stayed invisible, not knowing what the situation would be. At first glance it was not much different from when I was in Korea in the thirties: low white wooden buildings, the smell of night soil, rice paddies surrounding the town. But there was also the smell of burning wood, rubber, and gasoline, and burned out vehicles and dead humans and animals were strung out along the roads.

There was a checkpoint at the edge of the town manned by two men who looked too old to be soldiers. They were wearing the ubiquitous white pants and loose tunic of a Korean peasant and holding farm implements as weapons. With them was a young man in a mustard-colored military uniform holding a rifle; I couldn't tell whether it was to keep security in the town or to keep the apparently drafted old men from deserting.

I walked by, holding my breath and being careful not to step in any puddles.

I found no food and almost no potable water. I suspected the North Koreans had taken it all. The civilians were staying in their houses and soldiers patrolled the streets. I had to stop and rest after being invisible and maintaining my cloud for so long. I hid in a bombed-out house that provided some shelter. I found a corner and curled up and went to sleep.

About midmorning I was awakened by gunshots. I wondered who was shooting, since we were far from the battles. But it was too regular, not the sporadic shooting of battle. I wondered if someone was target shooting.

I would hear shots, then a long period of silence, then more shots.

I knew the smartest thing would be to stay where I was, but curiosity got the best of me. I went invisible and followed the sound of the guns, ending up at what appeared to be the city's jail. Soldiers had dug long trenches in the prison yard and were lining up people in civilian clothes in front of them. I could see that the trenches were full of bodies. Horrified, I couldn't stop watching, although I wanted to. I still couldn't believe that they were going to do what it was so obvious they had planned. Old men, women, and even children were lined up. Their hands were tied behind them with wire or rope and even cloth.

Men in uniforms were watching all this; I assumed they were the leaders.

Then five of the soldiers stood maybe twenty feet from the line and opened fire with their rifles. They weren't machine guns, so the soldiers had to pull the trigger every time they wanted to kill an innocent. The people fell backward into the trench, blood splattering everywhere.

I screamed and shot fire at the nearest communist solider. The flames knocked him to the ground and he screamed as he burned. The others turned, including the surviving civilians, to see where the fire had come from.

I was slowly becoming visible, I realized, but I didn't really care. I shot fire again, hitting the next soldier and setting his uniform ablaze. The leaders had pulled pistols, and the killers stopped shooting civilians and were aiming at me. I teleported across the prison yard and sprayed fire at every man I could see in a uniform. They all screamed, dropped their weapons, and ran in a panic if they didn't immediately fall to the ground. I smiled grimly: I had at least stopped the killing of apparently innocent civilians (I couldn't believe that many were guilty of some capital offense).

Then I ran like mad, and went invisible again.

I probably didn't do much good. The NKPA probably had plenty of men to dig the trenches and fire the rifles. But I couldn't just stand there. I was also sure I knew who had killed the civilians whose bodies I'd seen lying by the road.

The shooting never resumed, at least not that day. I waited until dark before leaving.

Before morning I got to Seoul on my cloud, crossing the Han River near a destroyed bridge and alighting in the southern part of the city.

For a city of a million or so people, Seoul was deathly quiet. I wondered what I would do if I heard gunshots. I couldn't save everyone the Communists were going to kill. Was it worth risking my life, and losing the possibility of being able to help Meyoung, to save a few?

I found a hidden spot and let the invisibility spell dissipate. Then I concentrated. The quiet of the city helped. I thought I could feel her, or at least some adepts, toward the north. I went invisible again and walked in that general direction.

The city must have fallen without incurring a lot of damage. There were soldiers and military vehicles on nearly every street corner, especially in the core of the city.

The city didn't seem to have changed much physically since my visit in the thirties, except it was much larger. When I'd been there before it was about the same size, at least in population, as San Francisco. But while the core of the city hadn't changed, the houses had crept up on the surrounding hills to the north. It seemed to have nearly doubled in size. There were some very Western-looking buildings that were new, perhaps built since the end of the war when Russia and the U.S. agreed to split the country at the thirty-eighth parallel. Many of the new buildings tried to affect Oriental architecture with modern building materials, such as a building I passed that was made of cinderblocks with a metal roof, but with the wide eaves like those found on a pagoda.

As I entered the Gwanghwamun district, I found a dark corner and stood quietly. Yes, there was at least one adept to the north, in the older part of the city.

Sticking to the shadows, I moved through the town. The streets were laid out haphazardly, but I remembered my way fairly well. And there were a few old landmarks I recognized.

Seoul had been just one of many cities where I'd looked for Nakamura or Meyoung, or both. I'd found neither.

When I defeated the adept and three samurai in Pusan, at the house where Nakamura's minions had tried to ambush me, the one samurai had told me Nakamura was in Mukden. So I had gone as directly as possible from Pusan to Mukden. That required traveling through Seoul since I had to take a boat from Inchon to Port Arthur and from there take the South Manchurian Railway to Mukden. Mukden was where the Japanese had started their war with China in 1931. The Japanese had taken the railway from the Russians in 1905 as part of the treaty that ended their war. Why the Russians had a railroad in the Chinese Empire, I didn't know, unless it was because the Manchu Emperor was so weak by then that he had little choice in the matter.

Then someone blew up some train tracks. The Japanese said it was Chinese terrorists. The Chinese said the Japanese did it. In any case, Japan used that as an excuse to invade Manchuria through Korea, starting the Pacific part of what later would be called World War II.

I had a truth spell on the samurai, so he thought Mukden was where Nakamura was. But either the samurai was mistaken, or by the time I had arrived there, Nakamura had left and there was no trace of Meyoung.

*** 

The house was one that, before the Japanese occupation, would have belonged to a government official or a *yangban*: a member of the high scholar class of pre-twentieth century Korea. A high wall made of stone blocks surrounded an inner courtyard and the house stood in the middle of it. As I teleported past the wall, I could see the main house clearly. The foundation was made of stone blocks. The walls were stone, wood, and plaster. The roof was done in classic Oriental tile, and paper windows were framed by dark wood. Pillars holding up the roof were decorated with grass writing. The fact that it was occupied by an adept had probably kept the North Koreans from expropriating it for a general to live in, or some such thing.

I ignored the smaller houses inside the wall. Traditionally they were for the servants and women. Besides, I could feel there was no adept residing in them. The strongest feelings I had came from inside the main house. It didn't feel like I remembered Meyoung feeling, but it had been nearly twenty years.

I climbed the stairs slowly and gingerly, thinking old stairs might squeak. In Japan the squeak would be intentional to warn the inmates of approaching spies or assassins, and a Japanese adept that might have lived here during the colonial period might have imported that idea. I didn't know whether Meyoung was here or someone else, but I hoped a Korean adept would be able to tell me where to find her.

The door slid aside easily and I was in the main room where the head of the house would greet visitors. The room was large, with a high ceiling cut across with wood beams. It had electric lights installed but they were off, and the room was dimly lit with candles on tables and the floor. Pillows were scattered about and I saw a very Western-looking chair. A silk and bamboo screen stood on the other side of the room. The adept I was feeling was behind it. I stepped slowly toward it, wondering if I should announce my presence. Everything was so quiet, as if all sound had been sucked out of the house.

"Joe?" a voice said. It was a woman's voice, but it seemed to be straining. It came from behind the screen

"Peg?" I asked softly, automatically calling her that name even after all these years.

"Yes, it's me," she said in the ancient language.

Something in her voice stopped me from rushing the screen and pulling her into my arms. She had spoken with no joy, no feeling at all, only as if stating dry facts about the weather.

I couldn't think of anything intelligent to say. "I got your message."

"Yes, I know," she said. Again, no feeling was expressed by her voice.

"You said you needed help."

"Yes," she replied.

There was a long silence.

I took a tentative step forward. "How can I help, Meyoung?" I remembered to use that name that time.

A laugh came from behind the screen. It wasn't happy, but bitter and angry and full of malice. I wondered briefly whether it was really her back there.

"Why can't I see you?" I asked.

"Do you know what Nakamura did to me?"

I frowned. "No, of course not. I spent five years looking for you."

"Liar!" she screamed. "You never came for me."

I was shocked. How could she not know? Rumors must have reached her. I'd walk into a town on Hokkaido or in Outer Manchuria, and even the local lessers would know about the wandering American adept looking for the head of the *Omi Uji* guild.

"What did he do to you?" I asked, my voice tight with the pain I was feeling.

"He made me kill it."

"Kill what?"

"Our child."

I stopped and peered at the screen as if I could penetrate what she was saying with my eyes. "Our child?"

"Yes, before it was born. I used a spell on myself."

"Our child?" I repeated stupidly.

"Yes," she barked. "I was pregnant when I left you."

"He had your name," I said, knowing that was how he had forced her to do his will.

"Yes," she said. "And I hated him for making me do it. And I hated you for giving me the child that I had to kill."

"Me?" My voice was like that of a hurt toddler.

"Yes. I've hated you for never finding me. For not even trying. You even became head of your guild and you never tried."

"I tried," I whispered.

"No!" she screamed. "He told me, you never came. He had spies in San Francisco; saw you with other women, laughing and kissing."

"It's a lie," I said. When I returned, yes, there were other women, most notably Beverly Morgan and Dagmar. But that had been after I'd spent five years looking for her.

"No!" she yelled again. "You lie!"

"Meyoung," I said. "I'm sorry." I knew nothing else to say. Why she believed Nakamura instead of me I did not understand.

"And he did something else," she said, seething with rage.

"What?" I asked, not really wanting to know. This was ripping me apart. A woman I loved had been abused, lied to, and controlled by an evil man, and I hadn't been able to stop it because of such a mundane thing as being unable to find her.

"He knew I hated him. I wouldn't touch him unless forced…with my name he could do it…and he hated that. So he brought forth an ancient spell of the *Omi Uji*."

"What spell?"

"He took my power."

"He what?" I'd never heard of such a thing.

"Took my power. I am no longer an adept."

"Oh, my god," I whispered. I realized how lucky I'd been on that dock at the Embarcadero.

"He could control me completely then. He used me as his *kisaeng*, for him and his friends. For entertainment of his friends."

I didn't know that word, but I could imagine.

"And when he tired of me, he threw me away."

My hate for Nakamura was seething inside me.

"Is he alive?" I asked.

She ignored the question. "But he just didn't dispose of me. That wasn't enough punishment."

She was quiet a moment, then she screamed: "He did this!"

The screen was flung aside and I could see her. Even in the dim light, the sight was seared into my soul. Her hair was gray and stringy, her eyes small and piggish while her nose was long. Her mouth was little more than a slit. She looked to be a hundred years old. She was wearing a *hanbok*, a traditional Korean dress with the waist of the full skirt just under the bosom, but I could still see that her body was misshapen. Her back was hunched, and she seemed mostly skin and bones. Her arms and legs didn't quite seem to be in the right place or point in the right directions. She didn't look human, but more like a monster out of a child's worst nightmares. I couldn't help but stare.

"Look at me!" she shrilled. "Look at what he did to me because of you! I hate you!"

"Maybe if you give me your name I can—"

"No!" she cut me off. "You can't. You don't know the spell."

She was right; there was nothing I could do. She could use a glamour spell on lessers but she would see through it, as would any adept. But no, I realized, she couldn't, not if Nakamura had taken her power. His humiliation of her was very thorough.

But if Nakamura had taken her power, why was I feeling the presence of an adept?

There was someone else there, I realized.

"Who else is here?" I demanded, my voice tight with apprehension. I made damn sure my *katana* talisman was in my hand.

A young Korean man stepped out from behind Meyoung. I hadn't been able to see him in the shadows. He was the one I had sensed.

Simultaneously, the north and south doors of the room slid open, and a man entered through each. They stopped masking and I knew they were all adepts.

Meyoung cackled. "And now I'm going to watch you die, *yuhbo*."

The Korean adepts were not as powerful as I, and individually would not have been a problem. But three of them simultaneously could be too much even for me. I could still probably beat them but it would be difficult and dangerous and why risk it, I thought. Meyoung had set a trap for me, to kill me, because of her hate for me. There was no reason for me to fight these adepts.

I looked up at the high ceiling. It was, maybe, twelve feet up, supported by dark wood beams. I aimed about three feet above that and prepared to teleport, hoping to materialize a foot or so above the roof. I didn't remember there being any trees overhanging the roof, and I hoped that was accurate. Even a small branch where I was going to materialize would kill me instantly.

I teleported, expecting to appear in open air. Instead I materialized just below the room's ceiling. I fell toward the wood floor, which now seemed forever below me.

Someone had put a very powerful secure spell on the room, one that wouldn't even allow teleportation. It might have been a group effort of the three adepts.

I grabbed for a wooden beam as I dropped past, but all I managed to do was rip the skin from the tips of my fingers, and drop my talisman. I hit the floor hard, and the breath was knocked out of me.

Meyoung was laughing. "We learned some tricks fighting the Japanese," she exulted.

I knew if I waited to catch my breath I'd die. I sprang to my feet as fast as I could and looked for the piece of a *katana* sword that was my talisman.

The Korean adepts were just watching, which I thought strange since this would be the perfect time to attack.

But they weren't just standing, I realized after watching. Two were going down on hands and knees; the third, the younger-looking one that had been behind Meyoung, was lying on the floor, hands pressed to his side and legs together. Scales grew on his skin and he slithered out of his clothes, now a snake more than six feet long with pale skin. The snake didn't have a rattle, but its mouth was big enough to swallow my head. And there are poisonous snakes other than rattlers.

The other two adepts turned into an orange and black tiger and a bear with long brown fur, ripping their clothes off in the process.

I'd never seen this before. I'd seen metamorphosis, of course, but not adepts doing it to themselves since the spells I knew were not reversible.

But different guilds have different spells.

I curled up in a ball and teleported above a beam, hoping I was small enough not to have my head hit the ceiling, which I assumed would knock me back down again. The secure spell would at least keep me from materializing in the ceiling.

I managed to materialize over the beam. From there I had a view of the room, and I scanned it for my talisman. I also felt safe from the transformed adepts below. The tiger paced under my perch, growling so low the sound seemed to be felt more than heard. It tried to jump up to reach me but couldn't leap high enough. After a few attempts he stopped, and looked at me with malevolent golden eyes.

The snake slithered up a post holding my beam, hissing and flicking out an arm-like forked tongue.

I ignored him and searched out my talisman, a suddenly small-seeming piece of metal on the large floor.

The snake reached the beam and started to slide onto it toward me.

Then I spotted my talisman, right where the bear was wandering back and forth on the floor. If he stepped on it, he'd probably know what it was. I didn't know if they kept their human intelligence, but I decided to assume he was smarter than the average bear.

I looked at the snake, now about a tongue-length's distance from me.

I dropped from the beam, landing on the bear. I shoved it aside, scooped up the talisman and shot an airbolt at the animal.

The fur on its side parted, showing I'd hit it full on, but the bear just turned and rushed me.

I teleported across the room, near a door. I grabbed the wood frame, but it seemed to bite back. Yes, still a secure spell present.

The snake had dropped to the floor with a squishy thud. All three animals were advancing on me. I shot fire at the tiger, and the flames stopped near it.

Damn, they could still spell and react like human adepts in these forms.

Fear made the hairs on the back of my neck stand up and tingle. For the first time that night, I thought that the odds were not in my favor.

I saw no escape other than to teleport to the other side of the room. They turned and looked at me with their different colored eyes.

The snake turned into a bird. It wasn't a rukhkh, but more like an impossibly large falcon. The bear did the same thing, and both streaked across the room toward me, talons held out.

I shot a lightning bolt at the falcon to my right. It seemed to explode in a burst of feathers, and I hoped momentarily that I'd killed it. But it was flung backwards and slammed into the paper door, breaking it. It fell to the floor, and then changed back into a snake.

A broken door cannot be secured, not by any meta I know. I could escape if I could get to that door.

But by then the second falcon was on me, talons slashing at my face. My cheek was burning, and when I touched it my hand came away bloody.

I pushed the falcon away and teleported, picking a part of the room with neither falcon nor tiger, but that put me farther from the broken door.

The tiger leapt at me, mouth agape. I tried lightning with it, but seeing my hand come up, it ducked and the bolt missed. But its need to duck kept it from landing right on top of me and sinking its teeth into my neck. Still, it swiped at me with a massive paw, the claws ripping through my clothes and flesh, and knocked me to the floor. I hit the wood face down and quickly rolled over just as the tiger jumped on me. Its claws dug into my shoulders and it looked down at me, golden eyes looking rimmed with human-like glee before the head bent toward my exposed neck. Without thinking, I held my talisman in my fist, perpetually sharp end out, and slashed at the tiger's thick neck. Blood spurted from the wound, washing over my hand. I felt strange power enter my talisman and my arm. The tiger howled in pain and anger, jumping off me, which was so painful I nearly passed out, as he used my flesh for traction.

I crawled to my feet, ignoring the blood dripping from multiple wounds. The tiger had retreated to a corner. As I watched, its wound healed.

This meta was extremely powerful. In this changed state they could do anything an adept could do normally. I wondered how the tiger healed itself without a talisman.

Unfortunately, the tiger was between the broken door and me. While it was distracted healing itself, I shot fire at it. My flames seemed hotter and brighter, and the force slammed me to the floor while the radiant heat seared my face. The power from my talisman seemed suddenly increased. The orange arc slammed into the beast and its fur blazed orange as the flames spread across it like water.

The tiger changed back into a human who screamed as he died, filling the room with a nasty greasy smell of burning flesh.

As I tried to stand, a man-sized falcon knocked me back down, its talons ripping through my scalp. It turned in the air and headed straight for me. The snake slithered over my legs before I could stand again and pinned me down.

I slashed at the snake with the talisman. Red, human-like blood spurted from the wound. The snake tried to turn its head to bite me, but I cut it just below the neck. It seemed each drop of blood that touched my talisman increased its and therefore my power. The falcon tried to land on my chest with its talons, but I used my left hand to push it away. The snake was sliding away, leaving a trail of blood with its scale impressions pressed into it.

I quickly glanced around the room for the falcon. It was swooping at me. I shot lightning at it, and it crashed to the floor, dropping in an arc and then rolling along the wooden boards until it hit a wall. It changed into a dead, naked human.

I jumped up and sprinted for the damaged door. If I could get outside, I could escape. The snake, moving with speed I couldn't imagine, slithered around my legs, tripping me, and then wrapped around my chest before I could get up again. Its head was close to mine and it opened its mouth, revealing rows of sharp teeth. There were no fangs, but this thing didn't need poison to kill me. I couldn't fight it; my arms were pinned to my chest, my hands at my sides. I tried to cut it with the talisman, but even by bending my wrist I couldn't reach it. The only thing I could cut was my own thigh.

The snake squeezed me and I found it hard to breathe. It squeezed harder, looking at me with eyes that blazed with anger. The pain rose and I heard my bones cracking. It could have killed me quickly with its teeth on my neck, but it seemed to want to make me suffer.

I needed power. Every time blood touched the talisman, it got more powerful. I didn't understand that but I needed to use it. I couldn't cut the snake to get blood.

It squeezed again and my vision started going gray. It was impossible for me to breath.

I cut my thigh, as hard and deeply as I could. Blood gushed out over my hand and the talisman. I felt the power rise through my arm. My vision returned, and I ran a strength spell on myself. I saw fear in the snake's eyes as it apparently sensed my sudden surge of power.

I pushed out with my arms and the snake's coils parted. It hissed as if in pain and fell to the floor. I grabbed the head just under the neck and pounded it into the wood floor. The boards cracked and splintered under the pounding. The snake, as I held its neck, changed into a human around whose neck my hands were fused. Blood was smearing the boards. I stopped and looked at the dead adept. I looked at his hands, looking for the talisman he was using. It was there, as if when the metamorphosis had taken place it had been absorbed into the creature's body, available for it to use. That explained their powers.

I also recognized it. It was an American Indian arrowhead: my arrowhead that Nakamura had taken from me.

I suddenly felt woozy and light-headed. I looked at my leg to see blood almost gushing out of it. I put my hand on it and ran a healing spell. Blood had covered my shirt where the tiger had clawed me. My hair was soaked with blood where the falcon had cut my scalp. I tried to heal each wound, but combined with my loss of blood, the effort caused me to pass out.

I gained consciousness with Meyoung sitting on my chest, holding a knife in both her hands over her head.

I pushed her off me easily. The knife dropped to the floor and she curled up in a ball and wailed.

"I want you dead!" she screamed.

I felt nothing for her, not love, not pity, not hate. I only felt remorse that I had failed to protect her from Nakamura and now she had changed to this.

"Meyoung," I said loudly. "Who is this adept with my arrowhead?"

She sat up and looked at me, her sunken cheeks wet with her tears. For a moment I saw in her eyes the woman I had loved.

"Our son," she whispered. "Your son."

I looked at her, disbelieving.

"You said Nakamura forced you to—"

"I lied," she wailed. "He took him from me, raised him as his own, and taught him to hate you.

"But when he learned of his heritage, he rejected the *Omi Uji* and fought against them. But he always hated you and was happy to have the chance to kill you."

I looked at the dead adept. I couldn't believe he had been my son. He looked young, maybe still a teenager. Was it my imagination, or was his complexion paler than that of other Koreans? Was the epicanthic fold of his eyes not as pronounced?

I looked back at her. She had no power, I suddenly remembered. I hit her with a truth spell.

"Is this my son?" I asked.

"Yes," she replied.

I just stared at her. I was numb with pain. My son had tried to kill me at the behest of his mother, a woman I'd once loved. And instead, I'd killed him.

"Why?" I whispered.

"Because I wanted you dead," she cried. "And he wanted you dead." She was looking at our dead son.

"Why now?"

She actually smiled, showing a row of misshapen teeth. 'My son was strong enough, finally. And someone told me how to find you. Seems you've been spending a lot of time in Norway."

"Who?"

"An adept. Very powerful. He said he could fix me, give me my power back, if I lured you here and killed you." She suddenly started crying again. "But now he won't."

I hit her with the truth spell, again. "Who?"

She fought it, tried not to answer. I increased the power and asked again, "Who?"

Finally she burst out, "Thor. He called himself Thor."

I looked at her. I knew it was the truth. Or she thought that it was the truth. And it would have to have been Thor, as he was probably the only adept powerful enough to give Meyoung her power back. And if she had her power, she could heal herself and be beautiful again.

"Where's Nakamura?" I asked, knowing the truth spell was still on her.

"Japan, as far as I know."

"Alive?"

"Yes."

Good, I thought. I was going to take special pleasure in killing him.

I realized I'd been sitting on the floor talking to her. I stood and looked down at her. "What do you want me to do?" I asked.

She looked up at me. "What do you mean?"

"What do you want me to do?" I repeated.

She looked at me, her gaze steady. "Kill me."

"You don't want to live?" I asked, as if inquiring about her food preferences.

"No," she stated simply.

I walked to the broken door and slid it open. Night air rushed in, and I could see in the east the sun was starting to rise.

"Wait!" she cried out. "Are you just going to leave me?"

I didn't know if it was crueler to kill her or let her live. I suspected the latter. I just knew that there was a part of me that still loved her, and I couldn't kill her.

"Yes," I said, and walked out of the house.

# CHAPTER TWENTY-TWO

The gunshots started shortly after dawn. Again, as in Tae on, it didn't sound like a battle. There'd be a burst of gunfire followed by silence and then another burst. I could only assume the North Koreans were executing more people. After my personal battle, I had no strength to do a damn thing about it, which frustrated me further.

I went invisible and hid. I needed time to rest and heal and gather strength. And to think.

This adept calling himself "Thor" had wanted me dead. But Thor hadn't been heard from for centuries. The legends said that the Atlantean priests had solved the problem of mortality and could live forever. I hadn't believed it for one reason: no one had ever reported meeting them. Was Thor walking the Earth? And if so, why did he want to have me killed?

*Mjollnir*, I realized. He'd want it back from the Valkyrie, and I'd be in the way. I'd try to stop him just as I'd stopped Nikolai. But if Thor was as powerful as the legends said he was, he should be able to just brush even me aside as a nuisance. And if he'd been alive all these centuries, why now? So maybe it wasn't Thor. The only thing I knew was that I had to get back to Norway as fast as I could to find out what was going on.

I was startled by another burst of gunfire which reminded me I was still in Communist-held Seoul, Korea, and still too weak to even leave the city. I was about as far from Norway as I could get.

The map the American soldier had provided didn't extend as far north as Seoul. But I could follow Japanese-built roads and railroads south to Taejon, then east to Taegu, and then on to Pusan. From there, I'd use a persuasion spell to get the military to take me to Tokyo, preferably by airplane, to pick up Larsen, and then try to get the most direct flight to Oslo I could find. I wasn't sure how I could do that. I didn't know where one could fly to from Tokyo aside from Hawaii. Civilian aviation hadn't recovered from the Pacific War yet, and as far as I knew there was no way to fly across the U.S.S.R., which was probably the most direct route.

I decided it was stupid to worry about it. I should wait until I got to Tokyo and had some information. But if I had to, I'd return to the U.S., fly across the continent, and fly from New York, as I had in July.

I didn't even know if Pusan was still in American hands, even though Johnson had said they'd stopped the North Koreans at the Naktong River. Any situation in war was likely to change, Larsen had often told me.

I wished I could get a message to Larsen. He could start out early and get to Tromsø and perhaps scout out the situation. But if Meyoung had been right and Thor was now my enemy, Larsen couldn't help me much.

I found an abandoned and mostly unscathed house, planning to spend the day there recuperating. I expended only enough energy to mask; I didn't want any more Korean adepts to find me.

The home was a traditional *ondol* house, in which the flue gasses from the kitchen fire could be directed to a space under the stone floor. Since Koreans slept and sat on the floor, a heated floor in the winter helped keep them comfortable, especially since Korean winters can be brutal.

The denizens of the house, who probably had fled south to escape the Communists, had left the futon-like thin mattress and some of the large blankets behind. I covered the few windows with blankets, darkening the interior, leaned a futon against the wall, and sat with my back against it on the *ondol* floor.

I had just gotten comfortable when I heard noise outside the house. I didn't want to go invisible because that would mean stopping masking. I knew there wasn't an adept outside, unless he too was masking. My biggest fear was that it was a communist soldier.

But before I could decide what to do, the door opened and a woman slipped in. She was wearing a *hanbok* with a dark pink skirt and a white top. But it was dirty and torn. Her long dark hair was in knots, and dirt smeared her face. She was not very old, perhaps thirty, and I could tell that under all that dirt she was quite lovely. She didn't see me in the darkened room.

While masking, I couldn't even do a translation spell. "*Yo boh say'yo*," I said softly, hoping not to startle her.

It didn't work. She turned around with a gasp and surveyed the room, her face registering her fear. Finally her dark eyes landed on me. She gasped quietly, "*Mekook boon?*"

"*Nay*," I said, nodding. "Do you speak English?" We were both whispering.

"Yes," she said. "Why are you here? All Americans were to leave before..." Her voice dropped off.

"Before?" I asked.

"Before the *Inmin Goon* reached the city."

I assumed that was the commie army. "*Goon*" was a generic Korean word for military. "I was incommunicado," I said, smiling, trying to diminish her fear.

She looked confused. I guessed she didn't know that word. "I was out of touch with the embassy. I didn't get the word."

"So you've been hiding six weeks?" she asked. She sounded as if she didn't believe me.

I nodded.

She looked skeptical but didn't say anything. "Did you work at the embassy?"

I shook my head. "No." I really wanted to run a spell to stop her interrogation. I knew I didn't know enough about Seoul since World War II to lie effectively. What did Americans that weren't diplomats or the military do in Korea? But that would mean unmasking. So I tried to deflect her questions.

"Where did you learn English?"

For some reason, the question caused her to look as if she were going to cry. "My parents were Christians and sent me to the missionary school until the Japanese shut it down."

"You speak excellent English," I said, hoping to cheer her up and preclude her questioning me.

"Thank you," she whispered, covering her mouth and looking away. "That's how I got my job at the American Embassy."

I was happy I hadn't claimed to work there.

I hoped this wasn't a stupid question, but I couldn't imagine the entire city population of millions of people was hiding from the Communists. "Why are you hiding?"

Now she looked angry. "When the Americans left, they were in such a hurry they left their employee files behind. The *Inmin Goon* has been arresting and executing whoever worked for the Americans."

I let out an exasperated sigh, angry at the bureaucratic incompetence. I never understood why lessers trusted governments so much when they are just made up of very fallible humans. In fact, often the most fallible humans, it seemed.

"Now if you don't participate in rallies in support of the Communists, you don't get a food ration, if you are lucky."

"If you are unlucky?" I asked stupidly

A volley of gunfire in the distance seemed to answer me. She winced at the sound.

We were both quiet for a moment. Perhaps her eyes had adjusted to the dim light, but suddenly she gasped quietly, looking at my leg. "You're hurt!"

I glanced down at my bloodstained and torn pants.

"It's fine," I said. "I did it a long time ago climbing a fence, and it's healed now."

She looked dubious, but didn't ask about it again.

"By the way, I'm Joe Kader."

She looked as if she were trying to place the name. Apparently giving up, she said, "Kim Eunju."

She stayed with me through the day, telling me in a soft voice of the horrors she'd witnessed under the Japanese, and now the worse horrors under the Communists. She'd seen and felt more terror in the past six weeks than in the twenty years or so of her life under the Japanese.

She was sleeping when I left, curled up on one of the futon-like mattresses, a blanket around her shoulders. She was quite lovely and an educated and intelligent woman. Especially for a lesser, she impressed me with the depth of her soul. I hated leaving her, but trying to take her would only risk both our lives.

I ripped one of the house's blankets in half; it was the perfect size for a flying carpet. It took less skill and meta to keep a carpet in the air than a cloud. The drawback was that a carpet was more likely to draw unwanted attention. I could mitigate that by flying higher, but the higher one went, the colder it got, even though it was August. And then there were airplanes and radar to worry about, too, especially in a war zone.

I changed my mind about following roads and decided to head southeast until I found the east coast of the Korean peninsula. Then I'd head south to Pusan and decide from there how to get to Tokyo, depending on which army I found there: U.S. or North Korean.

I wondered briefly whether Brother Wagner was still proselytizing there.

When the sun went down completely on my second day in Seoul, I sneaked out of the house so as not to wake Miss Kim, spread out the half a blanket on the ground, and invoked the correct spell. The blanket floated off the ground and hovered about three feet over the dirt. I climbed on. I sighted Polaris and aimed my carpet southeast. The carpet leaped into the sky at my command. I went higher and higher, so high I was in the clouds. There was no moon, so I felt nearly invisible in the mist: invisible, but cold. I kept the carpet going straight, using the North Star when I could see it for course corrections.

The landscape below me was a stygian void. I decided because it was a war zone, no one was showing lights.

As the quarter moon began rising I worried that I'd perhaps gone too far. Korea isn't all that big, and a carpet can move pretty fast. So I flew lower, hoping to see a landmark I recognized.

The moonlight wasn't much help, so I used a spell to help see in the dark. Then it was apparent I was over a rice paddy-lined plain between low mountains to the east and south. At least I wasn't over the Sea of Japan, I thought happily.

I stopped the carpet, hovering a few thousand feet above the surface, and pulled out the map. I tried to orient myself. I was sure the mountains to the east were the coastal range, the Taebaek Mountains, and the ones south were the Sobaek Mountains. There was a river just to my west, which I assumed to be the Naktong. And that meant I was probably pretty close to Taegu and not far from Pusan. It also meant I was hovering over the battlefield, unless the battle had moved. I could see no evidence of fighting on the ground below me. Had the Reds taken Pusan, I wondered.

My thoughts were interrupted by a low drone. The sound shook my bones, it seemed, and was growing louder by the second. I turned to look north. If I hadn't had a spell to see in the dark, I probably would never have seen it. It was an airplane that looked as if two planes had been stuck together. There were two fuselages, two canopies, and two huge propellers. It was painted black or dark blue, and a large pod hung down in the middle between the props and fuselages. And it was coming right at me.

I flattened myself on the blanket and dropped as fast as I dared toward the ground. The drone turned to a roar as the machine streaked over me. Air slammed at me and I was nearly knocked off the carpet, which would have been fatal at this altitude.

The plane was flying away—I could see its two tails and a small wing between them—but then it turned in a long arc and headed back for me.

They must have spotted me and were wondering what the hell I was. I looked for a cloud to hide in, but they were too far above me; I'd never get there in time. I assumed the plane had weapons, but I wasn't sure they'd fire on me. Nonetheless, I didn't want to take the chance. I went invisible, hoping the floating blanket would rouse less suspicion and they wouldn't fire on it.

I thought the plane was going to ram me, but it passed a few yards to the north of me. The blast of air from its passing flipped the blanket and I hung onto it with my hands tight in the fabric, my feet dangling down over the ground below. I was glad I hadn't brought Miss Kim, since she'd be dead now. I couldn't have kept us both on the carpet.

When I got it upright again, my fists refused to open at first. I raced for the clouds as I tried to get my hands to relax.

The plane turned a few more arcs, then, seemingly unable to find me, headed southeast.

I followed, although it quickly sped out of my sight.

Pusan Harbor came into view. It, too, was nearly black, but there were enough low lights for me to see. Also the moonlight reflected off the harbor and I could see it was full of ships.

There were also more planes around, including ones like the one that had accosted me. From the white stars on the side, I decided they were American planes. I didn't know if that meant Pusan was still in American control or not.

I dropped quickly to the city, landing between two small houses. I was in a residential neighborhood much like the one I'd fought three samurai and an adept in years ago. I left my blanket rolled up beside a house and walked east toward the city center.

It wasn't long until I came to an intersection patrolled by two armed guards. They were Korean, but I didn't know whether they were South Korean or North Korean and the uniforms didn't help me much, although I had to admit their clothes looked more like the American uniforms than those I'd seen on the communist forces. But I wasn't going to risk my life on that.

I hit them both with a persuasion spell and walked up to them, also preparing a translation spell. I used a glamour to disguise my blood-stained clothes and hair.

"Where are the Americans?" I asked in Korean.

They both turned and looked at me, surprised.

"Halt!" one said, almost but not quite pointing his gun at me. I decided he was doing that on purpose, not wanting to be totally threatening but wanting to have his weapon close enough so that he could quickly change his aim and shoot me. "Who are you?"

"I'm an American civilian," I said.

"You have password?" the other said in English.

"No," I replied, also in English. "I'm a civilian missionary. You know Brother Wagner? I work with him."

They both looked at me. I switched to Korean. "I'm a missionary. I need to see the American commander."

"Yes," the second one, the one I presumed to be the leader, said. "You need to see the American commander." The spell I was working on them was causing them to be quite agreeable, but I got the feeling they had no idea how to get me to the Americans.

"Take me to your commander," I suggested helpfully.

The leader looked at the other soldier and spoke in Korean. "Ee, run to the platoon command post. Tell the sergeant to come here."

The other soldier saluted, bowed, and ran off.

\*\*\*

The sergeant, a stub of a man with scars on his face, took me back to their command post. There, a lieutenant who look like a teenager used a phone about the size of a shoebox and with a crank on the side to talk to his commander. About an hour later, a jeep showed up and I was driven to another command post. There a captain radioed an American unit and another jeep, this one driven by what looked like a prime example of American corn-fed youth, picked me up and took me to his headquarters.

A few hours and more jeep rides and more persuasion spells later, I was standing in front of a tired and irritable major just as the sun was coming up.

"Who are you?" he demanded, looking at me.

"Joe Kader. I'm a missionary."

"All civilians were to be evacuated. Didn't you get the order, Kader?"

I shook my head and fingered my talisman. "No, I was traveling near Taegu, incommunicado. I was communing with nature, as it were, and didn't know of the trouble until I heard the fighting. I have been trying to get back to Pusan since."

The major was trying hard not to believe me, but the spell I was working wasn't letting him. I didn't know how many holes there were in my story. It could have been completely unbelievable.

250

"Fine," he finally said. "I'll have a jeep take you to the Navy's operations and they'll put you on a ship for Yokosuka."

"I really need to go to Tokyo and to fly," I said, putting more power into the spell.

"You'll have to talk to the Air Force about that," he said.

"Can you tell me where to find the Air Force?"

"Their liaison officer, Colonel Stratton, is in the next building over," he said, sounding as if he would be glad to be rid of me.

"Thank you."

After I used a powerful persuasion spell, Colonel Stratton put me in a jeep that went to an airfield. He looked confused as I walked out, as if he wasn't sure why he'd agreed to my demands.

I was loaded on a "C-47," the same plane that forces you to climb uphill to find your seat that I'd flown from Oslo to London on and had been in during the war; World War II that was. Larsen had called it a DC-3, but apparently the Air Force had its own name for it.

This was the most primitive version yet. There was a fold-down metal seat on the side of the wall. That meant flying sideways with a seatbelt to keep you from sliding down toward the back of the plane.

But it dropped me at Haneda and I walked outside, much as I had when I'd first arrived in Japan...had it only been a little over a week ago?

The hotel near the Imperial Palace was indeed open, having suffered little damage in the war thanks to its location; the Allies never bombed the palace. The clerk gave me Larsen's room number and I knocked on his door.

He opened it, looked at me with wide eyes, and pulled me into the room, nearly giving me a hug in the process.

"Sir," he said enthusiastically, "you're back."

"Yes," I said. I let the glamour dissipate and Larsen looked at me shocked.

"Oh, sir," he stated looking at my blood-stained clothes. "Are you okay?"

"I'm fine," I growled. "Healing spells."

"Did you find her, sir?"

I shook my head. "No, it was a trap. The girl I loved died years ago, apparently."

Larsen looked sad. "I'm sorry, sir."

"Me too," I stated simply.

"It was a trap?" he asked. "Who?"

I looked at him. "Thor."

"Who?"

I smiled grimly. "Thor."

"The Norse god of thunder?" Larsen asked.

"Actually, Thor the giant killer," I said.

He looked at me, confused.

"It's a long story. I'll tell you on the way."

"The way where, sir?"

"Norway," I said. "We need to get there as fast as we can."

\*\*\*

You wanna go where?" the Air Force sergeant asked in a thick southern drawl.

"Oslo," I said, "Norway."

"Now," the sergeant said, "we have civil flights to Honolulu, Anchorage, or Okinawa. Which will it be?"

"Do you have flights to Hong Kong?" Larsen asked.

I looked at him. "Hong Kong?"

"The B.O.A.C.," he explained. "The girl in London said they fly there; they must fly back."

I smiled at him. "Thank you; I'd forgotten that." I turned to the sergeant. "Any to Hong Kong?"

The sergeant looked exasperated. "Now I just told you, you can take Pan American to Honolulu or Okinawa or Guam, or you can take Northwest to Anchorage. That's it."

"Pan American flies to Hong Kong from the U.S.," Larsen explained patiently.

"Well, if you haven't noticed, there's a war on," the sergeant stated, drawing out each vowel nearly to the breaking point. "If you want to go to the U.S. and fly to Hong Kong from there, you're welcome to it."

"Do they fly there from Hawaii?" Larsen asked.

"I have no idear," the sergeant said, sounding exasperated.

"What about military flights?" Larsen asked with forced patience.

The sergeant's eyes seemed to be trying to escape his skull as he peered at my warrior. "Y'all are civilians. You can't go on no military flights."

I fingered my talisman, and later that day we were on a yet another DC-3/C-47—Larsen confirmed that they were the same basic plane, just civilian and military designations were different—and heading for Hong Kong.

We landed at a combination civilian and military airport, walked to the civilian terminal, and booked a flight on the B.O.A.C. to London for early the next day.

A taxi took us to a nice hotel, the Peninsula. In my room I felt safe enough to try something. I invoked a spell of far seeing, trying to see Dagmar and talk to her. It would have helped if I'd had some object of hers, but I was never really into keepsakes. I worked on the spell, forming it, projecting my own power to try to reach her. But every time I thought I had it, the spell would collapse. The fourth time, I felt a power like I'd never felt before. It wasn't Dagmar; I didn't know what it was. I gave up, knowing I'd have to make the trip in order to be able to talk to her.

The next morning Larsen and I returned to the airport for our flight.

The plane had four engines, and in order to enter it you had to climb stairs rolled up to the door near the craft's rear. To my eye it looked like a four-engine and larger version of the DC-3. Inside it was much more spacious, and there were two seats on each side. There was no beam to step over at the wings as in the DC-3.

Larsen and I sat on the left side of the plane, placing our hats on the shelf above the seats. I let him sit by the window since I didn't really enjoy having a constant reminder next to my elbow that I was flying in a machine made by lessers. An attentive and attractive stewardess brought us refreshments and newspapers, the *South China Morning Post*. The war was, of course, front-page news. The Americans claimed to have stopped the communist advance and formed a perimeter around Pusan at the Naktong River. They were holding off the NKPA's "human waves" of attacks with "napalm" and other air attacks. North Koreans were still trying to infiltrate over the river, and in fact held the "Naktong Bulge" east of the river. Counter-attacks had so far failed.

There was some speculation about Red China attacking Taiwan or even Hong Kong. There was also worry that Russia might make a move for West Berlin, or even the Allied zones of West Germany.

There was a brief article about the scarcity of rice. Both Japan and Red China couldn't meet their own needs, but rice exporter Siam had resumed pre-World War II production levels. Burma and Indo-China had not.

I put the newspaper away, glad there were others in the world to worry about such mundane things.

My curiosity was tickling the back of my brain, so after a few hours of flying I asked Larsen about the airplane.

"I think it's a DC-4, sir," he said. "It looks like a C-54 Skymaster, which is the military version."

"'DC'?" I asked. "Like the DC-3? They do rather look alike."

"Yes. They are made by the same company: Douglas." He paused for a moment. "That's very good, sir, to recognize the similarities. Pretty soon you'll be able to tell a Ford from a Chevy."

I laughed. "Don't count on it."

Larsen laughed with me.

"I did," I said lightly, "see a strange airplane in Korea."

"Really, sir?" I could tell he was interested.

I described the airplane that had nearly hit me, the two propellers, the two fuselages and canopies, the strange pod hanging down in the middle.

"Sounds like you encountered a Twin Mustang, an F-82, I believe," he said after asking a few questions about the back, or tail, of the plane. "The pod houses the radar. I don't know whether they would have picked you up on radar. But in any case, it seems they saw you and were probably wondering what the heck you were."

He chuckled.

"What?" I asked.

"I would have liked to have heard their debriefing."

He laughed at that for a few minutes and then looked out the window.

Larsen was quiet for a few minutes, then turned from the window and looked at me. "What's this about Thor? I thought he was a myth, like Apollo or Zeus."

I suppressed a smile. He was right; Thor was like Apollo or Zeus, but none were myths. I was, however, regretting having told him anything about Thor. It was one of the guilds' oldest and more important secrets.

"Not here," I said. "In private, maybe."

Larsen looked disappointed.

The trip took thirty hours with stops and plane changes in Calcutta and Cairo. The Calcutta to Cairo leg was in an airplane that had sleeping berths like the ones in a railcar, which allowed one to sleep, although the comfort was marginal. The stewardess did bring my breakfast to my berth. We landed in London in the late afternoon on yet another aircraft.

We had to stay overnight, again. If Drake knew I was in London, he didn't do anything about it; we went unmolested during our short stay.

The next morning we flew to Fornebu on SAS, again on a DC-3. I was amazing myself by being able to recognize machinery. It was three weeks to the day since we'd left Fornebu for London.

I turned to Larsen as we stepped out of the terminal in search of a taxi. "Take the flying boat to Tromsø. I'll meet you at Dagmar's house. Wait a week. If I don't show up..." I let my voice trail off.

"Sir?" he asked, looking concerned.

"If I don't show up, go to San Francisco and tell Louis I'm dead and Thor killed me at Valhalla. He'll know what that means."

Larsen gave me the same look as on the dock at Hakata Bay in Japan; hurt mixed with fear. But it was fear for my safety, not his. This time he didn't protest. "Yes, sir."

Larsen took a taxi; the "Flying Steamer" didn't leave until morning, so he'd spend the night in Oslo before going to its pier. I had another idea on how to get to Valhalla. I took another taxi into Oslo, found a furniture store, bought a rug, and had a second taxi drop me on the edge of town.

In August in Oslo there's not a lot of nighttime, but luckily Norway's interior is sparsely populated. Also, I wasn't too worried about lessers seeing me. Adepts do try to remain discreet, but sometimes circumstances force one's hand. I once fought a battle on a flying carpet over San Francisco in daylight. That had almost pushed World War II off the front pages of the newspapers the following day.

I looked at the daylight sky, laced with ruddy clouds, and realized the flaw in my plan. Without the North Star, I would have trouble navigating. I plucked a pine needle from a tree and ran the appropriate spell; it bent and pointed north. I tried to aim my carpet in that general direction and took off, wishing I could run both spells simultaneously. Or, at least, that I'd remembered to buy a compass.

The sun went down about eight-thirty by my watch. By nine I could find the North Star, found I was a bit off course, and aimed to the left of it, trying to put a little westerly into my direction.

The moon hadn't risen yet and it seemed I was passing over a black, lifeless land. I went higher, hoping to miss any mountains. But of course, higher was colder.

I wasn't worried about finding Valhalla. If Thor was there, I'd start to feel his presence if I even got close. Add to that Dagmar and the Hammer, and I could probably feel Valhalla from halfway up the country. And once I saw it, I'd recognize it.

As a sliver of a moon rose, I stopped the carpet and hovered in the air. Staying quiet, I felt for the presence of power. I felt nothing, so I continued flying a little west of north.

It started getting light at about three in the morning and soon I couldn't see Polaris. I could see I was over rugged mountains typical of northern Norway. Again I hovered. And I felt it, to the west and north. I changed directions.

When the sun rose at about 4:30, I could feel Valhalla well enough that I didn't need to hover. It was like a beacon, guiding me in. I dropped down into a valley and before me saw the snow-capped mountain. In a flat spot about halfway up the mountain was a hall thatched in gold shields, reflecting the morning sun.

The grassy floor of the mountain valley was littered with rusting relics from Hitler's army: helmets, rifle barrels, vehicles. I supposed the Valkyrie were fortunate that the Nazis hadn't been able to get tanks up here. I then realized I was thinking tactically. Must have been spending too much time with Larsen.

I landed at the base of the mountain. Flying in on the carpet would be rude under normal circumstances. In the current situation, it could be deadly.

The entrance to Valhalla is a crack in the side of the mountain that a narrow trail passes through. I climbed the trail, spotting at a distance two Berserkers guarding the entrance, as always. As I got within hailing distance, I worked up a translation spell, assuming they'd be speaking Norwegian.

They were dressed as Berserkers traditionally are: chain mail, breastplates, holding golden shields with large swords at their sides. They had no modern weapons, which was unusual since Dagmar had ordered Berserkers to start using them.

"Halt," the one on the left, the larger one, said. "Who approaches *Volhöll*?"

I stopped and raised my right hand, showing it contained neither weapon nor talisman. "Francis Kader to see Brunhild."

"Brunhild is seeing no one," the Berserker replied. I recognized him. His name was Nils and he'd been outside Dagmar's house in Tromsø that day. He had been Dagmar/Brunhild's personal warrior. I wondered why he was here on guard duty and not with her.

He made a motion with his gauntleted hand and I put my arm down. "I think she'll see me."

"Brunhild has ordered none are to enter *Volhöll*."

"Could you please ask her?"

"She has made her orders clear," he stated. "None are to enter, no exceptions."

It would have been an act of war to use a spell on the warrior of another guild, but I was getting close to doing so. I put my left hand in my pocket and touched my talisman.

"Please," I said, my teeth clenched.

"I'm sorry, I cannot."

I stepped closer and spoke softly. "Nils, tell me, please, what is happening here."

The Berserker's eyes flashed with emotion for a moment, but he continued to stare straight ahead. "All is well," he stated simply. The way he said it, I knew it was a lie, a lie he wanted me to disbelieve.

Act of war or no, I touched him and he fell in the trail. The other Berserker was drawing his sword when I got my hand around his arm. He joined Nils on the ground. They weren't dead, but they would sleep a while and wake up with a bad headache.

I sprinted up the trail, between walls of bare, black rock that seemed to close in on me. Funny how I'd never noticed that before.

I hit something and was thrown back, landing on the gravel of the trail. I lay there a moment, trying to get my breath and figure out what the hell I had run into. An invisible wall? I wondered. Could have been an airbolt but where did it come from? I climbed to my feet, although it was more painful than I could believe. I walked forward slowly, my hands in front of me. There was nothing there. I started walking faster.

A man dropped into the crevasse in front of me, towering over me. I guessed he was at least seven feet tall. He was dressed as a Berserker would be, but was larger and had no sword; instead *Mjollnir*'s short handle was in his belt. I could only think that this must be Thor.

"Who are you?" he demanded in the ancient language, and the walls shook with his voice.

I stood as tall I could, reaching about his chin level, and looked into his dark eyes. "I am Francis Kader, head of the American Meta Association, the largest guild in the world."

He threw back his head and laughed, his long dark hair undulating with his mirth.

"You are Kader," he stated, looking down at me. "Kader, whose lover betrayed him to the Germans and lay with another woman."

256

I looked at him, wondering how he knew that and why he was saying it. Had Dagmar told him? I couldn't imagine.

"Kader," he continued, "who couldn't fight to keep the woman he loved from leaving with her master. Who couldn't find him after searching for five years, even though he sits in the Root of the Sun in Capital City, and still he can't find him. And then his lover tried to kill him."

That Dagmar wouldn't know. He must be Thor, for he'd set up the trap with Meyoung.

"Let me see Brunhild!" I demanded. Despite my wishes, my voice was getting shrill.

He again laughed. "Yet another lover who has betrayed you. She is no longer yours. She is mine."

I had my talisman in a near death-grip in my left hand. I pointed at him and flames leapt from the fingertip. And they sputtered and died a few inches from me.

He was still laughing, laughing at me. I wanted only to shut him up. I threw an airbolt at him. It seemed to dissolve as it left my hand. I shot lightning, and I was momentarily cheered as it hit his breastplate. But he simply stood there, as if I'd hit him with a feather. I pointed to the ground at his feet and the gravel and stones and dirt started twisting around his ankles. He stepped out of the trap and looked at me, his mouth curled in a contemptuous smile.

"Seems you are not powerful enough to stop me, either, Kader."

I ran a strength spell on myself and physically attacked him. He pulled the Hammer from his belt with inhuman speed and used it to knock me back with a blow to my chest. I lay on the ground, trying to catch my breath as he strode toward me.

He pointed at me and for the first time since facing Nakamura in San Francisco those many years ago, I was paralyzed with fear.

He swung the Hammer.

I was flying. It was as if I were only a bug and he'd flicked me with his finger, and I was flying backwards through the air. I smashed into a granite wall, slumped to the ground, and passed out as pain washed over me like a heavy rain.

# CHAPTER TWENTY-THREE

Larsen looked at me with shock on his face when I came into the room. I knew I looked like hell. My clothes were tattered and dirty. I was limping painfully. Healing spells were not ending the pain as they should. I'd woken up in the same marshy valley where I'd fought the Transylvanian. I had no idea how I'd gotten there. My talisman was still in my pocket but it didn't seem to have any power left. It was as if Thor had drained both it and my powers.

I'd walked to the main road and hitched a ride to the ferry to Tromsø. From the ferry I had walked to the house.

"Sir!" Larsen cried out and helped me to sit at the table. "What happened?"

"We're taking the flying boat tomorrow," I said ignoring his question. "I know where Nakamura is."

Larsen hesitated. "Who's Nakamura?"

I looked at him, realizing he'd never known the whole story of Meyoung. "Someone I've wanted to kill for a very long time." I couldn't reach Dagmar; that was obvious. But I could at least kill Nakamura after all these years, assuming my loss of powers was temporary.

"Where is he, then?" Larsen asked, looking at me as if I were a hurt child in his care.

"Tokyo."

"Sir," Larsen said softly, "you don't seem to be in very good shape."

"I'll get better," I said, grimacing with pain, hoping it was true. If it wasn't, I was finished and probably dead. There were still elements in the AMA who would like to kill me and take over in the way Fitzgerald had taken over from Newmark and I had taken over from Fitzgerald (although I hadn't killed him, I'd killed Reynolds, who had killed him).

But Thor had defeated me easily; I was almost powerless against him. He blunted my most powerful spells as easily as I would manipulate a weak-willed lesser. There was no way I could fight him again, as he would easily kill me. I had no idea why he'd let me live this time. I was one of the most powerful adepts in the world, and it wasn't enough.

Larsen started packing and phoned the local DNL office to get tickets for the Flying Coastal Steamer.

I sat and watched the flames in the fireplace and the feral shadows they cast about the room. I felt powerless and helpless for the first time since I'd been in that hospital dying of an infection from my burns. I didn't know what Thor had hit me with but I'd never been unable to heal myself, at least not when I had a talisman.

We had to catch the "Flying Coastal Steamer" the next morning. I felt slightly better. Larsen offered me aspirin and in desperation I took it, swallowing the bitter pills with a glass of water. Hadn't had to do that since before I'd become an adept.

We were leaving the house—Larsen had found us a local taxi service to take us to the flying boat pier—when Nils drove up in one of those local cars. The taxi driver, seeing Nils, put our bags in the trunk of his car and got inside.

Larsen reached under his jacket and I whispered, "Easy."

Nils extracted his large frame from the small car. He was wearing denim pants with a button-down shirt and a loose leather jacket. I wouldn't glance twice at him on the streets of San Francisco, except for his size.

Larsen moved his body between Nils and me. I could feel his tension and I understood it. For the first time, I couldn't protect myself; Larsen was the only thing between any threat and me.

Nils put up a hand, showing it was empty. "I have a message for Mr. Kader," he called out.

I looked at him and wished I could put a truth spell on him. If I'd had the power, I would have.

"What?" I asked.

Nils reached into his pocket and Larsen tensed, his right hand at his hip where his gun was holstered.

Nils extended his hand. I could see it held a piece of paper.

I touched Larsen on the shoulder, which was something like touching a wound spring, and stepped around him. I took the paper from Nils.

"Thank you," I breathed.

Nils nodded. He looked sad, somehow. He turned and entered the car, backed it around, and drove away.

Larsen seemed to slump as if he'd just finished exercising. "What is it, sir?"

I unfolded the paper. It was covered in Dagmar's neat handwriting. It was in the ancient language except for the names and Norwegian words:

\*\*\*

"Frank, I am sorry. The adept priest calling himself 'Thor' has returned to claim *Mjollnir*, *Volhöll*, and the Valkyrie Guild. He forbids all contact with other guilds, including yours. I am sorry, but the Valkyrie must obey the Æsir in all things. I risk his wrath by sending this note with Nils on the excuse that we need supplies. I can only hope he finds you.

Dagmar."

\*\*\*

I wadded it up and threw it away.

Larsen looked at me and then at the paper where it sat in the mud, soaking up the dirty water.

"Let's go," I said, keeping my voice level. I climbed into the back seat of the taxi. A few minutes later Larsen followed.

"What took you so long?"

"I was making sure the house was secure."

\*\*\*

We stayed overnight in Oslo, and from Oslo we flew to Stockholm. From there we started a thirty-hour journey on a plane named "Alrek Viking"; Larsen said it was a DC-6, yet another airplane made by the Douglas Company. The plane was mostly unpainted except for the airline's name, a stylized Viking dragon ship masthead behind the pilot's window that melded into a line running the length of the fuselage, and some sort of coat of arms behind the door.

The flight was to Calcutta via Copenhagen, Zurich, Rome, Damascus, Basra (in a country I'd never heard of called Iraq), and Karachi. The plane then went on to Bangkok, but we changed to the B.O.A.C. at Calcutta and flew to Hong Kong.

By the time Larsen and I got into a taxi to the Peninsula Hotel, I was feeling fine physically. I was, however, drained mentally. It had been just over a month since I had battled Nikolai in that field and I hadn't stopped moving for most of that time.

"How are we going to get to Tokyo?" Larsen asked in the taxi. "There are no commercial flights from here."

"I guess we'll have to convince the military," I said.

"I don't know if they fly every day," Larsen said.

"We'll have to see."

Larsen hesitated, looking out the window. I could tell he wanted to ask me something.

"What?" I prodded.

He turned to look at me. "Are you up to it, sir, I mean, convincing them?"

I smiled. "Yes, I'm fine, now."

He looked relieved, but still I could see he was worried.

"I wouldn't be looking to face down Nakamura if I were still weak," I added.

\*\*\*

It helped that Britain had joined the war on the side of the U.S. They had flights going to Tokyo, including a "Short Sunderland" flying boat that, except for the military paint job, looked like a smaller version of the "Flying Steamer" in Norway. Unfortunately, it was going to Iwakuni Air Force Base, which was on the southern end of Honshu, not too far from Fukuoka, where I'd caught the smuggler's ship to Korea.

Another military flight was needed—and of course that required a persuasion spell on a British officer—to get to Tokyo, this one on the seemingly ubiquitous DC-3/C-47. Since it was a military flight originating from inside Japan, we didn't need to go through customs. Larsen laughed that we'd slipped through the cracks, having avoided customs at Iwakuni by not leaving the base.

We took a taxi to the Tokyo Station Hotel, the same one I'd had Larsen wait in, near the Imperial Palace.

"How are you going to find Nakamura?" Larsen asked at dinner that night in the hotel's restaurant. The food was imitation American, unfortunately. "Tokyo's a big town." He pulled out a map he'd bought. On one side was Tokyo and environs; the other side showed the whole of Japan. It had both English and Japanese writing on it.

I looked at Larsen. "If you were in San Francisco and wanted to find the local guild, what would you do?"

Larsen stopped to think. "I'd ask, politely, at a Chinese apothecary shop. Or a fortuneteller or palm reader's, maybe. Even if they weren't in the guild, they would probably know how to contact it."

"Exactly," I said. "I think we'll start at the black market. I think right now in Japan, people on the edge of the guilds are also likely to be living on the edge of the law."

Larsen nodded his understanding.

Finding the black market was easy. I wondered how "black" it could be given that it occupied several acres of Tokyo real estate and was as obvious as an open sore.

However, it was not as easy as I'd expected. Larsen and I both were eyed with suspicion and surprise. Both of us were taller than the tallest Japanese, and they seemed to look at us as circus freaks walking among them. I wondered how they'd react to Nils.

With a few polite inquiries we found several herbal medicines stores operating quite openly. But the proprietors claimed to have no knowledge of the guilds, even after I'd used truth spells on them.

Walking along, tired and thinking a cold drink would be very nice, I looked up and laughed. Larsen joined in. We had come across the Happi Go-Go Luck bar.

"Can I buy you a beer?" I asked Larsen.

"Sure," he replied.

When we walked in, the place pretty much ignored us. It was full of Americans and Japanese, although the Japanese seemed to either work there or be working there. All the Americans I saw were in uniforms.

There was an empty table, and Larsen and I sat down wearily. A Japanese girl, on cue it seemed, sat down next to me, smiling.

I shook my head and she didn't move.

I looked at her. "No," I said in English.

She still didn't move, but continued to smile and look at me. She was pretty, but with too much makeup and a dress that looked like a child's idea of evening wear.

"*Nain*," I said, switching to Japanese.

Still, she smiled at me as if she didn't hear me.

I was working on a translation spell when she began speaking, softly, in the ancient language.

"Wait here; someone wants to meet you."

I stared at her. I couldn't understand why an adept would be working as a prostitute. She was very young and it wasn't a glamour; I'd see through that. As she stopped masking, I felt her strength. In a way this reminded me of my first meeting with Dagmar, who like this girl was young, petite, pretty, and powerful.

She stood and walked away, and sat down next to an American in a sailor uniform. He put his burly arm around her and pulled her close with a beery laugh.

I looked at her, wondering.

"What was that?" Larsen asked.

"An adept. She asked us to wait."

He looked as surprised as I felt, looking over at her.

"What the hell is she doing, then?"

"I don't know." I couldn't think of any reason an adept would need to resort to prostitution to survive, even here.

I felt another adept walk in. It was a Japanese man wearing an old battered uniform, including the hat. Again I was surprised. This is not how I expected a member of the *Omi Uji* to appear.

He glanced at the girl, still in the clutches of the boisterous sailor. She looked at me and he walked over, sitting down next to Larsen across the table from me.

He didn't even look at my warrior, but spoke directly to me. "This is the second time you've come to this city recently; what are you looking for?" He spoke in the ancient language.

I looked straight at him and hoped my eyes didn't show any bewilderment. "I seek the former head of the *Omi Uji*; he called himself Nakamura."

"I am not *Omi Uji*," the man said.

I was taken aback. I had learned years ago during my travels in Japan that the Japanese adepts were all united into one guild, the *Omi Uji*. "Who are you?"

I could see him hesitating. "We are the *Muraji Uji*."

"I thought there were no other guilds in Japan."

"There aren't."

I looked at him. I detected no mirth or deception. He seemed to believe what he was saying. But his clothes, and the female adept working as a B-girl, were incongruent with everything I knew about guilds.

I decided to ignore it. "Do you know where Nakamura is?"

"I do not. I know he is not in Tokyo. He disappeared about four years ago."

I almost said, "But Thor said he was here," but I stopped myself. I looked over at the girl. "Why?"

He smiled. "How better to hide than as the faceless, worthless, discarded people? No, she doesn't sell herself, although she does get money."

That was easy to understand. The men might even think they had a wonderful time. "Why are you hiding?"

"We have always hidden from the *Omi*, since Hideyoshi unified Japan and chose the *Omi* as the only *Uji* allowed. The *Omi* were very strong for four hundred years until the end of the war. They bet too much on the success of the Japanese militarists. Now they are weaker and we are growing stronger."

I looked at him still, his black eyes blazing. I'd had no idea about this part of the history of the Japanese guilds. I'd heard of the *Muraji* but I thought them a legend or a myth, or at least lost to history. Like Thor.

"Thank you," I said, "for the information."

"When will you be leaving Tokyo?"

"I have to find Nakamura first."

"He is not here."

"My information says otherwise."

He looked at me intently. "I can tell you are powerful, Kader *sensei*. I do not know where Nakamura is now. He hasn't led the *Omi Uji* for over a year now."

Before I could respond he stood and walked out, masking as he did. I watched him go, wondering.

"What was all that?" Larsen asked. He seemed as if he were waking from a dream.

I almost laughed. "I'm not sure. But he says Nakamura isn't here."

"But you said—"

"Yes." I cut him off. "I need to think about this. Let's go."

The old woman had walked up by then and looked at us. When we stood to leave, she started yelling. I didn't bother to translate it; I pretty much knew what she was saying.

Larsen and I tried to find our way out of the black market.

As we walked I explained what the adept, the *Muraji Uji* had told me about Nakamura.

"Do you think he's dead?" Larsen asked.

I shook my head. "Thor said he was in Tokyo."

"Thor sent you on a wild goose chase before," Larsen pointed out. I'd told him what Meyoung had told me.

"And that's another thing," I said. "That makes no sense. He's powerful enough that he shouldn't need to send me to Korea to be ambushed. I still don't know why he didn't kill me." The fear I felt at talking about him was a sour taste in the back of my throat.

"Maybe Miss Dagmar won't let him," Larsen conjectured.

I frowned. "You could be right, in a way. Perhaps he's worried that if he kills me, he'll lose her loyalty."

We passed another bar, but the name was written in Japanese; actually in *Kanji* and Kana, the two Japanese phonetic alphabets. I didn't know them as well as I knew Korean *Hangul* but I recognized the *Kanji*. The bar must have been called "Tokyo something" since the first two *Kanji* were those for "Tokyo."

I stopped walking and looked at the sign. "Damn!"

"What, sir?" Larsen was looking at me.

"He was using a translation spell," I said.

"Who, sir?"

"Thor. Damn, I'm an idiot."

Larsen was looking at me as if he agreed. "Sir?"

I pointed to the sign. "The word 'Tokyo' is made of two *Kanji*, or Chinese characters. Let me see your map."

Larsen pulled the map from his jacket pocket and I turned it to the Tokyo side. At the top "Tokyo" was written in English and *Kanji*. "See these two *Kanji*? That means 'Tokyo':

"The first one..." I pointed to

"...means 'east,' and the second one..." I pointed to

"...means 'capital.' So 'Tokyo' means 'East Capital.'"

"Yes?" Larsen asked, sounding perplexed. "East of what?"

"Peking, I think," I said. I didn't tell him that "Peking" means North Capital in Chinese. "But that's not important. When Thor told me Nakamura was in Japan, he said 'Root of the Sun.' If you're using a translation spell, you tend to get literal translations." I turned the map over to show the whole country. "These two *Kanji* mean 'Japan':

"The first *Kanji* is 'sun' and the second, literally 'root.'"

"I thought Japan was the Land of the Rising Sun," Larsen objected.

"Yes, that's what those two *Kanji* mean together. But literally, they mean 'sun' and 'root.' Thor must have made that 'Root of the Sun' and I figured he must have meant Japan. I mean where else would Nakamura be? Certainly not Korea or China, now."

Larsen smiled broadly. "Oh, it's like, uhm, butterfly. Literal translation sounds like flying butter rather than a pretty insect."

I looked at him. "Yes, exactly. But, Thor said 'Capital City' which I assumed meant Tokyo, the capital of Japan."

"'Capital City'?" Larsen asked.

I pointed to the map. "Those *Kanji* there literally mean 'capital' and 'city':

Larsen looked at the English. "Kyoto?"

"It was the capital until the Meiji Restoration and its name literally means 'capital city.'"

"So Nakamura's in Kyoto."

I smiled at Larsen. "Yes. We're in the wrong city."

\*\*\*

We had passed through Kyoto on the train to Fukuoka. It was the last large city before Kobe. I decided the easiest way to get there was to take the train again.

Kyoto was a city of ancient temples and shrines, not to mention the Kyoto Imperial Palace. Larsen explained that the Allies hadn't bombed it out of deference to its cultural and historical significance and the Japanese's wise decision to place nothing of "strategic value" there.

We found a new Western-style hotel near the rail station, built for the tourist trade they were hoping would start coming from the States.

"Same drill?" Larsen asked as we walked to our rooms.

"Huh?"

"Try to find herbal shops or the black market?"

I shook my head. "I don't think that's necessary. A visit to a shrine should suffice."

He looked at me quizzically.

I smiled at him. "Have a good rest, Larsen. You will need it."

The next morning was bright and warm. Kyoto tends to be hot and humid in the summer, and Larsen and I were both sweating when we reached the shrine's *tori'i* gate. I knew we'd just started our exercise, because this was the Fushimi Inari Shrine. *Tori'i* gates always looked vaguely like a *Kanji*, to me, and this one was huge, at least twenty-five feet tall. I turned to Larsen.

"Do what I do."

"Yes, sir."

"And I need more money." I usually carried a few dollars and some coins for tips and such, but Larsen had the bulk of my cash.

"How much, sir?"

"A hundred dollars should suffice."

Larsen reached into his coat and brought out his money clip and peeled off a one-hundred dollar bill. I folded it and placed it in my trouser pocket.

"Ready?" I asked him.

"Yes, sir."

I bowed before the *tori'i* and then walked through, watching Larsen out of the corner of my eye. He made a clumsy attempt to bow and followed me. I walked on the left side of the path past the stone guardian foxes wearing red cloth around their necks that looked like bibs. I passed the main temple, which was just after the second huge *tori'i*, to seek the pathway up the mountain. It passed under countless *tori'i* with the names of those who had donated them written on vertical posts. At places there were so many that it was like passing through a tunnel. And there were statures of foxes everywhere, in different shapes, sizes, and attitudes. Some were large and frightening, others small and cute.

Because of the muggy weather and the hills, the hike was slow and unpleasant. Larsen did better than I, but he said he wished he could take off his suit jacket. He couldn't; it concealed his weapons.

The Fushimi Shrine is not just one shrine, but many shrines for many deities. I found the one I was looking for and was glad it was near an *ema*.

Again, I bowed before passing the small *tori'i* marking the entrance to the shrine.

At the purification fountain I used the dipper to rinse my left hand, then my right, then my mouth, and then rinsed the dipper. Larsen did the same, after I gently reminded him to rinse the left hand first.

As we approached the sanctuary, I whispered to Larson, "Just watch." He nodded his understanding.

I stopped in front of the sanctuary and bowed. Then I walked toward it, staying to the left of the path. I rang the round bell by pulling the cord hanging from it. I reached into my pocket and pulled out the one-hundred-dollar bill and tossed it into the offering.

Then I bowed low twice, clapped twice, and bowed again, not quite so low. I brought my palms together in front of my chest in a gesture not unlike the one my mother used when praying in the church in Grand Forks. I clapped again, using the fingers of my right hand to hit the palm of my left. I again put my palms together and stood in silence. This would be the time for an adherent to make a prayer or wish. I found myself wishing to find a way to defeat Thor, despite myself.

I bowed low again, stepped back about three paces, and bowed again. I backed up farther before turning to walk away.

"What was that, sir?" Larsen whispered.

"Showing my respects."

I walked to the nearby *ema*. I purchased a wooden plate shaped like a fox's head from a priest and wrote on it in English with the provided paintbrush, "Nakamura" and the name of our hotel, and "Kader." I hung it on the *ema*, a four-sided structure that almost looked like an information kiosk one might find at a railroad station, except for the wooden plates hanging from it.

Larsen and I then walked out of the Fushimi Shrine. Once past the *tori'i* at the entrance, Larsen looked at me. "Will that work?" He'd stopped whispering.

I nodded. "It will here."

"And what do we do now?"

"We wait."

"And the hundred dollars?"

"I wanted to get the *kami's* attention."

Larsen frowned. "What's a *kami*?"

I smiled. "Never mind."

Larsen looked confused.

"You have weapons?" I asked.

"Of course."

"Good. You'll probably need them soon."

Larsen waved down a taxi, which was a tiny vehicle. I didn't know why the Japanese insisted on making their cars so small.

We crawled into the back and I told the driver the address of our hotel.

"*Hai!*" he said bowing from the neck, and then drove off at a speed that made walking look fast.

I rolled down the window to try to get some air.

"Why," Larsen asked, "couldn't you do that shrine thing in Tokyo?"

"Doesn't have the right shrine."

I could tell by the look on his face that Larsen didn't understand but he didn't ask any more questions. He was smart enough to know that if I was being evasive I wouldn't answer his questions anyway. In Japan, religion and meta are combined in a way unlike that of any other country, except maybe Tibet. The shrine was to the *kami*, or deity, the ancient Japanese adepts believed provided their power. And modern adepts still go through the motions of honoring that *kami*; whether out of tradition or out of actual belief, I do not know. But only at that particular shrine could I contact the *Omi Uji* through the *ema*.

My hotel room was on the second, and top, floor. To help with the heat, I kept the window open. It was a new-design: the bottom pane tilted out letting air in, but making it all but impossible for a human to get through. I put an alarm spell on it, nonetheless. I also placed an alarm spell on the door. I didn't really need to; I didn't sleep anyway.

The door alarm sounded in my head and a bright light appeared in time to see the door knocked off its hinges. Two men stood blinking in the light. They were holding pieces of black metal I presumed to be weapons, except the box part that held the bullets was on the side rather than the bottom as I was used to seeing.

That they were weapons was confirmed when they started shooting blindly into the room. Blindly, because I knew they couldn't see anything past my light spell. The flash from their guns splattered the room with angry shadows and I could see furniture and walls being battered by the impact of the bullets.

Blood flashed brilliant red in the light, coming from the head of the man on the right. He fell as if pushed over, his gun silenced.

"I need one alive!" I called out above the noise of the guns.

Blood sprayed from the knees of the second man and he crumpled to the floor.

The room's lights came on and Larsen, still holding his smoking gun, bounded over from his hiding place in the corner and ripped the guns away from both warriors.

I could then hear the one breathing hard, wheezing. Larsen grabbed him roughly and pulled him into the room. The man yelled with pain as his knees were dragged across the wooden floor.

Larsen tried to close the door but the frame was too damaged. He settled for leaning it against the opening.

I was fingering my talisman, preparing the truth spell for the *Omi Uji* warrior, when the alarm spell for the window sounded.

"Damn!" I yelled turning to the window as glass came showering in. The warriors had been a distraction.

A man was crashing through the window. I could see the shimmering of his protection spell around him, warding off the shattered glass and keeping him from being cut.

Larsen turned, raising his gun.

"No!" I screamed.

Larsen fired several times in rapid succession at the adept, the bullets bouncing off his protection spell and ricocheting around the room with a twang and a whine. I found myself ducking to try to keep from being hit, although intellectually, I doubted that would help much.

The adept twisted in the air and just as Larsen stopped shooting, he ended the protection spell and aimed a finger at my warrior. Larsen was dealing with his weapon, putting a black metal box into the handle. He was doing it by feel or practice or both, because his eyes were on the adept. Larsen's eyes were full of fear, something I'd never seen before.

I aimed for the Japanese adept and fired an airbolt. But as I did, lightening arced from the Japanese adept's palm to Larsen's chest. Larsen was pressing a button on the handle of his gun and part of the device snapped forward just as Larsen was hit. The force knocked him back into the wall, cracking the plaster.

He slumped to the floor, his chest smoking, his gun falling to land on the carpet.

My airbolt hit the adept and knocked him down. He struggled to his feet and I pulled the air from him. He tried to pull it back, but his power was no match for mine.

I worked up a translation spell. "If you want to live, tell me where to find Nakamura!"

He looked at me, bewilderment on his face, before he folded up and dropped to the floor. I kept the air from him long enough to ensure that he was dead, not knowing why he had never answered me.

I rushed to Larsen and took his head in my hands.

"Larsen?" I cried.

He opened his eyes and looked at me. He tried to speak, but all that came out was a moist gurgle.

I knew his name; I could heal him. I ripped open his shirt, exposing the blackened and crisp skin underneath. I put my talisman on the wound and invoked the strongest healing spell I dared without passing out. At that moment, I didn't think I should reserve some meta in case of another attack.

I heard movement in the room and turned. The wounded warrior had crawled to where Larsen had left the weapons and was picking one up and pointing it at me. I didn't want to kill him: he was my last link to Nakamura. I dove out of the way just as he fired. But that left Larsen exposed. His chest jerked spasmodically as the bullets slammed into it and he slumped over, his last breath escaping his mouth mixed with blood.

I said a very bad word in the ancient language and jumped across the room, not thinking now of my own safety. The warrior tried to change his aim, but I was on him too fast. I wrenched the gun from his grip and threw it across the room. It hit something and fired once, the bullet making a screaming sound as it shot around the room. I ignored it.

I hit the warrior with two spells: one that held him, one that made him tell me the truth. I did the translation spell on myself.

He looked at me with wide eyes, full of fear. I liked that look in his eyes. I walked over to Larsen's body and found my talisman, still on his chest. I ignored the corpse and returned to the warrior.

"Is anyone else attacking?" I barked at him.

"No."

"No more adepts or warriors?"

"No."

"Where's Nakamura?"

He started to rattle off an address.

I stopped him. "Do you have a car?"

"Yes."

"Take me there."

"I can't walk."

Persuasion spell: "Try." The word was more of a growl. I let the holding spell go.

Slowly he stood. When it looked as if he would stop because of the pain, I strengthened the persuasion spell.

He got to his feet, stood wobbling for a moment, and then fell. I guess he really couldn't walk.

"What's your name?" I asked him, trying to soften my tone.

He looked at me; he didn't want to answer, but the truth spell was still on him. "Haruo Nakajima," he whispered.

I put my hands on his knees and healed his knees.

He looked at me, gratitude in his eyes.

I put the holding spell on him again, this time tighter, making it impossible for him to move or even breathe.

"Deceive me, try to escape, or harm me, and I will kill you," I hissed at him, allowing all my anger and hate to flow into my words.

He couldn't move, but I could see his acquiescence in his eyes.

"We're going to your car." I released the holding spell and he stood, smiling at his healed knees. He pulled the door aside. The corridor was full of people, including the police.

"*Omi Uji* business," I said, showing my talisman and hitting the cops with persuasion spells.

They let us by.

The warrior drove me to a neighborhood that looked relatively prosperous. The houses were large and in good repair. I wondered how that was possible, given the poverty I had seen in Tokyo.

"He's in that house," the warrior said, stopping the car and pointing. The truth spell was still on him.

"Warriors?" I asked.

"No, I am the last."

"Adepts?"

"No, you killed his protector. You killed all but me."

"He's alone?"

"Yes. The *Omi Uji* will not help him; only those loyal to him, and I am all that's left. I think they told him where to find you in hopes you'd kill him."

I knew it was the truth. But why would the *Omi Uji* abandon their leader? In most guilds, a former leader was a dead leader. But if he was alive, why wasn't he still head of his guild? I didn't understand, but I knew where to get answers.

"Out of the car."

He led me to the front door, which was made of wood and paper, and slid it aside. The warrior took me to a side room. Lying on a futon on the floor, almost unrecognizable, was Nakamura. His hair was mostly gone, and he was thin and pale. He shouldn't have been older than fifty-five, but he looked like an ancient, shriveled-up man.

He looked up at me and whispered something I didn't hear. It might have been "Kader."

"What's wrong with him?" I asked.

The warrior still had the truth spell on him. "He was near Kobe when the atomic bomb was dropped. The effects he could cure using his skills. But later he developed cancer of the blood and bones. He detected them too late."

"Too late?"

"He could heal, but that would make him weak and the cancer would advance. He'd heal again, but get weaker still and the cancer advance further. It is a losing battle. He will die eventually. Soon, I hope. I can only control the pain." He gestured toward a box with a red cross on it. Drugs, I decided.

"Does he have a safe?"

The warrior looked at me as if he didn't understand.

"Where does he keep his papers and talismans?" I asked.

The warrior pulled an unlocked lacquer box from a shelf. "This is all the guild leadership let him keep."

I took the box and opened it. There were no talismans, but there were papers written in the ancient language with occasional *Kanji*. One paper described how to manipulate water.

Nakamura could manipulate water as easily as I could fire. That explained how he'd gotten out of the water so fast at the Embarcadero it looked as if he flew.

I folded up the paper and put it in my shirt pocket for later study. The warrior made no move to stop me, knowing it was the spoils of victory.

I looked at the man on the futon. "Nakamura?"

"*Hai*," he said softly. "Kader? *Ronin*?"

"Yes," I said. I had been guildless, or *ronin*, for years. Perhaps he thought I still was.

Nakamura just looked at me with eyes that radiated his pain and humiliation.

"What happens if you die?" I asked the warrior.

The warrior looked at me. "No one to give him his medicine."

"And without his medicine?"

"He dies in pain."

I touched the warrior and he fell to the floor, dead.

I looked at Nakamura. I wanted to say something, to tell him of the pain he had caused me. I wanted to tell him about Meyoung and how I hated him for what he had done to her. But it all seemed trite and meaningless.

So I told him about Larsen. "My warrior..." I hesitated in order to stop my voice from cracking "...my friend, is dead."

He didn't say anything. I didn't know whether he understood.

I looked at him and he returned my gaze. I knew I had his attention. "If you're lucky, you'll die soon," I said. "If I'm lucky, you won't."

# CHAPTER TWENTY-FOUR

It took money and persuasion spells, but three days later I was on a flight back to the States, Larsen's body in the cargo hold.

I still was struggling to believe that Larsen was dead. The typical attitude in the guilds is that warriors are fungible. I hadn't realized it until I told Nakamura, but Larsen was my friend. Yes, he knew about guns, tactics, cars, and airplanes. We had little in common. But without him, my world suddenly felt wholly empty.

Sitting in the airplane's lounge on the lower deck, looking over the expanse of gunmetal gray ocean, I thought about my life. There was little left in it. I'd lost Dagmar. I'd regained—I had thought—and lost Meyoung. I had apparently killed my own son. And now Larsen was gone. I could only return to San Francisco and run my guild, but somehow even that seemed hollow and fruitless.

I was hoping my posture and my scowl would discourage any loquacious passengers from trying to engage me in conversation. It worked, but that didn't stop them from talking near me. One large American with a southern accent was talking to another man.

"You mean we left Tokyo at 8:00 A.M. Wednesday and we'll get into Honolulu at 2:00 A.M Wednesday?"

"That's right," his companion said.

"Shoot, that's six hours before we left."

"No," the companion explained patiently. "It's eighteen hours after we left, but because we're crossing the International Date Line, we go back twenty-four hours."

The southerner just looked at him. "That don't make no sense."

I didn't understand it either, but I just didn't care. I seemed to have no reason to care. Something I'd heard in church many, many years before came back to me unbidden: "The thing that hath been, it is that which shall be; and that which is done is that which shall be done: and there is no new thing under the sun."

Meyoung was as good as dead. The woman I had known as Meyoung, or Peg, had died years ago after Nakamura's abuse.

Dagmar was controlled by, and perhaps the lover of, Thor.

I couldn't defeat Thor; I was sure he'd kill me if I tried again. He'd probably spend an hour insulting me first, though.

Nakamura wasn't worth killing.

And Larsen was dead.

They'd given me a satchel with his personal effects, minus the weapons, of course, which the Kyoto police had confiscated after I'd persuaded them they belonged to the dead men. I'd never looked at it. I'd carried it onto the airplane and thrown it onto the shelf above the seats. I wasn't sure why; maybe I thought I could return it to his family. But I knew nothing about his family. Adept habit: don't talk or ask about the past.

I walked up the spiral stairs to the upper deck with the seats and found mine. I pulled down the canvas satchel and pulled back the zipper. The seat next to mine was empty because I'd bought a ticket for it so I wouldn't have to sit next to anyone. I sat in it and pulled out items from the satchel and placed them on my seat. There was his wallet with some money, a California driver's license, and an old faded picture of a girl. He'd never talked about having a sweetheart.

There was his passport, stamped with all the places we'd gone. There were keys. Since I'd provided him a room in the Huntington, I wasn't sure what they unlocked.

And there was a dirty wrinkled piece of paper that had been folded neatly into quarters. I didn't recognize it until I unfolded it. It was Dagmar's note. Why had he hung on to that? I wondered. I was about to crumple it up again when I found myself reading it.

"The adept priest calling himself 'Thor,'" she'd written. Why had she said it in that manner? I wondered. All adepts call themselves by aliases. But why emphasize it with quotation marks?

And why would Thor forbid contact with other guilds? Of what would Thor have to be afraid? He had defeated me easily.

And why had he insulted me so? In all the legends of Thor, both those of the guilds and those of the Norse who turned him into a god, none spoke of him insulting his enemies. That sounded more like...

"Damn," I whispered.

***

Louis and two warriors met me at the airport. So did a hearse.

"Teacher," Louis said in respectful greeting.

"We need to talk," I said.

Workers were loading the casket into the hearse. "I've made arrangements," Louis said, speaking softly. "His body will be taken back to his family."

"Where's that?" I asked, realizing how little I knew about him.

"Salinas," Louis said.

I nodded.

"He was a good man," Louis said softly.

"Yes." I had nothing else to say.

We climbed into the armored Cadillac that Larsen had made me buy.

"Repaired?" I asked the driver/warrior.

"No, sir," he said, looking in the rearview mirror at me, "this is the new one you ordered before you left. The other is still in the shop."

I laughed bitterly. I still couldn't tell cars apart. Larsen probably would have known at a glance.

We drove toward the city and I briefly told Louis about everything that had happened. Then I said, "We need to go after him."

"Yes, Teacher, but you said he was too strong."

I nodded. "Yes, he was. I have to find some way to defeat him."

Louis nodded thoughtfully but didn't say anything.

\*\*\*

That night I slept in my own bed in my own hotel room at the Huntington on Nob Hill for the first time in what seemed ages, but was really less than a month. Two warriors patrolled the hall, and another was sleeping in what had been Larsen's room. I still didn't feel as safe as I would have if Larsen had been there.

In the morning it was time for research. I ordered all of the guild's books brought to me. Some were so old that only spells held them together, spells it was my duty to reinforce from time to time.

It was widely believed that adepts had first developed their abilities on Atlantis. There the adepts lived in peace with each other and studied their art. They mingled with the lessers, using their powers to free oppressed peoples living around the Mediterranean. They had ships, powered by meta, that reached the Americas, "the opposite continent which surrounded the true ocean." Attempted barbarian invasions were brushed off by meta attacks. It was said that the Atlanteans had powers that modern adepts had lost: the power to see the future, the power to control nature, the power to end the aging process and stop death.

But the peoples the Atlanteans freed were resentful of Atlantis' wealth and power, and they gathered a huge invasion fleet and attacked the island people who had been their benefactors. It was too large a force, and even meta could not stop them. The Atlanteans fled to the far corners of the world, becoming the gods of Greek and Norse myth, the priests of the civilizations of the Americas, the mythological founders of civilizations in Asia, or the wizards and warlocks and witches of myths and legends.

That much the books and manuscripts agreed on. What had happened to the lost island continent was a matter of speculation. Some books claimed it was unstable and held in place only by the spells of the most powerful Atlantean adepts: the priests. And when the invaders killed or drove off those priests, the continent sank into the ocean, ironically drowning the invaders. Others said it was simply a natural disaster. Still others said it was Iceland, and since the adepts could control the weather, it could be a warm tropical paradise for them. Or maybe it was Greenland.

And what had happened to the immortal adepts, the Atlantean priests? That too the books disagreed on. As Christianity spread, the adept-gods were forgotten, persecuted, or at least hounded by constant attempts at persecution. Some books said they had allowed themselves to die. Others said they went into hiding. Still others claimed that the immortals went into a deep sleep, hoping to wake when the world was more accepting of them. It was *Ragnarøkkr*: twilight of the gods: what Wagner had called *Götterdämmerung*.

I thought I knew who was at Valhalla claiming to be Thor. But I could not find a clue as to how to defeat him. When the gods had grown tired of his pranks, they had captured and bound him. That story might have been apocryphal, but if it was true, it took the combined forces of adepts more powerful than I to do it.

I was eating a light supper when Doc Addleman came into my suite.

"Frank," he said, "good to see you back."

I looked up and smiled at the old adept. He'd refused to leave his Arizona home where he helped lessers. But he did occasionally come for a visit, usually unannounced. He always stood out in cosmopolitan San Francisco in his jeans, plaid shirt, and cowboy boots.

"Hello, Doc, what brings you here?"

He sat on one of my leather couches. "Louis called me, told me what happened. I caught the first train out."

We looked at each other for a while and then he said softly, "Tell me what's going on, Frank."

I leaned back in my chair. I told him about the imposter at Valhalla. I told him of my defeat. I told him I had no idea how defeat the imposter.

"How did you beat the Transylvanian?" Addleman asked.

"Lightning bolt to the brain," I said.

Doc frowned. "There was more to it than that."

"Well, yes," I said. "There was quite a battle. He'd double-crossed me and set up an ambush."

"What saved you?" Doc prodded.

I thought a moment. "My abilities as an adept," I said. "And the car, some. But that saved me from the guns, the technology. I don't think I'm going to face technology at Valhalla."

Addleman shook his head. "Probably not. But you didn't defeat the Transylvanian alone." It was a statement.

"No," I agreed, "he had too many warriors. If it weren't for that, I would have been able to defeat him. So I asked Dagmar for help, and Louis and Henderson helped, too." And it had gotten Henderson killed.

"And you can't ask for help with this problem?"

I looked at him. "Without the Valkyrie, I don't think I could trust enough adepts to help me. It will take a lot of adepts to win that battle."

"There is one who could be a big help."

"Who?" I asked.

"Thor."

I laughed. "First of all, I don't know if he's alive, and second, how can I know I can trust him?"

Addleman looked at me. "You trusted me once before you knew you could."

I looked out the window at the darkening sky. "Yes, I did."

"And it saved your life," Addleman stated.

"Yes," I whispered. I looked at him. "But I don't even know whether he's alive."

Addleman gestured toward the books and manuscripts. "Then try to find him."

Then I said, "Hungry?"

"Sure," Addleman answered lightly.

I picked up the phone and ordered room service for him.

After he left, I returned to my reading, concentrating on finding a clue about Thor.

There was one recurring theme when it came to Thor: he was always killing giants or monsters or trolls. One manuscript even claimed he was Beowulf using a different name, as adepts often do.

But there were no giants or monsters or trolls left in the world. And what if he was sleeping the centuries away, as some claimed? Where would he be then?

Light was coming in the east-facing windows when I finally stopped. I had been reading and searching for nearly twenty-four hours and still had no idea where to look, unless I could find a giant that needed killing—other than the one at Valhalla.

"Good morning, sir," my new personal warrior said, coming out of his room. His name was Mason and he seemed competent.

"Morning," I mumbled.

Mason looked at me. He was a large man with black hair in a crew cut and deep, dark eyes. "Been up all night, sir?"

"Yes," I said.

"Hell of a way to greet the day, sir." He smiled nervously.

"Order me some breakfast, and then I'm going to bed."

"Yes, sir."

I leaned back in my chair and looked at the pile of books in front of me. There was no clue as to how to find Thor.

I ate my breakfast and fell into my bed. I was awakened later that evening by the phone in my apartment ringing. I picked it up. "Yes?"

"Sorry to wake you, sir." It was Mason. "There's someone in the lobby asking for you. Says his name is Krupp."

"Krupp?" I mumbled. Why did that sound familiar? Some far-off bell was ringing in the back of my memory.

"Vaughan says he's an adept."

"Who's Vaughan?" I asked, still not fully awake and still distracted by the familiar name.

"The young adept from Salt Lake City. You had him on lobby duty, sir."

"Oh, yeah," I said, brain cells starting to fire. Vaughan hadn't struck me as a very serious fellow. I'd thought lobby duty might sober him up. "What guild is this Krupp?"

"Won't say, sir, just insists on speaking with you."

I let out a long sigh, still lying in bed. "Give me fifteen minutes to get dressed, then have Vaughan bring him up."

"Yes, sir."

*** 

Mason was standing beside my chair when Vaughan brought Krupp in.

"*Danke*," Krupp told the young adept as he left. He was an old man, small and frail and bent over as if his years were weighing on him. He held his hat in his hands and looked at me with bright blue eyes. I could feel his power and decided he wasn't masking. He was surprisingly strong for one his age.

"Have a seat, Mr. Krupp," I said, trying to sound welcoming. I pointed to the old leather couch.

"Thank you," Krupp said, smiling as if it hurt to do so. His teeth seemed small and pointed, more like a serpent's than a man's. He sat slowly and deliberately. Then he looked at me again with those bright eyes that seemed out of place in his wizened face.

"What can I do for you, Mr. Krupp?"

He took a shallow breath. "My guild is Germanic, I'm sure you surmised."

"Of course." The name kept nagging at me, as if a string was tied to the back of my mind and the old man kept pulling it.

Krupp again smiled, showing those teeth. "You know some Germanic guilds were in league with Hitler during the war."

"Yes." I struggled to keep my voice even. The guilds that had helped the Nazis had much to answer for.

"It started very early," Krupp said. "Hitler was always interested in the guilds."

"Is it true he was a failed adept?" I asked, despite myself.

Krupp shook his head. "I do not know, and it doesn't matter. He wished the help of the guilds."

I just looked at him, for if I opened my mouth I'd probably say something to make him angry.

In turn he just looked at me.

"Is there something I can do for you?" I finally asked, my voice taut with controlled anger.

"Let me tell you a story," Krupp said with that serpent smile.

I nodded, hoping this would bring him to the point of this discussion.

"On March fifteen, 1938, Dr. Joseph Goebbels conducted a meeting at Watburg Castle near the small town of Eisenach," Krupp started. "Did you know this?"

I shook my head. "No, I didn't."

"Not surprising; it was a state secret. Goebbels invited adepts and…what is the word?…fakes, I think."

"Close enough," I stated. I knew what he meant—those who prey on ignorant lessers and give adepts a bad name: astrologers and clairvoyants and the like. Some have some small power and are friends of the guilds, even members. But most are charlatans. We tolerate them, as we care little how foolish lessers waste their money.

"We were loyal to the Third Reich, or we would not have been invited. You must understand: Hitler had seemed to save Germany, to make it rise anew from the ashes of the Versailles Treaty."

I waved my hand to dismiss his excuses. I didn't care why he'd supported Hitler; I only cared how this affected me and, more importantly, my guild. "Yes, yes," I said. "I understand." Although I hoped he realized that understanding is not condoning.

"We knew Germany was about to enter a large war," he continued. "That much was obvious, as tensions between Germany and England and France were continually growing. Although some claimed to know this through their powers."

He paused to take a deep breath, which seemed impossible with his small chest.

"We decided that Germany would need help."

"Help?"

He shook his head. "That's not quite accurate. We proposed Germany might need help in the unlikely possibility that America would enter the war. Goebbels rejected the idea immediately, boasting of the *Führer's* military might."

"What idea?" I asked, hoping to speed up the man's story.

He smiled at me. "Not until the events of August thirty, 1943 did Hitler and Goebbels agree to our plan. I assume you know what happened that day."

I nodded. I had been in Paris that day.

"It was only by bad luck, or perhaps I should say good luck, that I was not there. I was in Schweinfurt when the allies bombed it on the seventeenth. I believe there was a large ball-bearing plant or some such thing there. In any case, I was badly injured, and by the time I'd healed myself it was too late to travel to Paris by the thirtieth.

"Otherwise, we might have met then," he said smiling. "And perhaps things would have turned out different."

I smiled back grimly. Or Brunhild, Dagmar, and I would have killed him, too. "Perhaps," I repeated, hoping to encourage him.

"Hitler was enraged by your success and the loss of the Hammer, and I was called to Berchtesgaden to explain the idea that we'd had in 1938 and Goebbels rejected."

"And that was?" I prodded, hoping he'd at last get to the point.

"To enlist the help of an Atlantean priest."

I leaned forward and looked at him intently. "Thor," I whispered.

"Oh, no," he said, shaking his head. "Why would Thor help us? No, we needed a priest who would be happy to cause mischief."

"Loki!" I burst out.

"Yes," the man hissed. "We needed Loki."

"You found Loki!" I exclaimed.

"Yes," Krupp confirmed, "and he's claiming to be Thor."

"And living in Valhalla with the Valkyrie," I added.

"Yes, yes," Krupp confirmed as if this were old, well-known news.

"You see," he continued, "by the time we had located Loki and woken him, it was too late. The Red Army was entering Berlin and the Americans had reached the Elbe."

"Why?" I asked.

"Why what?"

"Why is he claiming to be Thor?"

Krupp smiled. "He's the prankster, a mischief maker. And he had always been Thor's student. He wished to be the master. When he learned the Valkyrie, Thor's female adept protectors, were weak, he planned to take over, posing as Thor."

"They know he's not Thor," I stated, hoping I wasn't giving Krupp too much information.

"The Valkyrie won't go against any Æsir," he explained dismissively.

"How do you know this?"

"He told me as much."

"Why would he tell you?"

"Oh, I was his protector. He was in war-torn Europe, and did not know the languages or the technology. It would be as if you or I found ourselves on the Moon. We grew quite close as I helped him escape to America.

"Once he felt confident enough to be on his own, he left me. When I heard 'Thor' was back at Valhalla, I knew it must be Loki."

"How do you know it's not Thor?" I demanded.

"Because I know where Thor is."

I leaned forward and probably sounded more anxious than I intended. "Where?"

"Where Loki was."

I was getting frustrated with the old German. "And where is that?"

"Yggdrasil."

I looked at him, sensing no deceit in his face. According to all my guild's books, Yggdrasil was a myth.

"Why are you telling me this?" I probed.

"I have my reasons," he stated simply.

"And they are?"

"My own."

"And where is Yggdrasil?"

Krupp smiled and fixed me with those blue eyes. "Atlantis."

\*\*\*

The plane, a Connie, landed in Reykjavik. We'd boarded it in New York after flying there from San Francisco. I'd taken this same trip to Norway, except we were stopping here this time. After so many times in Iceland, I was finally going to see more than the airport or airbase. Getting off, I was surprised by how cold it was. It was almost September and quite chilly.

Mason turned up his collar and grumbled, "Hate to see this place in winter."

I pulled my trench coat around my shoulders and raised the collar. Krupp smiled at the overcast sky as we waited for a car. I groaned when I saw it. It was one of those Army "jeep" things, its open top covered with canvas that smelled, and metal seats.

I looked at Krupp. "Is this necessary?" Krupp had made all the Icelandic arrangements, sending telegrams to West Germany and Iceland at my guild's expense. I'd sent a few telegrams myself.

"Yes," he replied simply, pushing the front passenger seat forward, making it swing up. He indicated that Mason and I should climb in the back where there was a tight, small bench seat with no place to put your legs. Mason muttered something about "Swore I'd never ride in one again," as he climbed in the back.

Krupp got in the front passenger seat. Our luggage was loaded on a second jeep, along with a pile of gear and another driver. We drove through Reykjavik in a little convoy.

The jeep reminded me of wagons I used to ride back in Grand Forks. It seemed every defect in the road was magnified and hammered into one's backside.

"There was a pothole back there you missed," Mason yelled at the driver over the engine noise.

The driver, a German, ignored Mason and followed Krupp's directions. I used a translation spell, but it hardly helped. The local names were practically a foreign language. There was something rather military in the way the driver and Krupp communicated. And once the driver called Krupp "*Mein Oberführer.*" "*Oberführer*" sounded very military to me. Mason had also noticed it, and I could see by the way his jaw set that he didn't like it.

"Where are we going?" I asked.

"The hotel," Krupp replied.

We only traveled a short distance into the main town. Reykjavik's architecture was similar to that of Tromsø: low squat buildings with sloping roofs to slough off snow. The streets were unpaved and were covered instead with black gravel. Mason, with his dark hair, seemed to stand out among the flaxen-haired natives. The women were indescribably beautiful, even in their thick sweaters, with blonde hair, blue eyes, and fair skin.

And I could feel what I'd felt every other time I'd been in Iceland. This young land was strong with meta. It was like being slightly drunk.

I tapped Krupp on the shoulder and spoke in the ancient language. "What about the local guild?"

"We'll have to avoid them," he stated simply, as if telling me to wear a coat when it's cold.

We stopped at a two-story version of the houses we'd passed.

It was the hotel, obvious because of the sign reading "REYKJAVÍK HÓTEL." After being assigned rooms, we met in the hotel's small restaurant.

"Tomorrow we travel to Fagurholsmyri," Krupp stated over our fish course. "It is about 400 kilometers from Reykjavik. That should take most of the day."

"What is our final destination?" Mason asked.

"Vatnajokull," Krupp said and started eating, indicating he was not going to answer further questions.

***

The road to Fagurholsmyri—unpaved and covered with black gravel at best, little more than a dirt trail most of the time—passed over volcanic mountains and then went into swampy coastal plains crossed with wide rivers and sprinkled with wildflowers and sheep. The sea was to our right, and huge steep mountains to our left. The land was barren and treeless. We passed a massive glacier as we drove through the town of Vik. Vik was a smaller version of Reykjavik with the same squat buildings. I was starting to wonder if they were ubiquitous in the far north.

Outside the towns we saw houses with sod for roofs and two of the walls. They reminded me of potato cellars I'd seen in North Dakota, only taller, and these were lived in. I supposed the sod made the houses warmer.

It was hard to enjoy the scenery, though, sitting in the back of the primitive vehicle. Even with the canvas roof up, it was too cold to be comfortable, exacerbating the discomfort of our seating.

After we'd passed through Vik, another huge glacier came into view in the distance. It dwarfed the landscape when first we saw it, growing across the horizon as we approached in our slow, rough vehicles.

Krupp leaned back and said over the noise of the wind, "Vatnajokull."

At one point the road was pointed straight at the white mass, which looked like a mountain of ice.

Finally, as the sun was setting and the temperature was following it down, we stopped in front of a two-story farmhouse. Like the rest of the buildings I'd seen, it was simple, and rectangular in all dimensions except for the steeply sloped roof. Windows were small and the front door was set back a bit, indicating the thickness of the walls.

Krupp got out of the jeep with a groan and walked to the front door. He walked as if he felt as bad as I did.

He knocked on the door and moments later it swung open. A golden warm light, quite a contrast with the darkening dreary day, fell out the portal and onto the dark green turf.

I could see Krupp's hand in his pocket as he talked to the older man who'd opened the door. A few minutes later, the man nodded and closed the door. Krupp returned.

"We're spending the night here," he said. "It looks large enough to hold us." He then yelled to the drivers in German and they both got out of the vehicles and started unpacking the gear from the second one.

I followed Krupp into the house; this time he didn't bother to knock.

The inside of the house was warm, with a fire in the fireplace and kerosene lamps providing light. The elderly couple had the look of those not exactly sure what was happening, but powerless to stop it.

Krupp had used a persuasion spell on them.

Mason walked in behind me and said, "Oh, good, all the comforts of home."

\*\*\*

In the morning the two jeeps were headed up a valley. Krupp again had commandeered the front passenger seat. I decided to sit in the second jeep's passenger seat, leaving Mason to keep an eye on the old Nazi. Krupp wanted something; he'd said so himself. I was pretty sure he'd come for it eventually, but only after Loki was no longer a problem.

The valley was deep, with dark green turf running up the sides from a rocky brook in the middle.

Slowly bluish-white ice came into view. Soon it was a wall, forcing the jeeps to halt. The ice looked layered, as if someone had smoothed out cake icing over and over. The creek was running out from underneath the wall of ice.

"This is it," Krupp said. He barked instructions to the drivers in German. Again I was caught off guard and decided to keep a translation spell going at all times.

"What?" I asked Krupp.

"A branch of Vatnajokull," he said.

"And what will we find here?" I asked.

He gave me an enigmatic smile.

"Did you know," he said, "that Iceland is one of the last places the Æsir were worshipped as gods?"

"Yes," I stated. I hadn't actually known that, but it made sense. Iceland had been quite isolated until modern transportation was invented. The "Æsir" was the name the lessers used for the Nordic "gods." Some thought it was a bastardization of the word for "priest" in the ancient language.

"So why are we here?" I asked Krupp.

Again he smiled enigmatically. Then he looked over my shoulder.

"Bring those axes and picks up here!" he called out in German.

I turned to see the drivers carrying tools in large green canvas bags. When I turned around, Krupp was examining the face of the glacier with much interest. "It's grown," he muttered in German. "We'll have to dig farther."

He lifted his finger and pointed. Fire jumped from the tip and splashed against the ice, causing it to sizzle. Steam rose in an angry cloud.

"Start there," he told the drivers.

They hefted the picks and attacked the wet spot Krupp had marked.

It took nearly all day. Krupp, Mason, and I watched as the two men hacked their way into the ice. Krupp would stabilize the glacier by melting the surface and then allowing it to freeze. I could tell this was tiring him, so I took a turn at it. It wasn't as easy as it looked. We stopped only to eat the lunch the farmer and his wife had obediently packed for us.

Then we went back to work.

The drivers kept working, hacking into the ice. Krupp kept mumbling something about the ice moving and how they had to dig farther. He and I took turns reinforcing the roof. I was getting better at it.

The drivers grumbled that Mason wasn't pitching in, but Krupp explained that he was guarding them, and their attitude improved slightly.

At about six by Mason's watch, Krupp made one last inspection of the tunnel.

"We're there," he stated flatly.

"Where?" I asked.

"Yggdrasil," he answered as casually as if he'd mentioned the time of day.

I picked up a flashlight and followed him into the ice cave. The ice was blue and shiny

Krupp led me to the end of the tunnel. At that point the men had dug down until they'd hit ground. Krupp pointed to a piece of wood in the soil. It looked like a tree branch about the diameter of my forearm that had been sheared off by the ice.

"What is that?"

"Yggdrasil."

I stared at him. "That's the 'world tree'?"

"Part of it." He took a deep breath. "It's too late to continue; we'll return tomorrow."

We walked out of the cave. The drivers were loading the equipment onto the jeeps, Mason watching them with a smirk on his face. We drove back down the valley to the farmhouse and again, Krupp used a persuasion spell on the occupants.

I used a persuasion spell on the old farmer to keep him from smoking. Krupp didn't comment on it; I'd done the same the night before.

Mason took out a red and white pack of cigarettes.

"Mason," I said sharply.

"Yes, sir?"

"Don't smoke in here; you know I don't like it."

"Sorry, sir," Mason said, replacing the pack in his pocket and walking toward the door. "I'll smoke outside. The cold will be bracing."

Again this was unremarkable; the same thing had happened the night before, even Mason's sarcastic remark. But that night, Krupp had ordered one of his drivers to accompany Mason. Tonight he didn't, the driver having reported that indeed, Mason had smoked a cigarette and returned.

The next morning, we returned to the glacier early. Daylight hours were still long, despite getting into fall. The sun rose shortly after we left the farmhouse at about six.

At the glacier, Krupp and his drivers entered the tunnel with the pickaxe and shovel. This time I decided to join them.

"Stay here," I told Mason. He nodded and sat in a jeep, watching down the valley.

"You armed?" I asked before leaving him.

"Yes, a 1911 under my jacket."

I nodded as if I knew what that meant and entered the ice cave.

When I reached Krupp, the men were digging in the dirt around the root.

"Can you make light?" Krupp asked. "These flashlights are damn useless." He pointed to the flickering bulb and then to his drivers. "They didn't bring extra batteries."

I nodded and looked around the cave. Icicles had formed overnight like stalactites. I broke one off and ran a spell on it. It glowed with a nacreous light, filling the cave. If it hadn't been an easy spell, I'd have suspected Krupp of trying to weaken me.

"How far…" I was going to ask how far they were planning on digging, when the ground caved in, making a hole about two feet wide. One of the drivers almost fell into it; the other grabbed his arm and pulled him back onto the stable ice.

"Put your light in there," Krupp ordered.

I bent down, holding the glowing icicle. There was open space through the hole. The only thing the light reflected off was the bark of another branch, this one thick as my leg.

I stood and looked at Krupp. "Now what?"

"We climb down."

I looked at him to see whether he was serious. In answer, he stepped into the hole and placed his foot on the larger branch. He pulled something from his pocket and it began to glow with a sickly green light. But it was bright enough that I could see more branches, and that there were plenty of handholds and places to put your feet. It should be no harder than climbing a tree was as a child.

Krupp descended, his light still not showing the bottom of the tree, if that's what it was, or the sides of the cavern the tree was somehow encased in.

I followed Krupp into the hole. His light source was strong enough that I didn't need the icicle anymore, so I dropped it.

It fell for many seconds, growing dimmer with distance, until I lost sight of it. I didn't know if it ever hit bottom—or if there was a bottom.

I broke off a twig from the tree and the end started glowing with the same pearly light as before. I liked that better than Krupp's corrupted green.

We climbed down the tree for more than a quarter of an hour. I was amazed; the bark was neither wet nor too dry. If it weren't for the absence of foliage, I could have believed this was a living tree. There were even winged seeds hanging from smaller branches. Other than the ceiling we'd climbed through, I never saw another edge of the cavern.

Krupp stopped at a natural platform formed by a "Y" in the branches.

"There," he said, pointing.

I looked up. To my amazement, there was a person—a man—lashed to a vertical branch.

"Who is that?" I asked, peering at the large man.

"Thor," Krupp whispered.

# Chapter Twenty-Five

As we approached the man, I saw others tied to the branches. There were men and women. Was this the last resting place of the Æsir? Something in the back of my brain spoke of Odin hanging from the branches of Yggdrasil. Is this what the myths meant? Was there truth in there somewhere?

The man Krupp had identified as Thor was large, at least the size of Loki, with long blond hair and powerful bare arms. He was wearing an armor breastplate and chain mail. There was a time when adepts didn't balk at weapons; the Hammer of Thor was originally an implement of war. The one incongruity was his face. It was ancient, shriveled, with slit eyes, nose grown large with age, and a gaping, toothless mouth.

The bark of the tree had grown around about half of him, making the ropes superfluous, which was good since they fell apart at my touch.

It took Krupp and me long minutes to extract Thor from the wooden body cast. I ran a strength spell to hold the large but surprisingly light man tight. As I held him, teetering on the branch I was standing on over the black abyss below us, Krupp tied a rope around Thor's chest and under his arms. While waiting, I looked around. There was another man-shaped depression in another thick vertical branch.

Krupp was done with the rope so I pointed to the depression.

"Loki," was all he said. "He was bound, but the ropes were rotted. Tree had grown around him and held him by then."

Lucky for him, I thought. That fall to whatever was at the bottom of this cavern would probably kill even him.

Krupp climbed up with the end of the rope. While I steadied Thor's body, Krupp and, I assumed, the drivers pulled him up with the rope. I climbed up, holding the body to keep it from swinging.

It took about half an hour, but soon Thor, Krupp, and I were back in the ice cave. I was breathing hard from the exertion and was letting the strength spell dissipate. I knew this was the dangerous part. If Krupp turned on me now, for whatever his reasons might be, I'd have to rely on my strength and skill. Krupp had put this whole expedition together without my help. And one of the drivers could have helped him get Thor out of that hole. So why was I here?

Mason entered the cave. I could see he was worried.

"Why are you here?" Krupp demanded.

"We've got a problem," Mason stated simply, addressing me.

"What?" I asked.

"Local adepts, I think. Two on horseback, one man, one woman, and five warriors."

Krupp turned to the drivers and started speaking quickly in German. I got the translation spell up fast.

"...the weapons."

"In the vehicles," one replied. "This idiot—" he meant Mason "—left his post."

"Maybe you Nazis should have told me where the weapons are," Mason said, in German.

I looked at him and he gave me a sly smile. I was impressed; he had been smart enough to keep that from Krupp and his boys.

"Let's go," I said in English. I pointed at Thor's prone body. "Leave him."

"What are you going to do?" Krupp asked.

"Talk to them," I replied, as if it were obvious. But my hand would be on my talisman.

I stepped out of the cave, Mason beside me. Krupp and his men followed.

In the valley near the jeeps there were two small horses with long manes, each ridden by a person. Both people were tall, lithe figures—one was male, the other female: a magnificently beautiful blonde woman. Her slightly curly tresses reached nearly to the saddle where she sat, and her eyes were deepest blue but seemed to change as she looked around and the light on her face changed. The male was a slightly more masculine version, with hair down only to his shoulders. They were both in the heavy sweaters and embroidered coats the locals seemed to favor.

The beautiful people on the horses distracted me, so it took me a few moments to notice the men along the valley walls, each holding a rifle.

"Mauser K98's," Mason was saying beside me. "Accurate and deadly. Bolt action, though."

"Meaning?"

"It will take them twenty seconds to kill us rather than ten."

I snorted. "That's encouraging. What about you?"

"I've got that nineteen eleven."

When I didn't respond he added, "Pistol, eight rounds."

That wasn't encouraging, either. I was pretty sure "round" meant a shot.

"Who are you people and why are you here?" the man on the horse called out in the ancient language.

I stepped forward. "I am Francis Kader of the American Meta Association." Those last three words were in English. I was trying not to look at the woman; she was so beautiful it was distracting.

The man's eyes flashed angrily. "And why are you in Iceland, Mr. Kader?"

They weren't masking and both the adepts were strong. I thought Krupp and I could probably defeat them, but the five warriors with rifles worried me, especially since our warriors were virtually unarmed. I'd taken on a larger group in Norway, but I didn't have an armored car here for protection.

"Our business is our own," I stated, continuing in the ancient language. "And we were just leaving for Reykjavik to catch the first plane to the U.S."

"Do you know what this place is?" the woman asked. Her voice was lyrical and soft, almost as if she were singing. It made my heart pound with a feeling of longing.

"It is a glacier," I said, trying to act stupid. Apparently they knew what was here, too.

"We spent too much time," Krupp whispered to me in English, surprising me because I hadn't realized he'd slid up next to me. "The glacier had grown."

I ignored him.

"I will ask you," the man was saying in the ancient language, "one last time; what is your business here?"

I let out a long breath and thought. I could see only one way out of this without violence. "Yes," I said, "I know what this place is—"

Krupp grabbed my arm so hard it hurt. I turned to look at him. I couldn't mistake the look in his eyes: fear and anger. He didn't want me to say why we were there.

Another sound came up the valley. I turned to see a form sitting on a broom moving through the sky. It was a woman with long dark hair flowing behind her as she flew through the air.

The Icelanders looked up and saw her too. Their warriors started watching her. Out of the corner of my eye, I saw Krupp's men moving toward the jeep with the equipment.

Just as the woman on the broom dropped from the sky, Krupp's men walked out from behind the jeep with submachine guns.

Anica stepped off her broom and propped it against a rock. She turned and smiled at me.

"Mr. Kader," she said in English. "Need some help?"

I smiled at the Transylvanian woman. Her dark hair and deep eyes contrasted with those of the Icelandic woman. I was glad Mason had told her the night before where to find us. She was probably high in the sky, watching, and came down when she saw we needed help.

The balance of power had just switched. Mason even held his pistol in his hand.

I looked at the male Icelander. "We were just leaving. We will take with us what we came for. Are you going to try to stop us?"

The woman looked at me, her eyes soft and blue and with no sign of anger or malice, but rather sadness. "This place is sacred to us." Her voice was as gentle as a breeze.

I looked at her. Maybe it was her beauty and her voice. Maybe I was the victim of some spell I could neither detect nor counter. I decided to be somewhat honest.

"What do you call yourself?" I asked the woman.

"Gudlang," she replied. "And this is Adalbörg." She indicated the male adept.

"Gudlang, do you know where Loki is?" I asked.

"Noooo!" Krupp hissed beside me.

I ignored him. Anica gave him a look that shut him up. He, too, could feel her power.

That broke Gudlang's composure. I could tell she thought she knew.

"Not where you think," I said.

"How is that possible?" she asked, her voice like that of a child viewing something mysterious.

I could feel Krupp tense beside me. He was preparing to fight.

"I don't know," I stated simply.

"Do you know where he is?" she asked, her eyes locked on mine.

I nodded.

"No, damn it," Krupp hissed.

I ignored him.

"He needs to be returned. He's a trouble maker," Gudlang whispered.

"I was hoping to kill him," I stated.

She shook her head, making those long locks undulate. "You won't be able to."

"But maybe I will," a voice said from behind me. It was a strong bass voice, speaking in the ancient language but with a strange accent.

I turned. Thor was standing at the entrance to the hole we'd dug in the ice. He was trying to stand straight, but I could tell he was weak, leaning against the ice for support.

The Icelanders almost fell off their horses and dropped to their knees. Their warriors, seeing this, lowered their weapons and dropped to their knees.

Krupp's men raised their weapons.

"NO!" I cried out.

Mason added "*Nein—halt!*"

Krupp's men looked at Krupp and he shook his head. Even he knew it was useless to fight our way out of this, now.

I looked back at the Icelandic adepts, prostrating before Thor. Did they still worship the Æsir?

"Loki has escaped," Thor continued, walking out of the tunnel. He was walking unsteadily, as if he'd drunk too much beer. "I will find him and return him, or kill him."

"Help him," I told Krupp.

The German barked an order at his men, and they set their weapons down and went to help the old adept. Each man got under a shoulder and lifted Thor.

The Icelanders rose to their feet, but kept their eyes cast toward the ground. Anica was staring at the old adept. She whispered, "A priest of Atlantis. So it's true: they are immortal."

Or at least very long-lived, I thought.

I turned to the Icelanders. "We will help Thor defeat Loki."

"We will help you," Gudlang said.

"The best help you can give is to help us get Thor to Reykjavik," I said.

Gudlang raised her gaze to look me in the eyes, something that was almost painfully beautiful. "We will help, and I will accompany Thor and help you in your quest."

"No," Krupp said in English.

"Yes," I said in English. Gudlang must have understood, for she smiled and nodded.

***

It was a logistical nightmare. The Icelandic Guild's disdain for technology extended to motor vehicles, so they insisted on taking their horses. I suggested flying carpets or brooms, but they didn't know those spells. They truly are isolated, I thought. World War II had opened Iceland to the rest of the world, but the world's guilds hadn't discovered it yet. The Icelandic guild would have trouble fending off even a weak guild such as Anica's. I worried that the Icelanders would soon be run over by a guild looking for breathing room. Like the Transylvanians. I worried that bringing Anica here might have been a mistake.

The Icelandic warriors had come in two cars that they had parked at the bottom of the valley because, unlike the jeeps, they couldn't traverse up the rough valley floor. I supposed I should have been thankful for the Icelanders' ways. Their slow transportation gave us more time to find Thor.

Thor absolutely refused to go near a jeep, once he realized they moved on their own and weren't some strange metal sculpture. I wondered how I was going to get him on an airplane for the trip to Norway.

At the valley entrance, where the Icelanders' cars were parked, Anica, Mason, and I got in one of the enclosed and heated cars. Our driver was one of the Icelandic warriors. The other four warriors piled in another car. Krupp rode in one of the jeeps.

Thor was placed on Adalbörg's horse. The animal looked as if it were straining under the load until Gudlang spoke to it and lovingly patted its neck. The horse then seemed to grow in strength.

But I'd lifted Thor; he wasn't that heavy, even with his armor. Was the ancient adept growing heavier and perhaps stronger?

Adalbörg kissed Gudlang on the cheek and walked back up the valley. She mounted her horse and the procession, two horses, two cars, and two jeeps, moved west. We must have looked strange to the farmers and the locals enjoying some of the last sunshine of the year in front of their sod houses.

Anica and I conversed in the ancient language, assuming the Icelandic warrior wouldn't understand us.

"Thank you," I said.

She smiled. "Of course. I owed you a favor. I believe you saved my guild."

I wonder if she included killing Nikolai as part of that. "Where are you staying now?"

"We are transients, moving from place to place as local guilds will tolerate us. We ask permission to come, to stay, and to leave."

I could tell she found this humiliating. "Could you merge with a guild somewhere?"

"And lose our culture and our history?"

I shrugged my shoulders. I wondered why those were more important to her than survival.

I changed the subject. "May I ask you something?"

"Yes," she whispered.

"The Transylvanians have a reputation, perhaps unearned." I waited to see if she'd understand.

"Yes," she said. "Necromancy. It is not entirely unearned. Vlad Dracul did experiment. It is even said he wrote a book, but it has never been found."

"About the power of blood?" Lessers feared "Dracula" because he drank their blood. "Consumed" would be more accurate.

"Blood and death, yes. Why do you ask?"

I told her about cutting the adepts and my leg in Korea and feeling more power. Her dark eyes grew wide.

"Yes, it's true. And what you felt, with your own blood and without killing, is just a shadow of the power possible."

"You have done this?" I asked.

She looked out the window as if finding basalt outcroppings very interesting. "This is a strange land," she said in English.

I knew the conversation was over.

*** 

We spent the night in a house owned by the Icelandic Guild. It was a sod house outside Vik, between the cold North Atlantic and the Mýrdalsjökull glacier. The inside was quite cozy, with wood-paneled walls and a fire in a stone hearth. It was nothing like a damp spud cellar that smelled of dirt that I remembered from outside Grand Forks.

The Icelanders fed us fish. We ate silently around the table, except for Thor's unhappy grumbling at the lack of mead. He ate little and looked tired, yet looking at his face, I could swear it was appearing younger. But it might have been the flickering light from the fire.

Even though it was one of the larger sod houses I'd seen in Iceland, the accommodations were lacking. The Icelanders insisted that Thor have one of the three beds. I offered to sleep on the wooden floor so Gudlang and Anica could have the other two. Mason, of course, made the same offer, and Krupp and his men reluctantly agreed. I think Krupp would have found a nearby farmstead for his lodgings but he wanted to stay close to Thor.

The Icelandic warriors were planning to sleep in shifts; still, there was little floor space left for all of us.

Then Adalbörg arrived and confirmed to Gudlang that indeed, Loki was missing, but the other Æsir were "safe," as he said in Icelandic, not caring that I was using a translation spell.

But that made floor space an even rarer commodity.

I said something about sleeping in one of the cars.

Anica growled and told me to stop being stupid and sleep with her; I'd be more comfortable and there'd be more space on the floor. So I did, holding her in my arms more because of the lack of room in the small bed than from emotion or desire; most of our clothes where still on. It was probably one of the few times that "sleeping together" was not a euphemism.

"Do you have any ideas for getting Thor off this island?" I whispered. "If he won't ride in a car, what will he think of an airplane?"

"A ship?" she asked.

"Unless it's made of wood and has sails, I'm afraid he'll refuse to board."

Anica was quiet. I could feel her breathe.

"We are approaching this the wrong way," she said finally.

"What do you mean?"

"He'll understand meta. Use a broom or a carpet or a cloud. It won't be as comfortable as an airplane or a ship, but he'll understand it, not fear it."

I thought about that. Then I had to chuckle. "Yes, of course." I would have kissed her, but I was afraid of where that might lead.

"We should stop going west," she said.

"We'll leave in the morning," I whispered.

\*\*\*

Anica and I related our plan to the others in the morning while Thor was consuming a large breakfast. In the light of daybreak, his face looked less withered.

Language was becoming a problem. Gudlang and Adalbörg didn't speak English or German, and Mason didn't speak the ancient language, and no one but the natives spoke Icelandic. So we spoke English, with the Icelanders using a translation spell to understand us.

"You're *verrückt*," Krupp said, exasperated.

I didn't ask for a translation; I caught his meaning.

"Do you have a map of Europe?" Mason asked Gudlang.

She shook her head and looked at me in wonder, those blue eyes rimmed not with admiration, but perhaps with astonishment.

"It's thousands of miles of open ocean," Krupp howled.

"If you're afraid, then take a plane," Anica said. "Kader and I intend to do this."

"A map would be helpful, and a compass," I said softly.

"I will accompany you," Krupp stated, sounding unsure. "I have maps and compasses."

"Of course," I said. I knew he wouldn't want to let Thor out of his sight. Or me. Or both.

Krupp had his men bring in maps. Gudlang pointed out our approximate position on the southern coast of Iceland.

Mason made a measurement with his hand and whistled. "It's right at about a thousand miles to Norway's west coast."

Ten hours at least by cloud I calculated. Brooms and rugs were quite a bit slower, but took less meta. A rug would take maybe fifteen hours.

"There's no place to stop," Krupp said, "if you tire."

"Big carpet," I said. "We'll work in shifts." I looked at Gudlang. "You coming?"

She nodded. "I go where he goes." She nodded at Thor.

I looked at Adalbörg. "You?"

"No, I must stay to…" he stopped speaking.

What the Icelandic Guild's relationship with the Æsir was, I couldn't decipher. Were they protecting them, keeping them safe for a time when the world would be more welcoming of them? But when would that be, if ever?

I switched my thoughts to the problem at hand. "We'll work in shifts," I said. "Four adepts, four or five hours each. We'll rest when we reach Norway. Then head for Valhalla." I looked at Thor, eating as if he hadn't for a thousand years, which may have been true.

"Is he strong enough to face Loki?" I asked Gudlang.

"I don't know. I don't think so."

"When will he be?"

"I don't know, but he gains strength by the moment; I can feel it."

I wondered why I couldn't. But I hadn't been trying to.

"We need a large carpet," I continued, "and warm clothes." I looked at Thor, still eating everything the Icelander warriors were cooking for him as if oblivious to our conversation. "And provisions."

"What should I do, sir?" Mason asked.

I had to think about that. Was it worth having him go to Tromsø? Probably not. "I need you to go back to San Francisco and report to Louis on what happened here and what we are doing."

"Yes, sir." He acted relieved. Perhaps he'd been afraid I was going to ask him to go on the carpet.

"My men will take him to Reykjavik," Krupp offered almost congenially.

"Oh, good, more time with the Bobbsey Twins," Mason grumbled. Everyone ignored it.

Mason pointed to the blob on the map that was Iceland. "Would it be better to leave from here, the eastern-most point of Iceland?" He did his measurements using his hand as a ruler. "That takes off about three hundred miles."

I looked at the map and nodded. "We'll make that a dry run: fly to there, and rest overnight before crossing the ocean."

I looked at Gudlang. "Is there a place we can rest there?"

"Yes."

"Good."

"Hell," Mason spat. "I'm an idiot."

"What?" I asked.

"You'll have to adjust for magnetic declination, especially at these latitudes. Your compass reading will be in error over that long of a distance."

He could have been speaking Icelandic for all of that I understood. "What do you mean?"

Mason looked at me. "The magnetic pole and the north pole do not line up, so compasses have errors. The error is called 'magnetic declination.' If you are navigating by compass, it will make your course different from what you think it is."

"How much?" Krupp asked, suddenly interested.

Mason looked thoughtful. "In France, it was about five degrees west; I don't know what it is here and how it will change as you cross the ocean."

"So what will this do?" Krupp demanded. I could tell this worried him.

"Assuming it's west here," Mason said thoughtfully. He looked at the map, then the ceiling, and made a 'T' with his hands, then turned them counter-clockwise. "If it is west, your course will be more northerly than you think."

"That's not a problem," I said. "We want to go north anyway."

"But it will make your course over water longer," Mason added.

"How much?" Krupp demanded almost shrilly.

"I don't know," Mason said, shrugging his shoulders.

"Will we miss Norway?" I asked.

Mason shook his head. "No, you'll just be a few degrees off. You'll be further north and your distance will be longer, but not hugely so."

"Are you sure?" Krupp asked. "These are our lives you're playing with."

"Even if the declination is east, you'll just go more south, but you'll eventually hit Norway. That looks like about a thousand miles of coastline; that's a huge target to miss."

I was starting to wish he hadn't brought this up.

"Without declination maps, we can't do much about it anyway," Mason finished. "But you'll be fine." He said that a little too cheerily.

*   *   *

A large carpet was found. It was made of wool and had a simple flower pattern. Neither Gudlang nor Krupp knew the spells and had to be taught. Anica's spell was unlike any flying carpet spell I'd ever encountered, but it worked. The carpet hovered a few feet off the ground as we loaded a large box of food—and strapped it down to the carpet by cutting slits in the fabric for the straps to run through—and Thor, who took one look at the carpet, smiled, and climbed aboard, sitting on the provisions box.

I helped Anica up, but Gudlang refused my help. She sat on the carpet at Thor's feet. Krupp climbed aboard, still looking unhappy about this plan.

"We'll follow the coastline to Seyoisfjorour," Gudlang decreed.

"How far?" I asked.

"Three, four hundred kilometers," she replied.

About two or three hundred miles: a good dry run, I thought, all over land in case something went wrong. A "dry" run indeed.

Not much did go wrong, other than having to reinforce the slits where the straps went through as the carpet began to rip. We arrived in Seyoisfjorour in about four hours, having left Vik in the early afternoon. The town was at the western tip of a fjord with the same name, in a deep valley surrounded by mountains. It reminded me of Tromsø. Gudlang took us to a house where we were welcomed warmly with food and drink and beds. Again, a shortage caused Anica and me to have to share the bed space.

Holding her, feeling her breath, made me long for Dagmar. I didn't know what Dagmar was feeling. She had written that note for a reason, had tried to warn me that it was not Thor but Loki she was dealing with. But what hold did Loki have on her? Was his power strong enough to hold her against her will? If so, I hoped Thor was as strong as legend had him.

The woman of the house sewed up and hemmed the slits the straps holding the box of food went through. Gudlang was satisfied it would hold. I hoped so; I'd seen what happened when a carpet fell apart underneath someone.

At first light, about 5:00 A.M., we boarded the carpet. Thor sat imperiously on the box of provisions, Gudlang at his feet. Krupp, Anica, and I sat in a triangle at the front. The person at the tip of the triangle "drove." I was a bit worried that Gudlang wouldn't want to leave Thor in order to take her shift keeping the carpet going.

I decided to "drive" first. I wanted to be rested when we got to Norway. Krupp had ulterior motives, and I had no idea when they'd come to the surface.

I flew the carpet down the fjord to the open sea, and then held the compass and headed east. I thought about trying to correct for Mason's "magnetic declination," but had no idea how to do so. I kept the needle pointed to my left, perpendicular to the direction we were going.

By the time the sun rose, Iceland was no longer visible.

The sea was gray with white flecks. The air was cold, and I could see white frost forming on Anica's dark hair. She looked at me, her eyes registering her misery. I didn't want to go too high because it got colder, but if I flew too low the wind was more violent.

There was a dark mass of clouds to our northeast. I looked at them, hoping we wouldn't meet them.

After four hours, I decided to rest. Krupp insisted on taking the next turn. We'd practiced this over Iceland and the carpet only drooped a few inches as we transferred from my spell to his.

I crawled back near Gudlang, curled up in a ball for warmth, and fell asleep, the stress of keeping the large heavy carpet moving and afloat having worn me out.

I woke with a start, feeling as if I were falling. At first I thought it was one of those dreams of falling I often have when first sleeping. But then I heard the screams.

I sat up quickly.

We were surrounded by black clouds. Wind was blowing hard against us. The carpet was tipping, and I could see Krupp fighting to keep it upright.

"Give it to me!" I cried, crawling toward him, afraid to stand.

The carpet tipped and I could see down. I couldn't see the ocean. The clouds made it look as if we were traveling sideways rather than straight.

"I can't; we'll drop!" Krupp yelled.

I passed Anica and looked at her face, which was white with fear. The temperature must have risen; she no longer had frost on her hair.

"Where's the compass?" I demanded, seeing Krupp was no longer holding it.

"I dropped it," he replied softly.

"Where?"

"It's gone," Anica said.

So we had no idea where we were going or where the storm was blowing us.

We dropped a few feet; then we rose quickly and nearly turned over. Anica started sliding toward the edge, and I grabbed her with one hand while the other clung to a fist full of carpet.

I looked back and saw Thor and Gudlang hanging onto the straps holding the provisions box.

"Give me the carpet!" I screamed at Krupp.

"Yes," he said. Now his face was white with fear.

Krupp released and I took control as fast as I could.

The carpet nearly buckled, and I fought to keep it from turning into a falling ball of fabric with us inside.

I got it level, my teeth clamped together in the effort and in terror.

I didn't know how we were going to survive this.

"Why didn't you go around the storm?" I asked Anica.

"We thought it better to not lengthen our journey. We didn't know it would be this bad."

I looked at her, damning myself for maybe killing her.

Lightning was crackling around us. I worried that if it hit the carpet, it might light it on fire. Or kill us outright. That might be preferable to falling who knew how far to our deaths.

I wondered whether I could dodge the lightning.

Suddenly, the carpet flattened out as if in calm air. The wind stopped buffeting us and the lightning was farther away.

Gudlang was chanting something I couldn't understand.

I turned to look.

Thor was standing on the provisions box and Gudlang was kneeling in front of the box and holding his feet, either to steady him or in some ritualistic pose.

Thor's face was completely young, strong. His mouth was full of white teeth. His blond hair was long and flowing. The arms that had looked muscled before appeared even more powerful, and they were spread out above his head.

And I could feel his power. It washed over me like an ocean wave. Perhaps the storm was adding to the power of the "God of Thunder."

"Fly!" he bellowed in the ancient language. "I'll hold the tempest from us."

"I don't know which way to fly!" I called back to him.

"Valhalla is that way," he said, pointing with an outstretched arm back behind us.

We had been going in the wrong direction, if he was right about the direction of Valhalla.

I turned the carpet and flew. It could have been a calm summer's day around us. But less than fifty feet from us, the storm was raging.

It took what felt like ages but according to my watch was only two hours to leave the storm behind. Thor stepped off the box then, and with Gudlang keeping the carpet moving, we ate the fish sandwiches and drank the water (and beer for Thor, but he declared it undrinkable).

I looked at Gudlang. "I think he's ready to face Loki."

"I will bind the prankster back where he belongs!" Thor bellowed. Almost everything he said was a bellow now.

I didn't say that I would rather have Loki dead. How dead depended on what he'd done to Dagmar.

\*\*\*

Thor's sense of direction proved flawless. It was nearly nightfall when we crossed the rugged Norwegian coast and landed outside a small coastal village.

Gudlang and I walked to the town and asked a local where we were. She pointed to our location on our map. We were much farther up the coast than we'd planned.

She also told us of a place that took in boarders.

The proprietors were agog at Thor. The problem was that Thor was dressed as if he were in a Viking costume drama. I hadn't thought about putting him in modern clothing; the Icelanders just seemed to accept that that was what he should look like.

We used persuasion spells to convince them that Thor was just an actor on his way to a play and liked to stay in costume.

Krupp used a Swedish passport and name. Germans were still not welcome in Norway.

Gudlang stayed in the same room as Thor. I don't know whether they slept together (in either sense). I doubted that they made love, as I suspected Thor would not have been a quiet lover.

Anica and I again shared a bed. I was exhausted and fell asleep before she'd even climbed under the covers.

Krupp apparently slept alone.

# Chapter Twenty-Six

I woke up curled around Dagmar, except her body was wrong, too long. I slowly came to the realization that it was Anica, not Dagmar.

She was sleeping peacefully so I carefully removed my body from hers. I was glad I'd woken up before I'd done more, thinking she was Dagmar.

I had to travel down the hall from our room to get to the toilet. When I came back Anica was still asleep. I dressed quietly and went down to the house's common areas. My watch said it was nearly 7:00 A.M. but that was Iceland time, meaning it was 8:00 here.

Our hosts, a middle-aged husband and his wife, greeted me in Norwegian as I walked into the kitchen. I pulled up a quick translation spell.

"...and your wife slept well."

"Yes, she is still sleeping," I replied. "We had a difficult and tiring journey."

"Yes," they said. I could tell they thought sleeping so late was some sort of sin or base decadence.

"The large one, Thor, left early this morning," the wife said.

"Where?" I tried to keep the worry out of my voice.

"I do not know."

"Was his wife with him?" Gudlang, I meant. We'd all, except Krupp, posed as married couples.

"No."

"Damn," I said in English.

I turned and bounded up the stairs to Thor's room and pounded on the door. "Gudlang, wake up!" I was using the ancient language.

She opened the door a crack and looked at me sleepily. The trip had been hard on her, too.

"Thor's gone!" I cried.

"I know."

"We need to find him."

"No, we don't. He'll be back."

"When?"

"Soon."

"How do you know this? Did he tell you?"

She shook her head, making those long blonde locks undulate. "I know."

That was the second time she'd said something mysterious about Thor.

"He needs to hunt. He's in the forests around the village looking for game. He'll return when he finds some."

"And you just know this?"

"Yes," she whispered.

I decided to be rude. "How do you know this? He could be heading for Valhalla."

"I just know. I don't know how. Ever since he came out of the ice, I..."

"You what?"

"It's as if I can hear his thoughts. Not like words, but like pictures, emotions. He has caught an animal and is on his way back."

"Breakfast?" I joked.

"He thinks so, yes."

I wondered how we were going to explain that to our hosts.

\*\*\*

Our hosts were less than happy when Thor dropped a bloody deer in their kitchen and demanded in the ancient language that they prepare it for a feast.

Some money and persuasion spells mollified them to an extent but we ended up leaving in a bit of a hurry. Again we traveled via our rug, leaving the empty provisions box behind.

We went north up the rugged coastline, passing over fjords and bays and inland waterways. I thought about going to Tromsø, but decided I could be recognized and Thor would cause a stir that might reach Valhalla.

When I started feeling Valhalla, we found an empty valley in which to hole up. Krupp built a fire using wood and a fire-throwing spell, and we sat around planning.

I drew a crude map in the dirt.

"There's one entrance to Valhalla," I explained. "It's a narrow mountain trail and we'll have to go in in single file."

"Thor should lead us then, as our strongest," Krupp added.

"No," Thor said forcefully. "There's another way."

"Yes, by air," I conceded. "We can cut the carpet into pieces. But I worry then about their Berserkers' guns." Suddenly I wished Dagmar hadn't decided to start allowing Berserkers to use modern weapons. But when I'd fought Loki they hadn't had any so perhaps he wasn't allowing it anymore and we could use that to our advantage. "But I was thinking we could use that as a distraction."

"No," Thor again persisted. "There is a tunnel."

"A tunnel?" I asked

"Yes, a secret entrance. Comes up beside Valhalla."

I smiled.

\*\*\*

Then came the logistics. I wanted to use the carpet as a distraction, and Gudlang as the weakest adept in our troop—our troop of very strong adepts—

was the logical choice to fly it. But she refused to leave Thor's side. Krupp, the second weakest, also refused.

In the end we decided to forgo the carpet as a distraction and all go through the tunnel with Thor in the lead.

We remounted the carpet and Thor led us to the east of Valhalla. At these altitudes and latitudes, even in late summer the mountains had snow on them; some of it seemed fresh.

Thor directed me, flying the carpet, to a ravine between two steep mountains. Everyone was masking except for me. That couldn't be helped. I suppose we could have approached the ravine on foot, but that would have taken a day or two and none of us, except maybe Gudlang and Thor, were up for a hike in the wilderness, especially since we were out of provisions.

Landing, we rolled up the carpet and put it under a pine tree, expecting never to see it again, but leaving it for a backup in case we had to make a quick retreat. The ravine was a narrow crack with a box end at the top and a few sparse trees. Snow lay under the trees in the shadows.

At the box end of the canyon, Thor spread his large arms and chanted in the ancient language. It was something akin to "Open Sesame," but more nonsensical.

There was a low rumbling from the walls of the ravine from loose rocks shaking down, and Thor kept chanting. The rest of us gathered in the middle of the dry streambed, hoping to avoid any falling debris.

The box end of the ravine cracked and then, with a great fall of dirt and rocks, split open and fell away, revealing a dark passage into the side of the mountain.

Once the rumbling and the dust had settled, I picked up a stick and made the end glow, and tossed it into the passage.

The sides were rough but the walls were straight, and the corner at the ceiling was close to a right angle.

"Dwarves," Thor rumbled, "carved this for me."

"They did good work," Krupp said, coming up behind us.

Norse mythology is full of dwarves doing the heavy work for the Æsir: forging weapons, building things, mining gold. But there was nothing in human history that corresponded to dwarves, and I didn't think the myths simply meant people of small stature, i.e., a modern dwarf.

I wondered whether somewhere the word for "lesser" in the form of the ancient language the Æsir used was somehow interpreted as "dwarf" when the Æsir became legend and legend became myth. That would make the dwarves of mythology just lessers.

I picked up another stick from the ground and held it high as the end lit up. It illuminated only a few feet of the tunnel, leaving the rest in gloomy darkness.

"How far?" I asked, thinking we'd come a long ways on the carpet.

"Ten (*somethings*)," Thor replied, using a word in the ancient language I'd never heard before.

"I wonder how many kilometers that is," Krupp said sardonically.

"About eleven," Gudlang said from behind us as she walked up. We were all speaking the ancient language, since it was the only common tongue.

Krupp let out a long sigh. "And probably uphill the whole way."

"Probably," I said, wondering how many miles that was and looking for another solution. Maybe we could fly the carpet in here.

"Come, enough chatter," Thor bellowed, striding into the tunnel. Gudlang passed around Krupp and me to follow, I let Krupp go ahead of me so I could watch him, and Anica brought up the rear, holding my hand. A few yards in, Thor found a torch and lit it with a fire spell. That gave us more light, but that just showed the endless walls of the tunnel ahead of us.

We kept walking, the entrance growing smaller and fainter until it finally disappeared. Anica's hand was tight on mine. I felt pangs of guilt as Anica and I became emotionally closer, but I also felt abandoned by Dagmar.

The further we got into the tunnel the staler and more oppressive the air became, and the more the walls seemed to move closer and the roof lower. But Thor could still stand tall without hitting his head or brushing his shoulders on the walls. The torch threw off a red and malevolent light that reflected off the black basalt walls.

At one point Krupp asked for a break. I was wishing we'd brought some supplies, particularly food and water. Larson would have thought of that, I realized, feeling a bit depressed and missing my warrior.

We leaned against the walls—Anica sat on the floor—and rested, but Thor was almost not able to stand still.

"What's at the end of this tunnel?" I asked.

"Valhalla," Thor stated.

"Where does it come up in Valhalla?" Suddenly I realized I should have asked these questions earlier. Again I missed Larsen.

"Side of the canyon."

I nodded, thinking. Vallhalla was a flat spot on the south side of a mountain, the hut thatched with warriors' shields in the approximate middle. To the west side was a canyon that ran down the mountain. It was used by the Valkyrie for shelter, they having built modern houses in it, albeit without electricity or running water. But the houses beat the ancient hut. This meant we could come up in the middle of one of their houses. No, I decided, if they built on top of the tunnel, they would have discovered it and would have the exit either guarded or sealed up. In either case, this trip had been for nothing.

When Thor's patience was exhausted, we resumed our trek.

The air became almost unbearably stale and the walls started dripping with water, making the floor slick. Just when I thought the end would never come, Thor stopped.

"This is it," he said, his voice booming in the cavern.

I pushed my way forward. "Can we get out?"

"Of course," Thor replied.

I took a deep breath, which in this air didn't seem to help much with the way I felt. "Okay," I said, gathering my thoughts. "Thor will handle Loki. The rest of us just need to keep the Valkyrie and their warriors busy."

"I will deal with the usurper," Thor rumbled redundantly.

He turned toward the door, spread his arms as wide as he could in the tunnel, and spoke the same nonsensical words he'd spoken in the box canyon.

"Wait!" I cried out. "We should use a spell of far seeing—"

Too late: the door swung open inward, forcing us to scramble out of the way, and sunlight streamed in, blinding all of us.

Thor burst out as soon as the opening was large enough for him to fit. Gudlang ran after him, I followed, and Krupp and Anica brought up the rear.

I could still barely see in the bright sunshine of the cloudless day, but I couldn't miss Thor rushing up the canyon toward the hut with the roof thatched with shields.

As my eyes adjusted I could see better. Even though it was early September, there was snow on the top of the mountain. Every time I had come here there was snow. It seemed to be permanent. But I didn't know whether it had already snowed this early in the season.

There weren't any people around as we moved past the modern houses toward Valhalla. Thor bounded up the canyon.

Two warriors, Berserkers dressed in chain mail and armor much like Thor's, tried to stop him as he came to the flat spot in the mountainside. He brushed them aside as if they were dry reeds in his path; each flew a few feet before landing on the ground with a thud. They remained unconscious and I didn't know whether they were alive or dead.

"*Hors de combat*," Krupp growled, sensing my trepidation. I didn't want anyone killed and I didn't like his cavalier attitude.

As I reached the fallen warriors, Thor was almost to Valhalla itself—the hut thatched with shields. Three warriors appeared with raised battle-axes. Thor shot airbolts at the three before they even got close, knocking them down. Two tried to rise again but by then Thor, moving with unbelievable speed, was on them and hit them with his fist. They didn't move again.

Loki rushed out of the hut, buckling on a leather belt with *Mjollnir* hanging from it. Dagmar followed, looking disheveled, hair a-tangle, traditional clothes askew. I had the feeling that she and Loki had been making love, and the anger grew in me. I could feel it increase my powers. She was followed by more blonde Valkyrie, all in chain mail. The Valkyrie were supposed to be female warriors.

"You!" Thor howled like a hurricane wind, pointing at Loki. "I bound you once, and I will do it again."

"Old man!" Loki shot back, drawing the Hammer and pointing it at Thor. "I have been free for years gathering strength, and you, old man, can't have been free for long. Plus, I have this!" And with those words he held the Hammer up above his head. "Come for me, slayer of Lit!"

I could see Thor's anger building. Lit was a dwarf whom Thor had killed in what was universally considered a cowardly act. Loki was obviously trying to insult the true owner of the Hammer.

Thor roared so loudly I thought he might cause the snow on the mountain to avalanche. He pointed at Loki and green light crossed the space between them. Loki seemed to catch it with *Mjollnir* and push it back toward Thor.

I'd never seen this kind of meta before. It appeared to be pure power directed at another. Loki was pushing it back with ease when I realized: Thor didn't have a talisman!

But it didn't seem to matter, for suddenly Thor's light intensified and became almost blinding and started to crackle in the air, which started to smell the way it does during a thunderstorm. Loki was knocked back and slammed into the ground.

A young Valkyrie raised her hand as if to attack Thor and Dagmar stopped her, knocking her hand down and looking at her intently. I didn't understand why Dagmar had done that but I was glad the Valkyrie were staying out of this fight. In combination with Loki, they could probably overwhelm Thor. And the rest of us didn't have to fight the Valkyrie, a fight we would probably lose.

Thor advanced on Loki, keeping his light pressing down on him. Loki let Thor get close then swung the Hammer blindingly fast, striking Thor in the leg.

The ancient priest howled and his light faded. Loki rose to a sitting position and swung the Hammer again, this time hitting Thor on the upper thigh where he had no armor. Thor stumbled and almost fell back, his light fading entirely. Loki scrambled to climb on top of Thor, held the Hammer over his head, and brought it down repeatedly on Thor, hitting his chest, arms, and head.

"Damn," I whispered. I looked at the others. Gudlang was crying, watching Thor's defeat. Krupp and Anica were staring, surprised. Krupp's mouth was agape and he said a very bad word in the ancient language.

I looked at the Valkyrie. They were just watching the spectacle impassively. I looked at Dagmar for a glimmer of desire to help us. She just looked at me, her face a mask.

"We have to help!" I cried out, not sure there was much even four adepts could do against such power as Loki possessed. Fear knotted my insides as I remembered what Loki had done to me the last time I'd tried to fight him.

Anica rushed to one of the fallen warriors and pulled a small knife with a jewel-encrusted handle from inside her clothing. She neatly and expertly sliced the man's neck, blood spraying over her. Her reaction to this was almost erotic and I could see the power build in her. But she didn't stop there; she bent down and drank the blood spewing from the man's vein. I could not turn my eyes away as she rose to her knees, blood dripping from her mouth, the power in her evident not only by how beautiful she looked, but also by the fire in her eyes.

"*Mein Gott!*" Krupp whispered. "A vampire."

He was right. Not the kind of the lessers' horror stories and movies, but a real vampire, one who used necromancy and blood to increase her power. She hadn't been completely honest with me back in Vik, I realized. The power she wouldn't speak of was the power of death.

Loki stepped off Thor's prone body. I didn't know whether the Atlantean priest was dead or just unconscious. Loki looked at me and laughed, bellowing, "You!"

"We have to attack him, now!" I called out.

Gudlang attacked immediately, the anger and sorrow screaming out of her. She shot an immense airbolt at Loki, but he simply brushed it aside.

"We have to do this together," I tried but Gudlang was too overwhelmed by grief and anger to hear me as she attacked again, with the same result. She might as well have been throwing glass at a rock wall.

Loki chuckled, strode to her, and hit her with the Hammer, knocking her to the ground. I felt for her, knowing what that felt like.

Dagmar was looking at me with wide eyes, but I averted my gaze from her. Still the Valkyrie did nothing to help Loki, or us.

"Attack him!" I cried hoping Anica and Krupp would follow my lead. I shot fire at Loki.

Anica joined in, her flames hot and intense, almost blue, as it arced across to hit Loki. Krupp used another attack: the ground swelled up and clawed at Loki's feet.

Loki pushed fire back at Anica and me. I ducked it in time, but Anica took the full force of it. She was thrown as if she were made of air, smacked into a rock wall, and fell to the ground, her hair and clothes on fire. I ignored Loki long enough to pull water from the air to douse the flames, but Anica was unconscious. Her breathing indicated that she was alive but I didn't know if she could stay that way as her skin turned red and seemed to boil before my eyes.

Meanwhile Loki stamped his feet and the ground swelled up around Krupp and climbed to his neck, immobilizing him.

"You again!" Loki called, glaring at me. He looked at Dagmar. "This is the one you tried to betray me to with your note. What a pathetic being."

Dagmar seemed to shrink before him and it became obvious that she was under his power as much as the rest of us. No wonder the Valkyrie weren't helping him. They were probably afraid to go against him, too.

I looked up at the top of the mountain. I don't know why; perhaps the beauty of it drew my eye before I was sure I was going to die. The snow seemed to be barely hanging on, perched on the edge above us, and I was surprised the noise of the battle hadn't caused an avalanche.

Snow.

Snow is made of water.

I turned and ran. I could hear Loki behind me, running, laughing, each of his footfalls shaking the ground. I sprinted into the canyon and the first house I found, flung open the door—of course it was unlocked—and found a rug just inside. I jerked the rug from the floor and tossed it into the air and leapt upon it. I flew out the door just as Loki ran up. He grabbed for my dangling legs, but missed. I felt his fingers on the fabric of my pants.

I shot for the mountaintop as fast as I dared, clinging to the rug.

Loki shot fire at me and I swerved; it missed me by so little the fringe on the rug smoldered. I stopped and hovered, watching him as he went to the Valkyries' stables, untied one of the white horses and mounted it, spurring it into the sky. The horse was flying, its legs a blur in the air as if it were running.

I turned and fled higher, hoping he would follow me. I could hear the horse snorting and breathing behind me as Loki drove him hard to catch up. I stopped below the field of snow and hovered, one hand holding the rug, the other in my pocket on the *katana* talisman.

Loki flew up to the same level as I.

"Why don't you run, little man, and leave me your woman?" he mocked. "You don't have much luck with women, do you?"

He was under the snow hanging off the side of the mountain.

I ran the spell I had learned from Nakamura's papers, moving as much of the bottom layer of snow as I could toward him without passing out from the effort. The snow dropped and hit him, nearly knocking him off his horse.

But that was all; the snow then fell to the mountain below us, useless.

He looked at me, eyes glaring with anger. "I'm going to kill you slowly," he said, so softly I could barely hear him.

He spurred the horse so that it charged toward me in the air, holding *Mjollnir* over his head as if to pound it down on top of me.

That was when the rest of the snow let loose, crashing down on him. The first of it knocked him from the horse, which managed to scramble to safety. Loki screamed and lost his grip on the Hammer. I swooped in before it could fall and grabbed it out of the maelstrom of snow, managing to escape the edge of the avalanche. I could feel the Hammer's power flow through me.

But the full brunt of the falling snow, unknowable tons of it, landed directly on Loki, smashing him to the mountainside and rolling him down it. I watched as he was buried under the white billows of roiling and boiling snow, his angry, pained bellow drowned out by the roar of the avalanche.

The snow roiled down the mountain, but ran out of momentum before entering Valhalla.

I swooped down quickly, more because I was exhausted and afraid I wouldn't be able to keep the rug in the air much longer or hang on to *Mjollnir* than because I was hurrying. Landing, I looked at Dagmar, who was smiling at me strangely, but I ignored her and rushed to Anica. I knew that if she was alive she could heal herself, but I didn't even know whether she lived. I took her hands and placed the Hammer in them, hoping for a spark of consciousness that would feel the power of the world's most powerful talisman.

Her eyes fluttered and then opened, looking at me. She smiled slightly and then groaned in pain.

I smiled: she was still alive and the Hammer could help her to heal herself.

I watched as she closed her eyes again, but this time her breathing was obvious. Her lips moved as she invoked a healing spell, and as I watched the burns began to heal.

I felt a hand on my shoulder and turned and looked. Dagmar was standing behind me. Over her shoulder I could see Gudlang moving as if in great pain, but she was alive. Krupp was digging himself out of his prison of earth. But Thor was still lying prone on the ground.

Dagmar must have seen where I was looking, for she said, "He's alive, but he needs *Mjollnir*."

"Can it wait?"

Dagmar looked at Anica, pain crossing her face as she made an assumption, partially correct, about Anica and me.

"He won't die," she said simply.

"Then he can wait," I stated. I brushed past her to go help Gudlang. Actually, I just wanted an excuse not to be near Dagmar. My feelings were conflicted and even I had noticed that the first thing I had done after landing was to rush to Anica.

"I feel strangely weak," Gudlang said, putting her hand on my shoulder to steady herself. I could feel how her power was diminished.

"It'll come back," I whispered. "Give it time."

She looked at me questioningly.

"I, too, have been hit with that Hammer."

She smiled, looking almost relieved. "Loki?"

"Dead, I think. In any case, we have the Hammer, and without it he's much less powerful."

I heard a scuffle behind me. I wheeled around in time to see a filthy Krupp jerking the Hammer from Anica's hands as she lay on the ground. Anica fought back, but was too weak to hold on. Dagmar rushed Krupp, but by then he had the hammer by its short handle and smote her with it. She flew back almost as Gudlang had when Loki hit her. Dagmar crumpled to the ground. I tried to run to her, but Krupp turned and blocked my way, looking at me.

"Now!" he cried. "Now it's time for revenge!"

I looked at him, my hand in my pocket on my talisman. "What are you talking about, Krupp?"

"You and that Valkyrie"—he indicated Dagmar—"destroyed the Third Reich. You killed my lover in Paris. But with the Hammer of Thor, I can help bring the glory of Germany back to fruition!"

When he'd told me back in San Francisco that his reasons were his own, I had suspected something like this. But in the denouement of the battle, I had forgotten to keep an eye on him.

I didn't know how much meta, if any, he had expended in escaping from his earthen prison. I did know I was on the edge of passing out after having flown the carpet and brought the snow down on Loki. And he had the Hammer, the world's most powerful talisman.

I wrapped my fingers about my talisman, the piece of samurai sword, and ran. I ran blindly away from Krupp. I didn't want him hitting me with the Hammer.

Krupp must have sent an airbolt after me because something knocked me to the ground, smacking me down next to a fallen Berserker whom Thor had brushed aside.

I tried to stand but Krupp was on me, holding the Hammer over his head with both hands, grinning at me as he stood over my body.

I could think of nothing to do but swung my hand with my talisman, perpetually sharp edge out, and slashed across his belly. Blood oozed, but Krupp just touched himself and it stopped. But that bought me a little time. I grabbed the first thing I could find to parry a blow from the Hammer: a sword the warrior was holding. I picked it up and swung it upward just as Krupp brought down the Hammer. The two pieces of metal clanged together and sparks flew from the meeting. Krupp looked surprised and angry. He lifted the Hammer again.

I ran him through, stabbing with the sword. Blood again spurted from the wound as I rammed the blade in to the hilt.

Krupp staggered back and I thought for a moment he might drop the Hammer. But instead he grabbed the sword's handle and pulled the bloody blade from his body, and dropped it. The bleeding stopped again when he touched the wound.

I got to my feet and shot a weak fire at him that caught him unawares and lit his clothes and hair on fire. He pulled moisture from the air to douse the flames; then, raising the Hammer with both hands, he came at me again.

I heard Dagmar say something in Norwegian that sounded like "*Drep den tyske*" and saw out of the corner of my eye that she was sitting up with the help of a couple of Valkyrie. I found myself celebrating that she was alive, even though I thought she wouldn't be for long if Krupp killed me now.

I didn't have the time or energy to invoke a translation spell, so I didn't know what she said. But I saw the effects.

All the Valkyrie, who had been passively watching this battle, attacked Krupp.

Airbolts knocked him to the ground and fire splashed over his body. I had to get away from him to avoid being scorched myself. Every Valkyrie except Dagmar was flinging meta attacks at the German. He was briefly able to stop the flames from burning him with a protection spell, but that weakened as the assault continued. Suddenly he screamed as his body began to burn. Then he was eerily quiet.

Only then did the flames stop.

I staggered to Dagmar, amazed at the carnage of the battles. Anica was alive but hurting; Gudlang had crawled to Thor and was weeping over him.

There were five fallen Beserkers, though only one that I knew of—the one whose throat Anica had slit—was dead. And Krupp was a cinder.

Dagmar was on her feet, but practically fell into my arms as I approached. I held her close, suddenly realizing how much I had missed holding her.

"I knew he wasn't Thor," she breathed. "But he had the *Mjollnir* and we couldn't fight him."

I didn't ask how he had gotten the Hammer.

"Thor," I said.

"He needs the Hammer," Dagmar confirmed.

I let her go and went to Krupp's body, ignoring the smell of it. I picked up the Hammer, its handle hot, and carried it to Gudlang. She took it from me and placed it in Thor's hands. The priest's fingers closed on the handle and I thought I saw him smile.

I went back to Dagmar and pulled her into my arms again. I purposely didn't look at Anica but I saw that she was holding her knife, which must be her talisman, and healing herself.

"My Berserkers," Dagmar whispered. "Are they all dead?"

"I don't know," I answered honestly. "Only one I think, but I don't know."

A rumbling on the mountain interrupted us. We both looked up to see Loki climbing out of the snow. He bellowed as he got out and looked down at—even from that distance—me.

"Damn," Dagmar said.

I looked at our condition, and no one was ready to fight Loki, even if he didn't have the Hammer anymore.

But we did. I rushed to Gudlang as fast as my weary legs would carry me. "I need the Hammer."

She shook her head, "No." We were speaking the ancient language.

I looked up the mountain; Loki was bounding down it, growling as he did, seeming to make a beeline for me.

"But Loki," I said.

"Thor needs it," she said simply, as if a giant adept wasn't climbing down a mountain to kill us.

I said a very bad word in English.

Gudlang didn't respond.

I turned to Dagmar. "The Valkyrie?"

She shook her head. "We will not—cannot—fight the Æsir."

That explained how Loki got the Hammer and controlled the Valkyrie. But it did me little good.

"Gudlang," I tried, "can he fight Loki?" I meant Thor.

"No, he's too weak." She then stood, leaving the Hammer in Thor's hands. "But together we can defeat him—all of us."

I shook my head. "Anica can't fight him, and the Valkyrie won't. It's just you and me." She was recovering from being hit by the Hammer, and I was recovering from fighting Loki and Krupp.

"So be it," she said. I had the feeling she would face the gates of Hell to protect Thor.

I looked up the mountain. Loki was beyond the snow and climbing down the rocks. At least he should be weary when he gets close enough for a fight, I thought hopefully.

Then I had an idea. Krupp hadn't been using his talisman, but the Hammer when he'd fought me. His talisman should hold some power. I could use that to increase my strength. I hurried to his body and, ignoring the stench that rose when I did, dug in the charred remains near where I thought his pockets would be.

I found a hot rock. But there were markings scratched into it, indicating it was a very old and powerful talisman. Just holding it I felt stronger; not strong enough to take on Loki, but stronger. I held Krupp's rock in my left hand, my samurai sword talisman in my right and returned to Gudlang, still standing near Thor.

Loki was getting closer, stopping occasionally to look at me, perhaps to see if I was still there.

Thor suddenly moved. I could tell by how slowly he did it that it was a strain. He sat up.

"Kader," he said in a low voice. I'd never heard him speak so softly, even when he'd first come out of the ice tunnel; I had to strain to hear.

"Yes, Thor?"

He strained to lift a hand and signaled for me to come closer. I did, looking into his clear blue eyes.

"You don't need two talismans," he stated.

I was about to protest when he continued. "Do you know the absorption?"

I shook my head. "What do you mean?"

"Technique to absorb all the power of a talisman at once."

I looked at him. Is this possible? I thought. "Tell me how!"

Thor had me place my sword talisman on the ground and hold the rock with both hands. He told of the spell, how to invoke it. I did as he taught, holding Krupp's talisman tight. I felt the power suddenly flow through me. It was as if I'd never fought that day. In fact, I'd never felt more powerful. I opened my hands and they contained only dust that blew away on the gentle breeze.

I stood and watched Loki, my nerves tense as if I had electricity running through me. I didn't know how long this spell would last.

Loki was almost to Valhalla. I scooped up my talisman and waited impatiently, pacing back and forth. Dagmar walked closer—she moved as if in great pain.

"By our traditions we cannot attack the Æsir," she said softly, looking at me with soft, tear-rimmed eyes. "I never expected to see one. But I must honor our traditions, or I cannot be Brunhild."

I nodded my understanding. But then Loki drew my attention as he got on the scree field and rushed down it to the flat area that was Valhalla. He looked at me again and pointed his finger. I ducked the flame even as he shot it. And I noticed it wasn't very hot and barely reached me. He had been considerably weakened.

I shot an airbolt at him, knocking him down. I rushed toward him as he got up with amazing speed. Rocks from the scree field suddenly popped up and flew at me.

I'd never seen this meta before, but I put up a protection spell as the rocks hit me. They bounced off harmlessly, and it seemed this attack had tired Loki still more.

Gudlang tried attacking, but her lightning bolt seemed to fizzle a few feet from her hand. I was surprised she could muster that much, as when I had gotten hit by the Hammer I'd had no power for days.

I raised both my hands and shot an airbolt at Loki again, as hard and fast as I could. It slammed him to the scree. I shot lightning at him and that made his body jerk.

I realized the dirt was growing around my legs as Loki rose to a sitting position. It was clawing at me as if to pull me down. I stamped my feet and the ground gave way, and I was on solid soil again. But this had given Loki time to shoot an airbolt at me. It knocked me back and I crashed into the wall of Valhalla. I pointed my finger at Loki.

"No fire!" Gudlang called out. I glanced at her. She was supporting Thor, and I could tell the order had come from him.

I switched to lightening, again hitting Loki. He jerked hard and twisted, falling face down in the scree. I waited for him to move again. When he didn't, I approached him slowly.

Thor and Gudlang both walked to Loki's prone body, Thor leaning on Gudlang, and Thor turned Loki over to face him, raised the Hammer, and brought it down on Loki's chest. The impact seemed to echo off the mountains.

They turned to me as I drew near and Thor said, "He's powerless now."

But for how long? I wondered.

***

Mason climbed out of the hole where Yggdrasil was. He had a tool belt around his hips dangling with chrome-plated pieces of metal whose function I could only guess.

"That stainless steel strapping ought to hold them forever."

Adalbörg followed him out, carrying a glowing piece of ice for light. He wouldn't use a flashlight. "Loki, Thor, and the other Æsir are sleeping and secure," he said. "As it should be, until the world is ready for them again."

I didn't mention that I thought that might never be.

We climbed into vehicles called "Land Rovers" that my guild had rented—except for Adalbörg, who insisted on riding a horse—and returned to the sod house near Vik owned by the Icelandic Guild.

Dagmar was waiting just inside the door. She looked up with anxious eyes.

"It's done," I said.

"And by the end of winter, the glacier will have buried the spot," Adalbörg expounded.

Later that evening, we sat around a long table with intricately carved legs as a fire crackled and popped in a fireplace, the light making our shadows seem like live things. Dagmar was to my right, Anica to my left. Anica had healed herself but her hair was shorter, as it hadn't grown back yet from being burned off. Around lessers she'd probably use a glamour but here one was useless and unnecessary.

Adalbörg and Gudlang were at the far end of the table.

"Then it's settled," Adalbörg said. "Our guilds are at peace."

"And the Transylvanian Guild will move to a permanent home in the U.S. Northwest, under the protection of my guild," I stated. Anica had stated she wanted mountains like in her homeland, and I thought Northern Idaho/Western Montana was mountainous and isolated enough for them.

Papers were executed with the proper spells to keep them secure, and we broke up. Anica gave me a hug, Dagmar eying her as she did.

Just then Mason came out of the back of the house smiling broadly. "The Icelandic warriors have a shortwave radio," he said. "I was able to get the BBC. The Americans landed at Inchon yesterday."

I smiled at his excitement and ignored the feelings being reminded of Korea brought up in me. "Good," was all I said.

I took Dagmar's hand, grabbed our coats, and walked outside with her. I wanted some privacy.

It was chilly even though the sun hadn't set yet at seven in the evening. I handed Dagmar her coat and wrapped mine around me.

"Now what?" Dagmar asked.

"What do you mean?" I was truly perplexed.

"I've seen the way she looks at you. And you gave her guild a chance to survive."

"I love you, Dagmar," I said simply, hoping to avoid discussions about sleeping together yet not "sleeping together."

"Even after . . ?" She let her voice trail off.

I wanted to ask "After what?" but I didn't. "Even after you tried to warn me, tried to tell me it wasn't Thor?"

"He wanted to kill Nils for delivering that note."

"How did he know about the note?"

"Far seeing. He was very powerful."

I nodded my understanding.

Loki was right. I hadn't had much luck with women. Except one.

I wrapped my arms around her and held her close.

"Maybe," she said softly, "your guild should take *Mjollnir*."

I let go of her enough to look into her eyes. "What do you mean?  You'd give up the Hammer?"

I saw nothing but sincerity in her eyes. "My guild is too weak. We'd be fighting for it constantly. No, correction, you'd be fighting for it constantly, like you fought Anica's predecessor for us, for me."

I shook my head. "Without the Hammer, the Valkyrie wouldn t be."

"We could exchange the samurai sword for the Hammer," she offered.

I thought about that. It was a tempting offer, and I knew she was sincere.

But: "No. I'll protect you. I'll protect your guild." I thought that once word got around of what had happened to Nikolai, knowing the AMA was protecting the Valkyrie would be deterrent enough that I wouldn't have to fight again. At least I hoped so.

"And I'll protect you, Frank," Dagmar said softly. "However I can.

I smiled at that. "If it ever comes to that, then yes." I couldn't imagine a situation where it would.

"Nothing happened between Anica and me," I blurted out.

She nodded, almost as if afraid to respond.

"And I need to tell you why I went to Korea."

She looked at me with her blue eyes. I knew this was going to hurt her, but I didn't want secrets between us anymore.

LOOK FOR THE NEXT BOOK
AGENT OF ARTIFICE
COMING NOVEMBER 1ST 2011

## ABOUT THE AUTHOR

S. Evan Townsend is a writer living in central Washington State. After spending four years in the U.S. Army in the Military Intelligence branch, he returned to civilian life and college to earn a B.S. in Forest Resources from the University of Washington. In his spare time he enjoys reading, driving (sometimes on a racetrack), meeting people, and talking with friends. He is in a 12-step program for Starbucks addiction. Evan lives with his wife and two teenage sons and has a son attending the University of Washington in biology. He enjoys science fiction, fantasy, history, politics, cars, and travel.

www.ingramcontent.com/pod-product-compliance
Lightning Source LLC
Chambersburg PA
CBHW021310250626
47155CB00002B/465